Absent a Miracle

Books by Christine Lehner

EXPECTING

WHAT TO WEAR TO SEE THE POPE

ABSENT A MIRACLE

❧ Absent a Miracle

CHRISTINE LEHNER

Houghton Mifflin Harcourt

Boston   New York   2009

For information about permission to reproduce selections
from this book, write to Permissions, Houghton Mifflin
Harcourt Publishing Company, 6277 Sea Harbor Drive,
Orlando, Florida 32887-6777.

www.hmhbooks.com

Library of Congress Cataloging-in-Publication Data
Lehner, Christine, date.
    Absent a miracle / Christine Lehner.
        p. cm.
    ISBN 978-0-15-101429-3
    1. Catholic women — Fiction. 2. Marriage — Fiction.
3. Friendship — Fiction. 4. Hagiography — Fiction. 5. New
York (State) — Fiction. 6. Nicaragua — Fiction. 7. Domestic
fiction. I. Title.
    PS3562.E439A27 2009
    813'.54 — dc22   2008053294

Book design by Joyce Weston

Printed in the United States of America

DOC 10 9 8 7 6 5 4 3 2 1

This is a work of fiction. All names, characters, places, and incidents are the product of the writer's fevered imagination, or in
the case of actual places, are used fictitiously. Any resemblance
to actual persons, living or dead, is entirely coincidental. All the
saints referred to do actually exist (in the loose hagiographic
sense of existence), but in some cases the details are changed.
For narrative purposes, the author has moved the months for
coffee picking and processing from winter to summer.

For CSB, YLG

Stranger things have happened.
> — Hubert van Toots, head librarian and
> provost, the Hagiographers Club of
> Gramercy Square and North America

I shall have many curious facts to relate concerning these mimetic resemblances.
> — Thomas Belt, *A Naturalist in Nicaragua*

The country and the people of Nicaragua are too much like other parts of Spanish tropical America, with their dull, lazy, sensual inhabitants, to possess any novelty. There is little that can be called adventure, and still less of geographical discovery.
> — From a review by Alfred Russell Wallace of
> Thomas Belt's *A Naturalist in Nicaragua*

Sainthood in itself is not interesting, only the lives of the saints are.
> — E. M. Cioran, *Tears and Saints*

Many things about this place are dubious.
> — Elizabeth Bishop, "The End of March"

❧ Prologue

Two young men, Abelardo Llobet Carvajal, a
Nicaraguan of an old landed family from the
ancient capital of León, already wise in the ways
of coffee, cattle, chickens, and sugar cane, and Waldo Fairweather IV, the older son of Waldo Fairweather III and Posey Fairweather, née Pinchbeck, from Catamunk and Bug Harbor,
Maine, an incipient inventor with a tortured family history of
inventions unrewarded, are sprawled across the sofa. The sofa,
acquired from the former residents of the suite — party-loving
members of the lightweight crew and one German scholar — is
dimpled, beer stained, and, at this moment, littered with popcorn. From their third-floor window in Quincy House they can
watch the completely predictable activity on the green.

Abelardo's English is perfect and at times he is more easily
understood, even with his accent, than his friend from Maine.
He says, "My sister is coming."

"Which one? Don't you have several? Have I seen a picture?"

"Only one would come here. Carmen."

"When?"

"She should be downstairs by now."

"You could have warned me. How does she handle squalor?"

"Nothing frightens her," Abelardo says.

When Carmen enters the room, it is as if the decrepit sofa,
the stained rug, and the tasteless posters all recede like a full-moon
low tide, and the space is taken up by beauty, scent, and wind.

For a week it is always the three of them, always together. Carmen goes to classes with Abelardo, and Waldo skips his classes to come along. She eats meals with them in the dining hall. Every evening both young men walk her back across the bridge to the turreted nineteenth-century guesthouse maintained by the diocese for Catholic visitors with ecclesiastical connections. Abelardo arranged the accommodations for his beautiful younger sister, who takes every opportunity to explain that she has ceased to believe in the Immaculate Conception, the Virgin Birth, the Shroud of Turin, and the Resurrection of Anyone. Waldo is undone and transformed. He sits up straighter. He keeps his jokes to the bare minimum. He takes cold showers whenever he can. Waldo falls in love.

On the seventh day of his sister's visit, Abelardo has an appointment with his adviser, and Carmen says she would rather walk along the Charles with Waldo. In no time at all, Waldo tells her she is lovely and enticing beyond words. Carmen tells him that she is a virgin and would rather not be, and she would love to go back to their suite and learn the ways of sex on their sofa.

They do. Carmen enjoys it more than she imagined, Waldo less so. But he is no less in love.

When Abelardo returns from his appointment, Waldo and Carmen are dressed and sitting under a pollen-dripping tree on the green. Carmen tells her brother that, thanks to his wonderful roommate, she is no longer burdened with virginity. Abelardo buries his face in his hands and stays that way for what seems like several minutes, at least to Waldo. When Abelardo raises his head, he says, "I knew this would happen. I should have warned you, Waldo. This is what I should have warned you about."

Waldo says, "I don't know what to say. Your sister is extraordinary."

"Say nothing. You don't need to say anything. I know Carmen, after all."

Carmen says, "You are both so serious. Everything is fine. Tomorrow is my last day and I would like to see the glass flowers."

That very afternoon the three cross Harvard Yard and go to the Peabody to see the glass flowers. Carmen is not disappointed. She is enchanted with the glass lady's slippers. Waldo tells her those flowers grow in hidden places in the Maine woods, though it is illegal to pick them because they are so precious. Abelardo explains they are members of the same orchid family whose tropical relatives grow all over Las Brisas, their coffee farm. Carmen says those look nothing at all like lady's slippers. She does not say what she thinks they really look like.

When Carmen Llobet Carvajal has returned to her convent school in the hills outside Matagalpa (where it pains the nuns to love her as much as they do, given her apostasy), when the air has ceased to rustle and her scent has dissipated, Waldo tells his roommate Abelardo that he would ask his sister to marry him in a second if only she were not so fearless. Abelardo would shrug if he ever shrugged. He tells Waldo it is a moot point because his sister will never again leave Nicaragua (though he is wrong about this) and, he asks Waldo (contradicting himself), how fearless can that be?

Part I ❧ Blizzard: Abelardo Llobet Carvajal

1 ❧ Alice Loses Whatever Jobs She Has

MY NAME IS Alice Ewen Fairweather. It used to be Alice Llovet Ewen, because Llovet was my mother's maiden name. All three sisters got the same middle name. I would have liked a middle name of my own, and briefly lobbied for Hyacinth. I stopped using Llovet when I became a Fairweather. Why? Because I was madly in love.

Given what happened, it would have been somewhat amusing if Llovet were still on my passport, because in Spanish, *v* and *b* are basically the same letter, writ small (*b pequeño*) or writ large (*b grande*).

About two months before Waldo and the boys went on vacation, I lost my job hosting *The Dream Radio Show*, Monday mornings for three hours on WBLT. ("Start your week by freeing up your subconscious. Tell me, Alice Fairweather, and our listeners in the tri-state area last night's dream, and we'll tell you the obvious.")

The events were not related in any way. I was sacked in December. You'd think that even the dimmest station manager would realize that it is especially in the trying holiday times that listeners need to be able to tell their dreams, live, and be reassured. But no, without the slightest consideration for the spirit of Baby Jesus or Rockefeller Center, Trudy Swatherton, in an act of generosity so rare it should have alerted me to the coming blow, took me to Joe's Rib Joint, and then she fired me. She canceled my show and left the itchy dreamers of the region with no outlet, no airwaves, no listeners, no disembodied voice beckoning them to unload the lingering memories of weird and disturbing dreams.

Trudy knew damn well I was a vegetarian and had been since the first mad cow scare. About the only things I could eat at Joe's Dead Cow Emporium were fried mozzarella sticks and hush puppies. I would have eaten fish (cooked or otherwise) but none were on offer. I sat there, huddled there, beneath faux-antique wagon wheels, branding irons, cow skulls, and horns, and Trudy ordered a pitcher of beer for the two of us and told me that my skills were wasted in talk radio. I had no idea what skills she was referring to, and I'm sure neither did she. Trudy claimed she wanted to let me down gently, but I knew better. I knew that she was worried I would reveal what I knew of her dreams.

People can rationalize all they want about the workings of the unconscious, but the truth is that we all feel somewhat responsible for the content of our dreams. And if our dreams are kinky or perverted or repulsive (and Trudy's were all of these), then it must be inferred that we are kinky, perverted, or repulsive as well.

I'm not a psychologist. For *Dream Radio* I'd had no qualifications whatsoever except a quick way with symbols and an empathetic nature. Well, I did have one thing: I was irrationally fascinated by dreams. I loved hearing people's dreams. Like my listeners, I had spent years waking up with the glimmering of a memory of a dream that tantalized and then wanting more than anything to tell it to someone, to say it aloud as a way of sealing its occurrence while dispelling its unnerving connection to the conscious me. Like my listeners, I had found that most people's eyes glazed over while their hands crept up to stifle the yawns. How many times had I said to Annabel and Audrey, "I had the weirdest dream. Do you want to hear it?" How many times had they answered, in unison or antiphonally, "No"? So many times that it was the morning mantra of our shared childhood. I fantasized that one day one of them would have a dream and want to share it, and then I would listen eagerly, I would be the Lady

Bountiful who harbored no grudges but listened attentively to the fleeting images. That had never happened. So *The Dream Radio Show* was the perfect job for me. I was happy to hear the dreams of perfect strangers, those strangers who were perfectly happy to tell me their dreams, what they could recall of them, because they knew I was interested. I had lots of repeat callers, and very few cranks. For those listeners who needed to hear it, I told them not to blame themselves for the occasional sick narratives or morbid surreal dramas that lingered in the morning. In this, they didn't believe me, no more than Trudy did. But they wanted to hear the reassurances. Apparently, being appalled by what one didn't even know one was thinking was part of the thrill.

During my four years at WBLT, our listeners had sent countless testimonials to the station, and over and over they had said that one of the most reassuring things about the show was that I was not a psychologist. That I was just like them: occasionally a dreamer, occasionally an insomniac, sometimes paranoid but always justified in being so, and benignly compulsive. I never tired of sharing these letters with Waldo and Ezra and Henry. They listened to them just as they listened to my dreams, with apparent interest and goodwill. They also made fun of me, but that seemed a small price to pay for the attention. Waldo liked to point out how my subconscious made puns. I told him that after all our years together, I still craved to hear his dreams.

At Joe's Carne Cafeteria, somewhere on my way from the table to the street door, the hiccups arrived. Somewhere in there, my poor vagus nerve (the wanderer, the nomad, the slippery hobo) became irritated and *ka-bang* (thirty-five milliseconds, so they say), the glottis snapped shut. I hate the hiccups, and I particularly hate getting the hiccups in front of someone like Trudy because I will try to mask them and pretend I don't have them, and that only makes them worse and prolongs the agony. Adios, Trudy. Adieu, Joe's Carne Crematorium. Au revoir, lovely WBLT.

I swallowed and tried to still the body jerks. I took a deep breath and imagined lead weights attached to my feet, keeping me rooted. I found I was in front of St. Winifred's on Seventh, and I went inside. I pulled open the heavy doors, and the darkness hit like a weather front. I stood still and let my eyes adjust, then moved into the nave and sat in a pew on the right. I exhaled. Had it always been there? Or had it just begun? The organ. There would be a longish baroque passage, and then the music would stop abruptly; rustling would signal the turning of pages, and then the music would start once more. Sometimes the same lovely passage, again and again. Sometimes another piece of music. I knew none of it and it was all beautiful, all surely written to raise the listeners' thoughts heavenward and, on this nasty December afternoon, succeeding in just that. After a long while I twisted my head around and peered at the choir loft. The organ's pipes loomed over the dim church interior. The railing hid the organist. No one else was there. Not another soul. How was this possible? It must have been the organist's practice hour, and I had just happened into the most peaceful and melodious spot in the entire city, when I needed it most. I even slept a bit, and dreamed of anthropomorphized vegetables (carrots, onions, and beets) copulating on Posey's Blue Willow plates while Henry played Ping-Pong on the kitchen table, the ball mere inches above them. But of course there was no extant radio show on which I could tell my troubling dreams to eager listeners.

The hiccups were gone. Thanks to the organ, I could take the train home without the weeping that seemed to embarrass fellow commuters. At home, Waldo and the boys were sympathetic. It must have struck them that without the *Dream Radio Show,* I would look to them, conveniently located at my own breakfast table, to satisfy my dream fascination. Waldo bit his tongue and did not repeat that I was practicing dreamology without a license or that my degree had been acquired by dialing 1-800-JUNG-R-US.

Henry said, "Tell me again why she took you to the Rib Joint. I think that is the most egregious of all. Actionable, I think."

For years Waldo and I had locked bemused eyes every time Henry had used one of the hundreds of vocabulary words he could not possibly have picked up at school and probably not even from us. But that time was past. Henry was now eight, and we were in awe of him.

Ezra, though ten, still crawled into my lap and said, "I'll tell you all my dreams, Mom. I think you're the best."

Right around then Waldo's mother called.

"I've just been reading about this hapless person who was mauled by his very own pet tiger. Really gruesome stuff."

"I think I missed this one, Posey," I said.

"I am so very, very pleased that you and Waldo have dogs. Dogs would never do anything like that."

"Well, actually—"

"Naturally I'm not referring to the Diebenkorns or the Rottenweiners. People like us don't have dogs like that," she said.

I tried again. "I don't think it's quite that simple—"

"I'm only saying it's a matter of what we're used to. And we're used to friendly dogs. Dogs you can sleep with in a pinch."

It was a family truism that Posey Fairweather, née Pinchbeck, frequently did not know how she sounded. *She Doesn't Know How She Sounds,* one of us would mouth to strangers at weddings or on train platforms. *She Doesn't Know What That Means.*

On the other side of the kitchen, Flirt and Dandy were curled up together on their plaid cushion, Dandy's slender nose resting on his sister's back, their breathing in unison, their aspect benign. They were taking a break, apparently, from their mutual inspection and licking of each other's genitals.

Posey had a point; she often did. That was the scary thing.

"This poor fellow had gotten this tiger as a baby, but it grew too large, as tigers are prone to do, and so he kept it in the next-door apartment, and each day opened the door just enough to toss in a few raw chickens. Just this once the tiger pushed the door wide open and mauled him. I've always said cats were untrustworthy."

"Would you like to speak with Waldo? He's right here." I handed the phone over, but Henry intercepted it.

Now the rest of us could go back to whatever we were doing—castigating WBLT for their shortsighted employment policies and wondering what would happen to all the dreamers of our metropolitan region who were not blessed, as I was, with Waldo and the boys, who each morning gave the impression of genuine interest when I said over my granola and blueberries: "I had the strangest dream last night."

Now, however, Posey would find out that I had been fired, and I really didn't want her to know that just yet. I didn't want to talk about it with someone who thought I'd been wasting my talents all along. But just what were those talents, anyway?

How often in life does one have the perfect job? Well, I had. I'd had it and I'd lost it.

About a month after that I started eating meat again, not very much and not very often, but somewhere in there was a palpable shift from the vegetable world to the world of flesh.

Waldo got paid to think of new and better ways to do the same old things, as well as of ways to do the things that were not generally considered possible. He got paid to tinker around with tools and tubes and hoses and grommets and items I could never name. Whenever forms required you to write in your occupation, Waldo got to write *inventor*. He worked for the research and development department of DSG Corporation, so called because their first successful product was a device that removed dust particles from the air in manufacturing plants, a device that was called the Dust-Sucking Gizmo, or DSG. He'd first worked for them in the city, but as they expanded, they moved the R & D department up the Hudson to Thumbtown, at which point we too moved and bought our house in VerGroot, two towns over. Dust sucking was naturally something of a specialty at DSG, and Waldo's first commercially successful invention was the Automatic Auto-Suction Friend. People with allergies loved Waldo. He was occasionally invited to speak at the Allergens of America annual conference, which was always held in May because that was National Allergy Prevention Month. Since I rarely went to the allergy conference, I never knew if Waldo shared his brilliant limericks with his sneezing audience, rhyming *pollen* with *swollen* and rhyming who knows what else, *dander, philander, slander,* and *oleander.* I assumed he did because of course that would only increase his desirability as a speaker.

Two months before the WBLT debacle, I had lost my other part-time job, teaching high school English to troubled girls at Our Lady of Precious Blood Academy. The semester had barely begun when Mother Apollonia told me the diocese had radically altered the English curriculum. Henceforth, my extensive knowledge of the writings and lives of the Catholic converts, especially, but not exclusively, T. S. Eliot, Evelyn Waugh, Graham Greene, and Thomas Merton, was no longer required. Henceforth, the school would be sticking to the tried-and-true narratives of the saints: Augustine's *Confessions,* Theresa of Ávila's *Interior Castle,* Thérèse of Lisieux's *Story of a Soul,* and John of the Cross's *Dark Night of the Soul.* I was as big an admirer of those texts as anyone, as I told Mother Apollonia, but I thought the girls in her care might need something else, something slightly more contemporary and accessible. And even more than that, I thought they needed to read stories that made it clear just how flawed most Catholics and most humans were, and yet all still deserving of grace. I argued for a more nuanced and entertaining view of the Mystical Body of Christ, and I was turned down.

I was fond of my students at Precious Blood. They were resilient and vulnerable, full of wisdom and full of shit. We had developed this weird pattern—which may have been another reason the diocese got rid of me, but how could they have known?—such that in almost every class one girl would make a great show of resting her head upon her desk and sobbing, twitching, or groaning. Then another girl would solicitously ask what was the matter. A long narrative would ensue, usually involving a cruel, fickle, and witless boyfriend; or a terminally ill mother; or an imprisoned brother; or a drunken, abusive father. Presumably the first time this happened, the story told was true, and probably even the second and third time. But soon they were complete fictions. It's true that I realized this long after the girls did, but I did finally realize it. Yet we continued. The girls continued with their theatrical poses, and their earnest questionings. We all continued to listen, even and especially as the stories became more and more outlandish. In my last month of employment at Precious Blood, my eleventh-grade class was regaled with escalating stories that went from the perfidious boyfriend who seduced the student's younger sister, to a boyfriend seducing a student's fraternal (as in "male") twin, to a boyfriend seducing a student's mother. It was beyond my capacities not to admire their inventiveness: details that included the contents of the boyfriend's pockets and his brother's favorite TV shows, and dialogue that was elaborate, colloquial, and often derivative of great literature ("I smell a hamster" or "You're nothing but a handful of dust"). These Homerically inclined girls would have great futures, if only I knew what they were. If only I could help them get there.

For almost four years I'd had these two part-time jobs, both of which had seemed ideal, as part-time jobs went, if you didn't consider how little I was paid. Aside from that, they were interesting and worthwhile—I thought they were worthwhile—and allowed me to be home by three in the afternoon, when Ezra and Henry returned from school, hungry and briefly ebullient. Was it that I'd been too pleased with myself? Had I neglected the all-important knocking on wood that Mami had drummed into us along with a fondness for nuts and figs? What if I had brought this double-whammy of dismissals upon myself?

One of my favorite girls at Precious Blood was Angela Sitwell. Angela made Mother Apollonia nervous; the mother superior knew Angela was up to no good, but she could never catch her in flagrante. Angela had a style all her own, and unnerving courage. She had two distinguishing marks, and she wore them both proudly: a vivid port-wine stain shaped like the Central American isthmus on her left temple, and her missing sixth finger.

One day I brought Ezra and Henry to school with me. The first thing Angela said was "Have you guys ever shaken hands with someone with six fingers?" Of course they had not, not that they knew of, not that I knew of, and suddenly their lives seemed emptier and paler without that very experience. In one moment Angela had created in their contented, privileged lives a void that only she could fill.

Angela let them trace with their small fingers the almost invisible scar that was all that remained of the sixth finger of her left hand. They couldn't get enough of it. Ezra in particular begged me to take him with me to my classes at Precious Blood, but scheduling was always hard. After all, he had school too.

So when I was canned from *Dream Radio* I had the sick satisfaction of assuming that now, finally, everything that could go wrong had gone wrong, and in spades. I'd lost two jobs for which I'd had no recognizable qualifications but was good at anyway. I had no idea what I would do next. If Waldo was such a great inventor, and I had no doubt that he was, couldn't he invent a job for me? If he could invent open-space videos for MRIs, magic magnetic moving picture hooks, a battery-operated wind-resistant umbrella, self-folding tortillas, and the Automatic Auto-Suction Friend, then surely he could come up with something I could do, that I might be able to do.

Apparently, putting me to use was a lot harder than inventing a device that allows one's car to automatically vacuum itself.

2 ❧ Monkey in the Middle

I WAS THE MIDDLE child. I was the one who came
after Annabel and before Audrey. I was born two
years after Annabel and two years before Audrey.
In those days, almost everyone I knew or went to school with
was separated from his or her siblings by two years. If someone
was not, it was regarded as an interesting anomaly. If he or she
had come several years after the previous sibling, the child was
invariably referred to as "the Surprise"; if he or she was an only
child, "Poor Thing" was the epithet.

As I was to learn with Ezra and Henry, this two-year interlude
meant that almost as soon as one child was weaned, the next was
conceived. Not exactly an epiphanic observation, or even rocket
science. More like a time-honored pattern that kept restless young
women on a hormonal high. This, at least, was my interpretation
of the procreative activity of thousands of years of human history.
For four straight years I was awash in hormonal surges. I was dangerously blissful. For four straight years I could have been a poster
child for hormonal surges.

That I was the middle child was not something people spoke
of in Santa Barbara or anywhere else I'd been before I came to
New England. Mami and Pop always called me their second
daughter, never the middle daughter. I never knew if this was
deliberate on their part, if they had consciously decided to spare
me the stigma of the middle child, or if it was just cluelessness.

So when the taboo was broken by the New Englanders, not
generally known as taboo-breakers, my sisters began to refer to

me constantly as the one in the middle. Before that I had been the hapless one in need of entertainment and social intercourse, all because I had once complained of being bored when left to myself one evening. For them, this phenomenon of birth order suddenly explained a whole gamut of behaviors. "She's the middle child, that's why she's so flexible," Annabel would say. Audrey would agree. "Like Gumby." Or Audrey would say, "Alice is pathologically social, you know. It must be because she's the middle child." And Annabel would add, "She can't bear to be alone. She needs to develop Inner Resources." You would have thought they were the first people in the Western world to notice that birth order matters.

That I was a middle child was the first thing Waldo told his parents about me. Or it may as well have been for all the attention they'd paid to anything he'd said before that. Waldo said, "Alice is her parents' middle child. They have three daughters." And both Posey and Three pressed their lips together even more tightly than usual before parting them to say, "We have no middle children."

Waldo said it might be a good idea for me to consider Maine and California as separate countries—which they surely would have been in any other part of the world, like Venezuela and Chile, or Germany and Spain—and then to think of myself as a foreigner; that way I would not expect to understand his parents' behavior, and I might even find it interesting, the way we found the rituals of Oktoberfest or Semana Santa interesting, or the Castilian lisp quaint.

"Why? Do you feel like a foreigner in California?" I once asked him. We were living in New York City then, on opposite sides of Spring Street. It was good that Spring Street was not too heavily trafficked, because many of our conversations took place in the middle of that thoroughfare.

"No, but that's because New Englanders never feel like foreigners, not anywhere. We can go to Turkmenistan or Timbuktu and know that we are the standard by which all others should be measured. We look around, comment on the habits and hygiene of the natives, on the foreignness of their language and attire. If they don't understand us, we just speak louder, because we know lots of people who are deaf. We are the norm," he said. "Plus, we are Red Sox fans, and Red Sox fans will always occupy the moral high ground because they lose, gloriously."

"You exaggerate everything," I said.

"You met Posey and Three. I hardly think I am exaggerating. Simplifying perhaps, but not exaggerating."

"You're a New Englander," I said. "Do *you* feel like that?"

"Let's just say that I never feel like a foreigner, which is either a curse or a blessing. But I don't think of you as a foreigner either. Of course, I am the rebel in the family. I've moved out of Maine, and I don't have a vegetable garden, and I'm marrying a papist from California."

"That's the first I've heard of it," I said.

"You thought I did have a vegetable garden?"

"Stop being amusing. If you even are. About getting married: I think I should be consulted."

And then Waldo shocked me completely. It wasn't like all the previous shocks of strange family stories and quirky behavior. It was physical. It was like walking into a plate-glass door headfirst. He fell, he crashed, really, down onto both knees, and said, "Alice Ewen of the western shores, O let us be married! too long we have tarried: But what shall we do for a ring?"

I don't remember what I said. Unlike Waldo's words, mine were neither memorable nor in rhyme. Of course I loved him to distraction. Never in my wildest dreams had I ever imagined a scene quite like this one, on a sidewalk in Lower Manhattan. The fact that he spoke to me as Pussy-Cat once did to Owl made it, somehow, only more profound. At one point I finally told him to get up and he confessed he might not be able to. He had done something to his knees, I forget now if it was the patella or the meniscus or the mysterious ACL. But the pain was excruciating. After two weeks of moaning and limping like the grandfather on *The Beverly Hillbillies,* he had arthroscopic surgery, and magically, the pain went away.

If Posey and Three ever warned him that a marriage between a first and a middle child was a dangerous reef, or that a marriage with a Californian of foreign extraction (more or less a redundancy) would be fraught with conflicts of values and misunderstood allusions, he never told me.

3 ⮂ Poor Sick Dandy

FOR MONTHS, WE HAD been planning this vacation to the Consummate Caves in New Mexico. Henry had been reading books and mastering the vocabulary of spelunking. Ezra wore his headlamp to the dinner table. But then plans had had to change, because Dandy was very sick, and even though I longed to witness Ezra's and Henry's spelunking adventures and hear their pithy commentary, I would stay home with the dogs. We all agreed there was no alternative. Not if we loved him, which we did, and if we wanted him to live, which we did.

Dandy became sick right after Christmas. He stopped eating, he stopped moving, and he was pale as a ghost. I'd never thought a dog could be pale, but then I saw how very possible it was. His tongue and gums were gray. His eyeballs receded into his skull. Because Donald, our vet, and his wife, Thelma, were taking their first vacation in six years—a Caribbean cruise sponsored by the American Agoraphobia Foundation—we spent New Year's Eve in the animal emergency room, along with an asthmatic cat and a lame Great Dane. Dandy then spent six nights at the Winifred Bates Memorial Animal Hospital. After Dandy had had two blood transfusions, a bone-marrow aspiration, steroids, and antibiotics, the hospital staff sadly sent him home to die. But he didn't die. We found a veterinary hematologist who prescribed a very experimental and expensive drug that required me to wear latex gloves when I administered it, which didn't strike me as a good thing. It struck me as a dangerous thing, and as a sign of all the dangerous things afoot in our medicated world. It struck me as a warning, if only I would heed it. But then Dandy's condition stabilized, and that was a good thing. Every week Waldo or I took him back to see Donald to get his blood analyzed. I made Dandy hamburger and waffles and scrambled eggs. He slept on Ezra's pillow, nose to nose with him. He was a long way from well, but he was far from dead.

There was no way we could leave him and disappear into underground caverns. We thought about it for a minute and a half. We considered the options. No kennel with an insurance policy, not even the Ritz of kennels, would take him. Our neighbor Bogumila, who was Polish and our street's enthusiastic advocate of herbal remedies for everything, offered to take Dandy in. But that was just too well-meaning by far. Dandy was too sick, and his medications were not simple. Nor were they herbal. And, really, who in her right mind would take on a family pet that could croak at any minute? What sane person could stand the guilt, even when it most certainly would not be her fault?

Speaking of guilt, we did briefly consider sending Posey a round-trip ticket and asking her to come and stay. She loved dogs and she was guilt-resistant. Waldo said if she wanted to, she could even bring Edgar Cicero, if he cared to come. Mr. Cicero was her second husband, and he didn't like to travel. In fact, he had not left the state of Maine in more than a decade. But it took mere seconds to imagine all the good reasons not to go down that path.

"She may not suffer from pangs of guilt," I said. "But I would never forgive her if anything happened. I wouldn't want to blame my children's grandmother for the death of their dog. That seems like a bad dynamic."

"There you go, Mom, anticipating the worst. Predilection is not always a good idea," Henry said.

"I assume you mean *prognostication*," Waldo said.

"Or just plain *prediction*," I said.

Henry glared at Waldo from under eyebrows that were already darkened and fast becoming a dominant feature of his face.

More discussion followed, and even some useful suggestions. All were rhetorical. Some were whimsical (the Plaza).

"I'll stay," I said. "I could use the peace and quiet. I can read a ton of books, and when I'm done with them, I can read the want ads."

"Promise you won't brood," Waldo said.

"I wouldn't know a brood if it bit me," I said.

"Seriously, Al."

"Seriously, I'll be able to eat anything I want."

Waldo said, "You already eat anything you want."

"How do you know? All these years I've been denying myself okra and garlic so as not to offend your delicate sensibilities."

"You hate okra," Waldo said.

"That's what you think," I said. "But really, really. It makes good sense. I don't even like caves. They're too slimy and—suggestive."

"I grant that it makes sense," Waldo said. "But not if you're going to be a martyr."

"I promise not to be a martyr. I rejected martyrdom decades ago," I said.

"You know what I mean," Waldo said.

I really did plan on enjoying myself, but I didn't want to entirely admit that. While I didn't want to make them feel bad, I could see the advantage of gaining some small foothold on the moral high ground in my relationship with Waldo and the boys.

Certain things were especially appealing. Like anyone who daily produced nutritious meals after consultation with the FDA food pyramid and epiphanies in the produce section of Stop & Shop, I longed to abandon that propriety and be left to my own devices. I could imagine a vacation of solitary sloventude: drinking coffee in bed and not changing the sheets if and when I spilled on Waldo's side. I could imagine scavenging in the fridge for those beckoning almost-moldy items tucked way in the back, and then daringly playing my own domestic variation on Russian roulette. I could imagine myself eating smoked oysters straight from the flat tin with the rolled-up top as I stood at the counter and read the obituaries and marriage announcements, ignoring the oil that spattered and soaked through the death at ninety-eight of a pioneer vaudevillian, or the merger of a Harvard MBA and a Princeton PhD in international affairs. I could imagine myself winning at *Jeopardy!*, night after night.

Besides, I was always looking for an opportunity to prove to Annabel and Audrey that I did in fact have Inner Resources. I planned that after the fourth day I'd call one of them and casually mention that I had been completely alone (I wouldn't mention the dogs) for days and say how much I had enjoyed my own company. I would tell her that I had taught myself a new skill, bookbinding or snowshoeing, that I had learned how to make pie crust and graft plants. (Maybe not plant grafting. Wrong season.) I would explain that I had taken up stamp collecting. I really had always wanted to take up stamp collecting, and somewhere in the attic was a box full of stamps I'd torn off letters, back when stamps were used on a regular basis. Stamp collecting was a thing of the past, because stamps were things of the past, which was all the more reason why I should take it up. And if Annabel or Audrey ever again referred disparagingly to my addiction to social intercourse at the cost of Inner Resources, I would mention my vast stamp collection and hint at all I had learned about small, obscure countries with no natural resources.

"Just tell me this: what if we come home and he's dead?" Henry sat up very straight and spoke simply.

"That's not going to happen," I said. Martyr or not, I felt a great weight, like rocks in a laundry sack, shift and settle upon my shoulders. Henry was the serious and retentive one in our house. If you said something to Henry, you damn well better mean it; he would drive you crazy otherwise. He brooked no excuses, no equivocation. From his infancy he had had the most prodigious memory. So much so that for a while we'd feared that he would end up like Waldo's brother, Dick, the idiot savant. But Waldo insisted Henry was most like his late father, Waldo Fairweather III, mainstay of the classics department of Swan College. Three, as he'd been known since the moment of my Waldo's birth, could tell you every good joke in Herodotus, but his face went blank when confronted with a grandson's knock-knock joke. Henry was not turning out like either his uncle or his grandfather, fine specimens though they were. Henry remembered things beyond count, but he understood that the rest of us were not like him. Still, woe betide the lazy parent who promised what could not be delivered, who swore to tell him later or to explain when they got home but had no intention of doing so. Henry would catch that parent up every time and demand only and exactly what had been promised. At the age of three, Henry was insistent. By the time he was eight, he was remorseless.

In this matter of being a stickler, Henry was profoundly unlike his older brother, Ezra. So it had taken a couple of years for Waldo and me to understand what we had on our hands. We experienced a sharp learning curve with this second son, this voice crying out in the wilderness from our very own kitchen table.

Ezra had been such a compliant peach, a dreamy soul who each day forgot everything he'd been told and re-imagined his life and reinvented the wheel. In no way did our sons resemble the classic archetypes of first and second sons, although God knows we looked for the signs, looked for resolve and ambition and conventionality in Ezra, and saw it not; looked for waywardness and rebellion in Henry, in vain. But perhaps the fault was in our searching.

"Can you promise?" Henry said.

I said what I believed I could do, what I could not fail to do. "I promise I'll guard him with my life. And he can sleep with me."

"What if he doesn't want to?" Ezra asked.

"We'll cross that tunnel when we get to it," I said. "And I told you, I didn't really want to go caving in the first place," I said. "I wanted to go to the south of France."

"You always want to go to the south of France," Waldo said. "What does the south of France have that the Hudson Valley does not?"

"French food and French hats. And truffles."

"Big deal, Mom. We have morels and *Grifola frondosa*," Henry said. "As you guys never fail to tell us. Ad nauseam."

Waldo raised his eyebrows and said, "He is far too young to have a taste for fungi."

"You're telling me?"

"It would serve you right if we moved to France and you spent the rest of your life bicycling around with a baguette in your basket," Waldo said.

Ezra immediately grabbed a loose crayon and drew two large circles that became the wheels of a bicycle, and then drew a basket on the handlebars, and then a tall, skinny woman with a ponytail, and finally, with a flourish, he drew an exceptionally long loaf of French bread.

"Enough already," I said. "One day we'll actually go to France and you guys will eat your words. Also frogs' legs. Meanwhile, I'll stay with the dogs, and you go have fun in some dark, slimy, moldy, vermin-infested caverns. The more I think of it, the better it sounds, staying here."

"Are you sure?" Outside, there was old gritty snow on the frozen ground and three inches of ice on the Hudson, but Waldo was eating black olives as if his feet were bare and the sun were beating down on his battered straw hat.

For someone who resisted the lure of the Mediterranean, Waldo certainly ate lots of olives. And there was his interesting habit of keeping several pits at once in the hollow of his cheek and then spitting them out in rapid succession. His mother frequently bemoaned this practice and claimed that she'd tried in vain to break him of it in his youth. Waldo insisted this was impossible as he had never eaten an olive until he'd gone to Italy, when he was twenty. To which Posey always responded, "Olives, cherries, what difference does it make? Small fruit, hard pit."

"Of course it makes a difference, Mother. One is sweet, the other is salty. If you can't distinguish between those two flavors, then life is hardly worth living," Waldo always replied. Not that he'd ever caused his mother, Posey Fairweather, Scourge of the Back Nine, Maven of the Garden Club and Delphinium Society, and All-Maine Ping-Pong Champion, to doubt herself or her ability to make distinctions.

"Of course I'm sure," I told Waldo now. "And it just so happens that, being ignominiously unemployed, I am completely free to dog-sit, to cater to his every need."

"Try not to dwell on it, Al."

"I don't dwell on it. I dream about it. I dream of knives and serpents."

4 &~ The Night Terrors

TWO DAYS BEFORE HE and the boys were to leave, Waldo called from work with a question. The telephone was anathema to him and he rarely called from his rabbit warren at DSG except to request some particular food for dinner. Waldo was subject to remarkable food cravings, and I always liked to indulge him. I was expecting to hear about seared tuna, or Fenway franks, or caesar salad. But I was wrong.

"How do you feel about a houseguest?"

In order to answer the phone I'd peeled off one of the latex gloves I had to wear whenever I suctioned and measured Dandy's medication into a disposable syringe. It had to be exactly 1.1 cc's. Too little might not be enough to save him, and too much was a bad idea, given that this was the most expensive drug I had ever heard of, never mind given to a dog. Sometimes I told friends that it was very costly, but I always lied when they brazenly asked, "Exactly how costly?" Susie Crench next door, for instance, came right out and said I had my priorities all wrong and that I should let the poor dog die a natural death. Hadn't I signed a living will? she wanted to know. "Well, give poor Dandy the same respect, and save some money while you're at it." And she was my best friend, my soul mate, my partner in culinary adventures, and the recipient of my lamentations about dogs, boys, and joblessness.

I said to Waldo, "Is this a trick question?"

"Of course not. So?"

"To whom are we referring? I have no problem with house-guests who don't smoke in bed."

"Good, he never smoked anything."

"Who?"

"We called him Lalo. Remember him? Abelardo Llobet Carvajal."

"Should I remember him?"

"Of course you should," Waldo said. "I take that back. There's no reason you should, but it would be handy. He was in Quincy House with me. You met him once at the Harvard Club."

"Keep going," I said. Bells were not ringing. I peeled off the other glove.

"He's Nicaraguan, from an old family. He had several beautiful sisters. You wouldn't know them. But they were spectacular. One in particular." One of the hardest things about a phone conversation with Waldo was imagining what he was doing when he called from the office. Maybe sit-ups on the floor, or catapult practice—anything to distract himself from the fact that he was talking on a telephone.

"I get the picture," I said. "Babes."

"You liked him, though. He's smart. Or at least, he's a brilliant farmer."

"How do you know?" I said.

"Because I know you, Al. I have plumbed your depths and come up with this fact: you liked my old pal Abelardo. Or you will like my old pal Abelardo. Who, it just so happens, has called because he's in New York for a couple of days and wants to come visit. I said the boys and I would be away but that you would love to have him for a night. It seemed like the right thing to do."

"Did you ask me?"

"No. And I realize that that may have been an oversight. But it's too late. He accepted."

"With alacrity," I said.

"Huh?"

"Could you just tell me *something* so that I can picture this guy? Any distinguishing characteristics? And not his sisters."

"He does have rather big ears. They didn't register when we were in school because he wore his hair long. Oh, and he studied to be a priest. But gave it up."

"He didn't study to be a priest at Harvard, I take it?"

"Hell, no. That was before. He was in seminary in Nicaragua or maybe some other country down there. But there was some crisis in his family, or some crisis to do with coffee, and then Lalo lost the calling, so he came north and studied medieval history. Which doesn't have much to do with coffee farming, but what does?"

"I don't know. Just as long as someone keeps growing strong coffee, so I can stay awake."

"So you don't mind if he stays one night?"

"Didn't I tell you about my plans?"

"What kind of plans can you possibly have? No, hang on. That came out wrong."

"What about eating tinned oysters and saltines in bed? Did you tell him that was my plan for the week?"

"He's only staying for one night," Waldo said, conciliatory. Papers crinkled suggestively somewhere. "Al, he's really a sweet man. You'll enjoy it."

"It's fine. So long as he doesn't mind about the oysters," I said. "Will you be home soon?"

"I need to finish up a project here but it won't be too late."

"Henry just informed me that I'd better pack you guys extra-heavy fleece jackets because it will be very cold in the hypogeal domain. He said he looked forward to abseiling to an exsurgence and getting intimate with cavernicoles. I hope you are ready for this adventure."

"Tell him to make me a glossary. That should keep him quiet for about twenty minutes."

"He keeps asking Ez if he'd rather be a clint or a grike," I said. "I can't find either of them in the dictionary."

Then the night before they left, Ezra walked in his sleep, again.

Each time it was a little different, but also each time there was the same oh-damn-I'm-not-dreaming-I'm-awake-but-he's-not sick feeling. With that acuity of hearing that parents develop when their offspring are young, Waldo and I stirred almost at the same time, milliseconds after Ezra's door creaked open.

One of the things my mother told me before she died was never to wake a somnambulist. And she knew. Her baby sister, my Tía Sofia, once sleepwalked on their balcony in Barcelona, was startled awake by a stray dog's barking, and tumbled off. She barely survived the fall.

Waldo and I tiptoed across our chilly bedroom floor and into the hall where Ezra, exquisitely oblivious in his dinosaur pajamas, glided toward the stairs. Usually he went down to the kitchen, opened the refrigerator, and poured himself some milk, always into a coffee mug. It was something I had had to see repeatedly to believe. Sometimes he ate an Oreo, but not always. Each and every time I found it so hard not to reach for him, not to bundle him into my arms and put him back to bed.

Waldo whispered, "Where's he going this time?"

"How should I know?" I said. "Oh, damn, he's going to wake up the dogs."

Like water finding the lowest point, Waldo slipped past Ezra and down the stairs. I knew where he was going; he wanted to be below Ezra on the stairs in case he fell. And he wanted to get there before the dogs were on the move. Then it was too late. The dogs had heard him. Flirt was at the bottom of the stairs with her tail thrashing, while Dandy sauntered out Ezra's bedroom door. Both dogs barked if a mouse farted in the night, so it was uncanny how Dandy did not bark when Ezra sleepwalked. But Flirt was another matter. Ezra was midway down when he appeared to jolt awake. He turned to run back but only got up one step before he tripped over his feet and fell, smacking his head on the tread.

"Oh, Ez," I said, and lifted him up.

"Don't wake him," Waldo whispered.

Was it possible he wasn't already awake? Waldo ignominiously dragged the barking Flirt into the kitchen. I led Ezra back to his room; his eyes were wide open and he was whimpering. But Waldo was right, he wasn't awake. Once he was under the covers, he turned his head back and forth. His whimpering continued at a lower decibel level. From the jumble that had all the pattern and rhythm of sentences but not the sounds or sense, I could very occasionally make out the words *not now not now not now not now.* Just those.

More than anyone I knew, Ezra lived fully in his sleep, in his dream-life, in his nighttime incarnation. When he was an infant, I'd nurse him, lay him in his crib, then stay and watch. And watch. There would be chores, telephone calls, and work beckoning just outside the door that couldn't even shut because it had been painted over so many times, but still I stayed. His room in our apartment was tiny, a former maid's room carved out of a larger former maid's room in one apartment of the three that had been carved from a larger prewar apartment. But there was room for his crib and a rocking chair I'd found on the sidewalk on Eighty-sixth and East End, and I was blissfully happy in that room. I loved to watch him sleep. His eyelids twitched, his fingers fluttered like an Indonesian dancer's, and his lips puckered, pursed, and then fell into a dreamy smile. Stories were unfolding, folding, and refolding, all inside that tiny head, or rather the not-so-tiny head attached to the tiny body with the tiniest fingers and toes. Could that be why I ended up hosting *Dream Radio*? Was it the memory of being warmly enclosed with napping Ezra in that tiny room that had spurred me to find employment in the early mornings listening to the dreams of those voices just emerging from the safety of sleep, just entering the clarity of day, and still between the two? Was it because I wanted to recapture that time of all-possibility, all-the-time?

As Ezra's body relaxed from the excitement of the sleepwalk, I lay beside him. I slept too.

Early in the still-dark morning I snuck back to our room, where Waldo in my absence had sprawled out and, like a Spanish conquistador, laid claim to the entire continent of our bed. I climbed in and rested my head in the crook of his arm, that warm, moist armpit place where he smelled most completely like himself. Whatever had gripped Ezra in the night, whatever it was he was now forgetting in the arms of Morpheus, still gripped me. Just on the very edge of the nighttime, in that thin line of light where morning was merely suggested in the east, there loomed an implacable void that I feared slipping into. In daylight I would be fine, but I knew only one way to keep away terror like this in the nighttime. Reaching down and taking hold of his warm penis, the muscle like no other, I held on tight and caressed the mushroom tip with my thumb. Waldo's penis was always ten degrees warmer than the rest of him, warmer by far than anything in the room or in the house. It seemed to exist in its private tropical climate, and always had. True to form, the magical hard-on came, and I climbed on top of Waldo and slid myself onto him. I knew he was awake by now and presumably pleased at where he found himself. But I could see he wasn't going to open his eyes yet, or let on he knew what was happening. He wanted this illusion that while he slept he was irresistible to the mysterious seductress and that even in his sleep he grew and thrust and gave pleasure in all the manly ways. Often that was fine. Wasn't that what marriage was all about? Being able to have sex in the middle of the night and not have to engage in conversation? Not entering the void? Or filling the void? Which was it?

Whatever it was, I'd clung just a little too desperately to it, ever since the week after Henry was born, when Waldo had told me that, to his great sorrow, he loved someone else. Edith Dilly, the daughter of his mother's golf partner. That was eight years ago, and now he said that he loved only me, and of course the boys. He said it repeatedly, and just as often I wanted to believe it. I had spent far too many hours of Henry's precious infancy obsessing about the wicked Edith Dilly and thinking of all the deserved and horrid things that could happen to her. It was so much easier, and safer, to hate her than to consider that Waldo had been willing to leave me and the boys and sail around the world, or at least up and down the eastern seaboard, with Edith Dilly. Everything was completely fine now. It was only in that chink between darkness and morning, between waking and sleep, that I caught glimpses of the black hole and backed away with horror, lest it suck me in.

But this night it was not enough to screw wordlessly, sleepily. I needed more. I needed him to pound the void out of me and give the emptiness no purchase in my body.

"Fuck me hard, Waldo. Oh, please. Fuck away."

His eyes opened. "Al!"

"You were expecting?"

"Roll over," he said. And I did. The better not to look at those eyes of his that I craved, his midnight blue eyes that could suck in the sturdiest soul, and I was not that. Looking into his eyes, I needed to grip the furniture to make sure I didn't fall in.

When we were finished, Waldo kissed the top of my head and softly pulled out and rolled off, back to his side of the bed. We slept through the heady light show of dawn. Darkness averted.

Ezra wanted chocolate chip pancakes for breakfast, and I made them too easily. That clued him in. He never seemed to recall anything of his sleepwalking, but I suspected that he knew something had happened because he often made extravagant demands at breakfast the next morning (ice cream on waffles, eggs and Oreo cookies) in the full expectation that I would comply. And I would.

Henry said, "Did Ezra somnambulate last night? Methinks I heard something."

"Are you sure we're related?" Ezra asked me.

"Don't be silly," I said. "And Henry, you don't have to be such a busybody."

"Well, did I?" Ezra said. "I assume I must have. Which would explain my dream—"

"There are altogether too many dreamers around here," Henry said.

Waldo said, "Since when do you find dreaming so objectionable?"

"I dreamed I was on top of a tall building and I had to make it lie down on its side so that I could walk to the base. The dogs were there but they stayed inside and watched from a window."

"That's really interesting, Ez," I said.

"See, Mom, you don't need that old radio show when you have us," Ezra said.

"She has you," Henry corrected. "But let's go! It's time for speleology! Stalagmites ho!"

I wasn't afraid of flying, but because I was irrationally afraid of missing flights, I always made my family leave plenty of time to get to the airport. Which we did for the cave trip. But there was a terrible traffic tie-up on the Whitestone Bridge, and so we arrived at LaGuardia an anxiety-producing fifty-seven minutes before their flight was scheduled to depart.

"Not to worry, Al. The boys and I have plenty of time. We'll be stopping at the sports bar for a few brews."

I watched them untie their shoes and await frisking. While one security guard glared beneath beetling brows, the others surveyed the world with studied indifference.

Twenty minutes later, I was on the Van Wyck heading home when Waldo called me on the cell phone.

"You know that traffic jam on the Whitestone?" he said. "It wasn't an accident."

"So?"

"It was a jumper."

"How do you know?"

"A lady in front of us in line told me."

"How did she know?"

"She said it happens all the time," Waldo said. "Plus she said he was standing on the railing when she drove past."

"She didn't see him actually jump, did she?" I said. I was shivering.

"I didn't ask."

"Maybe they talked him down."

"Somehow I think not," Waldo said.

"Well, it did seem weird to have all that traffic and no sign of an accident. Police cars and the ambulance, but no smashed-up cars, no broken glass."

"I'm not going to tell the boys."

"Good thinking. Why did you call to tell me?"

"I don't know. I must have needed to tell someone. And I thought you'd be interested."

"It doesn't matter. I like it that you called. Call all you want. Call me lots."

"Don't push your luck, Al. You don't want me developing an allergic rash."

"Very funny. Just concentrate on having a good time. And let Ez call and talk to Dandy all he wants. There's no reason not to."

"Henry just informed me that I should call him Chief."

"Chief what?"

"Just Chief," Waldo said.

"If you like. Just so long as you don't call him Hank."

"I always liked Hank."

"We've discussed this," I said. "Ad nauseam."

"Okay. They're loading our flight. Adios."

I realized I was crossing the Whitestone again and now traffic was fine, moving smoothly in both directions. In forty-odd minutes, all evidence of the jumper was gone, if you count traffic as evidence. I had read somewhere that most suicide jumpers change their minds midair. Halfway down, the jumper reconsiders the misery that sent him hurtling into the abyss, and it no longer looks so bad. The crushing weight of love lost is lifted from his back. He remembers a loving touch and the taste of a certain food and music that transports the senses, and he wants to give it another try. Then he hits the ground or the water, and blackness falls. How can this be known? Presumably because sometimes jumpers do survive, and then they tell us about their second thoughts. But can it be extrapolated from the testimony of those few that most jumpers regret the leap? This is something we can never know. Ah, the unknowables.

Chief? Chief, Chief, Chief. Where had I heard this Chief business before? When Henry was born, I'd wanted to call him Felix. Waldo had nixed the plan. He'd said, "What if he's not happy? It could be a terrible burden of a name to live up to." So my son was nameless for a week, Baby Boy Fairweather, until we'd agreed on Henry. We both had Henrys somewhere back in our families. Waldo's Great-Great-Uncle Henry claimed he'd invented the telephone and then been deprived of the glory by Alexander Graham Bell.

My second cousin Henry was a Jesuit out in California. He was quite radical, and we thought he might have been excommunicated or defrocked or something because he had written scathing articles about the impossibility of certain miracles. His life's work was disproving every instance he could find of purported incorruptibility—those stories about saints whose bodies still smelled like roses after they'd been dead for three weeks. Or three years.

In my life so far, I'd seen Cousin Henry only twice, once at a wedding and once at a funeral.

5 ❧ A Sus Órdenes

I STOOD ON THE chilly platform. The train's beams first appeared as specks of distant stars in the gray dusk, then snaked forward along the track I knew so well. In seconds they grew and became less like disembodied lights; they muted as they sank into the larger reality of the proboscis engine of Metro-North. The train roared in, and then stopped. In every car a door opened—the magic of a control panel. Exodus ensued. They stepped onto the platform, my neighbors, my friends, the parents of Ezra's and Henry's friends, some strangers, and one foreigner. The men and women in their dark suits and colorful scarves, the women stepping firmly in sensible shoes and sometimes in high heels. They stepped out with a purpose and direction. Almost all of them stepped out through the sliding doors of the train and kept moving in a seamless gait, not missing a beat. Only a few stepped out as if into the glare of the footlights. These few had slept all the way from Grand Central and for just an instant had forgotten what they were doing here; who were all these people sidestepping around them?

I recognized Abelardo immediately. And I instantly knew that I had never met him before. Our previous meeting, at Quincy House or elsewhere, existed only in Waldo's imagination.

"What a surprise!" I said, which wasn't what I meant at all.

"A sus órdenes," he said, with an almost imperceptible nod of his head.

Yet how easy it was to recognize him. Was it because he appeared to be from another climate? I will never know. Of course, he was much better groomed than anyone else getting off at VerGroot. That must have been it, and not some lingering scent of mangoes. His suit was so smooth, so achingly unwrinkled that I wondered if he'd spent the last hour standing up in the aisle. His shoes glistened in the fading light. I remembered my father cleaning his shoes on Sunday evenings, rapidly buffing them to that businesslike luster—the movement just a bit too quick to see, like the sharpening of his carving knife. It dawned on me that I'd never seen Waldo polish his shoes, had no idea if he'd ever polished his shoes, and I was sure he'd never taught our sons to polish their shoes. Neither had I. Abelardo's suit was dark blue, a shade of blue I immediately coveted, and his tie was patterned a tropical oceanic blue with not a hint of hyperbole. My neighbors must have spent their entire commute in awe of Abelardo's sartorial splendor; his first-class haircut and his demeanor that made it all seem so easy.

I should not have brought Dandy. The car smelled like dog, and Abelardo's was not a suit that should ever smell like dog. But of course my car always smelled like dog, whether Dandy and Flirt were in the back or not. All day long I'd been checking the color of Dandy's gums, so I couldn't leave him behind; if the train had been late, I'd have ended up sitting by the station itching to pull back his upper lips and see the hopeful pink color. One of the great things about dogs was that they didn't mind my gum-checking. Henry wouldn't have put up with it, not once, never mind all day. Ez would not have complained, but even he eventually raised his eyebrows when I took his temperature for the third time in as many hours.

It began to snow as we drove home from the station. In the space of the less than half an hour since I had left the house, the sky had become as opaque as a cataract. There would be no pointing out the sun plummeting over on the western shore of the river, as I usually did for new arrivals from the city. No sunset, and the snow fell. The flurries were large, and there was something serious about the way they landed on the windshield, each flake clinging to its individual uncloneable shape.

"You're in for a treat, Abelardo. It looks like we're going to have a little snow," I said.

"I've never been very fond of snow. And you must please call me Lalo. It is the tradition."

"Perhaps you'll change your mind this evening. I think the woods look lovely with snow, and we'll make a fire."

Naturally, Abelardo did not mention the fecund odor of moist dog, and I kept my window cracked open a bit.

Our driveway was uphill but not terribly so for the first one hundred feet. Then it flattened out and turned left toward the kitchen door at the western side of the house. The top of the incline was in the deep shade of two old hemlocks, and that was where ice patches always formed and ambushed me. But I was not thinking of ice as we drove to the house, and for once, I did not skid or lose traction.

Inside, I led Abelardo up to the guest room, otherwise known as Ezra's room. Henry's and Ez's rooms were each tiny and magical little kingdoms, as different from each other as the boys were. For reasons that had more to do with the resident's personality than the room's cleanliness, I had deemed Ezra's the more appropriate for stranger occupation, and I'd tidied it up. But as soon as I entered it with Abelardo and saw it with foreign eyes, saw the chart on the wall that named all the parts of the eyeball, and the neatly labeled collection of dried tree fungi on the top shelf, and the birds' nests cradling reconstructed pale blue eggshells on the shelf just below, and the well-thumbed Tintin comic books under the bed, and the lava lamp, and the cardboard box with pennies glued to every inch of its surface, both inside and out, I wondered if I had misjudged. But it was too late. He was gracious. I pointed out the bathroom, the only bathroom.

I had neglected to ask Waldo what Abelardo actually did, or

what I should do with him, or anything at all about him. Had he said something about coffee? At Harvard they had rowed crew together, and later were roommates. They were close in that way that men become close when they struggle together against the same arbitrary physical difficulty: a river, a mountain face, a storm at sea, an opposing team. Through Abelardo, Waldo had gotten to know several other wealthy and amusing Central Americans. And they, apparently, found Waldo's pale winter-loving Yankee-ness appealing. According to Waldo, they all went home to Guatemala or Nicaragua or El Salvador and dated one another's sisters. He'd always regretted that he had had no sister to enter into that social intertwining. I'd told him it all sounded a little too feudal and arranged to me. I'd told him it wasn't like that in Spain, where my mother's parents were from and where she had spent her early years cavorting among the olive trees. The truth was: I had no idea. Waldo had just laughed. Now I didn't know what to say to Abelardo. I didn't even know if he liked dogs.

For dinner that evening, I made carrot soup, chicken, and salad. My plan was to eat carrot soup all week long, along with my tinned oysters. I was eagerly awaiting those tinned oysters.

"You're not by any chance a vegetarian," I said before putting chicken on his plate.

"No, we have a cattle farm."

"That's nice," I said. "So you don't have a problem with chicken."

"We also have chickens. The *granjas* are near Chinandega and the *matadero* is in Tipitapa. That's an abattoir to you."

"That's nice too," I said. "I was a vegetarian for a long time, but then I found myself craving protein." It seemed more elegant to say *protein* instead of *flesh,* although that was what I had found myself craving. "And of course boys need protein. Lots of protein."

"There is also the coffee *finca.* Caffeine also is very healthy for young people, for blood flow."

It was only when Abelardo was chewing his food that I noticed the size of his ears. They were not nearly so pronounced as Waldo had led me to believe. But they were a long way from Henry's tender little apricots that I used to nibble after reading him *The Runaway Bunny*. And having noticed them, I needed to look away and examine the salad greens on my plate, the pale green spine of the romaine lettuce, the dark green spinach, the spermlike tendrils of alfalfa sprouts. What if Nicaraguans didn't eat alfalfa sprouts? What if they didn't consider alfalfa sprouts to be appropriate for human consumption?

Think of it as broadening someone's horizons. Think of Waldo eating garlicky frogs' legs in Paris and olivey rabbit in Provence, both worthy cultural experiences. So with my alfalfa sprouts.

"I am most grateful for this opportunity to visit with my dear friend Waldito," Abelardo said. "And so of course I am sorry he is not here."

"I'm sorry too," I said. You don't know how sorry.

"But what a pleasure to visit with his wife. It is a terrible shame about missing your wedding. Our national bird, *Aëdes aegypti*, intervened," he explained, and chuckled gently.

I laughed too rather than reveal my complete ignorance of the reference. Something about the pyramids? Didn't the Mayans build pyramids too?

Abelardo continued, "In college, we all thought that Waldo could do anything. That he would do anything. *Naturalmente,* we didn't know exactly what that would entail."

"But Waldo still can do anything," I said, thinking of his fingers, his tongue, his penis—surely not what Abelardo was referring to. "He doesn't always know what that anything should be. You'll have to come back when he and the boys return."

"Perhaps, but I am only in New York for a few days of research. It will depend."

"What are you researching, Abelardo?"

"My Great-Aunt Tristána. We believe, it is believed, she should be canonized; that is to say, she should be beatified first, but ultimately canonized. For the good of all. So I am here to see what I can do," he said.

"Your aunt was a saint?"

"Of course," he said. "That is why I am here."

"In New York?" I said. "What can there be in New York?"

"Oh, you have the Hagiographers Club, and I have been corresponding with the librarian there. His name is Hubert van Toots. They have the best library outside of the Bollandists in Belgium. And the weather in Belgium is even worse than it is here."

"I've never heard of this Hagiographers Club," I said. "In New York City? What exactly is it?"

"Never? How remiss of you. Neither have I ever been there, but that will all change soon. They have a wonderful library, thousands of books and treatises, all about saints and their lives. Of course, much of it is in Latin."

De gustibus. Amo, amas, amat. Dominus vobiscum.

"But can you eat there? What would a library about saints serve?" I said. I imagined oysters on halo platters, oysters in triptychs. How little I knew.

"Mr. van Toots and I never discussed food. Although I am sure he eats somewhere. The food in some monasteries is excellent. Though not all, no, not all."

"Your friend is a monk?"

"Not anymore. That is all I know. Oh, and he mentioned he was writing a monograph on the cephalophores—those are saints who carry their heads. After they've been cut off. Which is very interesting, but not pertinent to my Tía Tristána."

"It sounds like something a rock star would do."

"First that rock star would have to be decapitated."

"Well," I said. "This is all over my head." I checked, but no, Abelardo was not chuckling. Then he was.

"You are delightful," he said.

I was silenced, briefly. "So where is this place?"

"The address is on Gramercy Park. Do you know Gramercy Park?"

"Not really. Not at all. They have material about your aunt?"

"I am afraid not. All her things are in Nicaragua. But they do have everything about the canonization process. We need to study that, to master it. And then research other saints. Saints, like her, who never married. Who refused to get married because they had other plans. It is always good to find a pattern."

"Didn't you go to the seminary for a while? That's what Waldo told me," I said.

"They barely taught us anything about saints. It was an out-of-favor time for saints."

"Did Waldo know about your aunt? Did he know her?"

"He may have met her when we were in school, when he came to visit us at the *finca*, Las Brisas. She was very old, of course, but she hardly seemed to age at all. Because of her sanctity, I believe."

"He never told me anything," I said.

Abelardo said, "I find that shocking. He should have."

It was time for Waldo to call so I could tell him about Dandy and say good night to the boys. I had trained myself not to panic when he didn't call, because of his telephone aversion. Like his whole family, Waldo felt ripped off by Alexander Graham Bell's claim to the telephone's invention. Righteous indignation, he would call it. But that animus had never stopped Posey. (Of course, she'd been born a Pinchbeck.)

The phone was not ringing. After scraping off the bones, I gave the plates to Flirt and Dandy. There wasn't much, but they enjoyed what there was. Then I donned the latex gloves and measured out the cyclosporine.

"Are you diabetic?"

"No, this is for Dandy, the dog. See, it's an oral syringe."

"Is he diabetic?"

This struck me as humorous, although God knows he hadn't

meant it that way. "No, he has anemia, aplastic anemia. That's why I couldn't go with Waldo and the boys."

"And you love him very much."

"Well, he's our family's dog. Flirt too, but she's indestructible."

"You must tell me all about it. We have always loved dogs, in our family."

"It's kind of a long story," I said. "Or maybe not. But I usually make it long, I warn you."

Once I'd done the dishes, and made coffee with the beans Abelardo had brought from his family's *finca,* we went into the living room and lit a fire. Abelardo said fires were one of his fondest memories of college life.

I was just a bit incredulous. "You had fires in the dorms?"

"My senior tutor did. He was a very kind man."

I was glad to hear it. And that was how I came to tell Abelardo of a canine mortality obsession that had ended with my being home with Dandy while Waldo and Henry and Ezra explored dark, moist, and slimy caves.

"Basically, it is because I have already let two dogs die—I won't go so far as to say I killed them. But I could not leave Dandy. And yes, I know that no one would blame me if he died, but I would blame myself."

"Why would you do that?"

Why indeed? I thought. Guilt was generally considered a Catholic thing; certainly Waldo identified it that way, both my having it and his lacking it. But he also said that my clinging to it was all self-indulgence and drama. He had a point. He often did.

Before Waldo, I'd never had dogs or even known dogs. I compared my newfound canine devotion to the fervor of converted Catholics. No one who'd grown up with dogs or as a Catholic would ever behave so extravagantly. There was something tasteless about such excess.

I said to Abelardo, "I just would. I always believe that someone around here has to feel guilty, and since I'm the only one who feels that way, it is generally me. Did you have classes in guilt at the seminary?" Flirt and Dandy lay between us on the rug. Flirt was closest to the warmth of the fire. Dandy curled up on the chilly perimeter. It was always thus with these two.

"No. But we do study sin—or I would have studied sin, had I stayed longer. *Las estudias hamartologisticas,*" he said, and grinned. I had no idea what he was talking about and no idea why it might be grin-worthy.

He said, "But in the intervening years I have come to think differently on guilt."

"You probably think I am self-indulgent," I said.

"Is that what my friend Waldito thinks?"

Aha, I thought. He must have studied with the Jesuits. Aren't they the ones who answer questions with questions? Or is that the Buddhists? I had no intention of answering him. "You have to understand about the bulldogs," I said. "You know the Pinchbecks always had bulldogs?"

If you credited the family lore, the first Pinchbeck in the Americas stepped off the *Mayflower* accompanied by a bulldog. The fact that there has never been a bulldog who didn't get violently ill on a boat never bothered the storytellers. When I first fell in love with Waldo, they had a bulldog named Stinkerbelle. She'd inhaled way too much pot hanging around with Waldo and Dick.

Abelardo looked pained. "Yes, I remember La Smellista."

"Stinkerbelle," I said.

"Exactly. She attacked me the first time I went to Maine with Waldo. Dogs have always loved me—it is a family trait—so I petted her, expecting a friend, and she bit my hand. You can still see the scar, very faintly." He held his right hand up closer to the fire. The scar was impossibly faint. What struck me were his perfect fingernails. I coveted them. I sat on my hands. "Posey bandaged it quite nicely, but she considered it my own fault."

"Not unlikely," I said. "Posey has never held the dogs responsible for their bad behavior. It is entirely the owners' fault. Except in your case, when it was the visitor's fault."

"In my country, if my dog were to bite you, he would be shot. We are not so sentimental. That is because we are tropical, and we are a poor country. Also perhaps because we understand the hierarchy in nature."

"It's too bad you didn't meet Bubbles. Posey and Three got her after Stinkers, and she was a major improvement. She was the ring bearer at our wedding. Which was sort of wonderful, and sort of a disaster. Posey was in a state because Bubbles had almost died on the flight to California. Bulldogs don't do well in the baggage compartment. My family thought I'd taken affection for Waldo to unseemly lengths."

"Can affection ever be too great?" he asked.

"Let's not go there," I said. "But I really am sorry you didn't come to our wedding. Getting all those Fairweathers out to California felt like an accomplishment, something along the lines of the Treaty of Versailles. Or do I mean the Peace of Worms?"

"I too am sorry. I am sure I would have learned much, and understood more. But alas, I had dengue fever at the time. *Lástima*."

Abelardo's face was mutable, and deepening by the firelight. His eyes were terribly dark, either brown or black, but it was too dark to tell which. So I went on. "The thing about bulldogs is that, well, to the untrained eye, they were so ugly."

"Yes, that was remarkable about them."

But eventually I'd changed my mind. It was my religious conversion, or as Audrey said, the brain transplant. It was naturally due to Ezra and Henry, who loved their grandparents' bulldogs: Bubbles, Peewee, and the late, lamented Gwendolyn. It was inevitable that sooner or later they would want a bulldog of their own. And one day I relented.

"And then our first dog, Gertrude, was killed by a motorcycle. Because I trained her so badly," I said.

We'd named her for Gertrude Stein, who I think in real life had pugs, but they could have been French bulldogs. Posey was delighted that I was no longer depriving my children of the advantages of growing up with a bulldog, but she didn't think much of the name. She'd told me Gertrude Stein had had a Boston marriage. I'd told her that Gertrude and her Alice had always lived in France.

Abelardo tugged at his earlobe, something he did again and again and which may have accounted for their size.

Waldo claimed I did not dominate Gertrude, which was true. Which was the problem. She always rode shotgun in the car, and if we were stopped at a stoplight and there was a motorcycle next to us, she'd go bonkers. She'd bark maniacally and lunge at the biker. I'd learned to keep the front windows shut, but I feared for the strength of the glass. After my car pulled away, its passenger-side window would be opaque with saliva. It had become a scrim of doggy drool.

"You know we were at his brother Dick's when she was killed?" I said. "Do you know Dick?"

"He used to come and visit Waldito at our rooms in Quincy House. A charming young man. We spoke about agriculture. He was interested in avocados and mangoes. As you know, my family has always farmed, and I applauded his interest. But it seemed unusual. Since he wanted to stay in Maine, where I believe nothing grows but blueberries and pine trees."

"It's not quite that bad," I said. "Potatoes grow too. Maine potatoes are famous."

"I shall remember that."

There were no potatoes, though, at Dick's farm. There was nothing native to the state of Maine.

"Gertrude was killed by a motorcycle," I said. "She was trying to take him down. She hated motorbikes. That's how fierce she was. I could never be that fierce."

We'd been out front at Dick's house when a motorcycle came

along, its roar piercing the low hum of grass growing and flies napping. Gertrude had lifted her head and, almost simultaneously, had run out to the road.

"Do you think a dog is capable of hating?" Abelardo asked. "Saint Francis thought not."

"Whether she hated bikers or not, she got herself killed. It was Henry's first trauma."

Abelardo tugged on his ears, and I felt an irresistible urge to massage my own lobes.

"It's just that he was only two, but he claims to remember everything."

"I remember something that happened when I was almost three. It was Tía Tata's first miracle."

"She committed a miracle?" I said.

"She cured me."

"What did she cure you of?"

"The hiccups."

Of course I smiled. It seemed an odd joke, but who was I to judge?

"You think I am kidding. But these were terrible hiccups. I'd had them for days, seven days, in fact. I was unable to sleep. I was pale and weak. My mother was in despair, and then Tía Tata rubbed the small of my back and said a prayer, and they went away."

"You think that was a miracle?" I said.

"We know it was. I don't expect others to understand. It is our task, that they may understand."

"I don't want you to think I'm not sympathetic, because I am. I really am. I get terrible hiccups and I hate them. And Ezra got hiccups in utero, which, by the way, is not unusual. But . . . don't hiccups usually go away on their own?"

"That is a perfectly rational point to make. But that is not what happened." He paused, breathed so deeply a hiccup eruption seemed likely. He exhaled slowly. "Hiccups do *normally* go away on their own, of course. They can also be fatal. Pope Pius the Twelfth died of hiccups. May he rest in peace."

"Are you serious?"

"Serious as the pope."

"Did Waldo know about this? Not the pope, but your aunt's miracle."

"I'm sure I told him. It falls into the category of life-altering experiences. After all, we were roommates."

"He never told me."

"Of course, not being Catholic, he never really understood," Abelardo said.

"That *is* one thing you and I have in common," I said. "But I'm not a good Catholic. You probably wouldn't call me a Catholic at all."

"No. I would never say that. I would say that is for you to determine."

My stomach was growling. It would be very odd indeed if I started hiccupping just then.

"Now you have told me how one bulldog died," Abelardo said. "But you say you have killed two. Or not killed them. My apologies."

He poked the fire and threw on a log that hadn't been properly aged. The wood crackled. Sparks jumped and danced inside the fireplace like the damned in the last days of the plague.

"Are you sure this isn't boring?"

Abelardo leaned farther back into his chair, farther back than I thought possible, and pressed the fingertips of his right hand to the fingertips of his left hand and created the skeleton of a perfect dome.

"About ten months after Gertrude's untimely death we got Priscilla, but the boys called her Pilly. She was much more docile." I was prevaricating a little. I knew that. There was a way in which I was massaging this story in order to make myself seem both better and worse than I really was. Pilly wasn't really docile,

45

she was narcoleptic. Sleeping was her strongest suit. Her second strongest was pretending to be dead. I was always calling her name, hoping for a raised eyelid or a sigh, just to reassure myself she was still alive.

Abelardo flexed his extended fingers back and forth.

"You'd think Waldo would have called by now," I said. Flirt got up, circled the room, and then lay beside my feet. I loved her warmth. Dandy wasn't moving, again. In another life, I thought, I will have pet turtles. It doesn't matter if they never move. True, I killed pet turtles back in California, but I hadn't noticed. Not until they began to smell. Guilt had not ensued. Waldo told me that turtles lack the aging gene, which is why scientists are always studying them. Even that had not made me feel guilty about the dead turtles. "I tried his cell but he must have turned it off. He has a thing about telephones. You probably knew that."

"In college he would never answer the phone. He said he couldn't hear the ringing."

"Did he tell you about his Great-Great-Uncle Henry? The one who really invented the telephone?"

"He explained how Alexander Graham Bell was a fraud and that he'd stolen all his ideas from a distant relative. Are you saying this is true? Our other roommates—you know Jaimee Bolt and Ogden?—they began to attribute every famous invention or discovery to a relative of Waldo's. They found this extremely amusing." It must have been, because Abelardo chuckled audibly. "Didn't he tell you?"

"Not a word," I said. "Silent as the grave."

"Oh, yes. Isaac Newton did not discover gravity; that was discovered by Waldo's Cousin Daisy, who had a coconut fall on her head while vacationing in the Caribbean. And the steam engine was invented by his Uncle Freddy Fairweather, who lived in some river in Maine. The best one was Einstein. Or not Einstein. They liked to say that Einstein stole the theory of relativity from

Waldo's Grandmother Frances, who wrote it down on the back of a grocery list. He also had relatives who invented the radio, the ballpoint pen, aspirin, and, of all things, the sash window."

"He never told me," I said. "It must have been very funny. He should have told me. It would explain so much."

"About why he hates the telephone?"

"About why he is the way he is. Now, I just wish he would call. I can't believe I lost the name of the hotel. That is very unlike me."

"I'm sure he'll call soon. I too would like to speak with him," Abelardo said. "Is it still snowing?"

I went and opened the front door. Sometimes you couldn't tell just by looking out the window, because it was dark, or because the wind blew the snow around long after it had stopped falling.

"It looks like it. It's a beautiful night."

"I prefer the scent of gardenias."

"You could like both snow and gardenias," I said. It sounded like something I would have said to the boys: *Just because Max doesn't like yogurt doesn't mean you have to not like it. You can like both Max and yogurt.*

"But I don't. Alas."

The fire blazed on, soporifically.

"And so what about the other dog? She is also dead, I presume?"

"It was her eyes. Bulldogs are prone to all sorts of eye diseases. All those wrinkles make their eyelids turn inside out and then they get infected and full of pus." Abelardo shifted slightly in the armchair. "I'm sorry," I said. "I didn't mean to mention pus."

"Not at all," Abelardo said. His own eyelids were looking heavy.

"So one of her eyelids got infected, and even though I slathered it with antibiotic cream, the infection got into her system and one night she ran a terribly high fever, I don't know exactly how high because she died on the way to the vet."

I stopped and waited. What was I waiting for? Exoneration? Absolution? Forgiveness? All of the above.

Abelardo was so still I feared I had put him to sleep. So much for my tragic canine tales, I thought.

Finally he said, "I am sorry you didn't pray to Santa Lucia."

"Who?"

"She suffered terribly under the Romans, and her eyes were torn out. Surely you've seen the famous painting by Tiepolo of Lucia and her eyeballs on a platter. Before she died, they were miraculously replaced and she could see again. Better than before."

"You're kidding."

"She might have helped your Pilly. I wish I had known. I would have prayed for you."

"Next time."

Flirt and Dandy were giving me their signals, so I got up and let them out the front door. The snow was falling from the huge dark sky. Several inches gleamed white in the night, softening all the landscape's contours. I loved waking up to a snow-covered world. I loved knowing that everything had changed overnight, and that we, mere mortals, had had nothing to do with it. But I loved most of all to be with Ezra and Henry when they saw the snow out their windows, and felt safe.

"Do you know the poet Rubén Darío?" Abelardo said.

Where did this come from? Was this his long-lost brother, or a hero of the revolution? "No, I'm afraid not."

"He is the great Nicaraguan poet. He wrote a poem about Saint Francis and the wolf. 'Los motivos del lobo.' It's one of his most famous, rightly so. Most people think that it speaks of the wickedness of humanity as compared with the innocence of animals. But I think otherwise. I think Darío is writing that animals must be animals, and follow their instincts, and that we cannot attribute to them the motives that drive us."

I stood for a minute longer wrapped in the lacy chill that swooped past the open door, and then shut it very quietly.

"But I am not a literary scholar," Abelardo said. "I am just a coffee farmer."

"I'd like to see this poem," I said.

"You will."

"You must be very tired," I said. I knew that I wanted nothing more than to pull off my clothes and crawl into bed, and there, in solitude, wonder what Waldo and the boys were doing.

"I am. But tell me one thing: why are these dogs not bull-dogs?" Abelardo gestured toward the front door, and by extension the outdoors, without turning his face from the fire.

It seemed painfully obvious, so much so that I couldn't believe there didn't exist—somewhere out there—a better answer than the one I was about to give him. "Because they kept dying on me."

"You don't really think it had anything to do with you, do you?"

"I didn't want them to die. I was devoted to them. We all were. But still—"

"I had a very good friend, a Jesuit, and he told me that it was egotism to blame myself for sins I had not committed. That I was a glutton for guilt. It didn't sound quite that way in Spanish."

If I'd been eager to go to bed before, it was worse now. My toes twitched for the sheets. Abelardo's fingers on both hands were still meeting at the tips, rising and falling like a dying fish cast upon the beach. He added, "Of course I do not think you are an ego-tist. Not that at all. But the monsignor was good teacher, and a good friend of mine. So I often quote him."

"Okay. I really don't blame myself," I said. "I just feel respon-sible. There's a difference."

"I'm glad to hear it." Abelardo nodded and gave every impres-sion that he took me seriously.

I could hear Flirt and Dandy running back and forth on the front porch. "You must be exhausted," I said. Again.

I let the dogs in. Normally they were brown and white, but now they were completely white, and for all that they were burdened with a layer of snow, they seemed lighter than air. The snow was falling steadily. Across the driveway was the barn that was such a sorry structure it barely deserved the name. The roof wore a thick white cap. It pained me to see the snow when Ezra and Henry were not sleeping upstairs, were not dreaming of a snow day, of a brand-new day stolen from the clutches of the legislated, regulated days of public education.

"When will it stop?" Abelardo asked.

"Soon, I'm sure. I never listened to the weather report, but it seems to be tapering off."

"Then I will thank you for a most delightful evening," he said.

He went upstairs, and I heard the high-pitched squeaking of Ezra's door, so different from the low breathy groaning of Henry's floorboards.

The wet dogs smelled powerfully, and they were uncharacteristically still, as if it took all their strength to keep from barking out some secret knowledge with which they had just been entrusted. For a few silent minutes I sat downstairs. Had I just unloaded on this unsuspecting—but very well-dressed—foreigner the stories of my late, lamented dogs and my currently sick dog? Obviously he'd been being polite. Normal people (my friends and relatives, for instance) stopped me ages earlier. When Dandy had first gotten sick and was diagnosed, his looming death seemed to me a tragedy of Greek proportions. Waldo told me I was more upset about Dandy than I had ever been over one of the boys' illnesses. "But they've been so healthy!" I whined. I justified myself by saying that Dandy's illness was fatal (so we'd thought then) while the boys only fell out of trees or put foreign objects in their noses. But Waldo was right. Even Ezra had to whisper in my ear, "He's a dog, Mom. He's only a dog."

By telling Abelardo these things, had I revealed more than I cared to of my misplaced priorities and my tendency toward melodrama? Surely he would make the connection between the loss of my *Dream Radio* job and the onset of Dandy's illness. And what were the chances he would tell me his dreams early next morning?

6 ❧ Snow Was General

I F DREAM RADIO WERE still on the air, I thought, and if I were someone else who was not the host of *Dream Radio*, then I could call in and tell that host-other and all the sleepy listeners in the tri-state area my dream this morning. No such luck.

I drew back the curtains. It was still snowing. Maybe I had missed one weather report, or even two, but there had been nothing about this snow lasting through the night. Here we were, living in a new century in which every snowflake was predicted, charted, and analyzed. Yet these had not been. Not this profusion of snowflakes. Not that I knew of.

From the warm impress of my body that was greedily in the middle of the flannel sheets, I remembered Abelardo. What was I going to do with him? And why hadn't Waldo called? Did he even know about the snow?

There was only silence, thank God, coming from Abelardo's room, from Ezra's room.

I tiptoed downstairs to let the dogs out. The snow had drifted toward the back door, and I pushed it away with the storm door. Whirling snow flew in and blew me backward. Flirt and Dandy cowered behind the counter. "You're dogs, guys. You *have* to go out. That's the deal."

He's going back to the city today, I assured myself. He'll take the train in, and snow isn't so deep in the city, it never is. And then it's Oyster Time.

Abelardo was standing in the kitchen, looking somewhat bereft—but ever so crisp, buttoned, and tucked in—when I came in from clearing a path to the car and shoveling it off. Was I discovering in myself a latent attraction to a well-groomed man?

"Good morning. You slept well?"

"I enjoyed young Ezra's bed. It was unusual."

"What was unusual about it?" Globs of snow were melting off me, puddling the floor. This man needed his breakfast.

"I don't think I meant exactly that. I meant it was very soft. And the panic button was a nice touch."

"It's not a real panic button," I said. "Ezra and Henry both like disaster scenarios."

There was no way I was going to shovel the whole driveway. I figured I could clear around the car, start her up, and then rock back and forth a few times to generate enough momentum to get down to the road in first gear. It worked. It was no surprise that Emerson Street was slow going. I guessed it had been plowed maybe once the previous evening, and not again since. What was surprising was that Route 72 had barely been plowed either.

This could have been the result of recent shakeups at the Department of Public Works. For almost fifty years Max Stone had ruled the DPW like it was his private fiefdom; his was a benign dictatorship over the snowplows, graders, garbage trucks, and cherry pickers. He had retired early in the winter, in the full expectation that his son and right-hand man, Max Junior, would be named head of the department after him. Our town supervisor, however, for reasons he refused to say publicly, did not do so. He brought in a new man from outside the town. But Max Stone had no intention of going gently into his retirement. His letters to the local paper, the *VerGroot Sentinel,* aspired to and sometimes achieved new pinnacles of outrage. Waldo read them aloud each Friday and considered it a dreary week if there was no new indignant screed from Max Stone or his large family. Waldo's favorite letter, often cited, compared the merits of a well-plowed road to those of well-folded laundry.

Still, and notwithstanding my terror of ice, I considered myself a good driver in the snow and I safely delivered Abelardo to the train station. I surprised myself by being almost sorry he had to leave. I would not say he had begun to grow on me, but given that the storm was going to keep us all inside for a while, I caught myself imagining we two sitting by the fire. (Remember Annabel! Remember Inner Resources!)

The VerGroot station was a Gothic revival building of a silliness that belied its sturdy structure. "The station looks closed," Abelardo said.

"It can't be," I said. So I looked. There were no lights on inside, and a notice was posted on the door. "Damn."

DUE TO HEAVY SNOW AND HIGH WINDS, ALL TRAINS ARE CANCELED. Period. You'd think they might have inserted the word *temporarily*. But no such luck. It hadn't occurred to me to call first or check online. I never had before. Maybe there was more snow somewhere else, because our inches did not seem enough to warrant this egregious halt in public transportation.

"I guess I'll have the pleasure of your company awhile longer," I said cheerily.

"Snow was the one thing at Harvard I could never abide," he said.

"Really?"

"I could tolerate the bad food and the bad music. But the snow was terrible. The way it stays around."

"It's not so bad," I said, unconvincingly.

The drive home took much longer than the trip out. It hadn't seemed like so much before, but now I could see that the snow was pummeling the ground. The aforementioned high winds had found their way up the railroad tracks. So really the snow was falling horizontally, in millions of paths parallel to the curve of the Earth.

The situation on Emerson had not improved in the meantime. Getting up our driveway was going to be a challenge; I would have to get a running start. The good news was there would be no other cars on the road. As we approached I drove far onto the wrong side of the road, aimed at the driveway, shifted into first gear, and slammed on the accelerator.

The car didn't make it. About a hundred feet in I skidded and made an almost perfect one-eighty.

"Perhaps I can help you?" Abelardo said. He was whiter than the snowdrift I had driven into, if that was possible.

"Don't worry. I often don't make it on the first try."

The second try was a breeze. I was nervous about the icy spot, but we roared past it and then it was smooth sailing to the house.

"You will excuse me if I go lie down," Abelardo said as we crossed the threshold.

"I hope I didn't scare you."

"Perhaps I didn't sleep as well as I thought last night."

I was watching the television weather, all weather, lots of weather, when the phone finally rang.

But it was Posey. "Why haven't I heard from you folks?" she said.

"We're having a snowstorm," I said.

"Of course you're having a snowstorm. That's why I'm calling."

"Are you having one as well?" Posey and Edgar Cicero lived in Catamunk, Maine.

"We are not," Posey said, as if she were being denied a snowstorm that was rightfully hers. "I suppose the boys are out sledding. We simply have snow."

"They're not here. Remember? They went to see the caves."

"I can't be expected to remember everything."

"Of course not," I said.

"What on earth will they do in the caves?" she said.

"Whatever they want. They are fascinated by caves, and bats, all the limestone formations and all the dripping water. Honestly, I haven't a clue."

"You never told me what Waldo wants for his birthday."

"Nothing. I'm sure he wants for nothing," I said.

"Doesn't he need a new sweater? The last time I saw him he was wearing that same ratty blue one."

"It's his favorite sweater," I said. "He barely ever lets me wash it."

"When he was a boy I would have to do his laundry while he slept. I'd have everything back where he liked it in the morning, and he never knew the difference. And at least he didn't smell."

Years ago, whenever Posey disparaged Waldo's attire or personal hygiene, I'd taken her comments personally and assumed that I was deficient in my uxorial duties. Not Waldo. He heard his mother's comments selectively, and responded selectively; it was his way of loving her, by only ever hearing or recalling the aspects of her that he could love. For the longest time, Posey's critiques of Waldo's grubby clothes and unshorn hair had filled me with wifely self-doubt. However, this was one job I still had.

"I know, Posey," I said. "But I usually fall asleep before he does."

"That's the problem."

"Well, he's a grown man. I think he should be able to make his own fashion decisions."

"You're both so modern about those things. I put Three's clothes out for him every morning of his life."

I knew that. She had shared it with me many times.

"Does Mr. Cicero like his clothes laid out for him?" I said.

"I gave Waldo that sweater more than ten years ago. I really think he needs another."

"He loves whatever you give him, Posey."

She said, "I have to go now. Apparently, Mr. Cicero thinks he can shovel the walk without any help from me."

"Be careful, Posey. Remember your sciatica."

"It's bursitis. And tendinitis. But I can't let that stop me."

I let the dogs in and we settled down to our private revels with the weather report.

A dome of frigid air over the Northeast will organize snow.

There is a broad jet-stream disturbance slowly moving off the plume of humid air that will arrive by dawn, that arrived last night, that will last through midnight, that will go on forever.

Accumulations of up to four feet are expected, are regretted, are a thing of the past.

The roads, the schools, the massage parlors are closed, are opening late, are not opening at all. You are kindly requested not to drive unless it is another day, an emergency, a relief.

You will be asked the differences between a winter storm advisory and a winter storm warning and a winter storm alert. You will be asked to define a blizzard. You will be surrounded by snow.

The snow fell and fell. Everything was closed. I listened for the telltale rattle-and-clank-and-screech of the snowplow out on Emerson, and heard nothing. It struck me as remarkable how something as large as a snowstorm could happen so silently. Even the wind blew silently. Mere inches past the windows and doors, past everything but the warm interior of the house, was a complete whiteout. That morning I had seen the dark winter trees, their burrowing trunks and reaching limbs, delineated in the chilly white blanket. Now there was no shape out there at all.

The dogs refused to go outside. Waldo often pointed out that they were hunting dogs, and, as such, they were meant to be outdoors. He asserted that they should stay in the barn and never muddy up the house. Not that the boys or I ever paid attention. We were happiest in the proximity of a sleeping dog.

The snow made them clingier than usual. Flirt and Dandy were with me as I searched the shelves for dinner inspiration. I looked with longing at the tinned oysters and knew I could not serve them to Abelardo. The dogs were with me as I folded the laundry. I thought about taking this opportunity to clean and organize Henry's room, but I didn't want Abelardo to hear me rustling and thumping around up there, with the dogs, who would not leave me.

"When will it stop?"

I must have dozed off in front of the weather report. My eyes popped open. Flirt's tail beat a staccato rhythm on the floor. Dandy slumbered on. Of course it was Abelardo, down from his lair. He wore pressed khakis and a pale blue oxford shirt. Not winter wear.

"Tomorrow. Certainly tomorrow," I said.

"This is intolerable."

"Oh, it's not so bad," I said. "I'm sorry you're stuck here with me. I realize it's not all that exciting, but at least we're warm. Do you play Scrabble? Cards?"

"I wish I could see it as you do. As a diversion. But I have this problem that has only exacerbated with time. I need a warm climate. It is my tragic flaw."

"Tragic flaw? You don't think that's a little histrionic?"

"Not at all."

"I don't mean to be critical," I said. Well, then, what *did* I mean to be? "But isn't a tragic flaw more like being doomed to marry your mother?"

"I disagree. It was Oedipus's fate to marry his mother. His flaw was having the desire to do so."

"But he didn't want to marry his mother. Quite the contrary."

"He wanted to marry Jocasta, and she was his mother," Abelardo said.

"But—"

"Please excuse me. I should not argue with you. It must be the weather."

"I could turn up the heat," I said. Although I very much doubted the house could get any warmer.

"I'm not that cold. I just find the snow excessive. The way it falls and then stays on the ground."

"I guess we should be grateful we're not in the Antarctic, or the Arctic. Snow that falls there lasts for thousands of years, turns into glacial ice. Because it's so dry, I think."

"I'm afraid I have no interest in weather conditions at the extremities of the globe," he said. "My focus has always been equatorial."

"You write for a newspaper?" I said. Not very surreptitiously, I rubbed my hands up and down my thighs, trying to smooth out the damp rumpled corduroys. There were two smallish puddles where the snow on my cuffs had melted and dripped.

"I don't even read the newspapers. In that, I am like your president. But only that, I hope."

"I thought you said your focus was editorial."

He pulled at his left earlobe, a gesture I was beginning to see as emblematic. "I said *equatorial.*"

"May I ask you a question?"

"But of course, dear Alice."

"Stop me if it's too intrusive."

He just smiled. As if that were impossible.

"Why did you leave the seminary?"

"Aha. Yes. That was before I had undertaken this effort with Tía Tristána. It had nothing to do with this."

"Then why?"

"But if I consider it, the reason I could not stay is exactly because I could not make the choice, I could not dedicate myself, as she had. Without benefit of seminary."

My wet socks, draped over the radiator, were steaming.

"I realized, dear Alice, that I would not be able to forgo physical love."

Dear Alice? I asked, "So you fell in love?"

"Oh, no. But I knew I would some day."

"That seems reasonable," I said.

"I would say that the last thing it is, is reasonable." He vehemently tugged both earlobes. "Either love or faith."

"Of course," I said. "I wish Waldo would call. You'd think he'd be curious how we are managing in this snow. He must know about the snow, don't you think?"

"But isn't he in a cave?"

"Not all the time. I really wish he would call. I'm sure he'd like to talk with you," I said.

"One would think so."

That evening we sat again by the fire while the snow continued to fall. I stuck a yardstick in a drift by the back door; it sank in to twenty-six inches. Which meant that more than those twenty-six inches had fallen, because of the compaction factor.

Then when I got up to coax the dogs out-of-doors for even the briefest time, the yardstick was no longer visible. The whiteout was complete and blinding. Flirt dug in her heels. Dandy lay down and slept. They were immovable. I gave up, and spread newspaper down in the back hall.

"Why don't you tell me about your aunt," I said to Abelardo. "That is why you are here. The purpose of your visit. Not to keep me company."

"Yes, it is, but it is more complicated than it seems."

"That's true for everything except your dreams. And they are simpler."

"But in my aunt's case, it is vastly more complicated," he insisted. Again, his fingertips touched, pulsed in and out, became a dome, then a peaked roof, and then a dome again. There was not a frayed cuticle in sight.

"First, you should know that for generations the Llobets were always giving birth to boys. Boys are generally considered desirable, but there were always too many. Until my generation. But that is something else. Boys tend to fight, and there is the matter of inheritance, and farms being split up. So when my Great-Aunt Tristána Catalina was born, she was the considered the greatest of all possible blessings. That was in 1896."

Abelardo told me how very beautiful she was. He told me that her piety and serenity were an example to her brothers, her feckless brothers. He didn't mention the matador portrait by Sorolla.

"Then she refused to marry. It was not that she disliked the young men—and there were many. She had a clear vision of her life as an accretion of good works, and marriage was not part of it. But where—you may ask—did she get that vision?

"A person does not set out to be a saint. To do so would be— unsaintly, I think. But she wanted something else. Something other. Born rich and beautiful and beloved, she had to depart from the expected path in order to achieve sanctity. Virginity was only one component. But in the eyes of the church, a big one."

"But not essential," I said. "Marriage is a sacrament. Married people make more little Catholics."

"Exactly. And I can cite Saint Elizabeth of Hungary, Saints Waldetrudis, Adelaide, and Anastasia. Who all married and even gave birth. But I don't need to tell *you* that most female saints are virgins."

A little voice in my head asked: Why *me,* oh, Abelardo? Why that stress?

"Dear Alice, my country could use a saint. And Tristána Llobet would make an excellent one. She led a saintly life. Especially, she is renowned for her goodness to the dying and her uncanny prescience. Also, there were several miraculous cures while she lived. I have told you of the hiccups, and that is not the only one."

"She cured *more* hiccups?"

"More ailments. Also, since her death. Those are the ones that count."

"But isn't it a huge effort?" I applauded myself for not saying *pain in the ass.* "A huge struggle to get someone canonized? Isn't it the sort of thing that can swallow your life up and spit it out?"

"It is. It is," Abelardo said. Yet his agreement did not sound like it came from the voice of one whose life was being swallowed up.

"Does Dandy seem awfully quiet to you?" I said. "He is just way too still. I need to check his gums." I pulled back the upper lip of the sleeping dog and saw that his gums and inner cheeks were indeed very pale, not quite gray but certainly not pink. It was always so hard to tell. "Does this look pink to you? Or gray? What do you think?"

Abelardo's eyebrows elevated far up his forehead and, as much as was possible, he retreated deeper into his chair. "I don't even look in the mouths of horses," he said.

I released Dandy's pale lip. He didn't budge. Was it too soon to start panicking? When is a good time to panic? "Explain to me, please," I said. "Why exactly does your country need a saint?"

"It is no secret that Nicaragua has a host of political and economic troubles. With the exception of the lovely Violeta, we have been cursed with some of the most corrupt, venal, and vengeful leaders in the hemisphere. Not an insignificant claim. While a saint will not cure these things, it would be excellent for our morale. It could improve Nicaragua's image in the eyes of the world."

This time he pulled on both his earlobes. He went on. "I can't pretend I don't have my own bugbear, hobbyhorse, bee in my bonnet, as you say. A saint could counteract the inroads of the Mormons, the Pentecostals, the Seventh-day Adventists, the Latter-day Angels, the Jehovah's Witnesses, the Sabbatharians, and

the Snake Speakers. These Bible thumpers have had many converts because—and I will admit this—they are diligent; they have
taken many weak souls away from the church and from the sacra-
ments. I find this upsetting. They tend to be anti-Marianista, and
that is not the Nicaraguan way.

"Practically speaking, Nicaragua needs an infusion of foreign capital if it is ever to build a decent infrastructure, and yet
without a decent infrastructure most foreign investors are leery
of sinking money into a poor and politically unstable country.
It is an insidious circle. However. However." Abelardo let go of
his ears and reconnected his fingertips in their dome position.
"However, a Saint Tristána Catalina Llobet could inject a fresh
perspective into the situation. I do not think it is outrageous to
suggest that a newly canonized native saint—a virgin of a good
family—could be an enticement to new investors. A saint will be
the imprimatur."

On a small low table between us there was a mud-colored
ceramic bowl that Ezra had made in kindergarten. Inside Ezra's
bowl were several chocolates wrapped in colored tinfoil. Bogumila, our neighbor up the road, went back to Poland every summer to see her ancient parents. And every year at Christmas she
gave us these chocolates she had carried back from Poland. Poland
is not a country known for its chocolates. My boys loved Bogumila and had already promised to go with her to her family home
just outside Kraków as soon as they were old enough. She actually
made the boys swear on the heads of Flirt and Dandy that they
would not fail to make this pilgrimage to Kraków.

"Please don't misunderstand, dear Alice. I don't seek her canonization for personal or financial reasons. God forbid!"

Abelardo let his fingers slowly separate, and then he reached
out to take a chocolate from the bowl. He unwrapped it, neatly
put the chocolate orb into his mouth, neatly folded the tinfoil,
and neatly put it back onto the table.

I had watched all too eagerly. I picked up the used tinfoil. I unfolded it and smoothed it on the top of my thigh. I was anxious lest the tinfoil was ripped. But I should have trusted to Abelardo's delicacy. Smoothing it out, I saw the tinfoil was a perfect colored square. I could exhale.

When I was a girl in Santa Barbara, each year at Christmas a large straw box filled with dried figs wrapped in colored tinfoil mysteriously arrived at our door and then lived on the counter in the pantry. It was an annual Christmas gift from Pop's Turkish business colleague, also a mysterious figure.

We ate the figs, then Mami showed us how to take each colored tinfoil wrapper and smooth out all the wrinkles with a thumbnail. Using the index finger of one hand as a mold, she showed us how to roll it into a tube. She showed us how to twist it at one end to create the stem of the wineglass. And finally we learned how to splay the end of the twisted tinfoil to make the base of the glass.

Every year at Christmas, by the time we had eaten all the Turkish figs, we had sculpted dozens of tiny colored wineglasses made of foil.

And they functioned.

We would fill them with tiny amounts of water and spoonfuls of wine and hold the tinfoil stems between our little fingers and sip.

In those days Mami also pretended to sew her fingers together, to amuse us.

I made a wineglass from the tinfoil, in the old way, and set it gently on the table. Abelardo said, "Waldo is a lucky man. I see that now."

I said, "Waldo is the funniest man I know."

"I was not referring to his comedic side, developed though it may be."

Flirt lifted her head and barked. Dandy's head sank farther into their pillow.

"It's a complicated process to become a saint," I said. "And does anyone really care these days?"

"I care. We care," Abelardo said. Then he jumped from his chair and went over to the front window. Yes, it was still snowing.

"This has to stop soon," he said. "I have to get to the Hagiographers Club. I foolishly thought this would be an excellent time of year because the *cosecha* is winding down at Las Brisas. Foolish, foolish. But I must get on with my research because the de la Rosas think they have a saint in *their* family. She was nothing like Tata. It is disturbing how helpless we are with this snow. Is there really nothing you can do?"

"Nothing," I said. Was he kidding? I briefly wondered if there was some snow antidote that I had neglected to mention or avail myself of. Nope. Nothing came to mind.

"There was nothing like this when we were at Harvard," he said.

Well, you're not at Harvard now. You're here with me. But I didn't say that. I still expected the phone to ring momentarily, and I wanted Abelardo to tell Waldo what a lovely time we were having, and I wanted Waldo to appreciate just how friendly I was being to his roommate and how for not one but two evenings I was forgoing the anticipated pleasures of tinned oysters and *Jeopardy!* Hell, I would happily let the dogs in our bed, put the Weather Channel on mute, and reread the diaries of Robert Falcon Scott. I would not mention the allure of Abelardo's earlobes, as I looked forward to inhabiting the moral high ground in our marriage for a while. Was there anything so terribly wrong with that?

First he had to call.

Abelardo hung on to the painted wooden windowsill as if to the gunwale of a lifeboat. His knuckles were paler than Dandy's gums.

"At least when it is raining you know it. You can hear the rain beating on the roof. I would say that rain is more honest. It doesn't sneak up on you. There is nothing sneaky about the rain."

I said, "I would hardly call three feet of snow sneaky."

"If I had known about this snow, I would never have come."

"But we didn't know," I said. There was a twinge—just a twinge—of dismay that he didn't find my scintillating company sufficient compensation for the misery of the snow. I squashed the twinge.

Of course Waldo had left me a phone number or the name of the hotel. How could he not? He definitely would have done that. So where was it? I went into the kitchen to look at the refrigerator door anew. But there was nothing new, nothing that hadn't been there that morning, or the night before, or the previous morning. Only the plastic magnetic letters that the boys used to make up their words, funny words, invented words, and sometimes dirty words when they wanted to test me. No message from Waldo.

I examined every Post-it note on the desk in the corner of the living room, and found the long-lost number for the chimney cleaner, but nothing about their hotel near the caves in New Mexico.

I didn't want Abelardo to see me pathetically ransacking my own house for information I should have had in the first place. He might think that he was in less than competent hands.

"So, tell me again, what do you hope to learn at this Hagiographers Club?" I asked him.

"Don't you have any snowplows here? Why are you not plowed?"

"I'm sure the plows are on the roads. But our driveway we do ourselves. We just can't right now because it's still coming down so hard. But we will, don't worry, we will," I said. "But about your aunt?"

He was right to be anxious about the plowing. It was going to take us hours to shovel out. Usually all four of us did it, with frequent breaks for snowballs and snow angels. Waldo did most of the work. A few times after snowfalls, two or three young

Hispanic men came up the driveway with snow shovels slung over their shoulders and offered to shovel us out for what seemed to me a very reasonable fee. I assumed they were terribly home-sick for their tropical homeland, where it was warm and colorful. Once I suggested we hire them, and Waldo was horrified that I would even consider paying people to shovel for us. We had one of our East versus West, Maine versus California, Stiff-Upper-Lip versus Laid-Back confrontations, neither the first nor the last. Waldo prevailed.

It seemed highly unlikely that anyone at all would trudge up our driveway in the midst of this storm, which meant that soon, tomorrow, Abelardo and I would be shoveling. Occasionally, if there wasn't too much snow, I could toss a couple of sandbags in the back of my car and drive it up and down the driveway a few times and compact the snow enough so that we could get traction. It was all about traction.

"My aunt? There is a great tradition of virgin saints who oppose the wishes of their fathers to marry and choose Christ as their bridegroom. A very great tradition, and my Aunt Tristána falls directly into it."

"I know something about that. But mere spinsterhood hardly makes for sainthood."

"There are also the miracles."

"You were joking about the hiccups."

"I never joke. You can ask Waldo. I used to say things in jest, about the Fairweather inventors, for instance. Waldo said I was too literal-minded to ever get a joke. Or make one."

"That wasn't very nice of him," I said.

"On the contrary. He tried to teach me. He wrote jokes on index cards for me to use in tense situations, but they never worked as planned. Things always became tenser. Here is one I remember: There is feebly growing down on your chin."

"That's a joke?"

"Not a joke. A play on words. It depends on whether you think of one word as a noun or an adverb. It could never happen in Spanish. Waldo will explain it to you."

"I certainly hope so," I said. Did he know that my mother was Spanish? Surely I'd told him, and if not me, then Waldo.

The phone rang. The ring sounded different than usual: shriller, twangier.

I lifted the receiver slowly, because if it was not Waldo then I wanted to postpone that disappointment as long as possible.

"Finally!" Waldo said to me.

I sank into a chair. I could have wept for joy. That was my word he had just usurped, that was *my* relief. I said, "Where are you guys?"

"In New Mexico. Where else? What's going on? I've been trying to reach you since yesterday and there's been no answer."

"That's not possible," I said. "I've been waiting and waiting to talk to you, and I couldn't find your number, and—"

"Well, I'm not inventing it."

"But we've been here the whole time. Except when I picked up Abelardo at the train. Oh, and when I went back to the station, but there were no trains."

"What do you mean, no trains?"

I said, "There were *no* trains. The station was closed. The tracks were covered."

"They never do that."

"Well, they did this time, Wals. Metro-North had to wait until you were out of the state. Ask your pal."

It sounded like he wasn't speaking directly into the mouthpiece. Perhaps he was eating. Waldo liked to have things in his mouth. He said, "Is he there now?"

"That he is," I said, because he was right beside me. He couldn't have been any closer unless we'd embraced. An odd thought.

"So how are things going? I gather there's a snowstorm."

"Not just a snowstorm. It's a rather big snowstorm." Then I looked at Abelardo and bit my tongue.

Waldo asked me, "Is he standing right there?"

"Yes," I said.

"And how is he liking the snow?"

"He's been telling me about his Aunt Tristána, who will be a saint. Or will be once he gets to his club in the city."

"Now I remember how much he hated the snow in Cambridge. We could never convince him of its merits."

I said, "We were just discussing the snowplow."

"Are you plowed out yet?"

"Are you kidding? Watch the Weather Channel, please."

"The boys are watching *The Simpsons*."

I imagined them in their pajamas, Ezra's patterned with dinosaurs, Henry's with spaceships, seated Indian-style on the floor at the foot of some oversize hotel bed, staring with rapt fascination at the television fitted snugly inside the wooden cabinet. They loved Lisa Simpson and frequently quoted her. They would have loved her as a sister. In the shared hotel room, the television would be inside a cabinet under which would be the minibar. They would both have examined the contents of the minibar and discussed at length the pros and cons of eating the peanuts or the candy, computing how much those items cost relative to the nearby 7-Eleven. Of course they cost more from the minibar, so the question was, was it worth it? They would already have watched Waldo remove tiny bottles of gin and tonic and make himself a drink. (Yes, the same Waldo who would never pay anyone else to shovel his driveway.) He would say: *Live a little, guys.* Or something like that. But they would need more coaxing.

"At this hour? They must be reruns. Shouldn't they be in bed?"

"They are in bed. Watching TV. This is a hotel room. They're on vacation."

"Waldo?"

"What?"

"Intuit, please," I said. What I meant was "Read my mind. Don't make me say it. Please help me."

"Oh. You mean about Abelardo. Is there really a problem?"

"Very likely," I said. I shouldn't have to tell him, I thought. He should know this already. If there ever was a moment for a mind meld, this was it.

"I think the best thing is to get him back to the city as soon as possible. You've more than done your duty."

"I'm speechless," I said. This wasn't exactly true. What I meant was "What the hell do you think I would like to do? And why can't you solve this for me?"

"I don't know what I can do from out here. Would he like a plastic model of the caves?" he said. "Oh, never mind. How's Dandy doing? The boys want to know."

"I think he's okay. A little lethargic, but it could be the snow."

"Have you checked his gums?"

"Of course I checked his gums. I am intimate with his gums."

"And?"

"They're not all I could wish for. But I think they're fine," I said. I don't know why I lied about that particular thing. Normally I would have gone into great detail about his symptoms, as well as my anxiety. It must have been because Abelardo was still standing right there, pulling on both his earlobes. "Let me talk to the boys."

"They're asleep."

"Two seconds ago they were watching *The Simpsons*."

"That's what I thought," Waldo said. "But now their eyes are shut. They had a busy day."

"You haven't even told me about the caves."

"You should wait until the boys can tell you. Besides, they retain more than me. Henry may have found his true calling."

"Which is?"

"A geologist. A speleologist. He says he likes being under the earth—actually he's really only beneath the crust—and seeing how it's all put together."

I hissed, "So what am I going to *do*?"

"Is it that bad?"

"Yes."

"It's difficult, being out here."

"Thanks. Your mother called. She wants to know what you want for your birthday," I said.

"You told her nothing, I hope."

"I told her you loved that sweater she gave you last time," I said.

"Holy Christ."

"Wouldn't you like to speak with your friend Abelardo? He's right here."

I smiled and handed the telephone to Abelardo. He had to let go of his earlobes, which struck me as a good thing.

This is what I heard, in my snowbound living room: "*Mi amigo* Waldito! Mmm . . . *Es un barbaridad* . . . no . . . no . . . *que lástima* . . . The snow is unsupportable, you might have told me . . . do I understand? No . . . I think you met her that summer after our freshman year . . . yes, she was the one with the braids. What a good *memoria* you have . . . *Entonces, vaya con Dios!*"

I stretched out my hand, but he returned the phone to its cradle.

"You hung up?" I said. It was all I could do not to wring his neck.

"Waldo did. He said he was exhausted, looking after the boys."

"He's exhausted?" Bite your tongue, Alice. Now is neither the time nor the place. "I think it is time for us to retire as well. Don't you think?"

I was seething about Waldo hanging up. If this were a movie of a certain type, not a very good movie, then we in the audience would all know, as surely as we knew our menstrual history, that something was amiss. But this wasn't a movie. It was my life, our life. And what could possibly be amiss? They are having fun in caves, and I am stuck in a snowstorm with the grandnephew of a putative saint who thinks snow is the devil's work. I am taking care of the dogs, making sure that nothing is amiss.

A miss is as good as a mile. Who said that?

7 ❧ Nothing but Mystery

I T WAS DEATHLY QUIET in the morning. Dandy was breathing, but just barely. His gums were like the sky right before it snows.

The snow had stopped. All around was an unimaginable thickness of white, a monochromatic world that was beautiful and dazzling to the eye. It was suddenly a day for sunglasses. What had Thomas Hardy said—"a day which had a summer face and a winter constitution"? It didn't exactly apply. Everything was more than just itself. Every aspect of the landscape, of the weather, every nose, eyebrow, or ankle.

Dandy looked terrible. I was anxious about many things, but I was terrified to lose him while Waldo and the boys were away. Wasn't his well-being—his very survival—the whole reason I'd stayed behind, and wasn't that why I was here with Abelardo, he of the bad attitude about winter weather?

I called our vet, Dr. Donald Eco. He was a kind man who seemed as unwilling to give up on Dandy as I was. Their house, formerly Thelma's parents' house, was right in VerGroot. They had turned the old chicken coop into a small clinic, which was a great thing, as it meant I didn't have to take Dandy all the way to Winifred Bates Memorial Animal Hospital every time he needed blood or new medications.

Thelma answered the phone. I asked how she was doing with the snow.

"Splendid," she said. "We've all been stuck inside for days. It's been wonderful. For two entire days no one has considered going out-of-doors. I've been completely normal."

"I hadn't thought of that," I said.

"You are not alone," she said. "But I suppose you're looking for Donald."

I told Donald about Dandy. He said I should bring him in for another blood transfusion.

"I'll meet you there," he said. "Are you already plowed out?"

"No, but I can get through it."

Still, it was all silence. Not a peep, not a creaking floorboard, not a snore from Abelardo's, that is to say, Ezra's, room, or from anywhere else. Great, I thought. I'll quickly shovel around the car, and then just try driving through the snow to the road, which will surely be plowed by now, and I'll get Dandy to the clinic, and leave him there to be transfused, and be back before Abelardo is awake. It was a good plan, good in its simplicity.

But after I'd cleared off the car, loaded Dandy in the back, and then actually started moving, I glanced up at Ezra's window and saw Abelardo's horror-stricken face. He must have been pressed right up to the wavy glass pane because his features were slightly distorted, flattened and elongated. It was impossible to tell if he was naked or wearing shorts, and yes, I wanted to know. I should have stopped right then and gone back inside and explained to him what I was doing and shown him the note I had left on the kitchen counter, shown him the half grapefruit under an additional Post-it with his name written on it, and shown him the already ground coffee in the coffeemaker. But I didn't. The car seemed to have some momentum; we were making headway through the snow and I was afraid that if I stopped I'd never get going again. Not without hours of shoveling. So I kept going and got down to the road. Emerson had been plowed, but not recently. Very slowly, I drove to Donald Eco's clinic, a mere three miles away. Dandy was perfectly silent in the back of the station wagon. I would have liked to hear just a yip, a hiccup, or a growl.

But he was as silent as the snow. I don't know how long it took us to get there. There was no one else on the road and that was lucky because the car skidded prodigiously.

Mentally I composed a letter to the new DPW head that I'd cc to the *VerGroot Sentinel*. While understanding that the scale of this snowstorm made immediate snowplowing impossible, I would describe most poetically the public safety concerns of uncleared roads for those of us with children and those without, for those of us with four-footed animals and even those not so blessed. I would not mention frustrated Nicaraguan houseguests. I would not sound hysterical.

I made it to Donald's office intact. It must have been a lovely chicken coop in its time. The chickens must have counted themselves lucky to live in such a well-wrought and finely detailed abode. Until the moment of neck-wringing, that is, when presumably the architectural merits of their home had paled. Like the house, it was built in the Gothic revival style promoted by Alexander Jackson Davis with such success in the mid-nineteenth century. I knew this because when I'd first gone there I'd complimented Donald and Thelma on their gingerbread house. I'd waxed enthusiastic about windows wearing hats and the roof waving banners. I'd been corrected. "You're referring to the drip-mold window crowns, Alice," Donald had said. "And the ridgepole finials." There were no finials on the former chicken coop, now veterinary offices, but that building too was graced with lovely verge boards that hung from the projecting eaves like lace.

He was standing on the front step in a bright blue one-piece snowsuit, the kind normally worn by children.

"You made it!" he said.

"Of course I made it. Don't tell me you ever doubted."

"Let's just say it's a good thing I have some blood on hand, because no one is going anywhere today."

Dandy lifted his head sadly but otherwise did not move. I took him in my arms and followed Donald into the clinic.

"Where do you get the blood anyway? Several people have asked. I told them public-spirited dogs donated pints to the doggy blood bank. I hope I haven't been misleading them."

"Everybody asks me that," he said.

"They do? You mean I'm not the only one who lies awake at night pondering canine blood banks?"

"Sorry," Donald said.

"But seriously, where—?"

"From greyhounds retired from the track. Instead of being euthanized, they get to spend a year supplying blood for clinics. And then they're adopted by good families."

"I guess informed consent is not an issue with dogs," I said.

"It's better than being put to sleep."

"Why greyhounds?"

"They have a very high red blood cell count."

"But they're so skinny."

"All that running oxygenates the blood."

"I never thought of that."

Donald inserted the transfusion needles into Dandy's back leg and dosed him with a sedative, which I didn't think he needed. "You may as well go home," he said. "This will take hours."

"Is Thelma really enjoying this as much as she said?"

"More so. She weeps with delight when she watches the weather news."

"Maybe she should meet my houseguest. He is horrified by the storm—he seems to take it as a personal insult. Of course, he's from the tropics. But they have weather too. You would think."

"You have a tropical friend here? Now?"

"It's a long story," I said. "But I was joking. I don't think he and Thelma should ever meet."

After a fond adieu, I left poor Dandy at the clinic, splayed indecorously on the stainless steel table with a needle stuck into and taped to his leg, and headed home. Driving on the snowy roads was still painfully slow. But not slow enough.

Just as I was starting a wide swing so I could gun it up my driveway, I became aware of bright and annoying flashing red lights. A fully grown migraine had landed inside my head, right behind my furrowed brow. But the lights were not inside my head. Just at the entrance to my driveway was a VerGroot volunteer ambulance vehicle, its flasher widely circling, pinking the snow in every direction. Its wheels were so deep in the snow they were lost.

I swerved and *ta-da!* I was stuck in a snowdrift at the road's shoulder. The wheels spun merrily through the piled-up snow, as if they had nothing to do but just that: spin. They spun and gained no purchase and I made no progress. I stopped before digging myself in deeper and making it much worse, a wise and prescient course I would have found impossible to follow a mere ten years earlier. I didn't understand why the ambulance had to get stuck in my driveway, of all the driveways in VerGroot. I didn't understand why they had to be on the road at all in this weather. Did they have anemic dogs in desperate need of transfusions? They did not. I knew several of the members of the VerGroot Volunteer Fire and Ambulance Corps, and many of their dogs.

Teddy Gribbon was at the wheel of the ambulance. He got out and started walking toward me as I left my car and headed toward the driveway. We were converging. He didn't have boots on—he was wearing sneakers. This struck me as a problem. And a bad sign.

"We got a distress call from Mrs. Crench, next door," he said. He didn't look happy. His hands were deep in his pockets.

"Susie Crench? What could have happened to her? Damn."

"Nothing happened to her. She said you had a problem."

"I'm fine. I mean, the dog is sick so I just had to go to Dr. Eco's office. But believe it or not, I made it." I looked back toward my beached whale of a car. "What's with the roads anyway? It's pretty treacherous out here."

"We've had a massive snowstorm. The biggest snowstorm in decades. No one should be driving."

"I know, Teddy. What did Susie call you about?"

"She said someone was outside your house, shouting. Specifically, she said he was weeping and bellowing. She was specific. But she couldn't get over there."

"Oh, shit," I said. "Shit, shit, shit. It must be Abelardo. And Susie just had knee surgery—she's not supposed to go anywhere."

"Who or what is Abelardo?" Teddy was looking down at his sneakers, barely visible in the snow, with an expression of overwhelming sorrow.

It was normal for Teddy not to make eye contact. Susie and I had often discussed just what exactly was so weird about Teddy. Teddy wasn't especially smart but he did know everything there was to know about the volunteer corps, and he was the local expert on fire hydrants. Which didn't explain his presence.

I said, "He's Abelardo Llobet. My houseguest. From Nicaragua."

Teddy said, "Nicaragua is the largest country in Central America. But at forty-nine thousand, nine hundred and ninety-seven square miles, it is still smaller than our own New York state."

"I know," I lied.

"My vehicle is stuck in your driveway," Teddy said. "I told you three times that the nearest hydrant to your house is over two hundred feet, and because of the curve in the driveway it could be described as two hundred and fifty-four feet. I've left several messages with the county about this. The county is in charge of fire hydrants."

"I see. We can walk."

"It's two hundred and forty-three feet to your front door."

"But you're stuck in the snow."

As we walked I worried more and more and wanted to walk faster and get the bad news as soon as possible, because sooner or later I would have to tell Waldo that while I was at the vet's with Dandy, Abelardo had locked himself out of the house or gotten frostbite, and now his friend thought that, in marrying me, Waldo had made the worst mistake of his life. There is a limit to how fast one can walk in three feet of snow, no matter how dire the catastrophe awaiting one. But it takes no time at all to sympathize with polar explorers; it takes no time at all to imagine the exhaustion of slogging across crevasse-riddled Himalayan snowfields, or of climbing Andean peaks with no llama in sight.

Did such empathetic images prepare me for the sight of Abelardo Llobet in his pressed Brooks Brothers blue-striped pajamas splayed on his back upon the virgin snow in front of the house, making an angel? Not likely. Five newly imprinted angels glistened in the snow, almost a host of cherubim. Abelardo had been at this for a while. Or were they fallen angels?

"Do you know this man?" Teddy said.

"Abelardo! What are you doing? Abelardo! Didn't you get my notes?" I went over and took his arm. His pajama sleeves were icing up. Tiny icicles descended from his eyebrows and nostrils. He shook my hand off with enormous strength.

"No one told me that I would go blind in Heaven," he said, with difficulty. His jaw was stiff with the cold.

"You're just really, really cold," I said. "Let's go inside."

"Tía Tata smelled of gardenias when she was dead. We all know what that means," he said.

Teddy said, "No one told me about this."

"Christ, Teddy, no one knew. We have to take him to the ER. He's awfully cold, and he's not making sense."

"Does he want to go to the ER?"

"Does that matter?" I said. Abelardo had stood up and was leaping barefoot through the piled-high snow, clearly scouting for another suitable angel spot. Or was he?

"I can't see her. I can't see anything," he said. I didn't know much about eyes. His looked normal. As normal as coal gray unseeing eyes can look.

Teddy said, "Hypothermia is present when the body core temperature is less than ninety-five degrees Fahrenheit or thirty-five degrees Celsius. What is his body core temperature?"

"How would I know?" I said. "Abelardo, we're going to go to the ambulance and get you warmed up."

"Three days after she was dead, she still smelled of gardenias. There were always gardenias in the courtyard in León."

Damn Susie and her knee surgery, I thought. She would be much better at this than I am. Hell, wasn't she the one who called Teddy in the first place? I needed to talk with her, with anyone except Teddy or Abelardo Llobet. It would be nice if her husband, George, was home, but George was almost never home. He was a pilot for Available Airlines ("If you are, we are" was their slogan). But you'd think that George would be grounded for this snowstorm to top all snowstorms. And as it turned out he was, in Greenville, South Carolina.

I told Teddy I was going to go inside and call the VerGroot ambulance corps to send over someone to help us, someone with chains or four-wheel drive or sandbags or all of the above; and then I was going to call the Virginia O'Connor Memorial Hospital to tell them that Abelardo was on his way; and then I would call Susie.

Teddy said, "We have to look for the umbles. They're the signs of mild hypothermia: stumbles, mumbles, and fumbles."

"Just keep an eye on him," I said.

I called the ambulance corps for backup. They were on their way, I was told.

The woman answering the phone at Ginny O Memorial asked me if I knew how bad the roads were.

I dialed Susie next door. I could almost see her from my house. On days when the wind was right, I could definitely hear her. "What the hell is going on over there?" she said.

"I've got a snow-crazed Nicaraguan, and Teddy got stuck in my driveway. What do I do?"

"I'll call Herc and tell him he has to send over someone else from the corps. Teddy was not who I had in mind when I called. And where the hell were you, anyway?" Hercules Delafield, our esteemed mayor, had in his high school days loved Susie. He still did. He was constantly seeking occasions to assist Susie in any way. Alas, she wanted very little assistance. I imagined his delight at getting this phone call.

"At Donald Eco's with Dandy. He needed another transfusion."

"You can tell me about that later. As well as about your Nicaraguan friend. Are you aware how cold it is out there?"

"Very cold," I said.

I got out Waldo's favorite forest green parka, and his black ski overalls, and his thickest socks, and his L.L.Bean hunting boots, and a red-and-white-striped hat I'd knit for him but he'd refused to wear, and red mittens. Back outside, Teddy said, "Paradoxical undressing is a sign of moderate hypothermia. He needs to be hydrated and rewarmed gradually."

"I think we need to get him dressed," I said. "Abelardo, I brought some clothes for you. Aren't you and Waldo the same size?"

"There is nothing but mystery to be seen. That's why it's so important to have faith," he said.

"Can you put these pants on?" I said. He lay down on the snow and spread his arms and spread his legs and swished them back and forth as if he'd been making snow angels all his life, the movements were so smooth and practiced. I could imagine circumstances—a tropical beach, perhaps—where this might not be so disturbing, where it might even have a certain appeal.

"Your friend is not cooperative," Teddy said.

"Someone else is coming to help," I said. "Come on, Abelardo. You'll feel a lot better when you're warmer."

His body stiffened as I raised him up and started inserting his left arm into the parka's sleeve. Ezra had been like this as a baby, always resisting clothing in all its forms. The rigidity of his tiny limbs had impressed me. If in later life he applied this force to any task, what could he not accomplish? Because of my years battling Ezra's recalcitrance I now felt almost comfortable forcing Abelardo's freezing arms into the parka. The overalls would be harder. And they had to go on before the socks and boots. Forget the overalls, I decided, and hoped I wouldn't regret it. But the whiteness of his feet and the horror of his long yellowish toenails—Waldo had never mentioned these toenails—convinced me that he needed his feet covered immediately. It is remarkably difficult to put socks on feet that don't want to cooperate, on toes that refuse to contract and point.

Teddy said, "Most warm-blooded animals have a layer of fur, hair, or blubber that keeps them warm. We humans need to wear clothes."

I kept up the struggle with Abelardo's rigid feet, and finally managed to get the socks on. The boots were almost impossible.

"Teddy," I said. "Maybe if you could help him stand up I could get his feet into these boots."

"It should not be hard to remember the simple rules for cold-weather safety. We say *c* for *cover,* *o* for *overexertion,* *l* for *layers,* and *d* for *dry.* They spell COLD. If you can't remember that, you're not paying attention."

"Well, he speaks Spanish. He says *frío,*" I said. *F* for *fuck you,* *r* for *ridiculous,* *i* for *inane*—no, I never said that.

"I don't speak Spanish. I speak English and always have. English is the official language of the USA."

Through the gaunt and snowy trees that stood between Emerson Street and me, I saw red lights flashing, and could have wept for joy.

"We hid all her clothes and books away so safely, no one will ever find them. Bones are another matter," Abelardo said, preaching to the snowdrifts. His feet remained stiffened in their capital *L* position.

In the freezing cold, well below freezing, I stood between two people who couldn't speak to me or to each other. And it was my fault: I had failed in my duties as hostess and as citizen; I was deficient in the basic skills of COLD; I had ignored the signs of distress right in front of my nose while busily searching for color signs on my dog's gums.

Hercules Delafield was striding up the driveway. He was wearing tall fur-trimmed boots and a fur-trimmed parka and a Russian fur hat. At least it looked Russian. Handsome Herc, he actually looked at peace with his surroundings.

Hercules waved and shouted cheerfully, "What the fuck?" Then he picked up his pace. "Teddy, go warm up the ambulance," he shouted.

"I am so glad to see you, Herc," I said.

"I was hoping I might see Susie here."

"You would, except for her knee. She's supposed to be careful and this snow is . . . well, it's impressively deep."

"Well, that explains a mystery," he said, and with not the slightest interruption of movement, Hercules powerfully—but ever so gently—hoisted Abelardo onto his feet and then leaned over and put Waldo's boots on him. Why couldn't I have done that?

Within minutes—or was it a lifetime?—Abelardo was dressed and inside a warm ambulance, while Hercules, his younger brother Hector, and Teddy Gribbon valiantly wielded their snow shovels and worked to free the wheels from the driveway's deep snow.

Because of some arcane town ordinance, I was not allowed to ride in the ambulance. (Not so arcane; fairly universal, I later learned.) So Herc had Teddy shovel me out of my personal snow-drift at the end of the driveway, and as soon as I could get some traction, I skidded and slid to the hospital behind the ambulance, confident that surely, now, nothing more could go wrong.

Things were very quiet at the ER because, Nurse Gish said, no one could get there, no one in his right mind was driving. *Except you, Mrs. Fairweather,* she implied, *at your peril and ours.* Since I was not a relative of Abelardo's and did not even know his birthday (I later learned it was February 29. I might have guessed), I was not allowed in the examining room with him. I didn't want to go into the examining room. I wanted to explain to Nurse Gish and her underlings and Dr. Genet, wherever he was, that Abelardo had gone outdoors of his own accord, that I had done my best to look after him, and that he had arrived with a preconceived prejudice against snow and any kind of winter weather.

Hercules was mollifying. "Just let them do their business, Al. Shall I follow you home?"

"Does anyone here speak Spanish?" I asked. "His English is good; better than good, excellent. But Spanish is his mother tongue."

Herc said, "Have you ever wondered about that?"

"What?"

"Mother tongue and fatherland?"

"No, I haven't."

"I'll just drop in and make sure that Susie has everything she needs," he said.

"I check up on her pretty regularly," I said.

"Yes, but I might be able to help with things you can't do. Blow down her furnace, for instance. I know she often forgets to blow down the furnace when George is away."

I had no idea what he was talking about.

"But I can't just leave him here," I said. "Even if I'm useless, I'm all he's got."

"They can call you. Take my word for it."

So I left Abelardo at the Virginia O'Connor Memorial Hospital in hands that Hercules declared were "more than competent."

On the way out I ran into Gunnar Sigerson, who was on his

way in. That is to say, we collided. Gunnar's son, Toby, played Little League with Ezra, or had before Deb got Lyme disease and wouldn't let Toby play on any field that hadn't been sprayed for deer ticks. Which in VerGroot meant all the playing fields. One could only assume that this was a source of dissension in the Sigerson household, because Gunnar was happiest when outdoors. He was a hiker, a bird watcher, and a mushroom collector. Last fall we had feasted on his prize find, a thirty-pound *Grifola frondosa,* a hen of the woods. There was a picture in the *Sentinel* of proud Gunnar and the large brownish lump resembling dried fallen oak leaves. He was a whiz at tree identification, as well as a fount of knowledge about the medicinal uses of weeds. His parents were originally Norwegian or Finnish, one of those pale northern peoples, and Gunnar was always pink with exertion and sunburn, his nose generally peeling.

"Ouch!" I exclaimed, though I was startled rather than hurt.

"Alice! What are you doing here?" he said.

"You wouldn't believe me if I told you."

"Try me," he said.

"Later. It's a long story. What about you? I was told only an idiot would be on the road today."

Gunnar said, "You're looking at one of those idiots."

"You didn't drive off the road, did you?"

"No," he said. "But I think I broke my thumb cross-country skiing." He raised a purplish swollen thumb—it was quite hideous—and grinned shamefacedly.

"That looks nasty."

"It was my own fault. There's far too much snow for decent skiing. Maybe in a day or two, but I'll be having a little trouble zipping up my jacket."

And not only your jacket, I thought. Your jacket is the least of it.

"How did you get here?" I said.

"I drove. I never drive with more than one hand."

"How did I guess?" I said. Then I wished him good luck and went on my way.

Herc followed me home, red light flashing. He did not follow me up my driveway but continued on and immediately turned into Susie's. She would surely call later and berate me for not having warned her of his imminent arrival.

It seemed a thousand years ago that I'd last spoken with Waldo. In what cave were they now?

The phone rang and my heart leaped. Would they consider coming home early? Could I stop myself from asking? I was desperate to hear his voice, desperate to lose control.

It was Donald Eco. "Al, where are you? Dandy's been ready for ages."

"Oh my God. Oh, shit, shit, shit," I said. "I can't believe I forgot all about him."

"Neither can I," said Don testily. "I thought you were worried sick."

"I was," I said. "I mean I am. It's just that Abelardo went a little nutty with the snow and they just took him away. It was way too white for him."

"You're not making all that much sense."

"I know. I'll tell you when I come get Dandy," I said. "It may take me a while, though. I think I parked in a snowdrift when I got back from the hospital."

"Not too long, I hope," Donald said. "Thelma's decided she wants to go snowshoeing."

"She does? I thought she was so happy about the storm forcing everyone to stay inside."

"She was. Hell, this could be a breakthrough."

"Of course there won't be many other people out snowshoeing today," I said. Picturing the two of them in their matching Mediterranean blue snowsuits taking giant steps across the pristine snowfield, I saw a definite problem. "Won't you sink in? I don't think the snow is packed enough for shoeing." What did I know? I had never worn snowshoes in my life. I had strapped them onto Ezra and Henry and gone back inside to hot cocoa and *Lawrence of Arabia.* "Aren't you worried about the cold? There's a danger of hypothermia. Ask Teddy G if you don't believe me."

"Al, don't you get it? Thelma wants to go out!"

"Sorry. I didn't mean to be negative. I'm on my way."

8 ❧ They Called It Hypothermia

FINALLY, FINALLY, I WAS opening a tin of smoked oysters. I had waited so long to ingest these strange oily mollusks, these mysterious pearl-making nacreous creatures, and now that I was, now that it was possible, I naturally started thinking about botulism. I slid the appropriate slot of the key over the protruding piece of metal and started rolling back the lid, slowly winding the metal over itself. If not done carefully, if done sloppily, the rolled-up lid quickly becomes askew, concave at one end, attenuated at the other. The art is to keep all the edges aligned, all the time. This allows the slimy dark oysters, laid down neatly next to one another, like sleeping children in an orphanage, to be revealed in equal measure.

The phone rang. Take a deep breath. It was either Waldo or the Ginny O Memorial, and either way, I didn't want to sound hysterical.

"Alice, dear, it's Posey."

"Oh. Hello."

"What are you up to?"

"Well, I just shoveled the driveway and now I'm folding the laundry."

"You know I don't want to interrupt. But I am concerned about Waldo and the boys."

"Why are you concerned about them?"

"I was just reading about these deadly viruses we contract from animal—you know—waste, and I was thinking about all those bats in the caves. And how whenever there is one bat there are a thousand—they're very social creatures, and very useful too, but that's not the point. There is bound to be masses of bat guano in those caves."

"I wouldn't worry too much," I said. "It's a national park. I'm sure someone there is up to speed on the dangers of bat poop."

"Oh, I don't agree," Posey said.

"You're thinking of mice. Bat poop makes fertilizer."

"I think you should get them tested when they return. Doesn't Ezra stick his fingers into his mouth all the time?"

"When he was two or three," I said. "I'll mention it to Waldo when they get back."

"Waldo refused to get the Lyme vaccine."

"He doesn't like shots," I said.

"Don't you think he's a little old for that excuse?"

"Posey! I need to let the dogs in—they've been out in the snow for ages. Can we talk later?"

"Tell Waldo he should start wearing more red. His father looked very good in red."

"Thanks, Posey. I will."

I replaced the receiver gently, with trepidation, lest it ring again and again not be Waldo.

I stood at the kitchen counter and forked oysters onto stoned wheat thins and ate with pleasure.

Night had fallen when Waldo finally called. His voice was music to my ears, the only music I'd heard in days. I needed to hear some music.

"This has been a rather trying day," I said. "Darling."

"How are Abelardo's spirits?"

"Abelardo's spirits are in the emergency room. Abelardo thought there was altogether too much snow and had a bit of a breakdown."

"He did what?"

"You heard me. Teddy Gribbon and the others called it hypothermia, and maybe he had that secondarily, but I think first he was driven nuts by the snow. That's my diagnosis. An overdose of white and the absence of a miracle."

"Slow down, Al. Are you saying he's at the hospital?"

"Yes."

"Shit. Shit."

"My words exactly," I said. "So now what do we do?"

"Let me think." We exchanged lots more information, and in the end it was decided that Waldo would call Abelardo's family in Nicaragua while I called the hospital to check on his condition. I never told him about Dandy's transfusion or my discovery about the greyhounds' blood. Nor did I tell him that Thelma Eco had wanted to get out of the house and go snowshoeing. He told me that Ezra and Henry were blissfully happy, that they loved the caves, loved the stalactites and the stalagmites and everything in between. Their only distress, the only fly in their ointment, was that a snowstorm had occurred in their absence. I wanted to talk with them but they had fallen asleep watching *The Simpsons* again.

"But do they miss me?" I asked.

The phone rang again in the early morning. I was awake but not upright. My eyelids were still partially glued shut.

Ezra was on the phone first. "What did you tell Dad about Dandy?"

"I didn't tell him anything, but he's fine," I said. "He's going to be fine. Doc Eco gave him another transfusion. He's chipper, and his color looks good."

"Are you checking his gums, Mom?"

"Of course I'm checking his gums, sweetie. How are you? I miss you both so much."

"We miss you too. Are you giving them those special treats I left?"

"I will today. He wasn't very hungry before. Did Dad tell you about his friend Abelardo?"

"That he didn't like the snowstorm. Yeah."

"And something else. I let him sleep in your room. I hope you don't mind," I said.

"As long as he didn't touch anything."

"Well, obviously he had to touch some things, just in order to get into bed."

"Oh, Mom. Fingers are full of natural oils, you know."

"I know that, sweetie. Not to worry. Can I talk to Henry now?"

I had to hold the receiver away from my ear while Ezra hollered for his brother. "Henry! Get off the pot. Mom wants to talk."

"Hi, Mom. I wasn't on the pot," Henry said.

"How are you, pumpkin? I miss you."

"The caves are splendid, Mom. You should be here. Flirt and Dandy should be here, but I think it might freak them out when we lose track of daylight. I think they might be slightly nyctophobic. What do you think?"

"I'll have to think about that one," I said. "Are you warm enough?"

"Mom! My down parka is good to minus forty. Of course I am."

"I'd forgotten about that. Can I talk to your dad now?"

Henry said, "He's still asleep. Mom, get real. Do you know what time it is here?"

Of course he was right. If I thought it was early, then how much earlier was it for them? Not that Ezra and Henry followed any clocks but their own. I said, "Yikes. Let him sleep, guys. He needs his sleep."

"He made up a limerick—do you want to hear it?"

"You know I do. Please."

Henry began,

> *"Henry and Ezra were subterranean boys*
> *They wore parkas, headlamps, and corduroys*
> *They went on a mission*
> *It wasn't golf and it wasn't fishin'*
> *No, it was a cave they approached with such joy."*

I asked him, "Did your dad really write that?"

"We helped," Henry said.

"I kind of guessed." More than guessed. In its awkward rhythms I heard the random humor of the boys, and then I loved it even more.

I felt lumpy and almost perverse saying goodbye to them, knowing that it was still dark where they were, that everyone slumbered where they were, everyone except weirdoes and my two eager spelunkers. Even Waldo slept. Somewhere in that motel room, my Waldo slept and dreamed the dreams he would never remember for me, dreams he denied dreaming. Was it asking too much to hear his dreams? He obviously thought so, but I couldn't help myself. I could no more stop craving to see the images that decorated his subconscious than I could stop spooning him at night.

Coursing through Dandy's veins was fresh blood drawn from otherwise doomed greyhounds. Thelma Eco was snowshoeing in the great outdoors.

And chez Fairweather? Was I losing my taste for smoked oysters?

I called Susie, who asked me, "When are you going to visit your tropical friend at the hospital?"

I told her I didn't have any plans to return there just yet.

"What do you mean you're not going to see him? You have to go. He's a stranger in a strange land."

"He went to Harvard, for God's sake. He's not that strange. Just foreign."

"Don't be so literal."

"The truth is," I said, "I doubt he wants to see me. Susie, he was totally unhinged yesterday. I was a terrible hostess."

"All the more reason to go. It's unconscionable not to go. There's nothing more depressing than being in the hospital and having no visitors."

"How would you know?"

"I know these things," she said.

"Maybe you'd like to come," I said. I started to visualize Susie with me, and then realized I could not, not with her repaired knee and in her semi-ambulatory condition. Given that our houses were about two hundred yards apart, and given that we could see the lights twinkling on each other's Christmas trees, it was ludicrous that we ever telephoned at all. When you consider the immensity of the telecommunications industry, the vast resources expended to hook us all up to one another, and compare that to the ease and ancient simplicity of walking across a patch of grass and over some pine needles to talk with a neighbor, you can only shake your head, as does Waldo.

"No, thanks. Even when I am completely mobile I am not a good hospital visitor. Ask George. Ask my late, lamented mother. Hospitals do not bring out the best in me."

"I had no idea, Susie. How many years have I known you? What is it you do in hospitals? Pull out tubes? Fiddle with the monitors? Complain about the food?"

"No, I just start weeping and I don't stop. I have no idea why, and I can't seem to help it. It's like I enter an onion-chopping factory, and you know how I am with onions."

It's true. I knew how she was with onions. Pathetic.

I said, "But how about as a patient?"

"I've never been a patient. Other than getting the new knee. That was just engineering."

"Fine distinctions," I muttered.

"Are you chewing something?" Susie demanded.

"So it's unconscionable not to go to the hospital. But you won't come with me."

"Correct," Susie said, seated somewhere in her house, perhaps with her left leg elevated, presumably with her crutches within reach. But which chair, which room?

"Besides," she said. "Don't you feel responsible for what happened? I would." She was not at all subtle.

"Not so much responsible as guilty," I said.

"Call it whatever you like."

"I will. It's an important distinction."

"A lot of distinctions today, if you ask me."

Responsibility was a weight, a heaviness, but guilt I knew. I fucked up, people went mad, dogs died: I was guilty. But not because I had meant any of those things to happen.

The roads were plowed, or mostly plowed. Plowed far more than they'd been yesterday. The Ginny O was awash in activity. The lobby was filled with teenage boys hopping on their adjustable aluminum crutches, mothers with their swaddled babies, and then the Huge Ones. There were no fewer than a dozen enormous people in the lobby (I counted), vast obese persons, persons in need of doublewide wheelchairs. Two of them were attached to rolling oxygen tanks, but all were breathing with difficulty, walking slowly, if at all. Whenever I saw people that large—and I had never seen so many in one place—I had the unfortunate habit of wondering how they managed to perform the most intimate functions (reproduction, evacuation, lavation). Both made me nervous: my imagination and the Huge Ones.

Abelardo was on the third floor. He had a double room, and his was the far bed closest to the window. I couldn't see his roommate because all the curtains were pulled shut, pale blue curtains with a pattern of dark blue lozenges. Abelardo was propped up on pillows. A pile of thin blankets was pulled up to his chin; one lone arm was outside the covers and was switching channels on the muted television that extended from a retractable arm attached to the wall. When he saw me, he sat up, and as the blankets fell away I saw that he was wearing at least three cotton johnnies, one on top of another.

"How are you feeling?"

"Carolina! I was just thinking about you. About you I was thinking. Do you remember what I told you that night we sailed to Las Isletas?" He was speaking in Spanish, which I understood. But he wasn't speaking to me.

"But how are you feeling?" I said. "Are you any warmer?"

"Not when it's impossible to get warmer, Carolina."

"Shall I get you more blankets?"

"I know it was a terrible secret. A terrible secret it was. But I hope you remember what I told you. Are you wearing your crown today?"

"I don't remember, Abelardo, because I am Alice. I'm not Carolina. I don't know who Carolina is."

"Of course you do. You should have been Señorita Nicaragua."

I said, "It must be your eyes. What can you see now?"

"I told you about the only time I saw her. And you've kept the secret."

"But now? Now what do you see?"

A round nurse came in. If you took all her contours and put them together, you would make a perfect circle. She wore scrubs with festive little snowmen all over; the snowmen wore red and green scarves, and stylized snowflakes fell in perfectly symmetrical patterns between the snowmen. Her nametag said FELICITY BOWDEN, LPN. I asked her if they knew what Abelardo could see, if he could see.

"Are you his wife?" she asked.

"No."

"Are you family?"

"No, I'm—"

"It doesn't matter, because I don't know. I just came on this shift and I haven't read his charts yet."

"He has snow blindness," I said. "I'm sure it's temporary but I don't know how temporary."

"I have to ask you to leave now while I do his vitals."

"Goodbye, Abelardo."

"When you return, Carolina, I will try to recall that night on the lake, because it was especially hot then."

As usual, Susie had been right. It would have been unconscionable not to come, and yet I almost hadn't.

Dandy's color looked good, and so that evening I returned to the Ginny O for evening visiting hours. When I stepped off the elevator on the third floor, I saw the round Felicity Bowden, LPN, in conversation with another nurse in scrubs of a different hue. She looked straight at me; I smiled and nodded, but she did not acknowledge me.

Nothing had changed in Abelardo's room. The curtains were still pulled as tightly as was possible around his neighbor. Abelardo was still burrowed beneath his pile of blankets. There seemed to be even more blankets than earlier.

"Aha, it must be Alice," he said, in English.

"That would be me," I said, sitting down. "Were you expecting someone else?"

"Only you. You are the only one I was expecting. Perhaps under other circumstances I might have received a visit from Hubert, but the literal truth is we have never met in the flesh and I am sure he realizes that this is not the way I would want to create a first impression."

"There's still a lot of snow out there," I said, and tilted my head toward the window. Tactless creature that I was, am.

"A man could starve," Abelardo said.

"So. How are they treating you here?"

"I wouldn't say they were treating me much at all. I am not a matter of grave concern here. Neither my well-being, nor my taste buds."

"I don't think I've ever heard anything good about hospital food. Maybe I could bring you something, if I come back."

"Oysters. I would love some oysters. I've been craving oysters," he said.

"You're kidding."

"I am not kidding at all. I was planning to eat at Grand Central Station's Oyster Bar, which is a landmark in New York and an excellent destination. There is much profound that one could say about oysters, but I prefer to concentrate on the flavor and, especially, the texture."

"I wish I'd known you like oysters so much."

"Perhaps, but would anything have changed? Would I still be here, almost blind?"

"I forgot to ask about your eyes!" I said, mortally embarrassed. I'd totally forgotten anything was wrong with his eyes. Beware the eyes of the beholder. That was something Mami used to say, if ever she suspected any of us of succumbing to vanity. We were adept at hiding vanity. We thought.

"I see more of you now than I did before," Abelardo said.

"That's great. That's wonderful. Your vision has improved!"

"Before you were not here, and therefore I did not see you. Now I see the outline of you, and the shape of you. And it is lovely."

"Has anyone given you an eye test? When will you get better?"

"I've been praying to my Tía Tata, so I am confident I will be seeing like a vulture very soon."

"But you're also talking to the doctors, I hope. Do they have any medicines for you? Drops or something?"

All this time he had been immobile beneath his covers. He had a two-day stubble, which accentuated the bones of his face,

97

and he looked sexy in that Hollywood, I'm-too-cool-to-shave way. His dark brown eyes, lidded by those appallingly long lashes, looked perfectly fine to me. Which may be yet another good reason I am not an ophthalmologist: they looked beautiful. Had I really thought they were gray?

"Drops, yes. But also miracles. And your dog? How is your very ill dog?"

"Dandy. He's fine. He got a blood transfusion, which seems to perk him up. Sooner or later, his marrow should start doing the right thing and then he won't need any more transfusions. At least I certainly hope so because there is something a little strange about giving blood transfusions to a dog. Don't you think?"

Abelardo's right hand emerged and smoothed back his hair, his wavy brown hair. Should I offer to comb it? I wondered. Would that be too forward? Would he get the wrong idea? How much was normal protocol waived in the hospital? "Not at all," he said. "What is strange about it?"

"It just seems profligate. I mean, all those people who need blood and here we are pumping it into a dog."

"Are you so sure? It seems to me blood gets lost, poured out, spilled onto the ground with such frequency that humankind cannot be very worried about its loss."

"I wasn't looking at it quite like that."

"I speak as one who has seen the spilling of blood," Abelardo said. I assumed he was referring to the Contra war. How little I knew about him! Just yesterday I'd seen him go mad, half dressed in the snow, and today I sat by his bedside. Surely these were intimate acts. Rendering oneself vulnerable is always an act of intimacy. Yet I knew him not at all. I looked at his nose as if for the first time, saw how long and narrow it was; I realized that if that nose had been a fraction of a centimeter longer or narrower, it would have crossed the line and been a dangerous object, a pointy object capable of inflicting harm. But it rested gingerly on the safe side of the line, and was exquisite.

"I am so sorry," I said.

"What I am sorry about is that you will not meet my dog Panchito."

"You mean, because he is in Nicaragua?"

"No, because he is dead. He was attacked by the *abejas del asesino* and no amount of Adrenalin or prayers could revive him." Tears were actually pooling in the lower rims of his aforementioned deep brown eyes.

"I am sorry about your dog. You might have mentioned him the other night. When I told you about Gertrude and Pilly," I said.

"I didn't kill him. The bees did."

"Oh, and Waldo is calling your family, so they will know where you are."

"You will have to go see Hubert, of course. Please go see him, dear Alice. Because when I get out of here, and I certainly will get out very soon because I am not suffering from their specialty in suffering and they will quickly cease to find me interesting, I will have to make a retreat and a visit to the Virgin of El Viejo."

"Specialty? I don't think they have a specialty here. It's just a local hospital. Broken legs and inflamed appendices."

"Ah, but they do. I heard the nurses talking; the tiny one with so many holes in her ears, she told me: it's called bariatric surgery and it has nothing to do with barium or the barrio."

This explained quite a lot about the population of the lobby.

"Why don't you and Hubert just talk on the phone?"

"When you meet him you will understand," Abelardo said.

"But you've never met him yourself!" I said. "And I wouldn't know what to say to him. I know about three things about saints. Maybe only two."

His legs moved beneath the sheets. Really, just his feet, and of his feet, just the toes. I remembered those toes from his time in the snow. If I had offered him oysters that second night of the storm, would things have turned out differently?

"I really don't see any alternative. And something tells me that you and Hubert will get on splendidly. I feel sure of it. He will help you fill in the gaps."

"What gaps are you talking about?" I felt defensive, almost cornered suddenly.

So now he looked flustered. "That was a manner of speaking. I was speaking imagistically," Abelardo said. "And, dear Alice, the next time you come, I would like fruit. Any fruit would be nice, so long as it is ripe. I discovered this morning that Harvard is not the only place that will serve rock-hard melon."

"Poor you," I said. To have come so far, for such a fiasco.

"Poor melon. Almost any fruit would be appreciated. I do not expect mango or cherimoya."

"That's lucky," I said. "I was here this afternoon. Do you remember?"

"No, my dear, that wasn't you. Only Carolina de la Rosa was here earlier, and that was most likely my addled imagination, because she would never come this far north in these conditions. She is more averse to snow than I am."

"I was here. You thought I was this Carolina. Who is she?"

"Who is she indeed? Who does she think she is?" Beneath the blankets, his hands appeared to be shivering.

I said, "Couldn't you just tell me who she is? In the normal course of events."

"The normal course of events? The course of events is constantly being altered. Ask Waldito."

"Waldo is still in the caves," I said. "I'm just making conversation. I just thought it might feel like a relatively normal thing to talk about, and perhaps you would feel better."

"Feel better?" he said with a hoarse croaking sound. When he moved his head I saw that the tips of his ears were bright red, either very cold or very hot. Perhaps they missed his pulling and stroking.

"To talk about your friend Carolina. But I wonder if we could get you a cap. Here, you can borrow mine." I pulled my glow-in-the-dark green fleece cap from my pocket. He didn't respond. So I sidled between the bed and the curtain that separated him from his roommate and put the hat atop his head. This time, it was my hands that shook. It seemed a terribly intimate act; it seemed like something I would do for the boys, or for Waldo, who never wore hats. If it had been any other hat, a hat I had not worn minutes ago, it might have been different.

He actually smiled and said, "How do I look?" Those four words sliced through everything I'd thought about Abelardo before. The words were hesitant but also coy, as if spoken by a drop-dead-gorgeous young woman. Hadn't the Jesuits, masters of rhetorical questions and critical thinking, trained him?

Then I had the oddest sensation: that the building was being lifted up at one end and everything at that end was sliding toward the other end that remained on the ground, and so by force of gravity and a waxed floor I was involuntarily sledding straight toward Abelardo. I think at that moment I knew. Just knew. Not *what* would happen but that *something* would happen.

I held my breath, then said, "Henry always says I look like a traffic signal in that hat." It was the wrong answer.

"Not a stop sign, I hope," Abelardo said.

"Just the opposite." I sat down.

His hands emerged from beneath the multilayered counterpane, and he reached for the hat. He adjusted it microscopically.

"I'm curious about this Carolina you thought I was."

"Carolina de la Rosa?"

"Exactly. You said you told her a secret. Now I am all curious to know that secret."

"What secret?"

"I'm the one asking you. There was a night on a lake, if that helps."

"What lake?"

I wanted to laugh, he was so like Henry. "How would I know?"

"I can only assume it is the big lake, because Lake Managua is so polluted that I would never go on it, whereas Cocibolca is lovely. And of course Carolina is a Granadeña, so naturally . . ."

"Is that the one with sharks?"

"So they say. So they say. I myself have never seen a shark. The secret was my first vision of the saint. I told Carolina how I saw her in the chicken-sexing plant."

"Your first vision?" I asked.

"So far my only one," Abelardo said. "But I am still young."

"Speaking of vision—"

"No, I am speaking of Carolina and how she kept the secret."

"Will you tell me? What you saw in the chicken-sexing plant. Whatever a chicken-sexing plant is."

"Once upon a time my father and Uncle Esteban had a chicken farm. It was a good business for a while, so long as the domestic price was kept artificially high by placing heavy duties on imported chickens. The *granjas* were just beyond Chinandega; they were long and low with galvanized tin roofs and ceiling fans every six feet, or whatever was mandated by the ministry. There were so many chickens in there, and they were so close together they couldn't even turn around without scratching their neighbors or getting their wings tangled. And once upon a time my father thought I should learn something about the chicken business, and so he brought me with them to inspect the facility where they sexed the chicks."

Dare I say that my attention was riveted by the sexing, and not the vision? I would have more to tell Susie than I could possibly have imagined.

Abelardo said, "Do not think for a moment that I was interested in chickens, not sexing them, not feathering them, not plucking them. It is trees that I love, not overcrowded bad-tempered fowl. He should have taken Olga. Alas, Olga is a woman, and was a girl—and Papa could never comprehend how much better suited she was to the business. It is a great loss for our family, you know, that Olga could not be the one to take over. Poor Olga."

"You haven't mentioned Olga before," I said.

"You will have to imagine the Olga-that-was." The window overlooked the parking lot. One by one cars were leaving, mostly SUVs of indeterminate color. As one exited the lot, an arm in a red sleeve extended from the driver's-side window and waved frantically toward the rear. I looked to see what the arm was waving at so frantically, and there was nothing. Unless it was someone inside the hospital, someone, like Abelardo, in a room overlooking the lot, watching.

"Everything in there happened so fast, and from my earliest days I have been a slow observer. The conveyor belt spat out the chicks, the worker opened their legs, determined the sex, and threw the poor chick left or right, depending. All the sexers were women, naturally."

"Why naturally?"

"When you come to Nicaragua, you will understand," he said.

"Don't tire yourself out," I said. What I wanted to ask was how the sexers could tell a chicken's sex. Did they have identifiable genitalia? Naturally I was not going to ask Abelardo that question. It would have to wait for Susie.

"I only rest in here," he said. "I don't save any dying dogs."

"Neither do I."

"To continue: it smelled revolting. I was dizzy and nauseated, but I managed not to vomit. I shut my eyes very tightly. That's when I saw her: the inner sides of my eyelids were completely filled with a blue light. First the light was blue and then it took the shape of a standing chicken. Its wings unfurled. They were the wings of a heavenly creature. I kept my eyes shut then as much to keep the heavenly creature inside as to keep from vomiting.

I could hear the voices of my father and Uncle Esteban and the thudding of the chicks tossed aside, and even the squeaking of the conveyor belt that needed to be oiled. Only when the voices stopped suddenly did I open my eyes. This is the vision part. The blue light was still there, and the chicken was still there."

"But Abelardo, that's completely normal. You must know that. I'm sure there is a word for it. If you stare at something of a certain color and then shut your eyes, you see the same shape but in its opposite color, and vice versa if you open your eyes too quickly." To demonstrate, I squeezed my eyes shut and then popped them open. Nothing happened.

"Oh, Alice, Alice. Can you honestly believe I don't know that? It's called a phosphene, but this was not that. Please listen carefully. It was when the chicken opened its mouth to speak that I realized it was not the face of a chicken at all. Where there should have been a beak there were lips, quite red and sensual lips, to be truthful. The same lips that Sorolla painted. It was my Great-Aunt Tristána Catalina."

"As a chicken?" Unfortunately, my voice squeaked just then. Suddenly I felt guilty (again). What was I doing dragging old secrets and delusions from the lips of a hypothermic man?

"I know how it sounds, especially to a gringo. But why not a chicken? Chickens are God's creatures. Chickens were just the element in which I found myself, in which Tía Tata found herself at that moment when I was ready to receive the vision."

"I have nothing against chickens," I said. "I've even started eating them again. I think I told you that. I cooked a chicken the other night. Before all this."

"So you believe me?"

I hadn't considered that question yet. "Did she say anything?"

Abelardo opened his mouth. He really had such perfect teeth—nothing beaky about him! Then his lips closed over those perfect teeth. "No. She just looked at me."

The body in the bed behind the curtain moaned. It was either a moan or a groan. The sheets rustled and a weight shifted upon the mattress. Abelardo and I looked at each other as we listened. Nothing was clearer in my sight than Abelardo. Could he see me at all? He was looking straight at me. Or through me.

Then silence.

"Remind me what the vision of the chicken has to do with the Carolina you thought I was," I said.

"This *is* exhausting," Abelardo said. To me now, he seemed to be spitting out energy, all sparks and fireflies. "I told her all about it. One night going out to Las Isletas. I remember it perfectly. I can see it." A hand popped out from under the sheets, with its fingers tightly aligned, and he waved the hand in front of his eyes. "We were in an old wooden *lancha*—it belonged to a fisherman, Octavio; it was amazing that he could keep fishing because he lost many fingers in the war—and I told her about my vision because she seemed so interested. I had never told a soul before. And never since, until now. I can remember the lingering phosphorescent twilight as I told her and we drifted. The lake was very still. Ometepe was watching everything. The howler monkeys on Monkey Island were howling." He smiled for the first time in a long while. Between the snow outside and the artificial light in the hospital, time was not operating normally.

His smile enlarged and became impish. "There's just one problem: we have no twilight in the tropics, as you must know. As I know very well. So how can I remember it? No, there are two problems. Of all the people to tell in the country, why tell Carolina, who is part of a movement to push aside the claims and miracles of Tía Tata in favor of . . . of her own relative, of La Matilda? Those are my problems."

"She is opposed to your sainted aunt? Does she know something? Why?"

"Why? How absurd this all is. And I mean no offense, not to you. It is simply that no Nicaraguan—planter, poet, or pauper—could ever ask such a foolish question."

"Most of us are not Nicaraguan."

"Of this I am well aware. So of course you do not know that the beautiful Carolina Felicita de la Rosa Oberon—who was runner-up in the Miss Nicaragua pageant and would have won if it were not for corruption, which surprises no one—*that* Carolina is laterally descended from La Matilda Vargas de la Rosa. And in my country, especially in Granada, and especially among the de la Rosas, there is a belief that La Matilda should be canonized and preferably before Tía Tristána. They are wrong and deluded, of course, because Tristána led a profoundly more saintly life in the classic mold of virgin saints, as my research among the hallowed stacks of the Hagiographers Club would have shown, will show."

Now, at last, his breathing became shallow and labored. Those final passionate words were pulled from his throat by a thin thread, stretched to its limit.

"Don't think that I'm not dying to know about this rival saint in your country, but you seem wiped out. And I bet visiting hours are over." I stood up to leave. "Can I get you anything before I go?"

"When you return you must bring my clothes," he said. "And my suitcase. Please zip it shut and do not look inside."

"Of course. No problem. I can't believe I didn't think to bring your clothes before."

"I agree."

"Good night, Abelardo."

"When you return, you must call me Lalo."

The glow-in-the-dark green hat was still pulled down over his head.

Then I heard, we heard, *Yo soy Nicaragüense.* It was not Abelardo. The voice came from behind the blue curtain.

"What's that?" I said.

"He said he was Nicaraguan. He is my compatriot," Abelardo said. "*¿Verdad?*" And then to me, "Alice, please open the curtain on your way out."

I did. His roommate, he of hesitant groans and rustling sheets, was a young Hispanic man with straight black hair that cleaved to his skull, and wide Mayan cheekbones; half his face was hidden beneath gauze pads and bandages, in a way that made it very clear why he spoke with difficulty, why I had trouble understanding him. His eyes were watery and sad. Compared with Abelardo he looked tiny and childlike in the hospital bed.

"Adios, Alice," Abelardo said. There was nothing else to do, so I left. Though I was terribly curious. True, there were many recent emigrants from Central and South America in nearby Thumbtown, and no landscaping company or tree company or construction firm could manage without them. It seemed quite reasonable that there would be Nicaraguans among their numbers, but remarkable that one should find his way into the very same room with Abelardo Llobet, also of Nicaragua. Unless the hospital did such things on purpose.

I stood for a while outside the room, out of sight (not that it mattered much in Abelardo's case) but not out of earshot. I listened and was rewarded; I heard Abelardo say, in his crisp, elegant Spanish: *"¿De donde vienes? ¿Para donde vas? ¿Como te llamas y que tal estas?"* What? He had not mentioned he was a poet; nor had Waldo. Had this facility for easy rhyming forged a bond between the two Harvard boys? Was this one of the million things they had not told me, as opposed to the three and a half things they had? Was there a Spanish equivalent of a limerick? There were so many questions I still had for Mami.

Two chubby nurses wheeled past with a Huge One. To justify my presence, I pulled out and studied a list that had long resided in the bowels of my handbag: *milk, TP, vanilla, some kind of meat, OJ with no pulp, bread, olives, 100-watt light bulbs.*

The man in the other bed, the sad bandaged man, replied, *"De arriba vengo, para abajo voy, Rubén me llamo, y muy mal estoy."*

This was too much. Both poets! Both rhymesters!

In the hallway and the elevator and the lobby I averted my

eyes from the other patients and kept them focused on my feet inside their mukluks. The sky was black and twinkling, and cold was everywhere.

I found my car behind a grittifying snow pile in the parking lot, and went home. *In the snow, off I go, blow, throw, crow.* No, it wasn't working. The gift was in making it seem easy, and that I could never do.

I walked over to Susie's, each step making a crater in the snow as I sank to my crotch, climbed out, then descended again. In my parka pocket I carried a bottle of wine, a jar of tapénade, and a box of stoned wheat thins. It was slow going. I imagined myself in Lapland, doomed to survive on dried reindeer meat.

"You shouldn't have," Susie said when I came in, leaving my snow-filled boots to puddle by the door.

"I have a question for you," I said. "What do you know about chicken sexing?"

Susie looked suddenly radiant. She was sitting in a modern leather armchair, a famous chair, or at least one that I'd seen in magazines; it had a curvaceous wooden frame and it swiveled. All of which was a good thing if you had just had your knee replaced and were stuck indoors. She was wearing a body-hugging pink sweater and baggy sweatpants. Her hair, as usual, fell behind her in a long brown braid, thick as a rope that could tether an ocean liner. "How could you possibly have known that I actually know something about chicken sexing? I do now, anyway. You really are uncanny, Alice," she said. "Except when you're not."

"All things being equal, who else would I ask about chicken sexing?"

"Bogumila, all things being equal," Susie said.

"You know perfectly well I wouldn't ask her. Not if I had to say the *sex* word. So tell me what you know."

"Why do you want to know? Chickens have not been on your most-favored-nations list."

"It'll take a while to explain," I said, and went into the kitchen for a corkscrew, wineglasses, a plate, and a knife. The kitchen was spotless; every surface, including the inside of the sink, gleamed, unsullied by crumbs or smears. Either Susie was not eating or she was doing a bang-up job of cleaning while on crutches.

"What's with the kitchen?" I asked.

"Herc came over. He can't help himself."

"Really? How exciting," I said.

"As regards cleanliness," she stressed. "He's fanatical. So I let him."

"Oh." We both drank our wine. "How's the knee?"

"Before or after the pain meds?"

"That doesn't sound good."

"I like this wine. So explain."

I told Susie that, per her instructions, I'd gone to see Abelardo at the hospital and told her what had transpired. I did not mention the vision of his Aunt Tata as a chicken with a blue aura.

"It's actually quite an art, is chicken sexing," Susie said.

"And?"

"Of course, you can just wait until the chicks grow up and develop secondary sex characteristics, as in having wattles or laying eggs; and it's also possible to breed chickens to have different wing patterns depending on their sex, to make them instantly recognizable. But I doubt that's what you're asking about. What you want to know about is vent sexing."

"I do?"

"I have no doubt. And it's just as well you didn't ask your Latin friend. You would have both been terribly embarrassed. Whereas . . ."

I laughed. "Whereas between us, nothing is embarrassing and all is fair game."

"Until it's not," Susie said. She was not laughing.

"So tell me. About vent sexing," I said.

"It's not for the squeamish."

"Since when have I been squeamish?" I was getting impatient. I had the oddest sense that we were in a French farce and there was a lover hidden in the draperies. But there were no draperies. Only Roman shades.

"Fine. First thing you need to know is that chicken genitalia are internal. Not available to the naked eye. Basically, you squeeze the shit out of the newborn chicks so you can look up their asshole and see if there is a bump or not. A bump means a male. It's called a 'male process.' I'll have you know that vent sexing is considered an art. There were these two Japanese guys in the thirties who figured out how to do it, and they compared it to playing chess."

"You're kidding."

"I couldn't make this up."

I said, "Well, thank goodness chickens are vegetarians."

"They're not anything when they get sexed. They're just hatched."

"Fine, but at least they haven't been eating hamburgers. That would be revolting."

"More revolting," Susie said.

"And you know this how?"

"The same way I know anything. I read it in a book. About raising chickens. *Raising Chickens for Dummies*—my bible."

"Will you have to do this?"

"First I have to get the chicken coop, and then the chickens. And then hens have to lay eggs and then they have to hatch. Then I consider whether to try vent sexing or not. And I certainly could try it, and as long as I don't kill the chicks then no harm is done and it may turn out that I have a gift for it."

"This has been very helpful," I said. "How can I thank you?"

"You can't. You've already made my day. But you can take out the garbage on your way back."

"Consider it done," I said.

• • •

Later that night, while Dandy and Flirt slept silently beneath our bed, I lay alone between the flannel sheets and felt at the epicenter of some seismic gratitude for Susie's next-door knowledge. It didn't entirely wipe out all the guilt for Abelardo's madness in the snow, but it made me feel pretty good, a kind of all's-right-with-the-world, or all-would-be-right-if-Waldo-and-the-boys-were-home-and-Abelardo-were-safely-in-Nicaragua.

It should not have mattered that there was no one who wanted to hear my dream the next morning. In my dream Mami was alive. The report of her death had been a terrible mistake and she stood on the beach in Goleta, shivering a bit, dripping, while we all stood in a semicircle and examined a severed arm and clucked over the telltale shark-tooth markings. She was horrified that we had identified it as her arm. She was indignant that we had thought her arm looked like the arm in front of us, which was flabby and mottled, nothing like Mami's long, muscled arm, an enviable arm. We were all so glad she was alive, but she remained annoyed that we had made such an egregious mistake.

It was not the first time I'd dreamed that Mami was alive and that a mistake had been made, but this one was especially vivid, and called for an audience. What it called for was *The Dream Radio Show*. Was it possible that not only did I no longer host the show but *no one* hosted *Dream Radio*? The show no longer existed. Every single person in the tri-state area with a dream to tell was up a creek without a paddle.

For five minutes that morning it snowed again, fat luscious flurries that fell leisurely to the ground, that flitted in the air like showoffs, that took all the time in the world to display their infinite eternally dissimilar patterns. I thought, Enough is enough. I also thought that Abelardo would never get back to Nicaragua if it snowed again, and then what would we do? But after five minutes the snow stopped: bored, indifferent, its gaze blank and pitiless as the sun.

And five minutes later I was making a sloppy three-point turn, butting up against the snowdrifts that lined our road, because I had forgotten everything: ripe fruit, clothes, the suitcase. In the fruit department, all I had in the kitchen were bananas and pears: monkey food and northern food. I would be lying if I said that I efficiently gathered up his clothes and placed them inside his suitcase and zipped it shut without a second glance. I looked.

All my life I had managed not to know Abelardo and in particular not to know anything of his quest to see his great-aunt canonized, and now, suddenly, I could not even wait until visiting hours to return to the Ginny O to see him. This had nothing to do with guilt. Who was this Carolina de la Rosa? And why did she matter to him, and now to me?

The curtain between the two beds was pulled back all the way to the wall now. When I walked in Abelardo said, "Have you met Rubén Zamora?"

"*Con mucho gusto,*" I said to the poor man with the bandaged face. And then to Abelardo, "You sound much better this morning."

"Sounds can be very deceiving," Abelardo said. "They are open to interpretations. They are always filtered and always translated."

"Are you saying you're not really better?"

"As were her relics. Translated."

"Excuse me?"

"Tristána's things. When relics are moved from one church to another or when the body of a saint is moved, we say she has been translated. But not into a foreign language."

I thought about this. "I don't think translators get nearly enough credit for what they do. Especially poets. I'm not sure poetry can be translated. Unless by *translating* you mean moving the body of the poem from one place to another. Then it makes more sense." All sorts of things were beginning to make sense.

They were making sense in the same way that if you took LSD, it seemed possible to solve the world's problems, write an ode, and then comprehend all of philosophy in a single night.

"*Señor, por favor, dígale.*"

"He wants me to tell you."

From the looks of it, even to speak was painful for Rubén.

"Tell me what?"

"That he knew my Tía Tata. He is a believer."

"That's great. Kind of an incredible coincidence, though?"

"I do not credit coincidence. But if you must, the coincidence is that we share a country. Once that has occurred, I find it not at all remarkable that he knew Tía Tata."

"But isn't she dead? How long has she been dead?"

"Quite a while. Long enough. She died in 1982. Rubén was a young man then, but he remembers."

I smiled at him. But I was thinking of Henry and Ezra in the caves. This Rubén's earnestness reminded me of Ezra; even his bandage reminded me of Ezra. I wondered if he walked in his sleep. Abelardo should know.

"You said you'd tell me about your girlfriend's aunt," I said.

"She's not my girlfriend! Please don't ever say such a thing."

"Sorry. Carolina's aunt."

"Her name was Matilda Vargas de la Rosa, and she had a twin brother, Mateo. On the last day of the year of 1900, they were born at home, which is to say, in the de la Rosa mansion, catty-corner to the Cathedral of San Francisco in Granada. Someone told me that under the bed was a jar with every detached umbilical cord from every de la Rosa who had entered the world in that bed. There is no reason to believe that is not true, but I have always thought that if you counted you would not find as many umbilici as there were babies. But that is not really germane." He spoke slowly and clearly, as if I were deaf, or slightly stupid. "They say that the twins' mother, Doña Rosalinda de la Rosa Vargas, wanted them to be born on the first day of the new century, and that when the contractions started on the morning of the thirty-first, she drank herb tea and lay tilted in her bed so that her head was lower than her feet, but nothing availed. The twins were born well before midnight."

"I've never heard of tea to slow down contractions," I said.

"You will notice, my dear Alice, that the contractions did not slow down. Remember that people in my country are subject to all sorts of superstitions and beliefs."

"But not you?"

"In the matter of belief, you may say I am an omnivore. I believe many things. But I have also studied the sciences, and I know the difference. Now, my new friend here, Rubén, he believes that there are demons inside the active volcano of Masaya, and that the Virgin of Tipitapa weeps real tears every Friday, and that jaguars change into children and children into jaguars. There is a difference."

Rubén smiled when he heard his name spoken in the middle of an otherwise incomprehensible English sentence.

"So the twins?"

"From the very beginning La Matilda was the stronger, dominant child. Did I say that she was born first? She was. She ruled Mateo, who looked nothing like her; next to her, he was so fragile, so pale. But it was not enough to rule and control, she had to contradict every little thing he said, and ruin every little thing he wanted. She was not a nice child. Not all children are nice, though parents find that hard to accept. Then, to make a long story shorter, Mateo found his true love."

"Why shorten it? Why now? I like love stories."

"Oh, Alice, Alice. The only story I will embroider and lengthen will be Tía Tata's. Surely you know that? It's remarkable that I tell you this at all. It is only for Carolina's sake, and in case you meet her."

"Meet her?"

"It is true our paths cross very rarely, usually only in the event of natural disasters or funerals. Which are not so different."

"And the true love?" I asked. What about Abelardo's true love? Where was she? I tried to recall what Waldo had told me of their roommate days, if there had been any female names. I couldn't remember any. She was probably Nicaraguan. Whoever she was. Was this all a roundabout way of telling me that this Carolina was the one? No, my instincts said she was not; if anything, she was a red herring.

"Her name was Isabel de Sola Pacheco, and she was a revelation to Mateo, who thought that finally, at last, he would be delivered from the unkind dominion of his sister."

"Was she really that bad?"

"Please listen, Alice. I was speaking of Isabel. Like the Vargases she was a Granadeña. Her father owned three pharmacies and was very prosperous. Isabel had been educated in an excellent convent, but still, her family did not dine at the Vargases, they did not meet each other at christenings and weddings. Mateo decided it would not be wise to tell his family—and especially Matilda, whom he feared—and that he and his beloved must elope. They did. Mateo knew the padre in a small village on the northern side of the lake, Tecacilpa. So it happened that they were praying in his small parish church when Mombacho erupted and the village was wiped out by lava flow."

"You're kidding," I said.

"I beg your pardon," Abelardo said, and blinked. He was definitely seeing things this morning: me, the wall, the snow outside the window, cars in the parking lot. I realized that his eyes were moving now, and days earlier they hadn't been. "It was the first eruption since 1570, when a debris avalanche destroyed an entire village. Another village."

"It seems a tad melodramatic," I said. I didn't mention that I have been accused of melodrama myself, on occasion.

"I assume you know we have forty-three active volcanoes in my country. Active. And what seems melodramatic to you, accustomed as you are to nothing worse than a snowstorm or a mid-summer hurricane, was death to this young couple. And the rest of the village." Was this man completely devoid of irony? Was that what was required? Which one of us had just gone batty in the snow? Which one had carved angels in his pajamas? He continued, "After three days Isabel's father came to the Vargases' mansion and told Don Umberto Vargas that the bodies of their two children had been found in the debris of the church of St. Eulalia in Tecacilpa. By some miracle—so they said—Padre Diego had survived; he was badly injured, but he'd survived, and he related that before the disaster he had joined the two in holy matrimony."

"I thought the whole village was wiped out."

"Well, he survived. Almost always there will be some survivors. To tell the stories."

"Awfully convenient," I said. It sounded more cynical than I really felt. What I wanted was to hear what Abelardo felt. About all of this, about anything.

"Perhaps. Perhaps not. After the tragedy, Matilda had a change of heart. They say that when she heard the news she fell into a swoon, hit her head on the tile floor, and was unconscious for three days. She had been tatting when the news came—for a while she was considered the best lace maker in the region—and she pricked herself with a needle as she fell. You, my dear Alice, might say that such elements contribute to the melodrama of the tale, and I would not disagree. However, at her brother's funeral, La Matilda publicly acknowledged that she had mistreated her brother and swore to spend the rest of her life looking after young boys. That evening, so they say, she moved into a hovel just outside the walls of the Vargas mansion, and the next day she began traveling the country, by foot and by donkey, ministering to poor young men. In the end, she started several schools for boys, each one dedicated to a saint who had misspent his youth. Saint Augustine, of course, and Saint Eustachius and Saint Wulfric, and others I can't think of just now. But I'm sure I will remember them soon."

"That's okay," I said. "I don't need to know them all."

"As I was saying, word spread, and donations came from all over. For some unknown reason vast amounts came from one city in Germany, Stuttgart. Do you know Stuttgart?"

"I know it exists. But I've never been there."

"Nor I," said Abelardo. "There are no great cathedrals there. But someone in Stuttgart heard about La Matilda's schools and sent lots of money."

"And all this because she felt guilty about having been so horrid to her brother?"

"Because her brother and Isabel would not have died if she hadn't been so horrid, as you say. The very fear of her recriminations forced them to elope."

"But other people died in the volcano, under the lava. And they would have died with or without this Matilda. And the volcano would have erupted no matter what she did. Was it like Pompeii? Are they preserved forever?"

"No." Abelardo sighed. The nurse was hovering over Rubén Zamora's bed, but she was positioned in such a way—and her breadth was so great—that it was impossible to see what she was doing to him. It seemed almost rude, or heartless, to be speaking in English about matters Nicaraguan when Rubén was right there and could not understand. But still we spoke English. "Not at all like Pompeii."

"So she's your big competition?" I said. *"La competencia?"*

"If you choose to look at it that way."

"So why would you tell Carolina about seeing your great-aunt in a chicken if Carolina's related to this Matilda? Isn't that like industrial espionage? Or selling secrets? *Giving away* secrets."

"The only reason I might not describe my vision of Tía Tata is that it wouldn't be believed, might detract from a true appreciation of who she was."

"Can't they both be saints? Can you get a twofer deal?"

"No. They cannot. It was a good thing to start those schools, but Matilda's motives were never pure. Surely you can see that?"

"It's not as if I were there."

"Nor I, but I am capable of forming judgments."

"Is she still alive?" I asked.

"Of course not. Surely you know a person must be dead at least fifteen years before the canonization process can start."

"Surely? Surely that is not common knowledge. And yes, I assumed she was dead. I just thought I'd ask."

"I don't understand you, Alice," Abelardo said.

"I don't see what understanding me has to do with it. You just need to get better so you can canonize your aunt."

He said nothing, just smiled. His cheek creases made such perfect parentheses that I cocked my head and strained to hear that parenthetical phrase, that secret answer. *Nada. Silencio.*

"You are getting better, aren't you? I don't see any IVs in you. Your vision is back, isn't it? You're warm enough?"

"What is enough?" he said, and pulled the covers up closer to his chin.

"Abelardo?"

Barely moving his lips he said, "Lalo."

"Okay. Lalo?"

"Yes, my dear Alice."

"Lalo, in all this, what do you actually believe? Because none of this sounds like major saint material to me. Maybe I don't know saint material when I see it. That's probably the likeliest explanation. But still."

"Is that what troubles you? Belief? The possibility of belief?"

"Exactly!" How did he know me so well? And did I mind that he did? I said, "It's just that they both—your aunt and Carolina's aunt—what is it with aunts?—they just seem essentially ordinary. Better than average, but not extraordinary."

"Not at all," Lalo said. "In Tía Tata's case, her goodness was more than ordinary, and the good she did was far more than ordinary. But there is nothing wrong with being ordinary."

All this time a fruit-filled grocery bag and Lalo's brown suitcase with dark brown piping had been sitting on the floor beside me. Everything at the bottom of his suitcase was ironed and folded perfectly. On top of that was a yellow legal pad filled with pages and pages of writing in a very unusual scrawl, Lalo's, presumably. Had I seen the pad anywhere other than in his suitcase, I would have assumed the handwriting was a woman's. I didn't know the first thing about graphology, but that is what I thought.

"I almost forgot," I said.

"You might ask Hubert about that," Lalo said.

"Your stuff. And some fruit. No cherries, though."

"Ask him about what constitutes ordinary. Sometimes ordinary is the highest grace."

"You can send him an e-mail when you're better," I said.

"He's not comfortable with e-mail. He needs to make contact with an actual piece of paper."

Suddenly I remembered what had been lurking in the back of my mind all yesterday and today: when Pop was in the hospital, Mami visited every day. Once I went to see him after school and found Mami asleep next to him on the hospital bed, her head on his shoulder, her arm flung across his body. Pop was awake and he shushed me before I could say anything. Mami slept on.

Abelardo said contritely, "The fruit will make a great difference. Whatever happens, I won't get scurvy or beriberi."

"That's a relief."

"Why are you looking at me like that?"

"Like what?"

"Like I have two heads, or two noses."

"Ignore me. I can't always control my eyes."

"You have strabismus?"

"I have distraction," I said. "And now I have to go and check on the dogs. Dandy is doing very well, by the way."

Lalo lurched forward in the bed. "Now I remember what I meant to tell you. That disease your dog has? What was it? An aplastic anemia, where his marrow is not producing red blood cells. Well, my father has exactly the opposite. I was thinking about that last night."

"Your father?" It crossed my mind that he was suffering from delusions. That either he or I was suffering from delusions. That he was suffering from delusions, and it was my fault. That I had been so concerned with my dog that I had neglected the most basic responsibility of hospitality. That I was guilty of some biblical sin.

"Last night when dear Felicity was tightening the cuff around my arm I thought of my father's blood, of all the Llobet blood that flows in his veins and mine and my sisters'. But there is too much of his blood. He has too much of his own blood. His marrow is overproducing blood cells. He has polycythemia vera."

"Pollyanna Vera?"

"Hardly. Don't you see? It is the opposite of your dog's illness. I find that extraordinary."

"Isn't it a good thing to have so many red blood cells?"

Lalo's nose twitched. "Too much of a good thing. They are clotting. Every three weeks he must be phlebotomized. Bled."

"How medieval. And creepy."

"Many people feel that way about blood, but I do not. Snow, on the other hand. Snow is creepy."

Back to snow! "Which reminds me," I said. "What can I bring you? Next time I come?"

"Poetry. Some poems would be nice."

"Any particular poem? Or poet?"

"I don't suppose you have Rubén Darío? Or Lorca? No. In that case, I defer to your judgment."

As I was on the way out, mere steps from Lalo's bedside, on the other side of the flimsy patterned-cotton curtain, Rubén, in the other bed, beckoned me. When his closed fingers curled back toward himself, in an eternal gesture of *come hither*, I didn't recognize it. I thought he might be having a seizure or was trying to stop himself from falling out of bed. Then I saw his eyes, and knew. It was easy to see his eyes because they were about the only intact feature of his face; they stood out in stark relief against the white bandages that swathed his cheeks and nose. I went and stood hesitantly next to his bed. He spoke in Spanish. At first I thought he said "Look after me," which seemed sad and also a little cheeky, given that I didn't know him. But in that weird way that spoken words unravel inside your head after you've heard them and are revealed to be other than what you'd first thought, I figured it out. I'd thought I'd heard *Cuideme*, when in fact he'd said *Cuidele*, which meant "Look after *him*." There he was, with a gashed face and no understanding of what was going on and generally pretty bleak prospects as far as I could tell, as a presumably illegal immigrant in the frigid north at the mercy of lawn-mowing trends, telling me to look after Lalo.

I asked him why. "*¿Por qué?*"

Which seemed to really shock him. What kind of idiot was I? Because his aunt is a saint, he replied in Spanish.

"Yes," I said. "I will. *Sí, voy hacerlo.*"

For the rest of the day I did laundry and read soup recipes. I never actually made any soup, but I did fold every shirt geometrically, and I folded every pair of socks into each other and made perfect little balls. I tri-folded the boys' tighty-whities so that each reinforced crotch panel formed the neat center of a closed triptych. Then I read the want ads. Why was there such a call for hospital administrators in our state but not dream radio hosts? If I had had a radiology credential and five years' experience, I could have had my pick of employment opportunities. But I had no such background.

I ate a can of sardines for dinner, and brought Gerard Manley Hopkins into the hospital for Lalo. It seemed highly likely he knew the poems already, given his Jesuit schooling.

On my way in I greeted Rubén, pleasantly but distantly, because I was afraid he might want to talk again. I pulled the separating curtain slightly aside and cleared my throat to announce my presence. Lalo's bed was empty. Lalo was gone, as were the blankets and pillows and sheets. The room was like a fresh wound scrubbed clean.

I asked the nurse at the nurses' station and she said he'd been discharged because he was perfectly fine, and if I wanted to know any more I really should ask Mr. Llobet—not her. So I had to talk to Rubén after all. He didn't know, he said. He'd been asleep, he said. When I repeated that Lalo was gone, not to return, he didn't look nearly as bereft as he should have.

My house felt empty. I gave the dogs some cold cuts I found in the back of the meat drawer, and that perked them up. But it was short-lived, and not enough.

By the time Lalo called from the airport I had lost all taste for smoked oysters. And then he didn't exactly tell me where he was.

First there was silence. Then, "Alice?"

"Lalo! I've been worried. Where are you?" I said.

He was silent, again. Then I heard the ambient noise of delayed-flight announcements, and knew.

"I'm really sorry about what happened," I said.

"*Yo también*. No, it is for me to be sorry," he said.

"But you shouldn't have left without telling me. I could have taken you to the airport, at the least. How *did* you get there, anyway?"

"You have an excellent local taxi service," Abelardo said. "I explained to the driver about Santiago de Compostela, about which he was sadly ignorant. Notwithstanding the scallop shell dangling from his mirror."

"He had a shell dangling from a mirror?" Was it safe to let Abelardo fly home alone?

"He said it was an air freshener," Abelardo said. "They're calling my flight. Alice, you will please come to Nicaragua?"

"I don't know, Lalo. I'm so—I don't exactly know what I am. Waldo will be home soon and he'll want to know all about you. What shall I say?"

"Tell him I missed him, but not very much. Because I had you."

"Lalo! Can you see where you're going?"

"Thank God for the return of colors," he said. And then he was gone.

Would I ever be hungry again?

9 ❧ *Querida* Carmencita

WALDO'S LUGGAGE DIDN'T ARRIVE with him. According to the airline's Lost, Mislaid, and Abandoned Baggage Department, his battered canvas suitcase had gone west instead of east. The boys' duffel bag, full of rocks and tools and treasures, was duly spat out of the luggage tunnel and down the chute; it made it halfway around the conveyor belt before the boys swooped it up.

Waldo was tired and cranky. "I am never checking luggage again. These people are idiots. The more advanced the technology they have, the worse the service is."

"You may have something there. This may be a clue to the modern dilemma," I said.

Ezra said, "We couldn't carry them on, Dad. Remember? They wouldn't have let us through with the pickax."

"This is true. But I don't normally travel with a pickax."

We filled out the forms, circling the line drawing of the suitcase that looked most like Waldo's while agreeing that it looked nothing at all like the real thing. According to the airline's tracking, the suitcase was now in Cheyenne, Wyoming.

"If they can get it to Cheyenne, why can't they get it to New York?" Ezra wanted to know.

"Ah," said Waldo, his mood brightening. "It's all about intention, isn't it? Where do they intend it to go? And where does it actually go? When do those things converge? Do you know how many discoveries were made accidentally, while people were looking for something entirely different? Do you know how many inventions are the results of slip-ups in the lab?"

"We know, Dad," Henry said. "'More than we think. Enough to make us wonder,'" he quoted.

"We really do know, Dad," Ezra chimed in.

"Tell me about the caves," I said. "Did you love the caves?" Tell me something new, and warm.

Ezra said, "Why didn't you bring Flirt and Dandy?"

"Because I can't leave them in the parking lot. Someone might steal them. Not to mention that it's not very nice to leave them locked inside a car," I said.

"But I want to be sure Dandy is A-OK," Ezra said.

"He is. He had another transfusion and he's a prince. You'll see him soon enough."

"You could have brought them into the airport. Close your eyes and pretend they're seeing-eye dogs," Henry suggested.

"I've never heard of a spaniel seeing-eye dog," Waldo said.

"Plus that's not very nice. How would a real blind person feel if he saw you pretending to be blind just so your dogs could come to baggage claim?"

"That's good, Mom," Henry said. "For one thing, a real blind person wouldn't see me."

"What's the second thing?" Waldo asked.

I said, "I want to hear about the caves."

"They were awesome, as in, they filled us with awe. They really did," Henry said.

Ezra said, perhaps with some pity, "They were huge, Mom. Vast and cavernous. First there was light from the opening, but then there was no natural light at all, only electric lights. And my headlamp. My headlamp was brilliant."

"They were grandiose, Mom. And eerie, full of secret tunnels, hidden openings. And of course stalactites. And stalagmites," said Henry.

"Tell me again how you can tell the difference," I said.

"Sta*lac*tites, with a *c*, grow down from the *ceiling*. Sta*lag*mites, with a *g*, grow up from the *ground*."

"That's very good. I just wish I could remember it."

"It's CK, Mom."

Waldo mouthed, *Common knowledge.*

"Thank you," I said.

I looked at Waldo, who had plugged his cell phone into the car charger device and was listening to his messages.

"I thought your cell phone wasn't working. I thought that was why it was so hard to call home," I said.

"It wasn't," he said. "I forgot the charger."

"You never forget things like that."

"Well, I did this time."

"Mom, we could have done a better job with the names," Henry said.

"I didn't think they were so terrible," Ezra said.

Waldo looked up and said, "This is the bridge."

"What bridge?"

"The Whitestone. Remember the jumper when we were coming to the airport?"

"I thought you weren't going to tell the boys."

"They're not paying attention," Waldo said. Silence had suddenly descended on the back seat. The boys were playing Tetris on my cell phone.

"I hate to think about things like that. About changing your mind somewhere between the railing of the bridge and the cold, black water."

Waldo said nothing. He held his cell phone to his ear and seemed distant.

"Do you think more suicides jump into cold water than into warm water?"

"I have no idea, Al."

"I bet somebody does."

"You're not suggesting Lalo was suicidal, are you?" Waldo said.

That hadn't occurred to me. There was enough traffic that I felt compelled to watch both the car in front of me and the car behind, and so I couldn't really examine Waldo's expression. "God, no. But he definitely wouldn't have run amok in warm weather."

Waldo said, "You can't know that. The snow is just the *ostensible* reason he went a little batty."

"Why couldn't it be the snow? You said he always hated winter."

"You should know."

"But I don't know. He's your friend, Waldo. I just fed him and told him all about Dandy and all the other dogs I've killed."

"You did what? I still doubt that sent him off the deep end. You've got to stop talking that way, because—as far as I know—Dandy isn't dead."

"Of course he isn't dead," I said.

"Who isn't dead?" Ezra wanted to know.

"No one," I said.

"Lots of people," Waldo said. He looked out the window, and then reached over and stroked my thigh. Actually, first he patted the top of my thigh, and then the tips of his fingers slipped inward. Even through my blue jeans, I could feel his touch. His fingertips were warm, like electric eels.

"There's still a lot of snow on the ground, isn't there?" he said, as if noticing for the first time.

His canvas suitcase was delivered two days later at six in the morning by a haggard airline employee. I answered the door in my flannel robe. He handed over the suitcase and shook his head glumly as he complained, "You have a lot of snow here, lady."

"I know," I replied.

"You really should do something about it."

The pickax was not in the returned suitcase. Waldo said he was going to call the airline and complain.

That night, Waldo came glumly through the back door. His dragging feet, shod in frayed hunting boots—how had he left the house so disheveled? had I noticed?—seemed to barely propel or carry his body, his unrecognizable body, lumpen and misshapen like a Halloween gourd.

"What train hit you?" I said.

He sat down at the kitchen table with a muted thud that matched up to someone else, to some other man who outweighed the real Waldo, the lively Waldo, my Waldo, by at least a hundred pounds. Exhaustion spoke from his cheeks, emanated from the sleeves of his jacket, while his ears hung limply from his skull.

"Huh?" he said. And then, "I don't know. Things are imploding at work. Half the patent department quit today. Or maybe they got fired."

"Have you considered a vacation?"

"I just had a vacation. In the caves."

I handed him a glass of red wine and his mail. Between the notice from the Town of VerGroot regarding compliance with the leash law and a quasi-personal appeal for funds to restore several old farm buildings that, it had just recently been learned, were once a way station on the Underground Railroad, there was something of actual interest. There was an envelope addressed by a real hand, bearing a stamp that had been licked by a human tongue: a Nicaraguan stamp, featuring a lizard of an improbable color improbably posing in front of an erupting volcano. But it was not addressed to me, and there was no return name or address. I was still not a graphologist, yet I detected the strains of convent training in that handwriting, a convent later abandoned. The penmanship was elegantly curvilinear, but also naturalistic and freeform. The writer had used a fountain pen and purple ink. I had held the letter up to the light and squinted, all to no avail, as the sender had used a high-quality twenty-pound linen envelope.

Waldo drank slowly and read the notice about the leash-law compliance with far greater attention than it deserved. VerGroot had no need for a leash law. He sipped his wine.

"You got a letter from Nicaragua," I said.

"I see that."

"Do you think that is Abelardo's handwriting?"

"It doesn't look like it," Waldo said.

"That's what I thought too."

Waldo sipped his wine and picked up a teaspoon that had been left on the table.

"You don't think he's dead, do you? Don't you think you should open it, toot sweet?"

"Something tells me he's not dead," Waldo said. He was enjoying my impatience, too much.

"Fine," I said. "Just don't ask me what Posey told me about Dick."

"I won't. I already know what Posey has to say and I recommend taking it with a grain of salt."

"Just open the damn letter! Please."

And he did. Just like that. As if complying with my wishes, as if humoring my impatience and catering to my neediness, were things he did on a regular basis. He took a knife from the table and neatly slit open the envelope and removed two sheets of paper. One had print on one side and was covered with tiny handwriting on the other. The other was the size of a note card and bore the same handwriting as the envelope, the same purple ink, and also an inkblot. I could see the inkblot from where I stood.

"It's from Lalo's sister Carmen. She says she was rummaging through his jacket and found this letter he must have written when he was in the hospital up here. She thinks that we—though I'm sure she really means you—should see it."

"Which one is Carmen?"

"Which what is Carmen?"

"Is she the babe?" I asked.

"I thought I told you they were all babes," Waldo said.

I thought: She's not the only one rummaging in pockets.

"Here, Al. This is definitely meant for you. It's in Spanish. I had no idea his handwriting was so minuscule." He sighed. "That whole business with Lalo in the snow was certainly an object lesson about how people can totally surprise you. After so many years, they can do things you would never predict. If I had any sense, it would make me look at everyone differently. Even you. Maybe that should be, especially you."

Waldo handed me Lalo's letter. It had been folded and unfolded and refolded too many times. He had written it on the reverse side of the Ginny O Hospital's daily menu choices sheet, the sheet upon which he should have marked his preference for turkey fricassee over baked fish (species unidentified); should have marked his preferred drink: coffee, tea, or apple juice; should have indicated whether he wanted Jell-O or vanilla pudding. And if he was writing letters on the reverse side of the daily menu choices, then how did the nutritionists and dieticians and gourmet chefs, all toiling away in their shower caps, know what to feed him? Did he go hungry that day?

I read, or deciphered:

Carmencita, Instead of this, instead of this, instead of this, at this very moment, on this day at this time of day in any time zone under the sun, but most specially the one we are in now, I should be at the Hagiographers Club wearing that blue suit you insisted I get tailor-made in London. Do you remember? Of course you do, you remember everything. We were in London after that disastrous trip to Rome, after our appallingly rude treatment by that craven, limping, sputtering Cardinal Ratskeller? Even now I see him lumbering beneath the weight of his miter—he looked like the last gasp in a long line of incestuous unions. And then to pretend he didn't know us, that he didn't even know where Nicaragua was. "Ah yes, you're the East African country with those wild blue rhinoceri. Of course I remember the article in National Geographic. How I adore the National Geographic. Do you know it?" I would have liked to put his ring through his nose. He knew perfectly well our exact location on the isthmus. We had a rather heated discussion about the proper length of sleeves. From where I lie, I can see that blue suit and all that it represents in my mind's eye, dare I say that I see it as surely as Bernadette saw Our Lady by the spring in Lourdes? As clearly as Juan Diego saw Our Lady at Teotihucan? As clearly as Don Diego of Tezoatega saw the statue of Our Lady in the shadow of the guácimo tree? Does that strike you as blasphemous? That I would equate a sanctified vision of the Virgin with my own vivid vision of a blue tailored suit, a suit I am not now wearing. No, blasphemy has never troubled you. Quite the opposite. Let me tell you about this country hospital named for a local benefactress, one Virginia O'Connor, whose greatest lifetime accomplishment, other than endowing this hospital sufficiently to get it named after her, was to be the first and, possibly, the last woman to swim the length of the Hudson while towing a rubber raft bearing her pet poodle Flanders. Her accomplishments are engraved on a plaque in the lobby of this hospital that I am now allowed to stroll through, now that I am no longer deemed a danger to myself, or a threat to anyone else. If you can believe what you read, if I can believe what is engraved on the plaque, Virginia wanted to swim the length of the Hudson as a gift to her dog Flanders, who was dying of kidney failure. I am here in this small country hospital whose one mitigating asset might ordinarily be considered its lovely views of the countryside, but now the views are all of snow, snow, and only snow, mounds of snow, snow piled high against the trees, snow pushed and *soiled by the sides of the road, so much snow. Did my eyesight return merely that I might see snow again? My roommate here is Rubén. He too is a Nica. He was injured in an accident with a chain saw, not the kind of chain saw we have at the finca but another kind, larger and more dangerous, don't ask me how I know about this, I just know that these are more dangerous than anything we use, and accidents happen often and when they do, the damage to the human body is horrible to behold. I translate for him when the nurses want to know how he is feeling, if the pain is here or there, if he is allergic to anything, and other things as well which I cannot write even to you. He is in terrible pain from the laceration of his thigh and his hand. Also his face. I imagined that in the States they would change bloody bandages more often, more often than they would at the Clinica de la Virgen del Viejo. But this is not León and there are no Sisters with airborne wimples, but twice a week they do have a Pet Visitation Program, to assist with Emotional and Physical Therapy. Even if they ask, I will refuse to translate this flier for poor Rubén. No matter how much they plead for me to discuss the merits of the Pet Visitation Program, I will refuse. Poor Rubén did not come all the way from his small village to be back in a hospital with animals in the hallways. There are fifteen rooms on this floor and only three of them are occupied, including ours. In one room is the thinnest girl I've ever seen. She is nothing but anguish crying out to be fed, only it is her refusal to be fed that has brought her here. She has the face of an ascetic angel who has gone into the desert to fast and pray and battle her demons for forty days and nights. Rubén reminds me of something that happened on the finca. Do you remember? It was ancient Don Eustachio—he was Papá's best pruner, the best pruner of coffee trees in all of Nicaragua, is what Papá said—and I remember him stepping out from the cafetal, all bloody—so bloody that it was impossible to tell which limbs were attached and which were severed. He had a painfully thin daughter, I remember that too—we thought it was a tapeworm or parasites. Don Eustachio's injuries involved a machete and also an animal who startled someone. Was it a rabbit? I can picture a rabbit running for its life. Tía Tata was there when Don Eustachio had his accident and she bandaged him up so brilliantly and wouldn't let anyone ask him how it happened which she said was all we wanted to know and that was probably true. I wasn't there and neither were you, not really. But we could have been and we would have wanted to know how it happened. And now here is Rubén who is all bloody and frightened and not understanding a word that goes on around him, although he watches the television. Last night he pulled back the curtain that slides along a ceiling track between our two beds in order to give us an illusion of privacy. He was lonely and frightened, that is what I think, that is what I thought until I thought this: that it was not his loneliness that caused him to pull back the curtain that separated us, but his perception of my loneliness, his kindness and concern for my isolation and despair even as, to the untrained eye, I am the unharmed one, the intact one. I will ask him if they are related. Aren't we all related, you and me and all our cousins and all their cousins and so on until we own the country, that is, we are all related to each other but not to them, not to Rubén and Eustachio, that is our history and our tragedy, if we only knew it. He knows Tía Tata. A cousin in Chinandega prayed and was cured of a kidney stone. How do I know this?*

"Well, blow me down with a feather broom," I said to Waldo. "This guy's handwriting is an act of God. Or something."

"I don't think that's exactly what you mean," Waldo said.

"Then what do I mean? It's infinitesimal. Look at this!" I

waved the fragile palimpsest in front of him. "I've known pygmy mice with larger handwriting."

Waldo poured himself another glass of red wine. Color was returning to his cheeks. "Maybe it's some secret seminarian code."

"Well, is it?"

"How would I know?"

"Because," I said. "He was your roommate. Remember? I'm just the spousal appendage. This is all news to me."

"So you say, but you're in this up to your frothy eyebrows, Al."

"Well, I can't take it anymore. I need a magnifying glass," I said.

"Check the back-door basket," Waldo said. But I was already there. I knew I would find a large magnifying glass—it had once been part of a Sherlock Holmes costume—in a wicker basket whose contents also included shin guards, grass-stained Wiffle balls, chewed-up plastic dog bones, and a pair of clippers I'd been searching for. I knew I would find the magnifying glass in the basket by the back door because my sons, my sweet, incipient arsonists, my cherubic pyromaniacs, used it to magnify the rays of the sun and set dried oak leaves on fire.

I cleaned the glass thoroughly with my best rag that I never used without recalling the exact flannel nightgown it used to be.

"Why do you think she sent this to you? To make me feel guilty?"

"Nope. That is not Carmen's way," Waldo said.

"Or to better acquaint me with the inner workings of his psyche?" Never mind how Waldo knew what was or was not "Carmen's way."

With the perfectly clean glass, I finished:

Will I ever meet Hubert van Toots? Should I have contacted him? What is the protocol in a johnny in a snowstorm? I enjoyed so much our correspondence, and I have no doubt that he understands and not just understands but relishes our cause and the sanctity and miracles of Tía Tata. Who is this Hubert van Toots? Toot Toots Toot. What kind of name is that? Gringos always ask that question, of me, of each other. What kind of name is that? And I have to wonder, what is it they want, what reassurance? I know what they think they want, a provenance, geography, a category, but— Cita, I am so terribly terribly cold, is Mombacho erupting now? Cerro Negro? Could I just dive in? Where is Alice? You do not know Alice. You cannot know Alice. But you will.

And that was the end of that. Not an end, but a stop.
"You have to read this, Waldo. He is *your* friend."
"You keep saying that," he said. I needed to stop saying it. Somehow, some time, in that hospital room he had morphed into my friend, and his aunt had become my task.

Part II 🙰 The Hagiographers Club:
Hubert van Toots

10 ❧ The Hagiographers Club

AND THAT IS HOW I came to find myself inside the Hagiographers Club, home to Hubert van Toots and repository of the Western Hemisphere's largest collection of hagiographica. The collection originated in 1871 with the startling bequest of Agatha Lipton de Romero's personal library and had been laboriously built up by four generations of librarians, culminating in the present tenure of Hubert van Toots, universally acknowledged to be the most resourceful and erudite of them all.

The building was constructed, according to Agatha Lipton de Romero's precise instructions, and likewise financed by her startling bequest, in 1872 in the flamboyant Victorian Gothic style, in which *flamboyant* is a term of art and does not refer to outrageous behavior or a penchant for overdressing in splashy colors. There was something exuberantly medieval about it, as if the addition of one more detail (beyond the Gothic windows, the oriels, the alternating voussoirs and the intersecting gables, the polychromatic and patterned slate roof, and the clustered chimney pots) would send the building over the edge of architectural probity and into the realm of Disneyland or Las Vegas. It was on the cusp of something, and that was its brilliance. Not that I understood all that on first sighting. On that winter morning it was the overall effect, of secrecy and mystery and maybe just a slight nod to the fantastical, that I gleaned from the building of the Hagiographers Club. The details that contributed to that effect I would learn to name much later. And of course, there was no signage of any kind. Why *of course*? I had never noticed the club before, which seemed remiss on my part, if only because of the gargoyles. They were unlike any other gargoyles; they were early Christian saints slyly perched in both front corners of the building, eyeing the un-Christian and the unsaintly as they walked by, as they smoked their cigarettes, as they collected their dogs' feces in plastic bags, as they passed this repository of hagiographies and the people who loved them and never knew. Later I would learn that all the gargoyles had names and attributes and that the club members knew them all, but initially all I saw were carved stone faces in extreme pain or extreme ecstasy, probably both, such often being the sainted condition.

That first day I walked down Lexington from Grand Central Station. Was it like taking the early-morning train in for *Dream Radio*? It was and it was not. I tried to believe I was engaged, employed, that I had a task. But certain realities intervened: the time of day and the uncertainty. My plan was to sit for few minutes in the lovely and manicured Gramercy Park and gather my thoughts before braving the daunting doorman of my imagination. That proved impossible. No one could get in the park without a key, and I had no key. According to a tasteful and discreet plaque, the park had been designed by a Samuel Ruggles, who in 1831 bought the property, drained the marshes, developed the sixty-six lots on it, and then sold them with the stipulation that only residents of the square would have access to the park. Hence the need for keys.

So instead of sitting calmly and questioning the wisdom of showing up unannounced and unbidden at this hitherto unheard-of place in order to gain the favor of, or redeem myself in the eyes of, or again get to see, Abelardo Llobet, I walked twice around the perimeter of the park, until my toes were almost numb with cold, and then pushed open the heavy door, which offered no resistance. It had the best-oiled hinges I'd ever encountered. Really, they were miraculous hinges. It was a dark wooden door whose grain reminded me of sand dunes in Santa Barbara. I couldn't name the wood. Many elements of the Hagiographers Club would flout my desire to name them.

The daunting doorman of my mind's conjuring did not appear. There was no doorman, no visible human presence of any kind.

I stood very still, let my eyes adjust to the darkness, and listened for the guardians of the place, who would surely materialize to challenge my intrusion. My eyes adjusted and no one appeared. I was standing in a large wood-paneled foyer. To my right and left were closed pocket doors; the brass doorknobs resembled the gargoyles outside. Several yards in from the front door there appeared a wide stairway with deep treads and low kickers. The rake was soft and gradual and gave the impression of having infinite time and space. The carpet on the stairs' central pathway was worn smooth in all the logical places.

There was something mutely irrevocable about the closed pocket doors, so I climbed the stairs. They didn't creak. I wished they would creak and announce my presence, so no one would think I was trying to sneak in. But quiet prevailed. At the top of the stairs was another hall with a vast Persian carpet and more doors. Sooner or later I would have to enter one room or another, or else crawl ignominiously back to Grand Central. I pulled open the door in the center.

This was clearly the library: a sparsely populated, dimly lit room full of books. The only eyes that even flickered belonged to a handsome bearded man behind a vast table to my left. I assumed he was in charge.

"Good morning," I said. "Please excuse me for barging in like this."

"Did you barge in?" he said.

"Well, yes. The door was open and then I didn't see anyone downstairs."

"As you can see, most of us idle our hours away here, in the reading room."

"I'm not a member," I said. "And I don't know any members."

"We are a rare breed," he said, as if someone might ever suggest otherwise.

"But a man I know—really a friend of my husband, but my husband wasn't home at the time—he told me about this club. He was going to come here and research his aunt. But then he was laid low by a snowstorm." I never knew how to describe what had happened. I wasn't sure what really had happened. He went mad and made angels in the snow in his underwear? He heard voices? He had a breakdown on my watch?

"Slow down," he said. "This sounds intriguing. Who was this unfortunate man?"

"His name is Abelardo Llobet de Carvajal. He's not from New York, he's—"

"Of course. You are referring to Señor Llobet. We corresponded," the man said. "He was charming on paper. I am dismayed about this laying low. Would you care to elaborate?"

That was just what I did not care to do. "Not really. You could say he suffered a reaction, an aversion to the snowstorm. Then he went to the hospital."

"Perhaps another time."

"Pardon?"

"You'll elaborate," he said. "And now you are here in his stead."

"Something like that," I said. "Not really. I just thought I could try to do some reading and find something helpful for him. I thought I might be useful." I closed my mouth, then opened it to say *It's more than that. I am desperate.* I closed my mouth again.

"Is he still snowbound?"

"Oh, no. He's gone back to Nicaragua. He doesn't even know I'm here."

The man said, "He will."

I took a deep breath. There were exactly three other people in the room. One ecclesiastic-looking man, pale and excessively forlorn. Another man in blue jeans and a plaid flannel shirt with the sleeves rolled up. And a beautiful woman I could only glimpse obliquely, as she sat in a chair much bigger than herself angled to catch what little light came through the large colored-glass window. I said, "I am wondering if you will let me do some reading here. Some research?"

"Why not?"

"Because I really have no qualifications, and I'm not a member," I said.

He said, "It was a rhetorical question."

"Oh."

"My name is Hubert van Toots," he said. "You can direct your questions to me, and I imagine I will know the answers to many of them."

So Hubert became my guide at the Hagiographers Club. Hubert ran the club, was the head librarian, was the director; he also repaired the plumbing and screwed in the light bulbs, such as they were. But if you asked him what he did—as on at least three occasions I heard others ask him—he would reply, "Very little, but I like it here."

Years ago Hubert had been Brother Hubert, a Trappist monk. Then he left the monastery and fell in love with a man, the mysterious Martin. Or perhaps he fell in love and then left the monastery. He was not forthcoming with details. Martin was now dead, and Hubert lived in the Sutton Place apartment that had once belonged to Martin's mother, then to Martin's brother, and then to Martin. Aside from the saints and their relics, the things that most excited Hubert were his efforts to track down the original paint colors and original wallpaper of the apartment. He often spent his evenings repairing threadbare draperies and regluing chair rails. But I learned all of that later.

I told Hubert that because Abelardo's Tía Tristána had been an unmarried female suspected of performing miracles, I thought I should read about female saints who refused to get married and about their miracles. He raised his eyebrows and said, "There are always miracles."

I searched all my pockets for my favorite pen. To no avail. "How's your Latin?" Hubert asked me.

"Dominus vobiscum. Gallia est omnis divisa in partes tres."

He nodded sadly, knowingly. This lamentable state of affairs was only to be expected. Then, making a balletic arc with his hand, he pointed me toward the twelve volumes of *Butler's Lives of the Saints.* "Start with January," he said. "And read all the virgins." Then he added, "For God's sake, don't restrict yourself to virgins." From the beginning, I figured out that—rhetorical questions notwithstanding—when Hubert said "For God's sake," he did not use the expression glibly.

I followed his instructions and quickly intuited that hagiographers did not need much light in order to read. Perhaps it was the grace of their intentions or the saintliness of their research that illuminated the pages for them. But not for me. I found myself squinting and angling the book to catch any stray sunbeams that infiltrated the reading room, wondering how the only other female, the beautiful woman in the large chair who had not once looked up from her book, managed to perform this task so serenely.

The first appropriate virgin I found was Saint Pharaildis of the eighth century. She "secretly consecrated her virginity to God," but her parents gave her away in marriage to a wealthy suitor anyway. She refused to have sex with him, and as a result he treated her very badly. But "God protected her, until at last the husband died." Pharaildis shared her feast day, January 4, with Blessed Oringa, whose brothers beat her because she refused to marry. So she ran away and was guided to safety by a hare. Was it then that I noticed the quasi-miraculous appearance of hares in the lives of virgins? No, not then. It must have been later.

It was definitely later when I tried to connect hagiographical hares with the recurring incidence of harelips in a certain branch of the Llobet family, the Parrillas. They believed that the harelips were a direct result of the pregnant mother's interaction with the hare.

Somewhat more to the point was Saint Apollinaris, who disguised herself as a man and ran away to the desert and there led an ascetic life. Not until she was dead was her sex discovered.

A bit later in Butler's January volume I found Saints Julian and Basilissa, who were married to each other but lived "by mutual consent in perpetual chastity."

I was not overwhelmed by evidence of good deeds.

Waldo was kind enough to pick me up at the train that evening and asked me how it had gone. From the very beginning, from almost the minute he'd come back from the caves, he'd expressed doubts about the Hagiographers Club. He suggested it didn't exist at all but had been conjured up by Abelardo in a snow-induced dementia. I reminded him that the Hagiographers Club plan preceded the storm and the front lawn full of adult-size snow angels. Then Waldo took another tack: depending on what kind of day he was having, he suggested the club was either a sinister front for Luddite Soviet-style communists or else a meeting place for ultra-rightist papal minions intent on reintroducing hair shirts, cilices, and self-flagellation, assuming those had ever gone out of style. To contradict Waldo in one of his moods, to deny his quasi-paranoid fantasies, was only to encourage them.

Still, he'd agreed we should be concerned and even helpful. He just didn't see any way of being remotely useful, according to his inventive notions of what that constituted. Carmencita's letter had convinced him we had to actually do something. The Hagiographers Club was the only something we could think of. He warned me, "Don't think of this as atonement, Al. You have nothing to atone for."

Atonement had in fact crossed my mind. As a concept, it was anathema to Waldo, who was raised Episcopalian by Posey and Waldo Three. "The Fairweathers have been Episcopal since

Henry the Eighth had his brouhaha with the pope over divorcing that Spanish wife of his, and she probably had an appalling accent. Before that we were Druids," Posey told me once, a long time ago, before I knew enough about the Fairweathers and their ilk to get the joke. I was from California; what could I be expected to know? Since then I have learned that the Episcopalians of Catamunk do not believe in guilt or atonement.

The Ewens had been Catholic, but we'd stopped going to church and Sunday school after the business with Mami's irate letters about birth control in the diocesan newsletter. By the end of that heated correspondence, everyone in the diocese knew that she had three daughters and in her opinion they were all three in need of access to birth control. This may have been a generally acknowledged truth, but it was not popular when said aloud at sodality and altar guild meetings. So I retained very little Catholicism from my youth. But of what remained, guilt was preeminent. I had naturally glossed over my lapses when I applied for the teaching position at Precious Blood. Not that it should have mattered.

I told Waldo that it was almost impossible to read in the Hagiographers Club. On the way north I had been thinking about those long-dead virgins, Apollinaris, Oringa, and Pharaildis, and how their sainthood seemed to be all about what they didn't do. Noting the possibility of rhyming, I had tried to make up a limerick, but it was hopeless. Even the boys had a better fighting chance at composing five-line doggerel than I did. After my years in New England, I had developed a theory that Episcopalians were much better at writing limericks than Catholics, and not just because of Waldo. I had no scientific or empirical basis for this assertion. Just that their knowledge of Latin was unencumbered by the Latin mass and this freed them up to concentrate on five-line doggerel with feminine rhymes that often included words like *Nantucket, bucket,* and *fuck it.*

"But what is the place like?" he asked me.

"Dark. It's very dark. Actually, next time I may bring a reading light."

"You could borrow Ezra's headlamp. If you ask him nicely. He's very fond of it."

That night in bed, I couldn't hold my tongue any longer. I said to Waldo, "What do you think of the merits of virginity?"

"Are there any?"

He sank deeper into his pillow, and the length of his left leg against the length of my right leg was sexual and enticing in a way I knew I had to resist. I said, "I asked you first. All the saints I read about today were virgins. That's really their only claim to fame. Lalo's aunt was a virgin."

"Maybe there were no takers."

"No. That's not it. Among the saints, the virginity seems to matter most especially if you're very beautiful and there are lots of takers. Then you reject them in favor of the Heavenly Spouse."

Waldo turned off his light and rolled over into his spoonable position.

"I'm worried that we've neglected the boys' religious education," I said.

"Their religious education or sex education?" Waldo asked.

"Aren't they the same thing?"

"Can we talk about this in the morning? Or never. How about never?"

I turned my light off and curled myself around Waldo's warm, smooth back. It never ceased to amaze me how warm his back was.

Two days later I was once more at the Hagiographers Club. It was only my second time there and already it seemed meet and right to be wrapping my gloved hand around the brass doorknob and pushing forward. Already it seemed meet and right to go directly to the palatially dimensioned stairs and climb. Of course, I could barely see a thing. I had forgotten the dimness of it all, and I had forgotten to ask Ezra about his headlamp.

Hubert was at his desk. Opened in front of him was a book of Brobdingnagian proportions, written in an unidentifiable language. Hubert was engaged in an intense, whispered conversation with the forlorn clerical man, at the end of which conversation Hubert handed him a key dangling from a rubber-chicken keychain. The man loped away, and Hubert looked up.

"You again?" he said.

"I said I'd be back."

"But I didn't believe you," he said. "More virgins?"

"I'm afraid so."

Blessed Jutta of Huy wasn't a virgin but wished she were. At thirteen, she was forced by her father to marry. Five years and three children later, she was widowed. After that she longed for an especially austere and deprived existence, so she had herself walled inside a small room right next to the lepers' house. She lived there until she died, in 1228.

Saint Agnes was another adamant virgin. She was beautiful and in great demand, but her inclinations were higher. Her rejected suitors denounced her to a governor of Diocletian—he whose very name evokes vivid scenes of lions mauling Christians—and after failing to convince her to relent by means of the usual tortures, he remanded her to a brothel. But even there her virginity prevailed. Many young profligates made advances, but they were "seized with awe" in her presence and backed off. Only one young man persisted, but at the instant of penetration, he was struck blind. *As if by lightning from Heaven.* Agnes later cured his blindness with her prayers. (Concerning his sexual trauma, nothing was written.) She was ultimately beheaded. Now she's the patron saint of cleanliness.

Ezra came with Waldo to pick me up at the train that evening. "Ez," I said. "I have a giant favor to ask you."

"I refuse to wear that blue sweater from Grams. I'm sorry, Mom, but I just can't do it."

"That wasn't it. I didn't know you felt so strongly about it."

"Then you aren't paying attention. Her sweaters get worse with every birthday."

"They're not as bad as the ones she gives me," Waldo said. "The red one with moose? I think that was a particularly low point."

"It's the Maine motif," I needlessly explained.

"She's never given you anything with purple mice on it," Ezra said.

"She means well. She doesn't think I clothe you properly. But it's about your headlamp."

"I love my headlamp."

"I know. So it is with some trepidation that I ask to borrow it. And I promise to treat it well."

"Don't be silly, Mom. Of course you can. You know that it's the Cadillac of headlamps? Three light levels and five LEDs for superior versatility."

"I believe you, Ez," I said.

With the invaluable aid of Ezra's headlamp, and as signs of spring—pollen, rain, and awakening flies—crept up on us, I read about Saint Catherine of Vadstena, Saint Werburga, Saint Maxellendis, Saint Paula the Bearded, and Saint Uncumber (who probably never existed).

After settling down with my stack of books I would put on the headlamp, adjust the tension, and then switch on the light. I didn't make a show of it or try to draw attention to myself and this brilliant device; I didn't want to give the impression that I craved attention or approval. Yet I thought someone might ask about it. No one did. Once, a young nun looked my way and tilted her head slightly. I thought she was about to speak. She thought better of it. When she departed the library, I saw her ascend the narrower stairs that led to the upper floors. I could only speculate about what lay above. I would have been pleased if anyone had taken this opportunity to start a conversation; I would have happily told him or her all about Ezra, or Abelardo and his aunt; I would have happily exchanged pleasantries about the usefulness of lighting. But the opportunity never arose.

In order to convince her lascivious and warmongering brother, Enda, to change his ways and convert, Saint Fanchea promised him a beautiful maiden in marriage. The maiden, however, was dead; Enda was presented with a pale and rigid corpse. Strangely enough, this did the trick, and he became a monk. I could imagine a very amusing limerick telling this story. I could imagine it, but I couldn't write it. Waldo could, but Waldo was keeping an amused distance between himself and anything hagiographical. Surely someone in the English-speaking world had written limericks about the lives of the saints. One day I would ask Hubert, but not yet.

Meanwhile, I was shocked to read again and again of these sexless virgins, so many sexless virgins (yes, a redundancy, but it needs to be said), and also of the chaste marriages. I had no idea there were so many married couples agreeing to never have sex, to never see or touch each other, and I didn't see the point. But I kept going back to the Hagiographers Club, kept following Hubert's delicately pointed finger up and down the stacks.

In my red leather notebook I kept careful notes. I listed the virgin saints and others in their various categories. There were the saints who cross-dressed in order to avoid the unwanted advances of a man, or men in general. There were the saints who grew beards and became leprously ugly in order to thwart the ardor of a lover. There were saints who married but promised God and each other to live together eternally as brother and sister. There were the saints who ate nothing or survived on the Eucharist only, a form of self-starvation for which there is a special word: *inedia*. Of course, they would all be diagnosed with eating disorders today. But there they are: sanctified, canonized, sitting in Heaven at the right hand of God, fielding all the prayers that come wafting their way. Sometimes the hardest thing was determining into which category to place a certain saint, because she fit so many categories.

One night I woke up around two A.M. because I'd had a rotten dream about a chaste marriage and everyone wearing obviously fake wings, Christmas pageant wings. So I did the only thing I could think of. I started fondling Waldo, and soon he was inside me, and I held him tight and raked my nails up and down his back. Images of those chaste saintly couples, rigid and glacial on their separate sides of the bed, would not leave me. I saw Saint Amator and his not-wife, Martha. Theirs was slightly unusual among the saints and chaste marriages, because from the beginning, he was the one to instigate the chastity. They were meant to be married by the aged Bishop Valerian, but in his senile dementia he read the wrong service; instead of marrying them, he ordained them into the deaconate. No one except Amator and Martha realized the mistake. Immediately after the ceremony, Amator convinced his bride to take advantage of the error and take up a life of virginity. Soon she retired to the convent. How had he put it? *Oh, what the heck, since we're not married anyway, let's just forgo all that messy sex?* Amator became a priest. I found this story especially depressing; I imagined the young woman's longing for a real husband, and the cruel trick life had played on her. I imagined a few nights of co-sleeping, when Martha wakes and stealthily scrutinizes the soft sleeping penis of Amator. She fondles it, watches it grow, and feels it harden. Then she drops it and turns away from what she will never enjoy.

11 ❧ The Dangerous Ocean

THE DENIZENS OF THE Hagiographers Club never noticed my presence. I was forever looking up from my pages to watch and wonder; their indifference only increased my curiosity and inflamed my fantasies. The same characters came again and again, though one or two I saw once and that was all. The beautiful woman who had read her text so serenely on my first visit did not reappear. But mostly they were the same ones, there when I arrived and there when I left. I wanted to ask Hubert if the club had rooms on the upper floors for the members. I knew from the exterior that there were two upper floors, but that was all I knew. Perhaps there were monastic cells up there, each one inhabited by a saint in training. Perhaps, like some motels in California, each cell had a different hagiographic theme: the Hermit's Cave (dank and dismal); the Mystic's Chamber (painted black with UV lighting); the Do-Gooder's Leper Colony (foul-smelling and crowded); the Pole-Sitter's Perch (rising from the roofline); the Scholar's Scriptorium (a slanted desk, an inkwell, the de rigueur bad lighting); the Martyr's Den (boiling oil and lions). But Hubert's demeanor did not encourage questions.

In the matter of the papal nuncio, however, I knew I had to ask. Not that I knew then he was the papal nuncio. I was incapable of not asking.

Every time I went to the club that first month, I saw him, sitting in the far armchair in the central reading room—a large chair upholstered in cracked burgundy leather—a tall, slender man in clerical garb. And such lovely clerical garb: his collar was magenta silk, and he wore cuff links with fat garnets. Around his neck hung a ponderous golden chain and medallion. I would have happily examined him and his accoutrements, but that was not to be. His clothes were worthy of interest, but not of the most interest. All day long, he read texts in Latin and wept. He wept silently but continuously. He kept clean linen handkerchiefs in what must have been a bottomless pocket in his chasuble.

If there was one reason that I curried favor with Hubert—and there were many reasons—it was to learn about the weeping cleric.

On my fourth or fifth visit I watched Hubert and the forlorn cleric in close conversation with each other. The cleric leaned over Hubert's table to ask a question, sotto voce. He leaned over a long way. Then Hubert stood up, and they were eye to eye. They were both tall, aspiring heavenward.

Hubert's hair was dark, and he combed it back so that it undulated, like wheat in the wind. Were tonsures a thing of the past? Hubert had a small and pointed beard that on anyone else would have been called Mephistophelean, but his blue eyes were too soft and tender to tolerate such a satanic epithet.

When the whispering ceased and the weeping cleric returned to his chair, I threw caution to the wind, dashed over, and asked Hubert, "Who is that man and why is he weeping?"

"Who said he was weeping?"

"Of course he's weeping." I was trying to whisper like them but it came out as a hiss. "Something is terribly wrong. He is so sad."

"Something is wrong with his lachrymal ducts. He told me what his condition is called, but I've forgotten."

"You're kidding," I said.

"I would hardly kid about that."

"Well, I don't believe you. It's not just the tears. It's his whole face. He is lamenting."

"He has good reasons to be sad," Hubert said.

"So can you tell me? Who is he?"

"You didn't know?"

"That's why I'm asking you. How would I know?"

"He's Monsignor Giacometti, the papal nuncio."

"I didn't know there still were papal nuncios."

"Of course there are. What else would there be?"

"But why is he so sad?" I whispered.

"If you must know, his entire family just drowned. In that storm off Sardinia last month—do you remember?—they were great sailors, I gather. His brother was the Italian champion."

"His whole family?"

"Parents, brother, sisters, nieces, nephews. It was a terrible and sudden storm. They radioed for help but nothing was possible."

"No wonder he's weeping," I said. I could not turn around. How could I ever look in his direction again?

"That's his condition. I told you," Hubert said.

At the dinner table that evening, I told Waldo and the boys that I had heard the saddest story that day.

"It's Monsignor Giacometti, he's the papal nuncio at the club. He weeps all day because his whole family was drowned at sea."

"I thought priests didn't have families," Henry said.

"His parental family, his siblings and so forth."

"And they were all on the same boat?"

"Maybe something is wrong with his lachrymal ducts," Waldo suggested. "Maybe the stopcock is missing. The lachrymal stopcock."

"Hubert said sort of the same thing. But I didn't believe him."

Henry and Ezra looked at each other and erupted in staccato laughter.

Waldo said, "Cut it out, you two. When Dick and I were kids, Posey and Dad never flew on the same plane."

Henry stifled his laughter enough to say, "Never?"

"Not until we were both eighteen."

"I thought they never left the state of Maine," I said.

"How come you and Mom don't do that?" Ezra asked.

"Because flying in an airplane is one hundred and twenty times safer than driving on the Taconic Parkway," Waldo said. "Remember Alaska?" he said to me.

"But they were on a boat," Ezra said. "All together."

"Can we go to Alaska? To see the glaciers?" Henry said.

"It was probably a family vacation. People sail together all the time," I said. "But then there was a terrible storm. Off Sardinia. Do you know where Sardinia is?" I said to Henry.

"It's a hundred and twenty miles west of Italy and a hundred and twenty miles north of Africa. And it's full of extinct volcanoes," he said.

"How does he know stuff like that?" I asked Waldo. "Not from me."

"I read the encyclopedia."

"Al, why are you telling us about this?" Waldo said.

"Because it's so sad. That poor man is all alone now."

"There's always his good friend the pope," he said.

"That's not funny."

"I don't think the pope's stand on birth control is funny either."

"I didn't say it was," I said.

"It's criminal, is what it is."

"You're not going to get me to defend it," I said. "You and Mami would have been unstoppable."

It was dinner again—funny how meals occurred with such regularity, how insistent they were—and we ate enchiladas filled with leftovers from the past week. The game was to guess the single mystery spice that transformed said enchiladas from rolled-up detritus into something rather delicious.

"Allspice," Waldo suggested. Correctly, as it happened. "And when do we get to meet this Hubert?"

"Meet him? I hadn't thought of that. What a good idea."

"Bring him home for dinner."

"I can ask. He's at the Hagiographers Club. All day. Every day, as far as I can tell."

"Does he have a halo?" Henry grinned and held up his plate to hover just above his unkempt head.

"Only on formal occasions," I said. Yet again, I lamented the deficiencies in the boys' religious education. I had become aware of everything I had not taught them about their Catholic background. Even if they were never likely to darken the door of the local Catholic church, St. Hilda's, this seemed like neglect on my part. Sometimes we took them to the Episcopal church, St. David's, and they enjoyed the hymns. But without the lingering threat of mortal sin and eternal damnation, I found myself without the motivation to get them properly dressed every Sunday. Meanwhile, Waldo informed them that God resided in every living thing, including rats and leeches. Full stop. Posey used to be active in the altar guild at St. Barnabas-by-the-Sea, but she had never forgiven the rector for his oration at her husband's funeral, in which he had referred slightingly to Waldo Three's appalling golf swing. "It was so unnecessary," she said. Then Posey married Mr. Cicero, who was a Unitarian Universalist. He called himself a U-U, a yew-yew, a you-you, all of which the boys loved. Mr. Cicero informed me that U-Us don't believe in saints. Full stop.

Henry scarfed up a single pea that careened around his plate, pointed his thumb toward the kitchen door, and then, in synchronized motion that would have done credit to an Olympic water-ballet team, he and Ezra got up from the table, put their plates in the sink, and headed off in what we knew to be the direction of *The Simpsons*.

Waldo said, "Do you remember when Ez got that pea up his nose?"

"How could I forget?"

Waldo aligned all the silverware on the table and said, "Does any of this have to do with Abelardo?"

"Any of what?"

"The club you love so much. Hubert. The lives of the saints."

"Most of them didn't even have lives," I whispered. "They're legends. They were invented to fulfill some need we have." I wasn't answering him. Or was I? What did I, could I, possibly need with the stories of mystic virgins and medieval miracle workers?

"You know what I mean," Waldo said. I did. The extent to which reading in the club kept me linked to Abelardo, I wasn't thinking about, or even acknowledging. The thing about the saints was the impossibility of them, their lives and acts, and those impossible wonders were dryly recounted by Hippolyte Delehaye and Jacobus de Voragine and Alban Butler and countless others. These men were not fabulists. I was the fabulist. I read of those martyred virgins—going bravely and chastely to the stake, the lions' den, the hatchet—and I fantasized about sex. Mostly with Waldo. But not always. Sometimes it was a young man I had known briefly in Barcelona. Sometimes it was Audrey's high school boyfriend. And then others. What would I go to the stake to preserve? The boys. Not my long-lost virginity.

But it wouldn't be fair to say the hagiographies were merely a trope to translate the believers from their short brutish lives to the unknowable eternal. Because of the details. The details were profoundly rooted in the quotidian. The hares and the stags, the little boys in pickle barrels, the lechers and jilted suitors, the beer-swilling monks. It was the details I kept going back for, the details I scoured for in those pages—some brittle, some supple, all touched by the natural oils of many fingers.

"Not much," I said. "To do with Abelardo. Some. A little bit."

Waldo said, "There's something about Abelardo. There always was."

"He's a good dresser," I said. "I don't mean in a fey, metrosexual kind of way. He just fits his clothes perfectly. Except when he's in the snow. But besides that. When I saw him I realized how you and the boys wear your clothes like a foreign language."

"Finnish," Waldo suggested. "Or Urdu. And that's not remotely what I meant about Abelardo."

"I didn't think it was," I said. "I just wanted to tell you."

"I just wanted to say that since you like it so much you should keep going. Maybe you could find a saint back in your family history to study up on. No Fairweathers though, I'm afraid."

The other day I'd asked Hubert, not for the first time, if he believed—concretely, tangibly—in these saints he kept leading me to. He'd said, "I believe some of them existed, and some of them were very good. Many were what we would now call masochistic or anorexic or hysterical. I believe in prayer. Do I believe those things are connected? Not today."

12 ❧ Not Another Snowstorm

WHILE I WAS READING about Saint Brigid, who'd specifically requested a deformity so that she would be repellent to suitors, Waldo was getting news from Nicaragua. While I was reading about how Brigid's eye had split open and melted in her head, Waldo was speaking with Abelardo's sister Carmen, who he now admitted was the most beautiful of the beautiful sisters. While I was reading about how Saint Brigid, in what seemed to be a frat-party variation on the Miracle at Cana, had supplied beer for eighteen churches from one barrel, Waldo was hearing that Abelardo squinted whenever confronted with anything white but refused to be given a prescription for glasses. Carmen said to Waldo, "Our brother has always been dramatic. Of course you knew that already. But I think this has gone too far." While I was learning that Saint Brigid had cured a leper and two blind men, and the blood flowing from her head wound had caused two dumb women to recover their speech, Carmen was saying to Waldo, "He's taken this Tía Tata business to an obsession. But apparently I am the only one in this family who doesn't think we need a saint. I think we need a minister for tourism who isn't corrupt."

I returned by train from the Hagiographers Club, innocent of Waldo's conversation with Carmen. I was incredulous. "You actually spoke with her?"

"I had no choice. She called."

"How is Lalo? Does she blame me for the snow-blindness

event? Does she think I wasn't being properly vigilant? Is she wondering why I don't have a job?"

"Al, Al, slow down," Waldo said. "She's not into blame. That's not Carmen's way. She couldn't care less if you have a job. She wouldn't recognize a job if it bit her lovely behind."

"You didn't tell me you knew Carmen so well," I said. "Anatomically and otherwise."

"A figure of speech, Al. A figure of speech."

It would not be impossible to be ambushed by a figure of speech.

Then the days got cold all over again. I dropped Ezra and Henry off at school and took the train into the city. By the time I'd walked the twenty blocks to Gramercy Park, my toes and fingertips were past feeling.

I went through the foyer and stood still, waiting to thaw. One of the pocket doors was slightly open; there was a gap of perhaps a foot, and of course I looked in. It was a dining room, and the table was set for a formal dinner. The walls were red. A brass chandelier hung from the center of the ceiling, a ceiling painted with grinning cherubs. No, they were leering. I peered closer into the room because I wanted to assure myself they really leered. But I heard a door close on the second floor, and then I heard footsteps, so I jumped back and started up the stairs.

The warmth and bad lighting that laconically greeted me as I entered the library triggered a shudder of almost sensual delight. I was happy to be there. I had initially come to this place as a kind of atonement (never mind what Waldo had said about atonement) for allowing Abelardo to go mad on my watch, for neglecting a fellow human while ministering to my sick dog, and also out of curiosity, but by now I relished it. I loved the chairs, with their cushions molded to bottoms long gone, and the faded paintings of heroic saints, and the burgundy velvet draperies that exhaled ancient dust. And I was very fond of Hubert.

On that chilly day Hubert was looking exceptionally dapper, in a way that showed no effect of the frigid air outside. I imagined that he had been beamed directly to the club from his walk-in closet at Sutton Place.

I sank into my favorite chair, pleased to be someone who had a favorite chair in this place, picked up *Butler's,* and read of Saint Austreberta, who, after the usual ups and downs (threat of forced marriage, flight in the night), entered the convent, where she was miraculously immune to the flames in the bread oven.

Monsignor Giacometti must have come in while I was reading, because there he was—in *his* favorite chair—when I looked up from the pages. "Good morning, Monsignor," I said.

His sad, tearful eyes blinked before returning to his newspaper. On the reverse side was an article about a spike in incidences of Lyme disease. Was Deb Sigerson the only person I knew with Lyme disease? Gunnar would have had us think so.

Over and over again I read the same sentence about Saint Marina of Bithynia, who cross-dressed as a boy, behaved as a boy, became a monk, and was accused of impregnating the innkeeper's daughter.

The monsignor wept on. Was he reading the same sentence again and again also? It seemed impossible to sit there and not say a word to him. I couldn't do it. Even if what he wanted most in the world was to be left alone with his sorrow, still I couldn't not speak to him and let him know that there were human beings who might assuage his sorrow, if only he would let them. I stood up. I opened my mouth and imagined speaking. And then I stopped myself.

Some days it was just not possible to concentrate on virgin saints. I decided to catch an early train home. But before I could leave, I saw her. The beautiful older woman was perched on Hubert's desk. She was whispering urgently with him, but still he stopped me.

"Alice, I don't think you've met Camilla Hyde. Her specialty is the saints of Wales and Cornwall."

"Oh," I said, and redundantly introduced myself because I had to purge my mind of the only thing I knew about Cornwall: As I was going to St. Ives, I met a man, and he had seven wives, and so on. She had perfect cheekbones, like parentheses, and loose silver hair that cascaded onto her shoulders. Beneath night-black eyebrows, her eyes were a metallic blue that clashed with the lapis glow of Hubert's. I stared.

"Camilla's from Maine," Hubert said. "I told her you were from Maine too."

"I'm not from Maine," I said. "Waldo is. He's my husband." Hubert should have known all this very well by now. So I thought.

"Neither am I," Camilla said. "I used to go there in the summers with my first husband. But once he died I couldn't bring myself to go back. His family had a house there, but I found them so frightening. So laconic."

"Where in Maine was that?" I said.

"A small town on the coast. You probably don't know it. Bug Harbor."

"You must be kidding," I said. I turned to Hubert. "She must be kidding. That's where the yacht club is. It's where Waldo's from."

"It's this shrinking world," Camilla said. "You can't be safe. Anywhere. Now it will turn out we know all the same people. Frightful."

"My husband is Waldo Fairweather," I said, and considered that making this statement was as brave as stepping out of a moving airplane. Wouldn't any woman from there who was in a certain age range know Waldo, and wouldn't she then perforce have loved him, or at least longed for him?

"I used to know Posey Fairweather. We gardened. Together. And sometimes when she was training. For a competition. She would play Ping-Pong. With me."

"Posey? I should have known! Everyone knows Posey."

"I don't know Posey," Hubert said.

"That must be why you're so special," I said.

"She doesn't like to leave Maine," Camilla said. "Of course, she has good reasons. But still. To be always. In Maine."

"Actually, she doesn't mind leaving as much as her husbands do. Or did."

"Is that what she says now? Well." Camilla Hyde ran her fingers through her thick lovely hair, as if searching for something lost. "Please give her my best regards. When you see her," she said. What didn't get said—even as it bored a hole through my skull—was that, along with Posey, everyone knew the Dillys. Maybe not all the Dillys or every Dilly, but some Dilly or another. The Dillys had inhabited that concavity of the Maine coastline since the invention of the lobster pot. It was entirely possible that this elegant Camilla knew Edith Dilly or her mother, that she knew about Edith Dilly and Waldo, and that at this exact moment she was wondering why Waldo was married to me and how someone like me could possibly call herself a Fairweather. And that possibility made me feel exposed, as if someone had just walked into the bathroom while I was examining my crotch for Lyme-transmitting ticks.

Outside the club, as I should have known it would have, it had begun to snow. How did these things happen without my knowledge? Should I spend more time watching the Weather Channel? Or talking to Posey?

I walked out of the Hagiographers Club and it was snowing and I was wearing the wrong shoes. They were red heels with pointy toes. I wondered, not for the first time, what had compelled me to wear such shoes for this day, for any day to be spent in a badly lit but extremely comfortable library reading about virgin saints. The shoes were not mildly uncomfortable, they were remarkably uncomfortable, and wholly inappropriate to the task.

I knew exactly when I had bought them, and on what exact

occasions I had worn them, which were few. They were the first shoes I'd bought after my burst appendix, three and a half years ago. They were indecently expensive. Waldo was indignant when he saw them and asked how much I had paid. I lied and said, "Five hundred dollars." Of course that sent him into a tailspin and then I said that I was kidding, they were only two hundred and fifty dollars, which seemed quite reasonable by contrast. (This was a technique I had used before, with some success.) I'd thought about returning them to the store, but something stopped me. My departed appendix. The first time I wore them it had also been an April. It was a black-tie event at which Waldo was inducted into the National Society of Inventors. Whenever I'd doubted my presence at the event, I'd looked down at my feet. Why couldn't Waldo invent beautiful shoes that did not pinch my toes? Or high heels that did not make me wobble when I walked? How hard could that be? Every year since then I had worn them to DSG's employees' and families' Christmas party, and once to the opera. Never had I ever worn them during the day when I was walking any distance. So why today? They had been inappropriate that morning when I'd walked south from Grand Central, and that had been before the precipitation.

There was nothing to be done but walk north on Park and try to think about anything but the wet chill inhabiting my toes. Every pair of feet I looked at seemed to be shod in boots or rubbers or galoshes. Where were the ladies that were never seen without hose and heels? Never before had their absence been so pronounced.

The warm air of Grand Central washed over me. At that same moment, Flirt and Dandy were surely romping in the snow in their bare paws. Bare paws!

I had almost forty minutes until the next train and was giving serious thought to a hot toddy or an Irish whiskey, anything along the lines of alcoholic and warming.

"Alice!" I heard a voice behind me. "What's up, buttercup?" It was Gunnar Sigerson; he leaned down and kissed the top of my head.

"Gunnar," I said. "You startled me."

"I seem to be making a habit of that," he said.

"You are?" I had no idea what he was talking about.

"Last time was at the Ginny O," he said. "You had a frost-bitten houseguest."

"Waldo says I have a finely tuned startle reflex. Like a deer."

"There's nothing wrong with a startle reflex," Gunnar said. "It may one day ensure your survival in the forest. And then there is your eagle eye for mushrooms camouflaged in fallen leaves." This last made no sense, as I had not managed to spot one single mushroom when Gunnar took us out hunting fungi. I'd stood right next to a massive hen of the woods upon a carpet of brown and curling oak leaves, and Gunnar had needed to point it out to me. I hadn't seen what was right before my eyes. It was like one of those puzzles we did as children: "Find the Bunny Hidden in This Forest Picture." And there, sharing his outline with ferns and toadstools, was a perfectly clear Peter Cottontail. Gunnar had spotted three *Grifola frondosa*s that autumn day. He had also made references to their aphrodisiac properties and their resemblance to sexual parts.

"How's Deb?"

"Better," he said. Gunnar was much taller than me, and so I often had to stand back a bit in order to make eye contact, if I didn't want to get a crick in my neck. Less so today in my heels; I reached his shoulder.

Gunnar said, "So how is the hen of the woods?"

"She's freezing," I said. "Cluck, cluck."

"Let's go get a drink," he said. Gunnar wore a forest green parka with frayed cuffs and strange stains on the hood. On his feet were huge lace-up rubber boots with fur lining. Expedition boots. The boots of someone firmly rooted in the natural world, someone at ease in all climatic extremes. But most especially the polar ones.

We weren't the only ones in the station hoping to warm up; the Oyster Bar was steamy with people's breath. We ordered drinks.

"So what were you doing in town?" Of course he could reasonably ask the question because I was jobless, unemployed, a person without justification. Like everyone else in VerGroot, he knew I'd been sacked not once but twice. In VerGroot, when I walked down the sidewalk from the hardware store to the post office, no one assumed I was heading off to teach a class or to sit in a booth with headphones on, listening to the dreams of strangers. In the city, I walked along broad sidewalks and liked to imagine that strangers who saw me assumed I was doing just those things.

"I was at the Hagiographers Club," I said. "Reading."

"Is that the mysterious pursuit Waldo alluded to the other night?"

"When did he say that?"

Gunnar shrugged.

"There's nothing mysterious about it, and he should know. It's his friend who went slightly mad in the snow. At our house. While Waldo wasn't there." Either I had guzzled my drink or it was the gnawing of disloyalty that churned my stomach. Why say such things? How could I possibly explain Lalo?

"That was the day I saw you at the ER."

"Exactly. Your thumb is better, I hope."

"My thumb is fine. It continues to be a useful, opposable digit, and as such distinguishes me and my simian relatives from other creatures." Gunnar drank deeply from his whiskey and fixed his gaze on my hands, or rather my almost useless velvet gloves.

"Alice," Gunnar said. "You know I've always liked you."

"Great. I like you too. You and Deb are two of our best friends, even if she does think my dogs are a menace."

"Seriously. One of my fondest memories of you is that time we all went out to eat after some Little League game, and you went outside to smoke in the parking lot."

"I have absolutely no memory of that. I don't even smoke," I said.

"Oh, I remember it, all right. You didn't want the kids to see you lighting up."

"Well, maybe once or twice I'd have a cigarette, but I don't recall any parking lot."

"It was the Wayside Inn in Budville. You were wearing cutoff blue jean shorts."

"I don't own cutoff blue jeans. Not anymore."

"Tell me that you know what I mean," Gunnar said.

"I don't know what you mean," I said. "When you put it that way."

"I like you quite a lot, Alice."

"You mean like, as in *like*?" I said. And felt an idiot for saying it. Didn't this all sound way too much like high school? I'd been bad at it in high school. Apparently I wasn't any better now.

"Yes, that kind of like."

"I don't think this is a very good idea, Gunnar. I mean, we *are* both married."

"But—"

"And that's just for starters." I took my gloves off. My fingers were definitely warm enough.

"But you guys have an open marriage," Gunnar said.

I wasn't sure if I'd heard him right, but whatever I'd heard, it was wrong. "Whatever gave you that idea?"

"It's just that Waldo—"

"Waldo?"

"Oh, Christmas, I've put my foot in it now."

"Your whole damn leg. Gunnar, this is very strange, very strange indeed," I said. "Tell me."

"Maybe I shouldn't have started this," he said.

"Well, you damn well better finish it," I said. "What are you saying about Waldo? And don't worry. I can handle it."

"It's just that I've seen Waldo with—with Sheila, and I got the impression that you had to know about it also."

"Who the hell is Sheila?" I said. Even though this was clearly where the conversation had been going all along, I felt like ice had been injected into my bloodstream.

"You don't know?"

"I'm asking you, aren't I? No, I don't know. It probably isn't even what you think."

"I wish that were so, Alice. At least, I do now, if it upsets you." I believed him. I was fond of Gunnar. That time we'd looked for the mushroom, I was really happy. I'd wanted it to go on and on. He was one of the few men in VerGroot I had even tried to imagine naked. Whether that was because of Gunnar's attractions or the relative dearth of sexy men in VerGroot was open to discussion. I didn't want to imagine him naked at that moment. I wanted him to stay firmly clad.

"I'll tell you something," I said. "I know that many years ago Waldo did screw around, with someone he'd known growing up. And it was a huge crisis in our marriage. But we dealt with it, and everything is fine now. More than fine."

"I am so sorry to be the one telling you this. I am sorry that anyone is telling you this."

Both my hands were wrapped around my drink. Gunnar put his hands over mine. "What exactly are you telling me?" I said. "Just for the record, could you be as explicit as possible? Because I can promise you that my imagination can do far worse." I could hear how squeaky my voice had become.

Gunnar looked over at the information booth's clock and said, "Oh my God, we've missed our train."

"Oh, fuck," I said. "And I really want to go home."

"Alice, I've never heard you say *fuck* before."

"Fuck, fuck, fuck, fuck it all," I said.

"Alice!"

"So where did you see Waldo and this Sheila person?" I said.

"Are you sure we should talk about this?"

"Yes," I hissed.

"More or less right here. At the Oyster Bar."

"The Oyster Bar? He was at the Oyster Bar with someone else?" My voice cracked.

"Alice, honey, don't let's go there," Gunnar said.

"I'm not your *honey*. I'm not *honey* at all," I said, because I knew that if he got too sweet and sympathetic I would cry, and I would much rather be angry, be outraged, with him, or Waldo, or, preferably, the unknown Sheila.

"Does Waldo come into the city much?"

"Almost never, since they moved the R and D department upriver, except for the opera. But that doesn't mean he couldn't have had a meeting with someone. What did she look like? Did she look like an inventor? Inventive?"

"Actually, she looked a lot like you."

"Well, fuck him." Then I started crying. All that alcohol and warmth, and the waterworks were copious. Or perhaps it was just the invidious state of my feet: cold, wet, and unnaturally set in the Barbie position.

"I am sorry about this. Are you going to be all right?"

"Of course I am going to be all right. Maybe it was work related. Or maybe she was an old friend. How can you be sure it's what you think? What I think you think?"

"I'm not sure of much. Global warming, for instance. But of this I am, sadly, certain."

I said, "I'm not going to ask you how you can be so certain. And don't tell me when I do ask you."

"Do you want to catch the next train, or just keep drinking? Or eat? Would you like to eat?"

"So. How can you be so certain?"

"Are you hungry, Alice?"

"I need to get home," I said.

"Then let's go."

As we walked to our platform I thought of a thousand things, of Waldo turning toward me, or away from me, in the night; of evenings when Waldo came home late because he'd been so busy in his lab, and he'd be so energized by creativity that he'd sweep all three of us into his arms, and then the dogs would leap up and run circles around us, and we would catch his energy and enthusiasm, like a flu epidemic. I remembered how, about eight years ago, he'd told me—because he'd said there was no one else to whom he could confide such things, things that he was bursting with—that he was mad with love for Edith Dilly and wanted to run away with her and they'd live a simple life and be itinerant apple pickers. I remembered how Waldo had left Edith's letters to him lying around the house, as much as saying, *Read me! Read me!* And who was I to deny them? How breathy they were, full of random punctuation and capitals, like Queen Victoria's diaries, except that they referred to a certain sex act they shared, and, ah, the intimacy of it, a certain sex act I had always shrunk from. The whole thing had shrunk me, like a tribal warrior's prize head. Every step along the platform, swept along with all the men in their lumpen overcoats and all the women in their appropriate shoes, every step shook loose a raft of unwanted memories.

What else did I think of? I bet Sheila has a job. I bet she is gainfully employed and daily performs interesting and challenging tasks. I thought: If I had a job this wouldn't have happened.

When we step onto the train, this will stop, I told myself. I am not Anna Karenina. Far from it. This is a commuter train and my feet are freezing cold. Even if I don't have *Dream Radio* or my girls at Precious Blood, I do have Henry and Ez and the dogs and this saint project and, yes, Waldo, and I don't want to destroy it, or let it be destroyed over some floozy named Sheila. If there is such a person.

Here is the amazing thing: I slept on the train. One minute I closed my eyes to clear my brain, and the next minute Gunnar was shaking me awake because we were pulling into VerGroot.

"I meant what I said," he told me.

"Please don't remind me, Gunnar."

"Not that. But about how I feel about you. I'm just so sorry about all the other stuff."

"Gunnar, maybe we should just start all over when it's another day, when it's not snowing. Maybe it's a weather glitch in which all things go awry. You'd think I would know something about that," I said. I would never look at snow the old way again. Abelardo had changed all that for me. "Wait a sec. How did you know her name was Sheila?"

"I heard him talking to her."

"You heard him say her name, and he didn't see you?"

"It's hard to explain."

Our train groaned and stopped. Waldo waved at me from the car. With relief, with a catch in my throat, I saw the two smaller heads in the back seat.

"Is Deb picking you up?" I asked, and hoped the answer was yes.

"No, I left my car here."

"Goodbye, then."

"We got sent home early, Mom. It was a snow day. You missed a snow day. But it's okay, because we went to Bogumila's and she let us sled on her hill and then showed us how to cook sausage." The words tumbled out of Henry faster than he could catch them. What great lungs my son had.

"I didn't even know you liked sausage."

"We do now. She cooks them in beer."

"I suppose almost anything is good cooked in beer, or wine," Waldo said. "And how were the saints today?"

"The saints? What saints? How is sainthood possible?" What was wrong with my voice? Why couldn't I control it?

"Al? Are you okay? What's the matter?"

"Nothing. Sorry. Just a weather glitch. My feet got very cold today. I had the absolutely wrong shoes."

Waldo looked over and down at my feet. He raised his eyebrows and smiled with creeping self-satisfaction. "You *wore* those shoes?"

"Unfortunately, yes."

"Why? Don't tell me you had a hot date at the Fagfoggraphers Club?"

"That's not funny."

"Let's see these shoes, Mom," Ezra said. He leaned over the front seat. "Whoa, nice color."

"I think so too," I said. "I realize that one's fondness for certain shoes is irrational. I just wish there were a way they could be more comfortable. Imagine if they could magically revert to flats when I have to walk thirty blocks."

"Would that really be desirable?" Waldo asked. He was driving with his right hand, or rather a mere two fingers, on the wheel. Normally this bothered me terribly and irrationally. I did realize that this was a gender-specific trait, that all men and boys drove with only one hand, that it was something they could not help any more than they could help missing the bowl sometimes. Any more than I could help minding.

Breathe deeply. Hadn't they all come to collect me at the train station? Wasn't that a gesture of domestic goodwill that I should not take for granted? It was a dilemma. One day Ezra and Henry would drive, and no doubt about it, true to their gender, they too would each drive with one hand on the wheel.

"What?" I said.

"Heels that went flat."

"Absolutely."

"Because I think it may be possible—what if you had a heel

that telescoped out for a few inches, but could then slide back into itself to be much lower?"

"Could you really do that?"

"I'm thinking," Waldo said. "There would probably have to be some kind of latch, to fix the heel in either position. Or a retracting knob. Yes, that would be better."

"Sweetie," I said. "The soles of those shoes are angled up for the high heels. It would be impossible to walk on lower heels with a tilted sole. You'd fall backward, or maybe forward."

"Couldn't you have a flexible sole? Can I fool around with a pair of your shoes back at the house?"

"I guess so. I mean, it would have to be a pair I didn't mind you screwing around with, right?"

"Al, you have gazillions of shoes. You have more shoes than I have screwdrivers," he said.

"Dad has more screwdrivers than the hardware store," Ezra said. "Or at least more kinds of screwdrivers."

"Which is quite a difference," Waldo pointed out.

"Sure, you can have a pair of shoes," I said.

"How about us? Can we have some shoes too?"

"Absolutely not."

Back at the house, we sat down to dinner. "Hey, guys," I said, "I learned about some rather interesting saints today, called cephalophores. Any idea what they are?"

Waldo said, "Saints who are head cases?"

"No. And let the boys guess."

"They'll never figure it out."

"Give them a chance."

Henry said, "*Head* must be right. Head-eater. No, head-bearing? A head-bearer? Something like that?"

"Damn, you're good, Henry. I mean, darn."

Henry said, "I don't get it. We all have heads."

"It's actually about saints whose heads get chopped off, then they pick them up and carry them somewhere else. They *bear* their *heads* that way. There was one saint who was the oldest of twenty-four children—his poor mother—and when he was beheaded, he just picked his head right up and carried it a ways to a special rock near a fountain, where he laid it to rest, and you can still see the bloodstains on it, twelve centuries later." But it wasn't today that I'd learned of cephalophores. It was Abelardo who had told me. Why now?

How many drinks had Gunnar plied me with at Grand Central? Suddenly my food was moving around my plate with no help from my fork.

"I can't eat any more," I said.

Waldo squinted at me and said, "Are you tipsy?"

"Perhaps. I didn't think so, but now I wonder. I had a drink with Gunnar at Grand Central. My capacity apparently isn't what it used to be."

"Used to be? When did you ever have capacity? You get high just looking at wine."

"You know that's not true," I said.

Waldo said, "How was Gunnar?"

"He was fine. We talked about mushrooms."

"It's a good thing the boys weren't there."

Big fat snowflakes were still falling fast; I could see their progress as they passed through the beams of the light on the back steps. It was the kind of snow that wouldn't accumulate much. There was little hope of a snow day for the boys tomorrow.

It was unusual for me not to finish a meal. I was a charter member of the clean-plate club. But there it was, food on the plate, untouched. It had to do with those two syllables: *she* and *la*. I couldn't think of anything to say to Waldo that did not include the word *Sheila*.

Then Posey called, and in deference to my probable tipsiness, Waldo actually answered it, and I went upstairs to read with the boys.

They must have read to me in my bed, and I must have slept, because it was hours later when, with his usual grace and ease, Waldo stepped out of his pants as they puddled into two rippling circles at his feet. No one else that I had ever known got out of his pants like that. I never knew if this was something Waldo had taught himself to do, or if this was a weird skill he had developed as a weird child, or if he had been born with it, like the birthmark above his butt crack. We never spoke of it, because if we spoke of it we would also have to address his habit of leaving his clothes where they fell. For a man who kept his tools in meticulous order, arranged in ascending size so that they resembled a musical instrument upon a pegboard in the basement, it seemed outrageous that he could not pick up his own clothes.

As he stood naked at the window and before he came to slide between the sheets, I said, casually, "Do you know anyone named Sheila?"

He said, "Why? Is that one of your saints?"

"I asked you first. And there is no Saint Sheila, strangely enough."

"Why is that strange?"

"Because I think of it as an Irish name, and the Irish are so Catholic," I said. "So do you?" The longer this went on, the harder it was to appear nonchalant. I was clutching my elbows through the worn fabric of my plaid flannel pajamas. Several years ago Posey's friend's lingerie shop in Maine went out of business, and at the close-out sale, Posey had bought up her entire stock of flannel pajamas. I received a pair of red flannel pajamas the following Christmas and then again the next Christmas, at which time I recognized a pattern. Each winter I wore one pair constantly until the fabric disintegrated at all the key spots. By morning one of my elbows would be visible through the sleeve. Flannel pajamas made the best rags.

"Do I what?" Waldo said.

"Christ, Waldo. Know a Sheila?"

"I think I met a Sheila once," he said. "At some company thing."

"What was she like?"

"How would I know?" he said. "What's with the inquisition?"

"Nothing. Absolutely nothing. I must be overtired," I said. And I rolled onto my side and opened up Trollope's *Can You Forgive Her?*, which I had been reading for months. It was suddenly clear that I had to stop right then because if the conversation continued in any of its possible directions, I would certainly mention that I'd heard Sheila's name from Gunnar, or else I would bring up the infamous Edith Dilly, a subject that was equally painful for both of us.

"Oh, I forgot to tell you why Posey called," Waldo said. "Dick's getting married."

"Dick? As in Dick, your brother?" Now this was something to wake a person up.

"No, as in Dick at the post office," Waldo said. "What do you think?"

"And you just *forgot* to tell me *that*? You don't think that's a little strange? Not to mention that it's your brother. Who's he marrying? Is it a woman?"

"Yes. *It* is a woman," Waldo said, more defensively than I would have predicted. "It's the famous Sydney."

"How can your brother get married?"

"The same way everyone else gets married."

Trollope was closed upon my finger and I rolled over. "Don't be disingenuous. He's not exactly normal. Has he ever been with a woman?"

"I doubt it."

"Marriage is a serious step," I said. "For the innocent."

"Wait a second, Al. Do you think only female saints can be virgins?"

"That's not what I said."

"Maybe he's a secret Lothario, a Romeo of the North Woods."

"There's nothing secretive about Dick," I said.

"Unless he's so incredibly good at secrets that we have never once suspected."

"Could you be so wrong about your own brother?" I said.

"Probably not," Waldo said. "No, I think he is one of the truly guileless. You won't be surprised to hear that Posey knows her family, and in fact plays golf with her mother sometimes in Catamunk. So she approves as far as that goes."

"Do you know this Sydney?"

"It's possible that I met her sometime along the way. At the club. But I don't recall."

I pictured a youngish woman as tall and lanky as Dick, someone who could be called beautiful if only she were not constantly bumping into furniture or slamming her finger in car doors or spilling her soup down her dress; someone who generally had food in her teeth and buttoned her shirts askew, but with lovely skin, and fingers as delicate as a bird's skeleton. Would that be the right person for Dick? Would they mesh like pieces of Velcro?

13 ❧ A Spectator Event

T HE FIRST TIME I met Dick, Waldo wasn't even
there. It was because of terrible traffic on Route 1,
which could have been predicted.

Before that, I'd met Waldo in the spring of my third year
in lovely Providence, my third year in that place of Roger Williams's refuge from the Puritanical Bostonians. Waldo was down
from Cambridge and came to a party at my friend Michel's loft
in Fox Point. He came with Martina Loomis, an eerily beautiful
woman from the behavioral sciences department. She spoke with
a foreign accent even though she was American, or so she said.
She was already doing brilliant work with chimpanzees and sign
language, and the use of metaphors. At the party, during which
Michel brought out a particularly potent variety of Sin Semilla
pot, Waldo and I talked about tides and water temperature at
Rhode Island beaches, and the efforts to preserve and replant
some sand dunes. He also told me that as a boy he had been a
methodical hole digger. That is not the sort of information usually imparted, nor is it easily forgotten. While I was very susceptible to marijuana, Waldo did not seem the least bit affected. His
sharpness only increased while the rest of us blurred.

The next day he called me with two specific things to say. The
first was that Martina was not his girlfriend, that her only love
was chimpanzees. The second was to ask if I would like to take a
walk that afternoon, with him and his bulldog, Stinkerbelle.

"You have a bulldog?" I said.

"She really lives with my parents, but Posey and Dad are in Alaska, and the kennel refused to take her."

"Why are they in Alaska?" I asked.

"Good question," Waldo said. "I guess because it's still the United States. They won't find any foreigners living there."

"They don't like foreigners?" I said.

"Let's just say they don't like foreign countries. Oh, they like England, in theory. But basically, if it's not Maine, it's suspect."

"Now that sounds reasonable," I said. I didn't know what else to say. Who was this person so proud of his xenophobic parents?

"So, do you want to?"

"Want to what?"

"Walk with Stinkerbelle and me."

"Is it safe?" I said.

"Oh my God, yes. She does whatever I tell her."

"I should warn you," I said. "I'm not a dog person."

"That's okay. Stinkerbelle is not a person dog," he said. Which I found funny. It seemed that I had already agreed to go for a walk with him.

He arrived in an old wooden-sided station wagon, with Stinkerbelle sitting in the back seat. We drove out to Horseneck Beach and walked for hours. I couldn't bring myself to actually touch Stinkerbelle, who struck me as profoundly ugly, but by the end of the afternoon or rather the early evening, I was madly in love with Waldo. Or if not in love, then deranged with lust for him.

He fashioned a skirt out of seaweed for me. He could walk on his hands. We talked about every fairy tale we had ever read as children. We told each other about a beloved grandparent, and wept for their loss. At the far north end of the beach Waldo pulled off his T-shirt and then stepped out of his pants and walked toward the ocean. Somehow, he convinced me to join him. I had never skinny-dipped in Rhode Island before, and suddenly it seemed a good thing to do before I graduated and returned to

California, where skinny-dipping was not nearly as exciting, there being no aura of prevailing Puritanism to be counteracted. The water was freezing and the only reason I did not immediately run out screaming was this newfound desire to impress Waldo with my ruggedness, my worthiness to walk with a hardy New Englander. Happily, he did not stay in the water for long, and we both emerged blue at the extremities. I remember trying to avert my eyes from the sight of his penis, all wrinkly and curled up like a caterpillar responding to an alien touch. I tried, but I did not succeed.

Many months later I went to visit Waldo and his family in Maine. They had two houses in Maine, one in Catamunk, where they lived year round, and, twenty minutes away, another one on a rocky spit of land called Bug Harbor, where they went in the summer. The Bug Harbor house had a generator, which they turned off at ten every night, without fail, without exception. I could understand one house in a chilly Atlantic state, but two seemed excessive.

Waldo had gone to get corn for that evening's meal, because Dick would be home. "When Dick eats corn on the cob, it is a spectator event," Waldo had said. There were still times when I didn't know if he was kidding or not. And at those times I wondered what I was doing there in an old house in Maine with warped wooden floors and pictures of innumerable ancestors, each one looking more miserable than the next. Waldo left me with Posey. "Stay and bond with Posey" was what he said. Posey did not look interested in bonding.

"Take Stinkerbelle with you," I'd said to Waldo. "Please."

I said to Posey, "I'm looking forward to finally meeting Dick. Waldo's told me so much about him."

"What exactly has Waldo told you?" she said, and fixed her pale blue eyes upon me.

This was my own fault, and now what was I to say? That he was an idiot savant? That he could wiggle his ears and dangle a spoon from his nose? That he knew the Latin names for all the native North and South American fruits? That he was a virgin and a prude, more virginal than the purest nun and more prudish than a Lutheran spinster? "That he's incredibly smart," I said. "And very interested in farming."

"Speak of the devil," Posey said, because just then a tall young man walked in. He looked like Waldo in a warped mirror, the kind that made you skinnier and slightly off kilter, and tinted you pink.

"Dick, this is Waldo's friend Alice Ewen," she said.

I started moving my hand in his direction, then retracted it when it became clear that Dick was not going to move from the door frame.

"You're from California, aren't you?" he said.

"I am."

"I'm going to go to California very soon. To look at avocado plantations. Of course they're native to Mexico, but they have been very successful at growing avocados in California since early in the twentieth century, when they realized how simple it was to graft the trees. The horticultural name is *Persea americana* but it has nothing to do with Persia; it's spelled differently. Do you know Wilson Popenoe? He went on expeditions all over Mexico and Central America to find the superior varieties."

"We have a few old avocado trees in our backyard," I said.

"They must be the Fuerte variety. Or they could be Hass, which was discovered by accident from a failed graft in 1935. Or they could be Rincon—they do well in Santa Barbara. Exactly how old are your trees?"

"I have no idea," I said. "Older than me."

"Wilson Popenoe once, in Guatemala, ate nothing but avocado pears for three days, in order to disprove a local superstition," said Dick. "He did many fine things for agriculture but he was never able to significantly reduce the size of the seed. I, however, am working on it."

"Dick," his mother said. "Why don't you come in and let me give you a drink. I'm going to get a neck ache if you keep standing there."

Dick looked down at his mother and squinted. Did they know each other? Like Waldo, he didn't resemble Posey, although in this instance they were dressed almost identically, in khaki pants and a faded polo shirt with the yacht club burgee on the chest. In one of his perorations on Posey's thriftiness, Waldo had told me Posey bought yacht club shirts only when a particular style was discontinued and being sold off cheaply.

"I can see why Waldo likes you," Dick said, and came to sit on the chair next to me.

"You can?"

"Oh, yes. You can sail, you can speak Spanish, and you don't bite your fingernails."

"Actually," I said, "I don't know how to sail. But I would love to learn."

"And you don't really speak Spanish, do you?" Posey said.

"I do speak Spanish, but not as well as I should," I said. "My mother was Spanish. I learned from her and my aunt." I wanted to add: I can't help it. It's not my fault.

"I don't understand how anyone can speak that language," she said. "All those *r*'s and double *l*'s, and then the waves over the *n*'s." She pursed her lips just so, in a way that was identifiably un-Spanish, if nothing else.

"It's really quite easy," I said, apologetically. *"Muy sencillo."*

"Well, I have no interest in discussing anyone's fingernails. Dick, you can make your own drink."

He did not move from his chair but shifted that intense gaze from his mother to me. Where *was* Waldo? Posey finally stood up and went into the kitchen and made Dick a drink. "One for you, Alice?" she called out. "The sun is over the yardarm."

"No, thanks," I said.

Just then, at long last, in waltzed Waldo and Stinkerbelle. "Fuck the lumber industry," he said vehemently.

"Waldo, please," Posey said.

"I would have been here half an hour ago if not for a lumber truck that tipped over."

"Lumber trucks never tip over," Dick said. "They're too heavy."

"Tell that to our friends on Route One."

"It must have been something else."

I saw Waldo opening his mouth and then stopping himself. In the four-plus months I had known him, I had never once seen him do that: think better of his words. I was moved by the gesture, and struck anew by my physical longing for him.

It was dark by the time we sat down for dinner. Three, the ailing Waldo Fairweather III, served us white wine over ice cubes. Waldo said, "Alice's Spanish ancestors would roll over in their Spanish graves if they saw you doing that."

"Not at all," I objected.

"Alice has Spanish ancestors?"

"Her mother is from Barcelona," said Waldo. Hadn't he told them about me, that they found this so surprising, so disturbing? It's not as if he'd said, *Her parents are congenital idiots. Her brother's in prison for child molesting.* "Didn't you and Mom go to Barcelona once, Dad?"

"Ahem. That was before your mother. But we do have ancestors from Normandy," Waldo III said. "I think they spoke English." Later I learned that he'd said this in jest.

But at this point I was no longer concerned with anyone's Iberian heritage, because Dick had started in on his corn on the cob. First he rolled the corn round and round on a whole stick of butter. Then, rapidly and thoroughly, he ate the corn. Anyone would have stared in an effort to understand just how his teeth were operating. To no avail. His jaw was a blur of motion. When he finished with a piece of corn, it was completely denuded of kernels. Not one remained. Even a goat would have been hard-pressed to find anything edible on that cob. Then Dick drank down his glass of wine, and started on another corn. By the end of the evening there was a neat pyramid of seven stripped ears of corn on his plate.

That was the first time I'd met Waldo's brother, Dick, and since then I'd never thought of him without the image of those stripped ears of corn. What sort of woman could marry him? She was becoming interesting to me.

The snow was gone in the morning, and it seemed entirely possible that Sheila, along with everything else, had been a figment of my overactive imagination.

I brought Waldo his coffee and said, "When exactly is Dick getting married?"

"Sometime in June. Posey knows the date. You really should call Posey."

"Sometime in June? Sometime? This is not how people get married these days. They have to reserve the church and reception hall years in advance. And what about invitations? Don't they have invitations in Maine?"

"Calm down, Al. It will all come in due time."

I took a sip of coffee and almost spit it out. "Why didn't you tell me this coffee is mud?"

"I like it, honey. I was about to ask why you decided to make it so strong this morning."

"I didn't."

"It'll be on Slow Island. That I do know."

"That little island off the coast, near you guys?"

"The very same."

"Wait a sec. Isn't June blackfly season?"

"It is," Waldo said, sadly.

"You always say we can't go to Maine in June because of the dreaded blackflies."

"And it's true, but there are no flies on Slow Island. You could say it's its chief asset."

"No flies? How is that possible? I mean, flies fly. And if so, why hasn't all of Maine moved there?"

"They would, but the Sweets own the whole thing."

"Who are the Sweets?"

"Sydney's family. Sydney Sweet."

"So your soon-to-be in-laws are the only people in Maine who can safely venture out-of-doors in June?"

"Exactly."

Ω Not Exactly a Chapter but an Interlude

I CONSIDERED AT LEAST fourteen ways to start a conversation that would begin with Waldo's dispelling Gunnar's misinterpretation of the Sheila event and culminate in my resident panic taking a flying leap. There were serious flaws in all fourteen opening gambits, which ranged from (but were hardly limited to) False Assumptions to Begging the Question to Ad Hominem Attacks to Bathos to Hysteria.

So I told Waldo I planned to write Lalo a letter.

"Good idea. I always liked your letters. I'm sure he will too." We were sitting at the kitchen table. Waldo was eating pistachios and then lining up their shells, concave side down.

"How many letters can I possibly have written you?"

"Enough. Back in the dark ages you wrote me from California,

> *"There was a lovely lass from California*
> *Where the girls are babes and the boys are hornier*
> *One happy day Waldo flew in*
> *Found himself Alice Ewen*
> *If you don't like this rhyme I have one even cornier."*

"Holy cow, Waldo. Where did that come from?"

"Would it make you feel better to know I woke up last night pondering *hornier* and *cornier*?"

"I don't know," I said. Because I didn't. What Waldo pondered in the middle of the night was as mysterious to me as the internal combustion engine. But infinitely more alluring.

"The middle needs work," he said.

"I just don't think Lalo is an e-mail type," I said.

"That seems a safe guess. You're making assumptions, of course, but what else is new?"

"Do you think Gunnar is an e-mail type?" I asked.

"What does he have to do with it?"

"Nothing. Except that he mentioned something the other day. About running into you at the Oyster Bar," I said.

"When was this?" Waldo said. His row of pistachio shells crossed the table and was now coming back toward us, in the boustrophedon mode. I would have liked to point this out to Waldo, because one rarely gets an opportunity to use such a word, but now was not the time to wave my vocabulary flag, not if there was any hope for dispelling the dark shadow of Sheila.

"I don't know. You were with someone named Sheila."

"I don't know anyone named Sheila. Has it occurred to you that Gunnar could be hallucinating? Maybe it was a mushroom."

"Maybe," I said. But the panic was still there, anthropomorphized into a miniature person sitting on the edge of a volcano, dangling her legs in the crater. And I never wrote the letter to Abelardo. I started twice, but instead of telling him about diagnosable virgin saints, I wrote about Waldo and the Sheila he didn't know; I wrote about being unable to forget about Waldo and Edith Dilly and how when I thought about it I often had to lean against a wall or a tree because the ground would become wobbly. Or my feet uncertain. I tore those letters up.

And then, for days and weeks, life went on. I got dressed in the morning and wondered what I would make for dinner.

For days and weeks, I did the laundry as always. I separated the whites and the colors and I got a perverse satisfaction from removing the accumulated lint from the lint tray in the dryer.

I wondered if there was something useful that could be done with lint, if Waldo could think of something to do with lint. But Waldo was never there at the moment that I was doing laundry and considering the problem of all the unused lint in all the dryers all over America, and later on I never remembered to suggest that he might address this problem.

I folded everyone's clothes and put the clothes away in the drawers. Waldo's boxers and the boys' superhero underpants and puppy underpants and airplane underpants. There was something eternally intimate about folding their underwear. Not the washing so much as the folding. And they had to be folded in a certain way, in thirds so that there was a flat center panel, rather than in half and then halved again to make a quarter. Socks were also important. I was of the line-them-up-roll-them-into-a-ball-then-fold-the-inside-sock-into-the-outer-one school.

Every morning and evening I fed the dogs. I checked Dandy's gums and gave him his medications. He was off the medicine that required a syringe and latex gloves; now he was on prednisone. Waldo told me that Three had often taken prednisone for his allergies, and he'd liked it very much. He'd said it made him smarter. If it made Dandy any smarter, we couldn't tell. Usually in the afternoons I walked with Dandy and Flirt down the road to Susie's and up the road to Bogumila's. Sometimes I remembered to check them for ticks, but not often.

Life just went on and sometimes hours went by without my thinking of Waldo and Sheila. Was it possible she didn't exist? Sometimes I wanted to know everything about them: how often, what they said, what she wore; I wanted to know how her body compared with mine in every way, from the length of her toes to the curliness of her pubic hair to the muscle tone of her upper arms to the wrinkles around her eyes. Did she have wrinkles? Did she color her hair? Did she shave her underarms? Years ago Waldo had told me how much he loved the soft silken hair of a certain woman's underarms. Did they cleave together, and were they now cleft? I wondered if her mother was alive. I wondered how much she knew about me. I wondered how much she knew about Ezra and Henry. Had Waldo ever shown her a picture of them? If she ever spoke of Ezra and Henry, if their names ever crossed her lips, I thought, I would be inclined to murder her.

But most of the time, I did not think of Sheila, and I did not think of Waldo and Sheila. Most of the time, I did not even think about Abelardo, not even when I read about the virgin saints, their trials and tribulations and their wonders to behold.

As in Brueghel, as in Auden, as in Ovid, the little people just keep going on with their daily tasks, their laundry and cooking and dog walking, while tragedy falls from the sky or happens in a far corner of the painting. So it was with us, the Fairweathers, little people driving the carpool to Little League games, running out at midnight for milk, and watching *The Simpsons,* while elsewhere in the world regimes toppled, innocent souls were slaughtered, smokestacks belched out their poisons, and rainforests were mowed down and hoovered up; while on at least two continents at any given moment humans slaughtered other humans in the name of religion. In VerGroot we questioned the wisdom of the DPW's acquisition of a new snowplow, and most of the time, I did not think about Waldo and Sheila.

14 ❧ Pink Gums

"WHOA, SUSIE! You scared me."
I had been deep in the contemplation of the inside of my refrigerator. Then I'd stepped back and seen the dark outline of a person through the storm door.

"I was hoping to find some hamburger in there," I said. I knew damn well there was no hamburger in there, or if there was, it had been in the fridge far too long to be safely edible.

Susie let herself in. "Since when do you eat hamburger?"

"I don't, at least not yet. It's for Dandy. Look at his gums," I said. I reached over and took hold of Dandy's lip and folded it back to reveal the pale flesh beneath. "Do these look pale to you?"

"I didn't come over here to look at your dog's gums."

"Please. Just tell me what you think. I don't call that pink. Do you call that pink?"

"Fine. It's very pale pink, if you must know. Compared to what?"

"I'll show you Flirt's gums."

"I saw Gunnar at the town board meeting last night," she said. She sat in the one stable kitchen chair.

"I thought you swore off board meetings, after the defenestration incident."

"I know. I should have stuck to it. Then I started to feel sorry for Herc. He's too well intentioned for this world. He doesn't get that there are Machiavellian forces at work, undermining our little town government," Susie said. "So what is this about Waldo and some kangaroo?"

Huh? I stared at my neighbor, my dear friend, at her translucent skin, at the tips of her eyes that dipped down and might give the unwary observer the false impression that behind this face was a hesitant soul.

"What on earth are you talking about?"

"I was talking to Gunnar after the meeting," Susie said.

"About kangaroos?"

"Isn't *Sheila* Australian slang for a kangaroo?" Susie said.

"Not to my knowledge. But I've never been Down Under. Have you?"

"Only in my dreams," she said.

"Well, I hope you realize that Gunnar jumps to conclusions," I said.

"He's worried about you."

"Maybe he told you more than he told me. I'm not sure I want to know. Except I do. Okay, what did he tell you?"

"That Waldo is having a thing with this Sheila, and that you are clueless."

"Waldo doesn't even know someone called Sheila. Australian or not. I think it was mistaken identity. And. It's been years since Waldo has done anything like that."

As far as I knew, Susie was the only person in VerGroot who knew about Waldo and Edith Dilly, and for years she had been good enough not to mention it, knowing how much it pained me. "Al, I hope you're right. But you do know that when it comes to their dicks, men are not rational. They're slaves to testosterone."

"Are we so different?" I said.

"Estrogen is a different kettle of fish altogether. Wait until you get hot flashes." She fanned her face with her hand and leaned back in her chair as if swooning.

"Are you having one now?" I said.

"No, this is just for dramatic effect," Susie said.

I said, "Don't sex and love make us all act irrationally? Whatever hormones we subscribe to."

"Oh, don't tell me—you're having a thing with the hagiographer?"

"Not exactly. He's gay," I said.

She looked genuinely surprised. "You mean you've actually considered it?"

"Whoa, Susie. Let's talk about anything but that. How's your knee?"

"It is brilliant," Susie said. She kicked up her leg and described a circle in the air with her foot. Not that I could see her knee through her blue jeans; not that she had been in the habit of doing leg kicks before her knee surgery. "I'm going to take the plunge and order my chicks. Do you think Dandy and Flirt will behave? Not eat them for breakfast?" Which explained *Raising Chickens for Dummies,* but little else.

"Of course they'll behave," I said. "Are they going to be free range? What about all the airplane innards over there?"

"I haven't decided. George doesn't know about the plan yet. It could be fun to surprise him," Susie said.

"It could be . . ."

"And there is still the question of the chicken coop."

"I'm trying to picture you stepping out the back door and tossing chicken feed from your apron, like something out of Normal Rockwell."

"You laugh, but when I was working at Chase I used to fantasize about chickens all the time. I would read McMurray's Hatchery weekly specials online secretly, just like porn."

"Susie, what else don't I know about you? Please tell me now."

"If I can think of anything, I'll tell you. But I'm still concerned about Gunnar."

"I thought we'd exhausted that topic," I said.

"We've barely started. Then there is Gunnar and you. Something truly shocking."

"Oh, God," I groaned. "He's just imagining it anyways."

"So you say."

And then, to my immense relief, Ezra and Henry walked in the door and dropped their backpacks on the floor. Henry more or less followed the descent of his backpack and threw himself across Flirt's body. Ezra opened the refrigerator door.

"Can you make us popcorn?" he said.

I told Waldo that evening about Susie's plan to keep chickens; he immediately called her up and told her he would a design a chicken coop on wheels that could be moved around the yard in order to spread the fertilizing benefits of chicken poop.

"Interesting. Why didn't you make one for Bogumila?" Susie asked suspiciously.

"Bogumila's kind of rigid about certain things," Waldo said. "In case you haven't noticed. If they don't have movable chicken coops in Poland, then she can't have one in New York."

I went with Flirt and Dandy to the woods, each of us sniffing our separate ways. They proffered an antler, a relic. Molted in the fall, to be grown anew in the spring. I pried it from Flirt's jaws. She didn't object. She may have already established that it wasn't edible. I wanted to bring it home to the boys, so they could feel its weight, and see the scars from battles over a desired female. Up in Catamunk they had seen moose in the early mornings, and they had seen pictures of moose engaged in fierce combat, heads down, the huge antlers of one thrusting and jabbing at his rival's equally huge headgear. But here in their own backyard, the same rituals, of seasons passing and of the struggle for domination, were being enacted, again and again. And each time, a memento was left behind, a further accretion in the natural world. I touched the smooth bony shaft of the antler, as well as the ridges near its base, where it had separated from its maker.

I got home mere minutes before the boys returned from school.

I loved that rush of energy, wind, noise, and all the smells that arrived home with the boys. I loved to hear the back screen door brusquely pulled open, then the main door pushed in as the screen slammed behind them. I loved the clatter of backpacks thumping to the kitchen floor and spilling their contents. Each day fell out an imperceptibly different assortment of the same old things: books, notes from teachers, bits and pieces of lunches. It had only recently dawned on me that they might not carry backpacks forever, and that there might come a time when they would not allow the contents to innocently clutter the kitchen floor.

The following afternoon Ezra came through the door several steps behind Henry, dragging his backpack behind him. He told me he'd fallen asleep at school.

"What did Miss Higgins say?"

"She said she couldn't bear to wake me. Which was really annoying. Because all the kids say I snored on my desk."

"You never snore," I said. "Talk in your sleep, maybe. Didn't you sleep last night?"

"Not exactly," Ezra answered with averted eyes. "I didn't. Something was wrong with the bed, and I kept rolling over and over and trying to get comfortable, but I never could."

"Did you check to see if there were crumbs? Eating crackers in bed will do that," I said.

"No, Mom," he said emphatically. "There was nothing. I'm not a dope, you know."

"I know you're not a dope. Look what the dogs and I found in the woods," I said, and brandished the antler.

Henry took it and held it against his forehead. "How do I look?"

"Like you have a giant headache," Ezra said.

"Do you want to take a nap, Ez?"

"No, Mom. I already did. I told you."

"I'll change your sheets tonight. Maybe that will help."

But it didn't. The next morning the bags under his eyes were even deeper. I suggested that he stay home and rest, and maybe drink one of Bogumila's Slavic soporific concoctions, but he declined. And off they went.

I went upstairs and vacuumed his room extra-scrupulously, because maybe he'd become extra-sensitive to dust.

Dust was not the culprit.

15 ❧ Christina the Astonishing

HUBERT SAT AT HIS vast mahogany table, reading the *Daily News* and shaking with erratic laughter, like a washing machine with an off-kilter belt. "You look terrible," he said.

"Thanks."

"How are things on the home front?"

"Things on the home front are fine," I said adamantly. "I just bumped into a man on Lex with one leg. Or rather he bumped into me. And it upset me. Don't ask me why."

"Funny you should say that. I'm reading about a nun who bit off a python's head. The python belonged to a friend of hers and it was sick, so the nun was holding it for her, and then she just bit its head off." Once again, his body shook as he was overcome by the hilarity of this event.

"Maybe she's in one of those sects that eats snakes and then speaks in tongues," I said.

"She wasn't. And this was a live snake," Hubert said.

"That is truly disgusting. And don't pythons have big heads? I bet it couldn't even fit in someone's mouth."

"You'd be surprised what can fit in someone's mouth," Hubert said.

"Forget I said that," I said. "I think I'll just go read about some nice saints."

He grinned. "Then you've come to the wrong place."

"Very funny. Seriously, do you have any suggestions for me?"

Of course he did. That was the day I made the acquaintance

of Saint Christina the Astonishing. Who, while she may not have bitten the head off a serpent, managed to behave unsociably in other ways.

Christina's story starts with her death. She was about twenty-two when she had a fit, became catatonic, and was presumed dead. She was duly placed in an open coffin and carried into church for her requiem mass. Just as the mourners sang the Agnus Dei, she bolted up and flew to the church's rafters, where she perched like a bird.

Agnus Dei, qui tollis peccata mundi, dona eis requiem, and finally, *dona eis requiem sempiternam.*

Except that Christina was not about to have eternal rest, not then, not for a long time. While she sat up there on the beams, everyone fled the church except the priest and Christina's older sister, who was so devout that she would not leave until the mass was over. At that point, the priest made Christina come down. Perhaps he was a precursor to those heroes of television dramas, those policemen cajoling rejected lovers and bankrupts down from window ledges overlooking the canyons of New York.

Christina had fled to the rafters because she couldn't bear the stink of the sinful human bodies. Christina told the priest that she had descended into Hell, seen a few friends, gone to Purgatory and seen some more, and then visited Heaven. She said that she was offered the opportunity to stay in Heaven, but she'd chosen to return to earth and save some of the suffering souls with her prayers. All of this had happened while the churchgoers sang the Agnus Dei.

Alive again, Christina behaved like one deranged or tormented. She climbed trees and rocks and, still attempting to escape the miserable smell of her fellow humans, crawled into ovens. Even by the lax thirteenth-century standards, she was considered mad, and her neighbors often tried to confine her. But Christina always got away. Finally she climbed into a baptismal font and sat in the water, peacefully. She quieted down after that and lived her remaining years, almost half a century, in the convent of St. Catherine at Saint-Trond.

I asked Hubert, "Do you really believe she levitated?"

"Stranger things have happened."

"That's not what I asked."

"Someone believed she levitated. Several people did. I also believe we can make ourselves believe all sorts of improbable things. And that improbable is not the same as impossible."

"Pardon me," I said. "But did you answer my question?"

"Frankly," said Hubert, "what I find hard to understand—even believe—is not so much the levitations and apparitions as the suffering. The fondness for suffering. The seeking out of suffering. Have you encountered Lydwina yet? She may not have slept in her coffin, the way Mariana did, but she was the 'prodigy of human misery.'"

"What's so hard to understand about that? Suffering is the human condition, is it not?"

"Spare me your platitudes," Hubert said. "What is so saintly about suffering, I'd like to know. I worry that the church has veered in a terrible direction, glorifying suffering and misery. I understand all too well it's about identifying with Christ's Passion and death on the Cross. Because, you see, when we sanctify mere suffering and martyrdom, we lose the ability to be horrified."

"Did Martin suffer before he died?" I asked.

"Yes," he said. "And now we'll have no more of that subject."

"Sorry," I said. "I just thought—"

"Don't be. And don't." He turned abruptly and knocked over several books stacked on his desk. I couldn't see their titles but at least two were in Latin. They fell to the floor in a heap and out spilled dozens of memorial cards, those small black-edged cards with a photograph and the dates of the deceased, and sometimes a prayer and sometimes not. Now they dotted the carpet. Every photograph I could see was of a youngish man. I expected Hubert to spring to life and quickly scoop up the cards and remove them from sight, but he looked at them and blinked, as if he were equally surprised to see them.

"Are those yours?" he said.

"No."

"I didn't think so."

I didn't want to read about any more saints that day. It seemed that there was not a single thought in my head that was not selfish, gossipy, jealous, or just plain frivolous, and the saints were making me nervous. Afternoon light was piercing the dusty window beside Hubert's desk. Like gnats and mosquitoes briefly identified in the beams of headlights, here the dust motes flew in and out of the shaft of light, and for a time had a separateness and an existence so solid we could name every individual speck. And each speck, once named, would never again merge anonymously with the mass of generic dust motes. For better or worse.

On my way out I slammed into the corner of Hubert's desk with my thigh. The sharp corner drove into my leg with such force that I gave a cry of pain that sounded—to me, hovering just at the edge—like a growl. I turned away in order to catch my breath, my stolen breath.

"You're bumping into all sorts of things today," Hubert said.

"I think I should go home now," I said.

Hubert handed me a book beautifully bound in green leather. "Read about Melangell before you go, she's a favorite of mine."

"Any particular reason?" I asked.

"Just read."

Saint Melangell was the daughter of an Irish prince, a virgin, of course, who spent fifteen years alone in the forest. Until Prince Brochwel Ysgythrog came hunting, in hot pursuit of a hare. The hare took refuge under Melangell's skirts, and from there it turned and brazenly faced the dogs. Brochwel urged his dogs on—he really wanted that hare—but they drew back, whimpering. Brochwel brought his horn to his lips, but it was mute. Then he saw Melangell, who told him of having lived in solitary prayer without once seeing another human face. Brochwel was so moved by her story that he gave her all the land around. She stayed for another thirty-seven years. Hares always found a safe haven there.

I held out the beautiful book to Hubert and said, "Do you believe this?"

"About Melangell's hare. Of course I do."

"Not that. The part about being alone in the forest for fifteen years. Fifteen years!"

"People were not always so addicted to social intercourse as they are now," Hubert said.

"Human nature hasn't changed all that much in fifteen hundred years. A mere speck of time. And if she hadn't seen anyone in fifteen years, how could she still have a skirt for the hare to hide in? It would be in shreds."

Hubert said, "Must you be so literal?"

"Me? Literal?" I was hurt. "*Willing suspension of disbelief* is my mantra. *Willing suspension of disbelief. Willing suspension of disbelief.* But fifteen years. That really troubles me."

"She had Inner Resources," Hubert said. Now *that* shook me.

Perhaps Waldo could compose a limerick on this subject. *Melangell* might prove a challenging rhyme, but I was convinced that *hare* and *prayer* were made for doggerel.

Under Grand Central's vast stellar-studded dome, evoking colliding planets, dive-bombing meteors, and careening asteroids, I only recalled colliding with Gunnar and his briefcase full of bombshells. Stellar too was his remarkable ability to find mushrooms in the woods, right there on the forest floor. Once we'd walked under towering tulip trees and he'd spotted the brown honeycomb-capped morels mere feet from our feet. As soon as he pointed them out, they were completely obvious. Until that moment, they'd been completely hidden. They recalled to me things that existed only in the imagination: Hansel and Gretel's witch's cottage, priapic gnomes, hares hiding in the virgin's skirts.

But until the moment of Gunnar's bending down to gently snap off the morels at their base, I could no more see the fairy-tale gathering of *Morchella esculenta* than I could see in the dark.

It was dark when the train pulled into VerGroot. I called Waldo to see if he could pick me up at the station.

"Are you wearing high heels again?" he asked.

"No. That won't happen again soon," I said.

"Or maybe it will. Maybe there will be a solution to the problem of altitude and ankles."

As we sat down to eat, Posey called. I told her I'd met an old friend of hers, Camilla Hyde. I didn't say it had been days earlier. I didn't mention my sweaty terror that she also knew the Dillys and the sordid tale of Waldo and Edith. Then Posey surprised me, which was a good thing.

"Her?" Posey sputtered, a rare occurrence. "Good grief, she went over to the dark side."

"Posey, isn't that a bit melodramatic? She's only a Catholic. And I don't even know that for sure."

"You misunderstand me, Alice. I don't know quite how to say this. She's a Satanist. Whatever that means. But I have it on the best authority."

"How can you be sure of something like that?" I asked. With my free hand I indicated horns and then a tail for Waldo and the boys. They looked puzzled. "I didn't think there were Satanists anymore. I thought they were defunct, or debunked. Like alchemists."

"All I know is what I heard. And it wasn't pretty. A baby was involved. An infant. I would give her a wide berth if I were you."

"She said she played Ping-Pong with you."

"That was before I knew. And I beat her," Posey said.

"I find this very strange," I said. "She's very attractive."

"Of course she is," said Posey.

"But this isn't why you called, is it? Here's Waldo."

From our end of things, it wasn't hard to figure out the intended topic; certainly no more than one python in America could have had its head bitten off that day by a person, any person. Apparently it had made the Maine papers.

"I know all about it," I told them. "It was a nun."

"Posey didn't say anything about a nun," Waldo said.

Ez said, "I would spit it out."

"I should hope so," I said.

"People do eat snakes, you know. And locusts."

Ezra said, "They eat locusts in the Bible. Locusts and honey. You know, the one who lost his head."

Waldo was pleased to hear this. Clearly I needn't worry about the boys' religious education if Ezra knew the diet of John the Baptist in the desert.

"Well, none of you better bite the head off a python," I said. "Then your grandmother would have to read about it in the paper. Imagine her surprise."

"Her glee," suggested Waldo.

"I would do it under an assumed name," Ezra said. "Because I think perversions should be private."

Again, Waldo and I looked at each other. Ezra? While I'd often heard the little boys at VerGroot Elementary yelling to one another, "Pervert! Pervert! Wears a purple undershirt!," this seemed very different from the exclamatory and insulting use of the word; this seemed indicative of depths to Ezra of which we'd had no idea.

It was happening more and more, these little peeks into the mysteries of boys that in every case seemed like the tip of an iceberg, an iceberg full of secret knowledge and longings that would go away with them as they traveled from this safe haven of ours, with its dogs, Legos, and family dinners, to a larger world that neither required nor accepted a mother's note to excuse infractions or absences.

These boys already knew things we hadn't taught them; already they imagined things we couldn't understand, and they dreamed of things we could only imagine.

In the town forest, the boys ran ahead of us: limbs, limbs, and more limbs. It had not departed, the picture of Waldo and his Australian lover slurping raw oysters under Grand Central. Her face (which was like mine) softened and elongated to become a brain worm burrowing into my psyche. And like any good parasite, it did not kill its host. It merely sucked energy, sucked happiness.

So, if Waldo didn't know this Sheila, whom did he know? Maybe if I brought it up then, as we walked in the woods we loved, as Flirt and Dandy leaped over the pine-needled forest floor and chased small woodland creatures, Waldo would explain, really explain, and I would come to know where Gunnar had gotten those crazy ideas of his. As long as I wasn't saying anything, too much was possible.

I knew I would bring it up. Sooner or later. So why not in this place, at this moment? Why, oh, why would Waldo want anything but the life we led together?

Did Waldo have unmet longings I had no inkling of? And ditto me? Did I have unmet longings?

Flirt found a massive mud puddle and dove into it. Other dogs passed indifferently by the same mud puddles that called out inexorably to Flirt. She swooped up through the mud until it coated all her fur, and then she swooped down, so that no spot was missed. How could one help but admire her determination to achieve this pleasure, this satisfaction of the senses? That kind of determination, that sense of mission, even just Flirt seeking the coolness of a mud puddle, always impressed me. And mystified me. Because I feared I didn't have it, that determination. What did I want as much as she wanted the mud?

Was this what it was like for Waldo, with his Sheila? Or only with Edith?

"There's something I've been meaning to ask you, Waldo," I said.

"Shoot," he said. "But we should probably turn around now."

"You never want to turn around," I said.

"I have stuff to do."

"Do you love me as much as ever?" I said. It was not the question I'd meant to ask.

"That depends what you mean by *ever*," he said. Then, noticing the stricken look on my face, he said, "Of course I do. Ever, whenever, whatever. I love you, Al."

I slipped my arm though his, as if everything were resolved, as if everything were the same. As ever. We turned around.

It *was* the question I'd meant to ask.

16 ✤ Travel Is Broadening

THE SUMMER BEFORE I met Waldo, Annabel, Audrey, and I had backpacked around Europe for two months. This was in the early eighties, and I'd had a different lover in seven different countries, almost every country we visited. But not all. Each one of those lovers spoke a different language. They also ate different food for breakfast, and approached personal hygiene differently.

Before that summer I was barely a sexual being. I was a sexual pupa. All summer long I chomped at the edges of my sac, and then Waldo came along and I crawled out and promptly fell off the branch. With Waldo I was passionate and passionately monogamous. There was only Waldo. Of course I told him everything about my past. I was pleased to have a past to tell. But when I described for him my summer's adventures, they came out sounding like bits of fiction, like wishful thinking set into an itinerary. But it's all true, I insisted, you can read about it in Audrey's journal.

It was an educational summer. In England we'd hiked with Niles and his friends, all of them afflicted with speech impediments. In Flanders there was Franz, who lusted more for Memling's virgins than for me. Jan was the Dutch veterinarian. I've forgotten the name of the boy in Denmark; he paled (as did they all) beside Annabel's Boris, the itinerant storyteller with whom she toured for two weeks while Audrey and I soldiered on. We stayed with Ulrich in Munich; he lived with his grandmother and his grandfather, the professor of Egyptology. Giorgio, in Rome, was a low point.

Our *abuela* met us at the train station in Barcelona, which was the first surprise, because Mami had told us that Abuela was completely dotty by now. But there she was, dressed all in black. Even her straw sun hat was covered with dark purple grapes and black ribbons. It was the kind of hat that caused little children to point and stare, and dogs to bark.

We spent our days there with Abuela and her stories. She lived alone now with Dolores, who had been their maid forever, and even before. Like Dolores, we had already heard all of Abuela's stories, but we took secret note of the tiny ways she altered the tales with each telling.

Sometimes we wandered up and down the Ramblas and imagined what our lives would have been like if Mami had married a Spaniard and stayed in Barcelona instead of meeting Perceval Ewen and letting him talk her into coming out to California. We wondered what we might have looked like. But the truth was that we couldn't imagine any life other than our own, our brightly lit life in California, picking lemons and avocados, swimming naked at Red Rock, and smoking pot.

One day after lunch, when we were even lazier than usual and spreading ourselves across couches and chairs for a siesta, Dolores's grandson came by to take her off to some family christening or burial. His name was Orlando, and as soon as he walked into the dim living room where we were sprawled, we sat up straight and tried to look alert. Instinctively we knew that he was not likely to be enchanted by three recumbent girls from California. Annabel was best in such situations. We air kissed and made small talk about our trip. He wanted to know if we'd seen the Fra Angelico frescoes at the San Marco monastery in Florence, and Annabel said we had gotten lost looking for it. He asked how we'd liked the Bronzinos at the Uffizi; Audrey volunteered that the Uffizi had been closed. But the Baptistery doors? Surely we had admired the Baptistery doors? They were closed also, Audrey said. Then the tiny ageless Dolores came in, dressed exquisitely in black. Gallant Orlando gave her his arm, and off they went.

As soon as she returned, we begged to know more. "Do his parents live here in Barcelona too?"

"His parents—may they rest in peace—are no longer with us. They died in a car crash," Dolores said. Her face was implacable.

When Orlando returned for his grandmother the following afternoon he found us wide awake and well groomed. We sat on stiff chairs and inhaled the dust mites that lived in the tapestries.

"Dolores told us about your parents. It's terribly sad," Annabel said. "Was your mother Dolores's daughter?"

"No. My father was her only son," he said, and as he spoke he crossed himself quickly, so quickly we might have missed it if we hadn't been watching him so closely. "She told you about the accident?"

We nodded.

"It was terrible. I was driving the car. They were in the back seat. I was driving and I was wearing a seat belt. But they were not; they were not wearing seat belts and they always preferred to sit in the back when I drove them. Really, no one in Spain wears seat belts. I often wish that I had not as well."

"But it wasn't your fault," Audrey said. "You didn't mean for it to happen. You're the one left behind to miss them for the rest of your life."

"That is what everyone says," Orlando said.

"Orlando!" Dolores stood erect in the doorway. "It's time to go," she said. She called back to us, "Do not fail to look after your *abuela*."

We waited up for Dolores. She came in very late, after midnight.

"We're so sorry."

"You never told us."

"That's the saddest story ever."

"Why didn't you ever tell us?"

Dolores said, "I hope your *abuela* ate something." When we assured her she had, Dolores added, "You shouldn't trouble Orlando like that."

"He seems so nice, Dolores. But terribly, terribly sad."

"Of course he is sad," she said. "I wanted him to have a family. But he wanted to enter the seminary. Next year he will be ordained. Padre Orlando."

We never saw Orlando again.

And so instead of eight lovers, which was the number of countries we'd visited that summer, I had seven, which according to Annabel was six too many. But it seemed a shame that the one country where I might have expected to find a kindred soul, the one country where the native tongue was familiar and evocative, was the one country where I did not have a lover. Where I did not have sex.

Then I met Waldo, and I was glad I had not announced from the roof of Wilson Hall my summer's sexual escapades. I was glad that I could break them to Waldo gently, with the educational spin they deserved.

My sisters didn't get to meet Waldo until my graduation, a couple of years later. We all had dinner at a great Italian restaurant in Providence. I told them stories about corrupt Rhode Island politics, and about our corrupt mayor who had burned his ex-wife's boyfriend with cigarettes and was almost universally beloved by the city's voters. Waldo recited one of his more scathing limericks, in which he rhymed the mayor's name with *fancy* and *romancey,* and also, I think, *truancy.*

After dinner Audrey took me aside and said, "Oh my God—I know who he reminds me of, Al—that German guy in Munich. Ulrich. The one with the Egyptologist grandfather. He made terrible jokes too. My God, they were horrid. Not remotely funny."

"Don't you think Waldo's limericks are funny? And clever?"

Audrey looked at me with genuine disbelief. "You're joking. You're not telling me you think they're funny? I mean, I like Waldo well enough. He has many good qualities. Those dopey limericks are not one of them. Take my word for it, Al."

"Mami thinks he's perfect for me," I said.

"That's why you need us," Audrey said.

After twenty-five years teaching Spanish to the lovely and lithe blond adolescents of Miss Goodwin's Girls' Academy, my mother, Inez Llovet Ewen, retired and decided to learn to surf. After all, we did live in California. Her old family friends back in Barcelona believed that everyone in California could surf, and no acquaintance with the facts could convince them otherwise. Shark attacks were almost unheard-of in Santa Barbara, but no one told that to the shark that attacked our mother. Henry and Ezra were one and three when she died, but they claimed to remember her. They described her perfectly. They imitated her Catalan accent. They liked to hear me tell the story of the shark attack and then wipe away my tears. On our annual trips to visit Pop in Santa Barbara, Ezra and Henry never failed to make a pilgrimage to the Goleta beach and look for the shark that had deprived them of their grandmother. We insisted the shark in question had long since died, perhaps been eaten by a larger shark. Such excuses, such looseness with the facts of shark lore, did not fly with the boys, especially Henry. Henry informed us that the life span of sharks was long indeed. Great whites had been known to live one hundred years.

I missed my mother terribly. I'd almost told her about Waldo and Edith Dilly, when Henry was a baby and I was a wreck. But then I didn't, and then she was dead in the water. If I had only told her, then that knowledge could have gone with her, and gone from me.

17 ❧ Christina the Astonishing, Again

I SHOULD HAVE SHOWERED, but instead I clung to the lingering warmth of predawn sex, through breakfast, even on the train into the city. I ventured out unbathed because I needed a talisman against my fear of losing Waldo, and losing myself. It was not because I was inspired by any unwashed medieval virgin mystics.

Hubert was at his usual spot behind his desk. Was it placed exactly there to catch the late-morning sun? The light pierced the stained-glass window overhead, the one portraying Saint Rocco and his faithful dog. The amber of Saint Rocco's halo gave Hubert's face a yellowish cast. A foreign-language newspaper was spread open atop preexisting piles of newsprint and hagiographies and love letters. What weirdness had of late transpired between a religious and a reptile?

"You really should have lunch with me today," Hubert said. "I'm in a sociable mood."

I almost levitated out of my shoes. First, morning sex, and then lunch with Hubert. What more could I ask? Oh, yes, Abelardo.

A little past midday Hubert nodded to me where I'd been dozing over the Seven Sleepers of Ephesus and then dozing some more over the Fourteen Holy Helpers. I followed him downstairs past closed doors. So many closed doors: to my parents' bedroom, to Mother Superior's office at Precious Blood, to Waldo's closet.

Hubert slipped his fingers into the brass recess in the dark mahogany, and the pocket door purred softly past the triple crown molding and into the wall. There was the dining room I had secretly spied—how long ago? An oblong table was laid with white linen, polished silverware, and more glasses than necessary. The room was empty.

"I had no idea this was here," I lied.

"That is the idea," Hubert said. "Our kitchen is so small."

"Do you eat here every day?" I asked.

"Only on feast days."

We sat side by side at the table and soon a very young girl emerged through a swinging door that was flush with the walls. She was freckled and had an athletic body, with broad shoulders, defined calves, and a flat chest, yet she walked daintily, toes first. She wore scuffed bedroom slippers. She poured us water and wine and then tiptoed out. She returned with two bowls of clear broth.

"She looks like she was just let out of an Irish convent school," I said.

"Welsh," said Hubert. "We have a long-standing relationship with St. Bueno's-by-the-Waters. Each year they send us one of their orphans, and she works here for a year and then goes on to Fordham while another girl comes, so there is overlap."

"Are you serious? That sounds rather archaic. Like indentured servitude."

"Take my word for it. This club is the best thing that has ever happened to these girls," Hubert said.

"Are there really so many Welsh orphans?"

"Perhaps they use the word *orphan* loosely. Many of our girls have gone on to become pillars of New York society. One of them is seen nightly on television, minus her accent, alas. You would be surprised if I told you all."

"You are full of surprises." I sipped my soup.

"The soup is quite good here," Hubert said. "We used to have a cook who would only make dishes from a certain medieval recipe book, but he left us. I miss Gregor. You should have seen him in his starched white apron—he was so handsome. He's cooking in a monastery now. One can only envy the happy brothers." He smiled so sweetly. The creases at the corners of his lips were delicate brushstrokes.

"Don't you miss the monastery ever?"

"Eat your soup while it's hot," Hubert said. "How are your sons doing?"

"Great. Brilliantly."

"I look forward to meeting those two," Hubert said.

"Except for Ezra's sleeplessness. And the sleepwalking. He's a somnambulist, you know. The night troubles Ezra."

"And of course the famous Waldo. I look forward to his acquaintance. The inventive Waldo."

"How much have I told you about Waldo?"

"Quite a bit, my dear," Hubert said. "Not to worry, my dear. I respect the bonds of matrimony."

"Very funny," I said. The only sound was the delicate intake of soup. And the spoon's splashless entry into the bowl, like a perfect Olympic diver. "But I am worried about Waldo. About Waldo and a woman named Sheila. I probably shouldn't say anything to you about this, because you don't know Waldo and I wouldn't want you to think badly of him, because he really is so wonderful, and funny, and inventive and . . ."

"Sheila, you say?"

"Yes, do you know her?"

"I knew a Sheila once. She didn't believe me when I said I preferred men."

"All I know about this Sheila is that she prefers Waldo. If she exists."

Hubert said, "Are you going to start crying in your soup?"

"I should stop, shouldn't I?"

"Only if you want to. It may not be what you think."

The girl came out to remove our bowls. "What's your name?" I asked her.

"Christina," she answered. "I was named for Christina the Astonishing."

Christina returned with fish quenelles. They were whitish tubular blobs set in the middle of some very nice but slightly chipped English bone china plates and surrounded by a sauce only slightly less whitish. Hubert rubbed his hands together with hungry anticipation.

"What exactly are these?"

"Quenelles? You are in for a treat. They are baked fish mousse. Or occasionally, they are poached. But usually baked. Delicious!"

"What kind of fish?"

"That's the beauty of it—we never know."

"If you say so." I took a bite. They weren't bad, definitely tastier than fish sticks, but hardly worthy of Hubert's delight.

I chewed rather guardedly, leery of the presence of fish bones. For all her orphan-ness, Christina struck me as not likely to be vigilant about fish bones. Abuela had instilled in us a terror of death by fish bones. A childhood friend of hers, a young girl with hair down to her waist, had swallowed a fish bone and it had killed her. Abuela had demonstrated how her friend's eyes had popped out, how she'd gasped for breath, how her body had contorted, and how she'd fallen to the ground, lifeless, because of a fish bone. This demonstration preceded many meals of fish when Abuela was visiting in Santa Barbara. One of the great things about oysters is they have no bones.

"I'm beginning to think it's not a normal sleeplessness, but something else. Something external," I said.

"External to what?"

"To Ezra. What else?"

"Have you checked under his mattress?" Hubert said.

I imagined all the thin mattresses in all the cells in the monastery. "No. I mean, yes. There were no crumbs in the sheets."

"Perhaps there is a disturbance under the mattress. You've read *The Princess and the Pea*, haven't you?"

"A long time ago. We aren't exactly royals, you know."

"I merely suggest it because some people, myself included, keep things of value under their mattress, between the mattress and the box spring, if that is your bedding configuration. Relics and holy cards, for instance."

I said, "I don't think Ezra has any relics."

"Don't be too sure."

Christina was standing by the door, and her eyelids hovered halfway down her pupils. Her tilted stance suggested she might keel over any minute.

"Maybe Ezra's not the only one missing his beauty sleep," I said.

Hubert glanced in her direction, and said very softly, "She stays up all night writing her novel. Most mornings she tells me how many words she did the night before. She is diligent. And she says we're all in it."

"All? All who?"

"Well, me, of course. And the monsignor. Camilla Hyde. Our friend Señor Abelardo Llobet could have been in it, but the snow intervened. So perhaps you are. And others you don't know." He straightened himself in his chair and said in a louder voice, "There's something elemental, something instinctual perhaps, about keeping things under one's mattress. For better or worse, certain objects have powers."

"Like relics, you mean? Do you have any?"

"First-, second-, or third-class relics?"

Hubert looked wistfully at his plate as Christina cleared the table.

"Salad or sorbet?" she said.

"Salad, my dear," Hubert answered. "And remember what I said about tearing the lettuce leaves. There should be nothing on the plate too big for one's mouth."

"Oh, I get it," I said. "Every day is someone's feast day."

"Correct."

"You have lunch here every day?"

"Correct."

"Are you going to tell me about your relics?"

"Since you ask so nicely," he said. For just a moment I thought he was flirting with me. The moment passed. "I only have a few first-class relics. I cherish them."

"What exactly makes them so first class?" I asked.

"Their very existence. They are parts of the saints. Bones. And hair is also first class. But I have no sanctified hair."

"The hair on your head is just fine," I said. Inside I was recoiling. Dead hair—like those Victorian lovers' knots tied up in satin ribbon—revolted me. Bones, on the other hand, posed no such problem.

"So you have bones? Whose bones?"

"A finger bone of Bernard of Clairvaux. Not the whole finger, just part of his left ring finger. It is my treasure."

"Where does one acquire such a thing?"

"This was given to me by an aged nun in Brittany. It had been passed down in her family for generations, but they procreated less and less, and even when they did they often went into the convent or the priesthood, so finally there were no descendants left."

From behind the unsecret swinging door came a shattering crash, and then a thud. Hubert said, "Please excuse me," got up, and went through that door of mystery.

I was alone in the dining room. Was it strange that in all that time no one other than Christina had entered the room? That no one else had sat down to a meal of these overrated fish quenelles? I had not thought so until Hubert's departure. So there I was, not quite in tears amid the alien linen, silverware, and portraits. There I was, shifting from one butt cheek to the other on the cracked leather seats of the stiff-backed Gothic chairs. There

I was, running the pad of my index finger round and round the rim of my water glass, imagining all the tiny bone fragments that one finger could produce, imagining the leap of faith that the possession of relics had required in a world before DNA testing. I couldn't wait to tell Waldo about every tiny minute of this day and this lunch. It was about time he helped me figure out what I was doing at the Hagiographers Club, what I would do with all my notebooks full of color-coded notes, what was the point of it all, and what I would tell Abelardo. I would invite Hubert up to VerGroot so he could meet them all, and so they could hear about relics. Ezra and Henry would know what questions to ask. And clearly Gunnar was very mistaken. How could I have listened to him at all? Waldo loved me, loved our life, loved the boys. I would know if his affections were alienated. What was the alienation of affection? An alien was a foreigner, a stranger. Before she was naturalized, Mami had been a resident alien. I wanted never to be an alien, never alienated. Everything about our life was about being in it together, being citizens of the same world defined by our affections, our breakfast table, and our dogs.

On the street-side wall, between the deep-set windows with their tiny panes of glass, hung a painting of Saint Sebastian, that beautifully muscled naked young man pierced by arrows. His unearthly blue eyes looked heavenward. Was he seeking help against the pagans who surrounded him with their bows drawn? Was his mother there to see her beloved son's skin shot through, again and again? I knew that gay men loved images of Saint Sebastian, with his smooth skin, his pink lips, and his Roman nose, with his gently sloping shoulders and those shapely thighs. But why only gay men? I liked naked young men as much as anyone. It was somehow touching that this painting kept Hubert company every day at lunch. I couldn't wait to tell Waldo.

All day long I collected and stored up things to tell Waldo. I considered it one of my daily tasks. Was that why I came down to the Hagiographers Club? To entertain my beloved? To learn the stories of saints never encountered by Down East Episcopalians? Or to learn the story of Hubert? Did I keep coming back with some fantasy that I could have Waldo gasping for more?

The question would not have arisen if I were still sitting in my booth at WBLT and listening to the dreams of strangers. Or if I still regaled the girls of Precious Blood with the poetry of Gerard Manley Hopkins.

The silence from the kitchen was deafening.

How long had I been waiting? Long enough. If Ezra were here, he would be clamoring for more food, and stroking the dogs beneath the table, the imaginary dogs. If Henry were here, he would be able to hear every word spoken in the kitchen, assuming there were any words spoken, so sharp were his little ears. Either one would have said, *Mom, what's your problem? What are you waiting for? Just go find out.*

I pushed through the swinging door into a glaring white kitchen just as Hubert was coming out. We chest bumped, sort of. Just past his shoulder I saw the inverted cone of a light fixture hanging from the ceiling. It swung to and fro, casting an arc of light from one side of the room to the other, slowly, slowly. There was a wall of wooden cabinets painted white, and a large wooden counter in the center. Then I saw on the floor to my right, amid the green lettuce and red radicchio leaves, the shards of shattered china.

"Let's leave Christina to it, shall we?" Hubert said. And we did.

Across the room, in the portrait, Saint Sebastian's chest was moving, I felt sure of it.

"I don't think I've known anyone before who owned actual relics."

"You would be surprised. I think you would be very surprised," Hubert said. "There are so many. So many of them, and so many of us. The garments of the Little Flower, and Padre Pío, some wood chips of Marianna of Quito's coffin. One of my favorites is the dancing shoe of Blessed Humbeline. She's only a Blessed, but she was Bernard's sister, and she has the cachet of having been a reformed sinner. Oh, and lots more. You can't expect me to remember them all."

"Why not? And are those second- or third-class relics?"

"They're second-, because they belonged to the saint. Third-class relics are usually pieces of cloth that have touched the relics of a saint. You might say they are referred relics."

"What kind do you think Ezra has under his bed?"

Hubert chewed thoughtfully.

"Did I say he had a relic under his mattress? I think I merely suggested that were he to have a relic, he might very well hide it under his mattress. I would. And I do."

"I just worry that he's not getting enough sleep. Some people need a lot more sleep than others, and Ezra is one of them."

"Many of the suffering saints deprived themselves of sleep. For that very reason," Hubert said.

"What very reason?"

"In order to suffer. And you know what I think of the cult of suffering. But still, it is a well-known fact that sleeplessness can be the path to enlightenment, to visions."

"He's just a boy. He doesn't need enlightenment yet. He needs a good night's sleep."

The afternoon was wearing thin, and I was no closer to an answer. "Do you think Abelardo has relics?"

"I know he does," Hubert said.

"You didn't tell me," I said.

"You didn't ask. And I only just learned of them. The particulars."

"When did you talk to him?" I demanded. "Did he ask about me?"

"Yes and no."

I didn't trust myself to ask any more. I didn't trust myself to imagine what Abelardo kept between his mattress and box spring.

Did they even have box springs in Nicaragua? Before going home I said to Hubert, "Remind me to tell you what my mother-in-law said about Camilla Hyde."

I could never have allowed someone to leave on that note. The toleration of suspense was not my strong suit. I would have demanded an immediate revelation. I would have pleaded and cajoled. But not Hubert. He nodded sagely, as if he already knew and had always known.

18 ❧ How Grand Is Grand Central

WATER MAIN had burst and was flooding a subway tunnel in some distant part of the city, and because of that the northbound trains out of Grand Central were delayed. Sometimes it amazed me that I had come all the way from Santa Barbara to the eastern seaboard and that I regularly passed through the portals and hallways of Grand Central, that I could suggest meeting someone at Grand Central, that I could say I had been to or was going to Grand Central. It amazed me, and sometimes it allowed me to think that anything was possible; if I could become so familiar with Grand Central, and so intimate, then anything was possible. Even its name was implausible and presumptuous, or it would have been if the building were anything other than Grand Central. There was no specificity to it, no locating it in New York, in any city or state; it was not named for any famous person. It was simply Grand, and it was Central, as in the center of the world. I read the headlines and I contemplated fourteen different coffee drinks I could order; I sniffed flowers at the flower stand and then I went back to the kiosk to read more headlines. I stood on the balcony and looked at the gathering and separating, the threading and massing of the people in the great hall below. Colors spread and mingled. I could not say with scientific accuracy, but it seemed that almost as many women wore high heels as did not. That accounted for a lot of women stressing their ankles and hyperextending their calves, but it did look so lovely, it did impart a shape not possible in flat shoes. Beneath the glittering stars, I realized that high heels embodied the eternal conflict between beauty and comfort, the eternal link between beauty and pain. If Waldo could perfect the collapsing heel, he could surely make a fortune. So I thought.

I called Waldo to say I didn't know when I would get back, and he said he'd feed the boys mac and cheese again. They would be ecstatic. They would watch *The Simpsons* and eat mac and cheese, and Flirt and Dandy would lick their bowls clean. Even I longed for the comfort of mac and cheese.

It was long past dark when I finally got home. Gunnar was at the station, waiting for Deb. I hadn't seen her, either on the train or at Grand Central. But there she was, getting off the car just behind mine. So they gave me a ride home. As he shifted his car into gear, Gunnar said, "Two lovely ladies, returned from their urban adventures," which seemed to me a completely unnecessary comment. Deb asked me what I'd been doing in the city, and I said I'd been shoe shopping and then had had an early dinner with an old school friend whose husband had just died. Descending from the Sigerson vehicle, I realized I should have reciprocated with an inquiry about her day. But why? So she could lie back to me?

Upstairs, they all slept so soundly. Dandy snored beneath Ezra's bed, so I was certainly not going to disturb either one to search for an old finger bone. What exactly was I looking for? A relic of what?

Waldo was in bed, but not asleep. He was reading *One Hundred Years of Solitude.* I don't know how many times he had read that book. Often, he would read aloud his favorite parts to me, and they sounded so great that I would decide to finally read the book. But I could never finish it. That was one of the many differences between Waldo and me.

I went back downstairs, flipped through the Rolodex, and dialed León, Nicaragua.

"Abelardo Llobet, *por favor.*"

"He is not here. Is this Alice Fairweather?" a woman asked, in English.

"I am. Yes, it is."

"This is Carmen speaking. You have not yet met me, but I feel that I know you." Her accent reminded me of Mami's, which made no sense at all because they came from different countries on opposite sides of the ocean.

"Oh."

"Shall I give him a message when he returns?"

"Just say that I called, please. And regards from Hubert."

"From Alice, and Hubert. I'll tell him. He has meetings all week at the agriculture ministry," she said.

"How is he? Are his eyes okay? Is he warm enough?"

"Physically, he is back to himself. Physically."

"Good. I guess," I said. "Thank you. Goodbye."

"Isn't there anything else you want to ask? Ask anything you like," she said.

I could barely breathe. If I'd known what it was I needed to know, surely I would have asked it, but my mind had suddenly gone as white and blank as . . . as snow, of course. "I just don't know," I said.

"Alice? Will you say hello to Waldo for me, for Carmen?"

I went back upstairs, climbed into bed, and clung to his warm nakedness. He rolled over on his side; I curled around him and threw my left arm over his torso, opened my palm across his belly, gently probed his bellybutton.

"Waldo?" I said. "You've got to help me. Help me. Figure this out."

I nuzzled my face into his hair.

"Waldo?"

He slept, slept the deep sleep he claimed was dreamless.

• • •

Ezra yawned through breakfast. He yawned again and his features disappeared as his mouth widened into a chasm that could have swallowed everything else on his face.

"Tonight you'll sleep like a baby," I said. "I promise."

"Sure, Mom."

Waldo said, "Any more dreams, Henry?"

Henry glared at Waldo. "I never dream," he said.

"Whatever you say, Chief."

While Waldo invented great things, while Ezra and Henry sat in their classrooms with other itchy children, hamsters, gerbils, and God knows what and who else and counted the hours and minutes until the end of school, I entered Ezra's room. With trepidation, I pulled back his mattress. It seemed a terrible invasion of privacy, even a ten-year-old's privacy. Perhaps especially a ten-year-old's privacy, as his options for secret hiding places were more limited than an adult's. So I thought.

I don't honestly know what I expected to find: a dried-up old pea, a dead mouse, a dirty magazine, a nickel bag of pot, nothing at all. I did not expect to find a relic, a laminated holy card with a relic affixed to it, and that is exactly what I found. About six inches in from the edge, between the mattress and the box spring, was an ivory-colored card with a fuzzy photograph of an attractive woman with dark hair, intense eyes, and more intense eyebrows. I read: *Tristána Catalina Llobet Otanguez, 1896–1982*. Next to the date was a small dark square, smaller than my baby fingernail, smaller than a pea, which I realized was a piece of cloth. This, surely, was the relic. A second- or third-class relic, as I now knew. A piece of the fabric of an article of clothing of the much-bruited Tía Tata, upon whom so much rested, was causing all this trouble. That was what Hubert would have me think, and how could I think otherwise? Surely Abelardo had put it here. He must have put it here before the snowstorm. Or maybe the first night of the snowstorm. Possibly even the second night of the snowstorm, when he might have thought he needed this familial aid in order to get a decent night's sleep. It could only have been one of those two nights. And I could attest that this card, this relic, whatever it was, had not kept him from hypothermia, from snow blindness, from hurtling himself almost naked into a snowdrift.

On the back of the card was a prayer in Spanish, imploring the uncanonized Tristána's help in achieving greater closeness to the Almighty, and also pleading for good health.

I may have been Catholic in my youth, and for all I knew I still was, but this was a mystery to me. This was animistic and totemic, and compelling. I would demand that Waldo explain it to me. He would not, and then I would ask Hubert. The person I needed to ask was Abelardo. This was what I should have asked Carmen. Maybe Carmen knew this was what I should have been asking her.

"I think I may have contributed to the obsolescence of petroleum today," Waldo said as he delicately popped a broccoli floret into his mouth.

"No way, Dad," Ezra said.

"Way," Waldo said.

"You're not serious, are you?" I said.

"Somewhat. We're very close to perfecting the Compost-Car."

"You mean the Offal-Ator? The Garbage-Mobile?"

"That name got nixed, Chief. I told them it was your top choice, and on that basis alone, the brains in advertising took it off the shortlist. Eight-year-olds don't buy cars," Waldo said.

"But we will some day," Henry said. "They're not thinking ahead."

I said, "How are you doing with the collapsing high heels? The more I consider it, the more I think this could be your great work of genius. Your contribution to the world. Women and their ankles all over will cherish your memory."

"Do I really want to be remembered for facilitating silly pointy shoes?"

"Silliness is in the eye of the beholder," I said. "Besides, lots of people are remembered for all sorts of silly but useful inventions."

"I don't know, Al."

"Don't do it just for me. I thought you were enjoying the project. Did something—or someone—come along and sour your opinion of high heels?"

"Stop it, Al. Nothing of the sort," Waldo said.

"Stop it, both of you," Henry said.

"They think we should stop bickering," Waldo said to me.

"We're not bickering," I said. "We're discussing."

"I'm tired," Ezra said. The heaviness of his eyelids was palpable. The arms of Morpheus beckoned.

"You'll sleep better tonight," I said. "I have a good feeling about it."

Waldo gave me the Look. He had many looks, but they were all called the Look. This one said, *Don't make promises you can't keep.* I liked to think that I knew all his looks, that I knew the difference between *Let's go home now and screw up a storm* and *I hate this guy's guts;* between *Stop while you're ahead* and *Do not, under any circumstances, repeat what I just told you;* between *I love and adore you* and *I can't stand you.* I liked to think I knew all his looks, and he knew all mine, and that such intimate and exclusive knowledge was a foundation rock of our marriage. I liked to think that there was no one else in the world with whom he could communicate so well, so wordlessly.

"More broccoli?" I asked in general. "The pork chops are gone."

"Flirt hates broccoli," Henry said.

"How about some more salad?" I said to Ezra. "Remember about lettuce being soporific?"

"No," he said, with finality.

"What's for dessert?" Waldo asked.

"Since when are you asking about dessert? You don't even have a sweet tooth."

"But he has a sour tooth," Henry said and cracked up laughing. His laughter cascaded over him; he chortled and snorted and tiny green pieces of broccoli flew out of his mouth.

"That's not exactly funny, Chief." Waldo was sonorous, as if relating, with deep regret, the death of an aged but fondly remembered great-aunt.

"It's funnier than the riddles he made up in nursery school," I said.

"Why did the turtle cross the road? Because he saw a chicken," Ezra recalled.

"That's not as bad as I remembered," Waldo said. "Keep it up, Chief. Who knows? Maybe one day you'll tell a real joke."

I was fluffing my pillows, as I fluffed my pillows every night before squashing them into lumps that had the texture of wet newspapers. I loved my old down pillows. I traveled with them whenever possible. I knew, because Waldo had told me, that they were filled with pillow mites, that they harbored millions and possibly billions of microscopic creatures that lived in dead feathers and did nothing all day long but eat dander, excrete, breed, and die. According to Waldo, 10 percent of the weight of a two-year-old pillow was composed of dead pillow mites and their droppings. But he did not tell me if my twenty-year-old pillow was composed of 1,000 percent pillow mites. Waldo said that if I bothered to look at a pillow mite under a very strong microscope I would see something that would most certainly revolt me: the ovoid creature had a tough and translucent shell, eight hairy legs, no eyes, and no antennae. I could not imagine any circumstances under which I would look at a pillow mite under a microscope. I had coexisted with the pillow mites for forty-odd years, and if they were an essential part of my old down pillows, then so be it.

"Waldo," I said. "There's something I need to talk to you about, that we need to talk about."

"Honey, it's too late to grapple with our issues."

"It's never too late to deal with our issues," I said. What issues did he mean? The same ones I meant? Would it help if there were a Saint Sheila?

"You just say that because you're wide awake tonight. Did you take uppers or something?"

"I found a holy card under Ezra's mattress. That's what."

"What is a holy card?"

"Oh, come on, Walds. Don't tell me you've never seen one. When you and Lalo were roommates," I said.

"Honey, we were roommates at Harvard, not the seminary. We drank together, we played Wiffle Ball, we rowed, we played indoor soccer. Sometimes we talked about girls and existentialism and sports and girls, and even, on occasion, liberation theology. But never, to my recollection, did holy cards cross our lips."

"We used to get them at Sunday school when we were kids."

"I guess we didn't have them in Maine."

I said, "It has nothing to do with what state you're in."

"I beg to differ," Waldo said. "Your state of mind counts for everything."

"Whatever," I said. "And some holy cards have relics attached, little pieces of cloth. I just learned about those from Hubert. And—" I paused for dramatic effect. "I just found such a card under Ezra's mattress."

"So?"

"So? So, Ezra hasn't been able to sleep lately. And Abelardo must have put it there. It has a picture of his Tía Tata, who isn't even a saint yet. Not even close. And, and, a piece of cloth is stuck to it. Probably some fragment of her underwear. A relic. Or it would be a relic, if she were a saint. Which she is not."

"And you think this is why Ez has been having trouble sleeping?"

"He's never had trouble sleeping before. Except when he sleep-walks, which is a kind of sleep anyway. This is totally different."

"You think Abelardo put this holy card under the mattress in order to disturb Ezra's sleep?" Waldo said. His head sank back on his foam pillows, nice hygienic foam pillows with no resident pillow mites.

"Things affect Ezra that don't affect the rest of us. You know that," I said. It was true. Sometimes it was as if Ez were missing the last layer of skin that protected the rest of us. He was so tender. Tender on the giving and the receiving end of things. He felt a change in the weather, a breeze, a drop in the temperature before it happened. Once in the middle of the night there was a small earthquake, four point something on the Richter scale, with its epicenter on the other side of the Hudson, and Ezra felt it. He came in to tell us the house had just shivered. Of course we assumed it was a dream until we heard on the news the next day that the tremor had occurred moments before he'd come into our bedroom, all soft and warm in his spaceship pajamas.

"Yup. He's more sensitive than a seismograph. I just don't think this is the problem with his sleeping."

"Then how about this?" I said. "How about we wait and see tomorrow how he slept tonight? I'll bet you anything he will be fine."

"Anything?"

"Anything," I said.

"Five blowjobs. Whenever I want them," Waldo said.

"Within reason," I said. "I don't do BJs at your mother's. Not in those bunk beds."

"Granted."

"Good," I said. "And I get the converse. Or is it the obverse? Whichever. Because I'm going to win this one."

"Al, I hate to say this—" Waldo said.

"No, you don't. If you hated to say it, you wouldn't say it," I said.

"Fine. I'm delighted to tell you I think you're taking this all too far."

"Is this because I don't have a job anymore? Because I got sacked twice? You wouldn't say this if I had a real job," I whinged.

"That's another thing you're taking too far, the job thing."

"Don't patronize me," I said. "I'm going to invite Hubert up here for dinner. It's time you all met him. He was the one who told me to look under the mattress, because that's where he keeps his."

"I can't wait," Waldo said. "Can I go to sleep now?"

We kissed. I rolled over and kneaded my pillow full of pillow mites one more time, and slept.

But apparently Waldo did not sleep right away. Apparently Waldo was creating poems in his head. I heard this:

> *"There was in León one holy dame*
> *She cured the hiccups to great acclaim*
> *But when she was dead*
> *Her panties were shred.*
> *An undressed corpse was that holy dame."*

"I love it, Waldo!" I said.

"Thanks, Al. But we both know it sucks."

"I don't think it sucks. I think it's amusing. I would give my little finger to be able to write limericks."

"Be grateful, Al. It's bad enough when you can't get 'Wake Up, Little Susie' to stop playing in your head. Imagine putting all of life into doggerel, counting the syllables, playing with rhymes. It's a curse."

"I think they're wonderful," I said. "If I had your talent, I wouldn't be so ungrateful."

"There was a young wife of VerGroot
Who simply did not give a hoot
When her poor husband pled
As he lay in his bed
For an end to limericks in VerGroot."

And then we slept. Or I slept.

Later, I don't know how much later, I felt his hand on my bottom and his lips at my ear. "Put your hand on my penis."

"Huh?"

"Now," Waldo whispered.

"You don't have to get huffy."

I felt his tongue on my earlobe and knew where we were headed. "Far from it. I can't sleep. I'm horny and I'm desperate."

"Sometimes desperation is a good thing. Focuses the mind."

He took my hand and put it where he wanted it.

"I'm going to win that bet," I said.

"Fine," Waldo said. "Just focus."

I touched his penis. It grew and it hardened, from a turtle egg to a new carrot. *There* was a miracle.

19 ⁊ The Olfactory Sense

BEFORE I COULD ASK Ezra anything at all, Posey
called.

"Alice, dear? Have you had any bears at your
house yet? I've just heard about all the troubles you've been having with bears. You must be careful with those dogs of yours. I
doubt they would be a match for a hungry bear. Or a mother
bear."

"We don't have bears, Posey," I said.

"Of course you do, I just read about it in the *Gazette*."

"I don't know what to say, then," I said. I turned to Ezra and
Henry. "Hey, guys, do we have bears? Have you heard of any
bears around here?"

Ezra raised himself up as tall as possible, curled his hands into
paws, and growled.

"They think not, Posey. But we'll be careful," I said.

"One bear went right into someone's kitchen—the family were
all still asleep upstairs, and they had *two little boys*." She said this
with Hitchcockian emphasis. "The bear ripped through the screen,
waltzed in, opened up the icebox, and ate all the leftovers."

"Posey?" I said. "You can't believe that."

"Believe what? What can't I believe? I read it in the newspaper."

"No bear would open a refrigerator door," I said.

"Why not? You don't think they would?"

"Why would they? They can't know there's food in the fridge.
Fridges don't smell like food. That is their point."

"Of course they know about iceboxes. What do you think they've learned in all these years living in our backyards?"

"Posey, I need to get the boys off to school."

"They really should give those boys more time off. I think this early-childhood education is vastly overrated."

"I think that's referring to nursery school. Ezra's in fourth grade, Posey. He's ten."

"I know how old they are."

Waldo sipped his powerful coffee like it was ambrosia, took the offered phone, and said, "I'd love to talk, Mother. But I have to get to work. No, any color but green."

Ezra was halfway out the door before I asked, "How did you sleep?"

"Fine, Mom. Gotta go. Today is Opposites Day." Just like that.

I won the bet.

Hubert was finally coming up the river to have dinner with us, but as I was cooking that afternoon, all I could think about, in stomach-wrenching detail, were the cooking disasters of evenings past. The blueberry-balsamic marinated trout that was metallically inedible, the squid-ink pasta that had triggered a life-threatening allergic reaction in Morton V. Smart, and always, always the bloody chicken. *Bloody chicken* in our family was shorthand for a meal that had gone terribly awry.

Not that I feared I might poison Hubert that evening. But I did worry that he might find us to be pedestrian heathens. Waldo might, just for fun, say something blasphemous about the concept of the Virgin Birth, that being one of his favorite credos to debunk. I was not worried about Ezra and Henry.

Foodwise, I decided on grilled salmon and saffron rice and stuffed tomatoes. The boys loved stuffed tomatoes as long as I didn't put anchovies in them. And strawberries for dessert, because they were good for the complexion.

I called Waldo at work and asked him to stop and get charcoal on his way home. We were out of charcoal. We were always out of charcoal, and yet I never remembered to get charcoal.

"Couldn't you just cook it in the broiler?" he said.

"No. Waldo, please. This is important."

"Why such a tizzy? You make dinner on a regular basis. It's always fine," he said.

"I'm not in a tizzy. But he's never met any of you before. I want him to have a good time."

"Listen, Al, this guy lives alone with pictures of his dead lover, and has no one to talk to except the saints. How could he not have a good time? Of course he'll have a good time."

"Is that the impression I've given you? That he's some kind of mournful recluse? He talks to people at the club every day. No wonder I'm in a tizzy."

"But you're not in a tizzy."

"Correct," I said.

Waldo came home in time with the charcoal, and the boys, dirty and hungry and filled with secret glee, returned with Dandy and Flirt from wherever they had been, and then I went to pick up Hubert at the 7:02.

Everything was fine. The boys bathed without too much discussion. The grill did not go up in flames. The food was edible. The salmon was not incinerated.

I said to Hubert, "I've been meaning to tell Ez and Henry about Christina the Astonishing."

Hubert said, "The saint, or our friend in the dining room?"

"What is so astonishing about her?" Henry said.

"She was dead and then at her own funeral she levitated up to the ceiling of the church and sat in the rafters. She couldn't stand the stink of other human beings, so she stuck her head in the oven," I said.

"It is often pointed out, by pedants and others, that hygiene in the Middle Ages was notoriously lacking," Hubert said. "But to my mind, it has always been more than mere body odor that repelled her."

Ezra and Henry locked eyes, then averted their eyes from each other's. But the damage was done. They burst out laughing, and I knew exactly why. Those two words, *body odor*, were as amusing as any pie in the face. In the case of those particular words, it was more than just the reference to physicality that set off their reaction; there was the triple repetition of the *o*, and then the two hard-*d* sounds in the middle, as well as its iambic perfection.

"Did I say something funny?" Hubert said.

"No," Waldo and I said, more or less simultaneously.

Henry and Ezra said in unison, "Yes!"

"Oh, dear," Waldo said. "I'm afraid Christina might have found the company at this table objectionable." And then he held his nose.

I couldn't believe this was happening. The dogs must have farted, and the smell was—as Waldo said—objectionable. What did Emily Post suggest one should do in the presence of a fart? Pretend it hadn't happened. Do not draw attention to it. Surely she would say to most definitely not mention it. But Waldo, Ezra, and Henry were in the habit of mentioning such things, as well as classifying them.

"Where are the dogs?" Waldo said, and leaned down to look under the table. "Dandy! Flirt! You're going outside right now!"

They were not under the table. They were not in the room. I remembered then that I had put them outside before we'd started dinner. Whatever the provenance of the objectionable fart, it was neither Dandy nor Flirt.

"Yes," Hubert said. "Where are those beautiful dogs?" He turned to the boys. "Your mother is constantly speaking of those dogs and her attachment to them. Far more than she speaks of you two."

There was a weird silence. Hubert said, "I was just kidding. Your mother is admirably devoted."

Waldo came to the rescue. He said, with no apparent effort,

"Saint Christina was an astonishing lass.
She spoke at her own funeral mass
And rose up to the rafter
But it's what she did after
That caused all the hoo-ha and fracas."

Henry jiggled in his seat and said, "Way to go, Dad."

"How remarkable," Hubert said. "I don't think I've ever heard a limerick about a saint before. This opens up wonderful new possibilities."

Waldo said, "Alice can't abide it when I make up limericks."

I protested, "You know that's untrue. I love them. In my opinion, we don't hear them near enough."

Henry muttered, "Yes, we do."

"I had a dream last night," Ezra said. "Do you want to hear it?" Waldo and I stared in shared shock and surprise. In front of a stranger? This was something wonderful and strange indeed.

Ezra carefully laid his knife and fork onto his plate, in perfect alignment, and launched into the dream. "I am walking down the road toward Bogumila's house. A family of tall, skinny stick people lives there. There are rabbits on the road. They keep hopping in and out of the road, back into the woods and then back onto the road."

"Ezra has a thing about rabbits," Henry explained.

Waldo waved his hand distractedly. "Quiet, Henry. Let him finish."

"I didn't know you have a thing about rabbits," I said. How could I not know he had a thing about rabbits? Wasn't it the very nature of having a thing that everyone knew about it? Had I not been paying attention?

"You too," Waldo said. "Quiet."

"So there were rabbits in the road. It was a room at Gran's house. Dad was taking the pieces out of a combination clock-toaster, and then he was lying down and I wanted to talk to him. He was using a rabbit as a pillow. So I opened my mouth to say something very loud to make him wake up and let the rabbit go, but no sounds came out and then the rabbit opened his eyes and said that I should be quiet."

We all just sat there.

"Does anyone want more salmon? Or rice? There are more tomatoes."

"I'd like more of everything," Hubert said.

"That's quite a dream you had there, Ez," Waldo said. "It's too bad you can't call in to that excellent radio show that used to be on the air."

"I think it's really different to hear the dream of someone you actually know, and love," I said.

"Different from what?" Hubert said.

"From hearing the dreams of strangers. Strangers you can't even see."

Waldo said, "Which do you think you can make more sense of?"

"No question," I said. "A stranger's. With Ezra, or you, or anyone else I know, I can't keep myself from trying to figure out who is who and what it means."

"Remember Saint Melangell?" Hubert asked.

"Fifteen years in the forest? How could I forget?"

"The hare. The hare signifies in her iconography."

"Of course! I meant to tell Waldo, so he could rhyme *hare* and *prayer*."

Waldo said, "How about *beware* and *underwear*? How about —oh, forget it!"

Ezra said, "Is there dessert?"

"Strawberries and cream."

"Mom said you were an expert in saints who got their heads cut off," Henry said. "Is decapitation a common form of sainticide?"

"That's quite good, *sainticide*," Hubert said. "But it can't really apply because, you see, someone can only become a saint after he or she is dead. For at least fifteen years. So you can't kill a saint. You can, however, kill someone who will become a saint. Decapitation *was* quite popular in early Christianity. Diocletian was rather fond of it. But he certainly didn't invent it. Anyway, we just say *martyrdom,* period."

"Where did you hear about this?" Waldo said.

"Mom told us," Ezra answered.

"I assume she was referring to the cephalophores. I have something of a penchant for the cephalophores."

"Exactly," Henry said with delight. "That's what Mom called them too."

"I am working just now on an article about the Forty Monks of Magul. Perhaps you would like to hear about them?"

"Go for it," Henry said.

I had wanted this dinner to go off well, and I had wanted the boys to like Hubert, but now I was just a little unnerved because they seemed to like him so much. They seemed ready to tell him anything, things they might never have told me, and ready to hear anything, happily. Nor had Hubert ever told me about these monks.

Hubert began, "I am fond of this story because it is such a wonderful example of the miracle of cephalolalia, the speaking of a severed head. We believe it took place on August the fourteenth, which would mean that the monks were singing the first vespers of the Feast of the Assumption. I am sure such brainy young boys as yourselves know what the Assumption is"—they shook their heads woefully—"and as I said, there were forty monks at the monastery of Magul. As they were antiphonally singing their vespers, a band of bloodthirsty heretics broke into the church and cut off their heads. All forty heads. Having completed their heinous crime, then all their ransacking and pillaging, the heretics departed. The monks picked up their fallen heads, and those heads completed the singing of the vespers, back and forth, from one side of the chapel to the other. When they were finished, the monks laid their severed heads down upon the ground, and died their glorious martyrs' deaths."

Ezra and Henry were transfixed, and then Ezra said, "Could that really happen?"

"Chips off the old block," Hubert said.

"I don't think so," Ezra said. "*We* don't think so. But we're not saint people."

Hubert said, "No, you're not hagiographers. Are you asking if a hagiographer believes such a thing is possible? It can be true legend without being true history. I personally believe in miracles. Not all miracles. But always the possibility for miracles."

"Strawberries, anyone? I'll let you put the cream on yourselves."

"I'd rather put the cream on the strawberries," said Waldo. "If it's all the same to you."

"Very funny," I said. I turned to Hubert. "You can see the abuse I take."

"Why are the dogs barking?" Waldo said.

"Are they barking? I don't hear anything," I said.

Ezra said, "I'll go see."

"Can I eat his strawberries?" Henry said.

"You may not," I said.

Ezra went out the back door and into the darkness. As soon as we stopped talking, we could all hear the dogs barking. Ezra shouted, "Flirt got skunked. It's gross."

Waldo got up and went outside, muttering, "Damn, damn, damn that dog. She always has to stick her nose up a stinky asshole."

We heard him calling the dogs, and then he yelled, "Don't come outside. It's pretty bad. Al, we need tomato juice, and the stuff."

238

The stuff he needed was feminine hygiene spray. It worked better than tomato juice, but Waldo refused to buy it at our drugstore. I always made a point of telling the pharmacist, Larry Nachtagal, who had filled prescriptions for our family for years, that it was for the dogs. I told Waldo he too could easily explain it was for the dogs. He insisted that by explaining, I was only drawing attention to myself, and anyone in his right mind would assume that the feminine hygiene spray was indeed for me, and that I didn't even have dogs.

I certainly did not intend to pronounce the words *feminine hygiene spray* in front of Hubert.

Flirt wasn't very smart about skunks. I had to think that smarts had something to do with it, since Dandy never got skunked when she did. He stayed out of the way while Flirt barged right in, nose first. Poor brave Flirt: dashing home with stinging eyes, a face full of toxic odors, and her fur imbued with the bitterness of it.

Waldo was outside with Flirt, the tomato juice, the feminine hygiene spray, the hose, and a bucket. The boys stood on the back steps watching the unsavory process from a safe distance, and I delivered sponges and scrub brushes to Waldo. Just for a while, I forgot all about Hubert.

After two thorough washings of Flirt, Waldo said, "It's still pretty bad. There is no way she can sleep inside tonight."

Ezra said, "But Dad! What about the coyotes?"

"What about them?"

"We saw a coyote just yesterday. They like to eat dogs, you know."

"Only puppies," Waldo said.

I returned to the kitchen and saw Hubert gripping the table's edge with white-knuckled fingers. His face was mottled with red blotches, like an uneven sunburn. His beard had levitated up his chin. Oh, shit, I thought, he's allergic to salmon. I've never heard of anyone being allergic to salmon.

"What's the matter?"

"Is there a train any time soon?"

"In about thirty minutes, but if you're having a reaction we need to get you to the ER for some epinephrine."

"I'm afraid I am reacting rather badly. To the skunk."

"Oh," I said, unreasonably relieved.

He got up unsteadily, and looked around. "Is there a bathroom nearby?"

I showed him the way upstairs and then returned to the action out back. I said to Waldo, "Hubert is upstairs heaving, I think."

"Sensitive sort."

Henry said, "Is he barfing his brains out?"

"Quiet, Henry," I said. "We're not going to mention it when he comes down."

Ezra said, "He might like you to mention it. He might want to tell us all about it."

"You mean the way you do, Ez?" Waldo said.

A smile crept over his lower face. "Yes, just like that."

Hubert returned. The red blotches were gone and he was whiter than fresh snow.

"Shall we go to the train now?" he said. Hubert smiled weakly at Waldo and the boys. "This has been a most delightful meal. I am so gratified to have finally met you all. I'm sorry that we did not have the opportunity to discuss your friend Abelardo. I think it would have been so enlightening. But alas, that will have to wait for another time."

"It's a shame about the skunk," Waldo said. Hubert cringed at the word. "Unfortunately, Flirt is a bit stupid about skunks. We're all getting used to it, I'm afraid. Probably not a good sign."

"I could never get used to it," Hubert said. "I have an unfortunately sensitive nose, and a problem with stenches."

Ezra said gleefully, "Like Christina the Astonishing!"

Henry said, "Can you levitate?"

Waldo said, "That's enough, you guys."

Then Ezra asked when he would be coming back. "God only knows," Hubert replied.

We drove almost the whole way to the station without a word. I wanted to inquire after his well-being but could not figure out how to do it without reference to either skunks or vomit, so I said nothing at all. It was Hubert who broke the silence.

"Your sons are remarkably sanguine, my dear."

"Huh?"

"I have an ancient horror of skunks. Did you know that skunks can shoot their odoriferous liquid up to twelve feet? And they have exceptional aim." He shook his head as if considering yet another example of human fallibility.

"They've gotten Flirt a few times. More than tonight."

Hubert leaned slightly forward in his seat. He appeared to be scanning the road for obstacles. Then we parked at the station, and while we were waiting he told me a long and rambling story of getting sprayed by a skunk one night after an argument with Martin, who had locked him outside their cabin, and how miserable he'd been. Though it ended up being a pivotal moment in their relationship. Eau de skunk was for Hubert the diabolical equivalent of Proust's madeleines. After the incident with the skunk and Martin, Hubert had burned all the clothes he'd been wearing.

I leaned forward and inadvertently hit the horn button on the steering wheel. *Honk!* pierced the silence in the car, shattered the darkness, and startled us both.

"Sorry," I said. "Here comes the train." The twin lights were bearing down from the north.

"Please tell your sons I do not resemble Christina the Astonishing in any significant way."

"Consider it done," I said.

The train groaned to a stop. Hubert embarked and said, "Will I be seeing you at the club soon?"

"Where else would I go?" I asked. The question was not rhetorical.

"Nicaragua?" Hubert said. The train pulled away and drowned us out.

The boys must have prevailed on Waldo to let Flirt sleep inside, because when I got home she was asleep on an old towel in the kitchen, with the door shut.

20 ❧ Half the State of Maine Is Serious

WALDO BROUGHT ME COFFEE the next morning. "Flirt still stinks," he said. It was barely six.

"Oh, the ambient air, how it stunk,
And put Dandy and Flirt in a funk.
But who would have thunk
That a black and white skunk
Could cause such distress to a monk?"

"That is nothing short of brilliant," I said. The morning was pinkish in color. Grackles and swallows were singing back and forth, or antiphonally, as Hubert would say.

"You're losing your grip, Al."

"Why shouldn't I like your rhymes?"

"Because they drive me nuts. How would you like to have misspent your youth thinking of rhymes for *Trojan* and *anatomy* and *marijuana?*"

"*Nitrogen? Lobotomy?*" I said. "See how helpful I could be?"

"It's a curse. I put Flirt out. Don't let her back in today."

"I should call Hubert today. To make sure he's okay. What do you think?"

"Give him a day off, is what I think," Waldo said.

What I did not say was my dream. I dreamed that Abelardo and I were eating fruit off a helium-filled tray, and I watched him bite into a strawberry with bright green flesh. Electric green. He'd said, "Maybe your cherry will be blue."

It should have felt strange not to tell Waldo my dream, but I did not even want to. I wanted to tuck it somewhere safe and secret.

Then it was the evening. The pine planks of the kitchen table were rutted and worn smooth with use; the stains were a Braille guide to the history of our meals and the reinvention of the wheel.

Waldo was catapulting red and green grapes from a spoon, and then a fork. This worked only when the utensil had a sufficiently arched handle. First he placed a green grape on the handle end of a spoon lying on the table, and then he hit the bowl of the spoon and sent the grape flying. He marked where it landed with a small green Post-it. He repeated the operation with a red grape, and then again with both colors of grape but using a fork.

"I don't know the relative density of the grapes," he said. "And I haven't even bothered to weigh them. But it's important to see if there is a difference."

"You always have to have an extra set of variables, don't you?" I said, because suddenly it seemed true.

"I'm just trying to set up controls for the experiment," Waldo said.

"Waldo, we need to talk," I said.

"Talk away. We have nothing much to do except prepare for my only brother's wedding, an event which I hear has flummoxed half the state of Maine."

"Please be serious," I said.

"Half the state of Maine *is* serious."

"Waldo!"

"Sorry, I'm all ears." Whenever he said this, and it was something he'd said regularly over the years, Waldo took hold of his lobes and flapped them back and forth.

"So what is going on, and who is Sheila?" I said.

"You asked me about Sheila a while back. I don't know any Sheilas."

"Fine. The woman you're seeing. She-who-is-not-me."

He said softly, "Her name is Shirley."

"Shirley? Not Sheila?"

Waldo's voice was positively sepulchral. "It's just a name."

"Fuck, fuck, fuck you. I almost let myself believe everything was okay because you said there was no Sheila. Fuck you. Fuck everything."

"Everything *is* okay," Waldo said. "This is not the end of the world." It wasn't entirely or even almost true that I'd believed everything was okay. It was true that I'd played mental games, constantly weighing, on some imaginary scale of justice, the possibility of a real-life Sheila against the possible damage of driving Waldo away with my paranoia. After Edith Dilly, and after the end of the Edith Dilly affair, I had been hypervigilant and even, for a time, afraid of the dark. I'd thought I'd wanted Waldo to be sorry, terribly sorry, but the few times he'd mouthed those words, it was such terrible acting—like Unfelt Bathos—that I relinquished the thought. And finally, it was exhausting to be so miserable, and Waldo was so tender to me, passionate and funny, often simultaneously. So we went on, and I had reined in the melodrama. So I believed.

"Then what is it the end of?"

"It's not the end of anything," Waldo said.

I said, "How about the end of you and surely Shirley?"

"There was never an *and* between me and Shirley."

"Please don't get grammatical," I said. "Is there an *and* between *fuck* and *suck*?"

Next to the catapulting fork and spoon was a knife that had not been part of the experiment. I picked it up and balanced it lengthwise on the tip of my index finger.

"You see this knife?" I said. "I don't know whether to use it on me or you."

"Put it down, Al," Waldo said. "It's a butter knife, for Christ's sake."

"You're always the voice of reason, aren't you? You think I'm hysterical," I blubbered.

Upstairs all was silent. I had not said good night to either of the boys, a serious omission.

Waldo said, "Al, I never claimed to have a lock on reason. You're putting words in my mouth. Again. I wish you'd stop telling me what I'm thinking."

"Fine, fine, fine. I don't know what you think. I just know that whatever you're thinking, it makes me feel terrible that you love this Sheila/Shirley. I want to know about her."

"Don't you think it would be better to know nothing?"

"No. And even if it were, I don't care."

Sometimes it was shocking how a house filled with children and dogs, as well as uninvited rodents and insects, and surrounded by a countryside full of nocturnal creatures, hungry owls and roaming skunks, could be so terribly, terribly silent.

"Who is she?"

"Someone from the office. Not this office, from the Texas office. She'll be going back there soon."

"You're having an affair with someone from Texas?"

"Don't be that way, Al."

"What way?"

"Snide."

"Do you love her?" I said.

"Al, I love you. I'll always love you. But you're not a child and I can't tell you that everything will always be fine, because I don't know that."

"What about Ezra and Henry? Are you going to abandon them too?"

"I'm not abandoning anyone!"

"Just tell me if you love her." My nose was running the way it always did when I cried.

Waldo sat very still, and I cried noisily. He had never been particularly responsive to crying, one way or the other, but it felt better to cry. It was something I wanted to do.

"No," he said. "I don't love her. We have sex. I'm not proud of myself. It was a mistake. Honestly, Al. This—you—are what I want. Please let me make it up to you."

"You sound like a fucking contrite politician."

"That was low."

"You deserve it. I don't want you to see her again. Not ever."

"She's in the office, Al."

"I don't care. I don't care if she's the men's room attendant."

Suddenly I was squeezed dry as last year's toothpaste.

"Can we go to bed, Al? I promise you, this will be fine."

"Fuck you."

"I know."

Crying is like sex in this one way, that I always sleep well afterward. Or maybe it's not *well*, maybe it's just very deeply, deeper than the Marianas Trench, deeper than the Mammoth Caves, deeper than Hegel and Kierkegaard put together.

Then it was the evening before the day before Dick's wedding to Sydney. The rehearsal dinner was on Friday night at the yacht club, and the wedding was on Saturday in the nineteenth-century stone church on Slow Island, where Sydney's family had a house, a bunch of houses, and some of them had indoor plumbing. We were not optimistic about the weather. Winter lingers for a long time in Maine, and then it segues into a spring that is often indistinguishable from winter except that it is muddier. But not always.

Following upon spring comes blackfly season, also known as June. Only the tropics had bugs bigger than Maine's. Except, so I was told, on Slow Island. According to Waldo, who probably heard it from Posey, the wedding was being held this particular weekend in June so that Sydney—and Sydney's mother, the formidable Gabriela Sweet—could be sure that Cousin Harold would not show up. Harold had been in love with Sydney since they were young, but now he was a terrible drunk who had a penchant for making scenes at family events and complaining bitterly about the terms of his grandfather's will. He also had a permit to carry a gun. But Harold was brilliant as well, and that week in June he would be in Los Angeles filming *Jeopardy!* That date had been set and confirmed months ago; his mother, Sydney's Aunt Grace, a morose widow, had promised that Harold would be safely on the other side of the continent. If Sydney and Gabriela knew one thing, it was that Harold had long harbored the ambition to compete on *Jeopardy!* and win a fortune to compensate for the one he had been so cruelly cheated of.

Waldo flew up a day early to be with his brother and then go to the rehearsal dinner. I packed the boys' new suits. I wrote out the instructions for Dandy's medications for Bogumila, who had agreed to keep the dogs. This was a huge volte-face for her. For years she'd refused to let the dogs into her yard, on account of her precious chickens. Now, although her chickens were still precious, she had changed her mind, and not one of us knew why. Although I had my suspicions; I thought a fox was involved.

The night before the boys and I left, Ezra walked in his sleep, all the way down to the basement. I would never have known, and certainly he would never have known, had he not walked directly into Waldo's model for the Home Harvest-Helper, the pieces of which stood in angry disjuncture in front of his workbench. It was meant to be Dick's wedding gift, once it was perfected.

I didn't hear the crash, I regret to say, but I heard Flirt barking, and continuing to bark, and after her barks had entered my dream and morphed into a distant stormy ocean we were trying to reach, I finally woke up and knew something was wrong. I found Ezra seated at the kitchen table drinking milk from a coffee mug. Above his left eye was a scrape oozing delicate red droplets.

21 ❧ A Wedding on Slow Island

IT WAS LATER THAN I'd planned when we arrived at Catamunk. After playing several rounds of My Grandmother's Trunk and then counting all the Moose X-ing signs past the border, Ezra and Henry had finally fallen into sleep.

All was silent when we arrived at Posey's. I lugged the boys inside, tucked them in, and went upstairs. It didn't matter how carefully I tiptoed, the stairs always creaked. I climbed into the top bunk in Waldo's old room. He slumbered noisily on the bottom one.

Once, long ago, I had told Waldo I thought it odd that not only did he still sleep in the bunk bed of his youth, but I was expected to sleep in it as well. "Other people graduate to bigger beds—double beds, for instance—when they grow up and get married. That is normal."

Waldo had said he liked his bunk bed, and that I could have the top bunk any time I wanted.

"What I want," I'd said, "is to sleep in the same bed with you."

He'd said, "But we do that every night. This will spice up our nightlife."

"Well, at least you didn't say *our sex life*," I'd said.

Strangely, I came to like the bunk beds too. When I climbed the rickety ladder to the top bunk, into that secret space between the musty linen and the ceiling, the years dropped away. I don't know exactly what age I dropped to, but I know it was an age before responsibilities. I slept well up there in the stratosphere.

It seemed late when I awoke, up there in the stratosphere, and I panicked. Not Waldo. Waldo did not move when I climbed down from the top bunk and almost stepped on his face. He did not move when I knocked over the rickety bedside table with my flailing foot. The table fell to the floor. A splintered board came loose from its back, and its single drawer fell open and spilled its contents.

Finally Waldo moved and turned his head to look at the commotion. "Amazing," he said. "That drawer has been stuck closed for years."

Scattered across the rutted wooden floor and the worn carpet were the ace of spades, the ten of hearts, an opened package of Viceroy cigarettes, one of those plastic eggs containing Silly Putty, and two Sheik brand condoms. What had not spilled out were two hard candies that had melted and were eternally adhered to the bottom of the drawer. Sheiks were not Waldo's brand.

Posey was in the sunny yellow kitchen, finishing up the breakfast dishes. She looked me up and down and up again.

"Have you seen the boys this morning?" I said.

"Not only have I seen them, but I fed them breakfast hours ago. Ezra is a brave little man."

"Do you know where they are?"

"With Mr. Cicero."

"And where is Mr. Cicero?"

"They went down to the beach. They needed to collect rocks."

I poured myself some coffee. Posey said, "Mr. Cicero has given up all caffeinated beverages. Soon ice cream will be his only indulgence. I don't think I will be able to stand that. We Fairweathers have always been leery of anyone too abstemious."

"He still drinks, doesn't he?" I said.

"Yes, of course," Posey said. "But that is not an indulgence. It's a social lubricant. Speaking of which. Does Waldo have a drinking problem these days?"

"Waldo? He hardly drinks at all. I tell him that red wine is good for the arteries, that it's why the French live long and healthy lives, but he is indifferent to my pleas."

"I do not ask this lightly," Posey said.

"Do I take it he drank too much last night?"

"He started off the evening so well, made a lovely speech about Dick and agriculture and Sydney as a flower, but then he just disintegrated. Lurched into his limericks. Now, I like limericks just as much as the next person, but it all depends on time and place. Last night was most assuredly not the time and place for Waldo's dirty limericks."

"They were dirty?"

"They were indeed," Posey said.

"I didn't know anything about them," I said. I was miffed. Why hadn't he shared them with me beforehand? "Do you remember them?"

"I should hope not," Posey said.

"That's too bad," I said. "I really like his limericks. It's a mysterious talent, but a good one."

Posey had a point to make, and she made it: "He was overserved."

"So let's let him sleep this morning. To be on the safe side. But what about Sydney? I know nothing at all about Sydney."

"Sydney is just as she should be. She will do wonders for Dick. She's already gotten him in a foursome at the club. And he's going to race in the midsummer regatta this year. He hasn't done that since he was thirteen."

"Dick's a member?" Now I was speechless. Dick had never shown the slightest interest in joining the yacht club. To the extent that he expressed an opinion about anything, he considered the Bug Harbor Yacht Club to be archaic, badly managed, bigoted, unimaginative, and engaged in nefarious horticultural practices.

"Since last week. Sydney's father was the commodore a while

back, and her grandfather as well, I think. Now one of her brothers is the second or third flag officer."

"I would have thought Dick was more likely to bite the head off a live python than to join the club."

Just then, and not a moment too soon, Mr. Cicero, Ezra, and Henry walked in, breathless, letting the screen door slam behind them.

"Mom! We got the best rocks," Henry said.

"They have these long flat rocks, like tiny skateboards with no wheels," Ezra said. "They'll be perfect."

"How's the cut, Ezra?" The butterfly bandages were stained and curling up at their edges. My fingers twitched to touch them, but I forbore.

"Excellent. Couldn't be better."

"He's a prince, is that young Ezra," Mr. Cicero said.

"Just be careful, okay?"

Posey said, "What did you do with all the rocks?"

"Don't worry. The rocks are under control. We have the situation under control. Don't we, boys?"

"We do indeed," Henry said.

I went to find Waldo. His brother was getting married very soon, and there was much to be done.

The Sweets had hired several Catamunk lobstermen and their boats to ferry guests over to Slow Island. People gathered at the yacht club and boarded the sturdy fishing boats (the *Leda-G, Jolly Mon,* and *Mary-Q*), incongruously fitted out with folding chairs on their decks. Slow Island was fifteen minutes, and a century, from the mainland.

Inside the stone chapel built ninety years ago to honor a Sweet who'd gone down with the *Titanic,* I cried. Sydney was beautiful in her grandmother's gown. How an athletic young woman (the club tennis champion and a former all-American lacrosse player) could fit in that gown harking back to a corseted generation was mystifying, or miraculous. Where was Susie to wonder with me? Not here. She was in VerGroot, researching chicken breeds on the Internet. I wept as Dick, resplendent in his monkey suit, and Sydney, in silk and lace, made their simple vows. I was still crying when they dashed outside. Waldo handed me a handkerchief and did something with his eye that resembled a wink. But Waldo wasn't a winker.

"Weddings always make me cry," I said.

"They make everyone cry," Waldo said. "Except me."

"It's not like that. I'm feeling sorry for myself. Here they are, full of love and hope, and here I am . . . You just don't get it, do you?"

"I get it, Al. I get it. Forgive me. I love you. With this ring I thee . . . Oh, Al. I can be such a shit."

"I know," I said.

"But I'm your shit, honestly," he said. I almost swooned with believing him.

Fairweathers, Sweets, and friends walked up from the chapel by the sea to the cottage. The sandy road swarmed with bridesmaids and flower girls. It wasn't a cottage at all but a rambling gray-shingled house with porches and verandas on every side, and a hexagonal tower with views of the cold Atlantic in every direction; it was all limbs and no torso. I anticipated flaking wicker chairs and abandoned paperback potboilers on the porches, then, inside, the comforting smell of rotting timber and mildewed books. Surely there would be warped jigsaw puzzles with views of the Alps, chipped duck decoys, and seashells giving up sand. Upstairs in the children's rooms, spongy old *National Geographics* and the missing puzzle pieces trapped in the gaps between the wide wooden planks.

"Don't you think it's a little strange that you barely know this woman?" I said. Waldo was fiddling was his cuff link.

"We have years to get to know her."

"Who's that?" I pointed to a handsome man who had what

must surely have been the best haircut in the state of Maine as well as a five o'clock shadow. He wore a dark suit and dark sunglasses.

"A Secret Service agent," Waldo said. "Don't point."

"You always say that. Seriously."

"Seriously," Waldo said.

"And pray tell, who is being protected here?" I said.

"That's the whole point. We don't know."

"Did you tell Dick about the mechanical harvester you made him?" I asked.

"Did I tell him it was in pieces back in New York? No."

All of a sudden it seemed I had missed more than a dinner. "Are you going to tell me what you said at the dinner last night?"

Posey of the never-failing radar materialized and asked if I knew where the boys were. I didn't. I took the hint and went in search while she parsed the Sweet genealogy with Waldo and Pompey. Pompey Fairweather was Posey's late husband's brother. He lived even farther up the Maine coast than Posey.

I wandered, air kissed and pecked club members to whom I'd been introduced countless times and still couldn't name. I found the boys behind the house with Mr. Cicero, next to a rusty wheelbarrow full of beach rocks. With admirable concentration they were placing the rocks on the ground. They appeared to have a plan.

Mr. Cicero said, "It's going to be a cairn. In honor of the newlyweds."

"I thought cairns were like gravestones. Somebody's going to be pretty upset."

"Dear Alice, give us the benefit of the doubt. The boys and I are creating a thing of beauty to commemorate this day. Cairns are often used as trail markers."

"Don't worry, Mom," Henry said. "It will be a thing of beauty."

Of course it would. How could I have ever doubted them?

Ezra looked pale and tired. I touched the now-fraying butterfly bandage with my fingertip. He said, "Mr. Cicero told those fruity flower girls that I got punched in a fight. He told them that the other boy is still in the hospital."

"You didn't?" I said.

Mr. Cicero nodded. "If anyone asks you what happened, tell them you're sworn to secrecy. Say you could tell them, but then you'd have to kill them."

Ezra grinned weakly.

Rounding the house, I almost slammed into a waiter balancing a tray of champagne glasses, shimmering vertical flutes of bubbles. He pressed one into my hand and floated off. It was delicious. And there was more of it. Perhaps there was an as-yet-undiscovered saint in the kitchen, turning salt water into champagne.

I longed to find Waldo. Was he still with Posey? I thought: Sheila—no, Shirley—probably has a mother too. They all have mothers. No, not all.

I drank more champagne. I stood at the edge of the lawn beside a vast hedge of rhododendrons and watched the black rocks that jutted up from the dark blue ocean.

"On a day like today it's hard to give credence to the terrible northeasters that roil up the waves and batter this shore." It was the Secret Service man.

"Really?" I said. I thought then that I should stop drinking champagne. But it went down so easily, more like the idea of itself than the reality.

He showed a vast number of teeth. They sparkled in the sunshine. "Or maybe you think that's just a line?"

"I was thinking about the champagne."

"Red wine is much better for you. The polyphenols are an antioxidant."

"I was just saying the same thing. About red wine, not the polyphenols."

"Some reports say that the resveratrol in the grape skin acts like estrogen."

"Amazing." I extended my hand. "I'm Alice Fairweather. Dick is my husband's brother." Mr. Secret Service regarded my hand quizzically. I looked down; were my fingernails dirty? Then he took it.

"How nice to meet you," he said. "I'm Harold Sweet. Sydney is my cousin."

"You're Harold? The—?"

"That would be me," he said.

"But I thought—?"

"That I would be conveniently absent for this event? Not to worry. Nothing could make me miss a celebration of this stature in my personal hierarchy of emotional upsets," he said. He had not yet released my hand. "I live for trauma, and trauma lives for me. And now I can be doubly glad to have traveled across the continent to witness the nuptials."

"What about *Jeopardy!*? I'm a *Jeopardy!* fan myself."

"I wouldn't describe myself as a fan," he said. "Oh, no. Rather, it was my intention to clean their clocks and reverse the damage that has been done to me and my financial well-being by the manipulative harpies who took advantage of a senile old man and caused my grandfather to change his will."

"So what happened? Why aren't you in Los Angeles?"

"If the truth ever emerges, it will be a nationwide scandal," he said.

"The truth about what?"

"The last game. Yesterday's game. I threw the game and then took the redeye to get here for the wedding."

"You *threw* a game of *Jeopardy!*? How?"

"The same way people have thrown games since the first Olympics. I lost. I gave the wrong answer. The wrong question." His grin curled across his face like a garter snake.

The sun was still shining, and the ocean was still blue. But something in the air had changed, and it wasn't the temperature. Suited men and hatted ladies continued to form knots of conversation and then disperse. Where had all the flower girls gone? "I am getting hungry," I said. "I've had quite a bit of champagne. When do you think we will see any real food?" When I looked straight ahead, things were crystal clear, but the perimeter was fuzzy. The perimeter of my vision was where things were slipping off the edge, into deep water.

"I take it you have not been warned about the Sweet indifference to taste buds. Or lack of taste buds. It used to be recessive, but now it's a dominant gene."

"Are you saying you're not hungry?" I said, unable just then to imagine a condition that did not include an insistent appetite.

"You remind me so much of Sydney," Harold said.

"Take my word for it," I said. "I am nothing like Sydney."

Harold said, "You don't even know her. I have it on good authority that you never met her before today. Have some more champagne." Harold's arm shot out to retrieve a flute from a passing tray.

"I think I should eat something first," I said. "This champagne is lovely."

"Are you a champagne expert?" he said. "And you really do remind me of Sydney."

My stomach was growling and my head was spinning. I was lucky to be upright. And where, oh, where was my Waldo? Was food imminent? Ezra and Henry were coming round from behind the house. Ezra was pale as a bleached seashell, and one of the butterflies had come off. Henry was pink cheeked and giddy. I saw a champagne glass in his hand. "Uh-oh," I said. "That's my Henry."

"How old is this Henry?"

"He's eight. I have to go see him."

"Shall I find out about the food?"

"Oh my God," I said. "That would be fantastic. Yes, thank

you." If he found food, I would find him less objectionable. I would encourage him to return to *Jeopardy!* and seek his fortune.

Waldo reached Henry before I did. "Where have you been?" I whispered. "I met the cousin Harold. He's the Secret Service man. He's not that bad."

"I've been here. Where have you been?" Waldo said. "Lay off the champignons, Henry."

"That would be a mushroom, Dad."

I felt Ezra's forehead. It wasn't feverish. Far from it. It was cold and clammy. Shit, I thought. Ezra was always intense and completely wrapped up in the project at hand. He never perceived the treacherous exhaustion looming just ahead, and so he always hit it head-on, and crumpled. Ezra was like a morning glory petal or a spider web, a thing of nature that was beautiful and vulnerable to every darkening sky or passing wind. What kind of mother drinks champagne on the lawn with a black sheep while her ashen son builds a cairn out back? This was a Grade B Bad Mother Moment—bad but not irredeemable.

"We're going to go inside for a bit," I told Ezra. "So you can rest."

"But the cairn! Mr. Cicero wants to show Uncle Dick and Aunt Sydney the cairn," Ezra said.

Waldo said, "You're already calling her aunt?"

"Henry and I decided we would."

"Henry will come get you if anything important happens," I said. "Won't you, Henry? Ezra needs to rest. I don't want his cut to get inflamed or infected."

Ezra insisted, "I feel completely fine, Mom."

"Humor me, Ez," I said. "It's just for a few minutes."

That was another thing about Ezra: he acquiesced so easily.

There was no one inside to ask if it would be all right for us to recline on one of the three capacious, threadbare sofas. Behind the screen door was a roaring silence. Absent the duck decoys, the dim interior was eerily as I had imagined. Instead of ducks, there were stuffed fish mounted on wooden plaques. Dead stuffed fish girded the whole of the living room, which was almost the entire first floor. Through an open doorway I could see the kitchen at the back of the house, and beside it was the stairway leading up. There must have been thirty or forty of those fish. The swordfish and sailfish I recognized. And the wide-mouthed bass and striped bass. But what were all the others? Those long-dead fins undulated against the wall. It was time for some strong coffee. These fish had been there a long time. Tired bits of scales were flaking off, and several were missing their eyeballs. Which, frankly, was better than the eyes that stared at me. A long time ago some Sweet had been a passionate fisherman. And fully employed his taxidermist.

Ezra lay down on the couch and I stroked his forehead. In about two minutes, he was asleep.

I would have slept also, but each time I closed my eyes the room started spinning. So I sat very still and decided that soon I would get myself a large glass of water. I should have been drinking water all along. One of Mami's great life lessons was that the only way to stay upright at a wedding was to drink one full glass of water for every glass of champagne. Her lessons were ignored at my peril. Today was a case in point.

But my eyelids kept drooping, and Ezra slumbered on. His forehead was a little less cold and a little drier.

"I can't believe you lied to me. About that. After everything." The voice came from the back of the house, from the kitchen. I needed water—big-time—but I didn't move from my chair.

"You're hysterical. No one lied about anything." Another female voice.

"You said he wouldn't be here. You promised he wouldn't be here. And he is here. I call that lying."

"I couldn't stop him from coming. What was I supposed to do? Hijack the plane?"

"After fucking up? You could have warned me he was coming."

"Oh, please. Don't talk to me about fucking up. You're the one who screwed him in the first place."

Ezra still slept. Or so I thought. His legs and arms quivered and stretched as if toward something. Nothing caught the attention of a small boy quite like an adult cursing. But he slumbered on and rolled over onto his other side. I held my breath and watched. His right cheek bore the imprint of the needlepoint pillow.

There was no question now of barging into the kitchen for a glass of water.

Then came the scratchy tinkle of breaking glass, not much glass, but definitely broken. "Oh, fuck. Don't remind me. The fucker."

"Just calm down."

"I wouldn't have come if I'd known."

"Calm down. You're overreacting. No one here even knows about you two, and he's not about to bring it up."

"Sydney knows."

"Sydney's busy getting married. She didn't want to see him any more than you did."

"He never abandoned her in a bedbug-infested Mexican hotel. He never gave all her clothes to the local tart. He never gave her—"

"You have got to calm down. Nobody's disputing he's a shit. And you have no idea what kind of diseases he gave her."

"The worst thing she ever caught was cold."

They must have been standing just outside of my line of vision, in some part of the kitchen I could only imagine. Where was Posey when I needed her? My mouth was as dry as yesterday's toast and my stomach was growling louder than ever. But my head had stopped spinning and that was a good thing.

"Shit. Shit. Shit. How much longer will this thing go on?"

"God knows. Sooner or later they'll have to feed us. Although knowing Hammy, I'm surprised we didn't have to bring bag lunches."

I should have spoken up the instant I'd heard a voice, back when I could have made some concerned reference to my sleeping child. I should have done anything but sit there inert as a stuffed fish.

Then they were gone. The hinges squeaked and I saw the back of a flowered dress and a hat exiting the kitchen. It was a wide-brimmed straw hat with a ringlet of faux red cherries around it. The screen door slammed behind them.

First things first: I drank several glasses of water and wondered if they'd tested their well lately. I drank several more.

Ezra still slept. Piled next to the sofa were copies of *Down East* predating the Civil War, just a little swollen with dampness. I read two articles about gardening along the coast. The articles were separated by almost a decade, but both extolled the merits of foxgloves and ferns. Ezra slept on, and I decided to let him stay there while I went in search of sustenance. I am like the mother bear going out foraging, I thought. I am fulfilling some atavistic impulse.

Outside, the caterers had set up the buffet under the tent. Suited men and hatted ladies, unsteadily clutching their champagne flutes, drifted toward food. Waldo and I found each other.

"How's Ezra?" he said.

"Asleep," I said. "Where's Henry?"

"With Mr. Cicero. I fear the worst."

We finally ate. No, I was not an expert, but it seemed to me that the Sweets could have served less champagne and, with the money they would have saved, improved on the food quality. Waldo claimed that I never went to an event where I did not wish to rewrite the menu.

Somewhere on the lawn, people danced, cast shadows, fell wearily into folding chairs, and then got up and danced some more. The music rose and fell, like the waves.

Chilly air rolled off from the dark blue sea. It was time for Dick to get himself off on his honeymoon.

"Your bride's anxious to be alone with you." Waldo found Dick shifting awkwardly inside his tux.

"She is? Did she tell you?"

"I'm sure of it. Why shouldn't she be? She's lucky enough to have snagged the most eligible fellow in Maine."

"Don't tell her that," Dick said.

Waldo said, "Your secret is safe with me." He glanced over my way. "And Alice. Alice is the soul of discretion."

I nodded.

Dick said, "We will be alone quite soon. Once Sydney changes her clothes. She doesn't want to go to the inn in her wedding gown. That is not done. I should have known that." Dick rubbed his temples in his characteristic way, as if he were trying to massage bits of information into his brain. He continued, "So, once attired according to her druthers, it's twenty minutes by boat to the yacht club pier, and then five minutes for rice throwing or activities of that nature, and then it's a forty-minute drive up the coast to our inn. Sydney says no one should know exactly which inn we are staying at, but I can tell you, because you are my only brother and Sydney has informed all her sisters as well as some cousins: it's the Frog Hollow in South Tree Harbor. And so we should be alone in an hour and ten minutes."

"If I follow, you are assuming that Sydney will change out of her bridal finery in five minutes. I think we need to have a discussion."

Dick looked genuinely perplexed. "But Sydney gets undressed in a flash. I've timed it at twenty-eight seconds, and that includes folding her pants, or at least hanging them over the back of the chair. That was her best time, but it signifies."

Then it was Waldo's turn to be addled. "You've seen Sydney get undressed? Already?"

"Of course I have, Walds. What do you think? That I wouldn't have sex before embarking on a venture of this magnitude? That would be highly unscientific."

Waldo nodded sagely. "Good thinking, Dickie. Brilliant. You have laid all my fears to rest."

His relief on discovering that Dick was not a virgin was palpable. Only as he relaxed into his tuxedo did I figure out how tense he had been all that day. I hadn't realized. I should have realized that my husband was worried about his brother's impending introduction to sex. Which was a thing of the past. Had I worried about my sisters' deflowerings? I had not. A wave of love for Waldo washed over me, a man who took rituals seriously and then debunked them in rhyme. With the next wave came uncertainty: was it really love, or simply lust and longing?

Meanwhile, Henry was getting to that hyper-chatty stage that preceded a complete meltdown, and Ezra just needed more rest, period. So we three took the next boat from Slow Island, the *Mary-Q*. Her skipper, Rufus Bouchard, was a man of very few words. Actually none, but I assumed they could be produced when absolutely necessary. About fifteen other guests were onboard, and we all agreed that Sydney had been a beautiful bride.

"I have never seen a more beautiful bride," Henry said, with the air of a connoisseur. "I think white is so becoming on some women."

Several ladies looked sideways at Henry. They were thinking how interesting this child was, and when he grew up he would be perfect for a daughter or granddaughter.

"They loved the cairn," Ezra said.

A woman in a flowered dress and black Chinese slippers separated herself from the flock and clutched her hat in her hand. She had been looking intensely at Ezra all this time and finally, pointing to his cut, said, "What happened to his face? Poor thing."

"I sleepwalked into a mechanical harvester," Ezra said. "You should have seen it. I left it in at least a dozen pieces."

I said, "It wasn't like a farm harvester. It was miniature. He was indoors."

The woman said, "How intriguing." Her face animated with

interest. "I used to sleepwalk. I would go downstairs and sit in my father's favorite chair and balance teacups on my knees. I can still do it too. Balance teacups. It's harder than you think."

The woman's voice was familiar. Us with the fish, her in the kitchen.

"I could show you," she continued. "But not on a boat. Even if I had teacups here."

"Really?" I said.

"We had a dog then. But he never barked when I sleepwalked. He was a schnauzer named Hansi and he followed me wherever I went. Of course, it all ended with puberty," she said, with genuine sadness. "As so much pleasure in life does."

Above the deep-throated grind of the diesel it was hard to be sure I was hearing what I thought I was hearing. "Are you saying you enjoyed sleepwalking?"

"Absolutely. Afterward I couldn't remember anything—except my remarkable ability to balance teacups on my knees—but I somehow knew I had this other life, a parallel or alternative life, and it was very satisfying to know that."

"Ezra wouldn't say that." Ezra folded his arms over his chest and slid closer to his brother. "Or maybe he would," I said, suddenly aware of how little I knew. There was so much to ask. With each passing night, slept and dreamed, Ezra was distancing himself from his childhood and inching up on the years when he would hold his secrets close to his manly chest and when his inclination to tell his mother, to blurt things to his mother, would dwindle into a vanishing dust mote. I sat next to him on the *Mary-Q* and envisioned that timeline, like the horizon we would always approach but never reach.

While no one could have called the sea rough, the waves were inexorably moving up and down, as waves do, and the boat rode upon them, up and down.

Henry said, "Sydney and Dick loved the cairn. They said it was their favorite wedding present."

"When did you present the cairn?" I said. "How did it go?"

"Excellent," Ezra said. "Mr. Cicero made a little speech." His expression was opaque and his color gray. I thought I saw his chest receding in that tiny motion that accompanies nausea and precedes retching. Or did I imagine it? This too was feeling ominously like a Bad Mother Moment.

"He said stuff about how each rock was like a member of their families, and when they all get together they create this thing greater than all the little rocks, and more stuff about marriage. Honestly, Mom, I thought it was sappy," Henry said.

"But nice? You thought it was nice too, right?"

"Sort of," he said.

"I think I'm seasick," Ezra said.

"Put your head between your knees," I said. "Unless you want to throw up, in which case, lean overboard." We rode up and down the swells.

Ezra put his head down. He garbled, "I *really* hate being seasick."

"Next time I'll give you Dramamine. But it's too late now, and we'll be on land soon."

Henry put something in Ezra's hand. "You can hold my rock," he said. Ezra kept his head down, and closed his fingers over the rock.

"Wendy's overboard!" someone shouted. Then several people all said at once, "Wendy's overboard! Where's Wendy? She's overboard. Starboard! Starboard! No, port."

We were sitting toward the bow, and all this commotion was in the stern. Someone yelled at Rufus Bouchard, who pointed to the lifesaver, which was then thrown into the water. He turned the boat around. I couldn't see Wendy anywhere. I didn't know who Wendy was, but I assumed she could swim. I couldn't imagine a Sweet guest who couldn't swim. People were leaning over the stern, waving their hands in the air and shouting. Then I saw Sydney's Cousin Harold, the Secret Service man. He removed his shoes and jacket and pulled his tie roughly through his collar, then dove off the stern into the dark blue swells. The water temperature was probably in the forties or low fifties. I shivered and held Ezra closer to me. Henry ran toward the stern.

"Come back, Henry," I said. He couldn't hear me. "We can't help. Stay with me."

Everyone was shouting instructions to Harold.

Then, as shocking as a gunshot in the theater, there was Henry's still sweet, still little-boy's voice saying, "I see a hat."

Off the port side floated an ivory-colored straw hat with red cherries circling the brim. The hat rode the swells up and down. In the troughs it disappeared. As everyone looked and pointed, the *Mary-Q* heeled to port. Harold started diving. While he was wholly beneath the water, a silence came over the boat, and for the first time we heard the cackling of the radio, Captain Bouchard having alerted the Coast Guard. Then Harold surfaced, and the shouted instructions recommenced. He dove again, and again the voices abruptly halted while Harold was unseen below the dark sea. But this time we also heard a woman's gasping sobs, a woman in a flowered dress that was loosely covered by an oversize trench coat. Harold dove again and again as the hat innocently floated.

Henry was in the thick of the onlookers, the peerers, the watchers, the gazers, and the leaners to the port side. I didn't want to leave Ezra, who occasionally put his head up to see what was happening, and then replaced it between his knees.

Ezra lifted his head slightly now and said, "Did someone drown?"

"I'm sure he'll find her," I said. "We just can't see her now."

"I bet she was seasick too," he said.

"No, honey, nothing like that. You don't drown just because you get seasick."

"I know that, Mom," he said. "She just wanted to get off the boat, is what I meant."

Harold was still swimming about and still diving. The buzz of voices on deck diminished. The roar of the diesel seemed greater now that people were holding their collective breath. Faces changed. The forces of gravity and horror had, in equal measure, altered cheekbones and jaws, as it set in that Wendy was lost, that Wendy could not be anywhere other than beneath the dark water's surface, unseen and drowned.

And who was Wendy? One of the two women in the kitchen, but which one? I looked toward the stern. I could not see the lady who sleepwalked and balanced teacups on her knees.

Had Hubert been with us, there off the coast of Maine, there on the ungentle waters, he might have invoked Saint Adjutor, who protects against drowning.

Or Hubert might have called upon Saint Nicholas of Tolentino, the thirteenth-century Italian preacher who resuscitated a drowned man and caused a cooked cockentrice to fly out the window.

Given the straw hat riding the waves, Hubert might prayed to Saint Francis of Paola to intervene. Saint Francis was barely older than Ezra when he became a monk. But that wasn't enough hardship for him, so he moved to a solitary cave on the seashore. Francis never wore shoes, never washed, and never changed his clothes all his life long. The most miraculous thing about him may be that people were forever commenting on his "heavenly odor." In 1464, stranded in Sicily and unable to find a willing boatman to ferry him back to the mainland, Francis tossed his cloak (unwashed, unchanged) into the Strait of Messina and rode it back to Calabria.

Relic-happy Hubert would probably also have invoked Saint Josse, another patron saint of sailors, who likely never set foot in the water. His relics consisted of nail and hair clippings, lots of nail and hair clippings, because for a long time after his death Josse's hair and beard and nails continued to grow, and his followers continued clipping.

But Hubert was not there, and I was alone muttering the names of saints I did not know.

It was darkening. The Coast Guard cutter arrived with its spotlight and crackling radio. It pulled alongside the *Mary-Q* and the crew spoke with Rufus Bouchard. Someone hung a ladder off the side, and a shivering and wintry-white Harold Sweet climbed aboard the Coast Guard boat. Someone wrapped him in a blanket, and he huddled in conversation with a small man in a large life preserver.

Henry came back to Ezra and me, and sat very still, unusually still.

Maybe I should have just pleaded with Saint Elmo for aid, because Saint Elmo was the patron saint of those suffering from seasickness.

Hubert would have known which saint to address, but he wasn't there. He was at the Hagiographers Club, shuffling his holy cards. And Waldo, who'd won all the swimming ribbons at the yacht club when he was a boy, and who had once swum across the Hudson River to raise money for some disease, wasn't there either. He was surely with Dick and Sydney, and I wondered if it was remotely possible that they could have left on their honeymoon without knowing about the lost Wendy. If Sydney was on schedule, then they would be long gone. Or else today was just the first day in Dick's long future life of things refusing to go according to the best-laid plans of men and monkeys.

None of them was aboard the *Mary-Q*; I was, with Ezra and Henry, and I could do nothing but watch and hover. The ocean between Slow Island and the mainland became stiller than still.

22 ✌ Land Legs

TIME ALSO WAS STILL. Waldo already knew all about Wendy, all about Harold Sweet's dives; he knew more than I did. He knew who Wendy was.

"Ezra looks terrible," he said.

"He was seasick," I said. "Did you know her? What was her last name?"

"She was some distant cousin of Sydney's. They used to be close when they were young, and then they weren't. I heard about Sydney from Wendy."

"So what's her name? I am pretty sure she was the one talking to Ez and me about her sleepwalking."

"She sleepwalked? I never knew that."

"She said it stopped when she hit puberty. Does your knowledge of her predate her puberty? And what's her name?"

Waldo looked over my head, toward the harbor, and said, "Wendy Dilly."

"Dilly?" I was physically incapable of shutting my mouth. That's what it felt like.

"Don't get excited, Al." He pointed at Henry and Ez, trudging ahead of us.

"Who said I was excited? You should have told me. That's the least you could have done."

"It's a distant relation. I don't even know what it is. Practically everyone up here is related. You know that."

"So now your brother's new wife is related to your ex-mistress," I said. "I think I'm going to throw up."

"She wasn't my mistress, Al, and calm down."

"Then what would you call it? Paramour? Fuck buddy? Home wrecker? How about home wrecker?"

"Al! Henry can hear a mosquito farting in the next state."

"Good for him."

"I know this is hard. Just don't get so excited."

"If I were excited, which I am not," I said, "I would see absolutely no good reason to calm down."

"You're making a much bigger deal of this than it is. I haven't seen Edith in years and years. And I probably never will again. She moved abroad. It's not as if she came to the wedding."

"I think that after almost destroying our marriage, her appearance at your brother's wedding would have been an act of over-the-top chutzpah."

"We're still married, aren't we? She didn't destroy anything."

"Not for lack of trying."

Almost from the very beginning, from the very first time I'd heard of Edith Dilly and the part she was playing in my life, I'd blamed her. Susie—and others too—pointed out the irrational, biblical, antediluvian, misogynistic draconian-ness of blaming the woman. Also the delusional aspect of it. Letting Waldo off the hook. I saw all that and I couldn't help myself. I wanted to keep Waldo, and so, without considering the implications, I clung to him and blamed her. But I didn't let Waldo off the hook. I kept him there. I hung on.

And here we still were. Making rhymes, soups, and love.

Henry and Ez were at Posey's front door, already deep in conversation with Posey and Mr. Cicero.

Posey wasted no time. "Did she jump or was she pushed?"

Henry said, "I think she was pushed. I think her evil twin pushed her." Then he added, with obvious pleasure, "Her doppelgänger."

"Geez, Henry, you can't go around saying stuff like that."

"Don't worry, Dad," Henry said. "I'm eight years old. No one will believe me."

Posey said, "What is this child talking about?"

"I don't know," I said. "It's clear to me that I don't know very much at all. I think Ezra needs to lie down. I'll see you all later."

I didn't see anyone later. I fell asleep next to Ezra and neither of us woke up until morning. And I woke with relief, because of course it had all been a dream: the *Mary-Q*, the hat, Wendy Dilly.

"Pompey's coming over," Posey said. She was making French toast for Henry. Henry preferred his grandmother's white-bread French toast to the kind I made at home, the healthy kind with whole-wheat or thirty-nine-grain bread.

Ezra and Waldo wandered into the kitchen.

"Where's Mr. Cicero?" Ezra said.

"Taking his walk. He walks out to see the cows every morning at this time."

"Why couldn't we go with him?" Henry said.

"Because you weren't awake yet," Posey said. "You needed your beauty sleep. Especially Ezra."

I said, "Don't you think the cut looks much better this morning? The redness is down."

"What I don't understand is what a piece of farming machinery was doing in your house," she said.

"Enough, Ma," Waldo said.

"For such a smart man, Waldo, you do some extremely stupid things."

Waldo's hands were deep in the pockets of his khakis.

"Even I could have told you that farm equipment belongs outside."

"Can we have some French toast now?" Henry said.

"Mr. Cicero spoke with Frank Flood this morning—you know he's the commodore this year?—and he said that the Coast Guard had boats out there this morning. I heard it all from Cathy Flood, and you know what she's like."

Waldo said, "I don't. But go on, Ma."

"Of course you do."

I said, "Tell us, Posey."

"Cathy said at least two people saw Wendy jump off the stern."

"Who?" Waldo asked. Posey sipped from her American Hosta Society mug, then shook her head wearily.

"What kind of person jumps overboard on her way back from her cousin's wedding?" I said.

"Sydney was a rather distant cousin, my dear," Posey said.

"It seems extreme."

"Bad timing," Waldo said.

"Suicide is more than bad timing," Posey said. There was a café au lait mustache lightly adorning her upper lip. "I'm sure she'll regret it."

"I don't think so, Ma."

"I mean she would have regretted it. It's a shame she can't. They always do, you know."

"Do what?"

"Regret it. After they've jumped."

"I know," I said.

"She wouldn't be the only one," Waldo said.

"Poor drowned Wendy. And while Dickie is on his first honeymoon," Posey said.

"His first?" Waldo grinned.

"You know what I mean."

"Yoo-hoo! Yoo-hoo!" came the clarion call from the front of the house. It was Pompey Fairweather, come into Catamunk for the third consecutive day, a possible record for him.

"We're in the kitchen," Posey called back.

"We're the Kitchen Cabinet," Waldo said. "Conducting a postmortem."

Pompey had a copy of the *Mid-Maine Gazette* with him. It should have been no surprise what the headlines were, but we were surprised nonetheless: WEDDING GUEST OVERBOARD. The subhead read: "CG Searches for Body Thru the Night."

"Have you seen this?" He held the newspaper at arm's length, as if fearful of germs.

"I have not," Posey said. "Just tell me that Dick's name is not mentioned."

"I can't tell you that."

"I hope Dickie and Sydney aren't buying any newspapers."

"Sydney's a news junkie," Pompey said. "She brought along her laptop."

Posey looked furious. "Who told you that?"

"Her mother. Who should know. Don't get your knickers in a twist. Gabby and I had a lovely chat yesterday. I don't think we've spoken that much since before Veronica died."

"Watch out, Pomps. She always had her eye on you," Posey said. "Your Veronica never much liked Gabby Sweet, if I recall."

"Oh, you know women," Pompey said.

Since Veronica's death, Pompey had lived very much alone. Too much alone, according to Posey. Up in his own world, all those curmudgeonly traits that had lurked beneath the surface when the lovely Veronica was alive suddenly burst out and flourished in her absence. Posey considered she owed it to Three, whose devotion to his brother had been mysterious and wonderful, to regularly admonish Pompey.

Waldo said, "Poor Dickie. It can't be a good sign that she's brought a computer along."

"Don't be so sure," I said. "Things have changed since our romantic days and nights in an undisclosed location. Who knows what games she might have on that laptop?" Did Waldo remember our view of the Pacific and the bellowing of the elephant seals? Did he remember our game of full-contact gin rummy? The strip gin rummy? The Kamasutra gin rummy? Did he remember the forfeits?

"Solitaire is not a good choice for honeymoon card play," Waldo said.

He must remember.

Waldo said, "Ma, did you say who saw her jump?"

"I told you."

"No, you didn't."

Posey looked pointedly at him. "Sarah Dilly," she said.

"Would that be Edith's mother?" I said. But Edith had no mother. No longer had a mother.

"No, it's her sister. Her older sister."

"Oh." I knew from years ago that Edith had two sisters, like me. She also had brothers. What I wanted to say was *Why couldn't she have been the one to go overboard?* She and her sisters? Or, at the very least, why couldn't they all move to the Yukon and eat blubber forever after? Or Timbuktu? Why couldn't they all go to Timbuktu and be eaten alive by killer ants? Did they have killer ants in the Sahara? Anywhere but here in Catamunk with Posey and Waldo and all of us, here, where, sooner or later, sooner or later, sooner or later . . .

Edith was the past, and Sheila/Shirley was the present. It wasn't just the timeline that separated them. Even if I worried and wondered along the byways of VerGroot and in the waiting room at Don Eco's clinic and on the train and even in the hallowed rooms of the Hagiographers Club, I was oddly confident that Sheila/Shirley was the last of her kind. The thing about the thing with Edith was that any other escapade paled beside it. Waldo and Edith busted my heart. Edith I would happily have watched sink to the bottom of the cold Atlantic. Waldo I adored, and clung to. I would have jumped in after Waldo, a thousand times.

In my versions of my life, Ezra and Henry mended my shredded heart.

"Exactly how many Dillys are there in this town?" I asked.

Posey said, "Quite a lot. Too many, if you ask me. Mostly they live around Boston, but some are here full-time now."

The screen door slammed open, and in walked Mr. Cicero.

Much later I said, "We have a long way to go today, guys. Bogumila's meeting us at home with the dogs. I promised we'd be back at a reasonable hour."

"Now there is something we can discuss all the way home," Waldo said gleefully. "The meaning of *reasonable*."

Ezra said, "Are we there yet?" He and Henry cracked up laughing.

23 ✿ Said Dick to His Sydney, Let's Fuck

IT WAS ALMOST DARK when we pulled into our driveway. A hundred miles back the boys had exhausted their enthusiasm for alphabet games and punnish license plates. Favorites were: WASSIT 2U, IMB4U, EYE CAN2, and AMA BRAT.

Bogumila was sitting on the back porch with the dogs. Flirt's head was in her lap, and Dandy lay at her feet. Bogumila had her cup of tea with her, so presumably she had been there awhile. No steam rose from her thick mug with the faded picture of a Polish castle. But that did not necessarily mean anything, because sometimes Bogumila drank tepid tea with garlic for medicinal reasons.

"Dirty Flirty! Handy Dandy!" Henry shouted. "Hey, Bogumila!"

The boys leaped from the back seat, and the dogs jumped all over them.

"Welcome back to little VerGroot," Bogumila said. Without another word, she handed over a large brown paper bag.

"What's in here?" Waldo said with a funny smile that made me think he already knew. But I was wrong. Henry and Ezra simultaneously took the bag from Waldo, opened it, and retreated with theatrical expressions of disgust.

Bogumila shook her head. "Yes, Mr. Gunnar Sigerson brought them over a very few minutes ago. He said you would want them."

I peeked at the mushrooms. It was not immediately obvious that they were edible.

Bogumila glared at Ezra's cut and said, "I will bring him some cream from my country. It is smelling bad, but it will help the skin." Bogumila had a vast supply of Polish creams, liniments, ointments, and unguents, all lined up on a shelf just beside her back door where they were ever ready for emergency visits to her neighbors.

"That's so nice of you," I said. "Did the dogs behave for you?"

We were getting into bed. Waldo said he'd called Gunnar to thank him for the nameless fungi. "He sounded strange. He may be getting as strange as Deb."

"Gunnar is sweet on me," I said. It just came out. Like a hiccup.

Waldo said, "You're pretty sweet yourself."

"Thanks." I climbed into bed, and then got right out to check on Henry and Ezra. Ezra slept curled up, his wavy hair barely visible on the pillow above the counterpane. Dandy was under his bed. Henry slept on his back, sprawled. Henry's sheets and blankets rarely survived the night intact. Flirt slept on the rug at the base of the stairs. So back to our bed, our place of coming together in passion and drifting apart in dreams, our mutual ground.

"What do you mean exactly? Sweet?" Waldo said.

"Just what I said. Sweet."

"*Sweet* as in sugar? *Sweet* as in he likes you? *Sweet* as in full of cavities? *Sweet* as in your new in-laws? Which is it?"

"As in he likes me," I said.

"Since when?"

"I don't know."

"Then how do you know?"

"He told me."

"He used that word? *Sweet?*"

"What's with the third degree? I'm sorry I said anything," I blurted.

"Don't be," he said. "I assume you're trying to make a point. To let me know it can go both ways."

"It certainly does *not* go both ways," I almost shouted. "I just felt like telling you that Gunnar likes me. It was a bad decision on my part apparently, but there it is. I did it. And that's all there is to it."

"Well, it's kaput with Shirley, if you want to know."

"Kaput?"

"Over. *Tutto finito.*"

"I thought it was over before."

"It's even more over now. I just checked my e-mail."

"What? And she dumped you? By e-mail?"

"If you want to put it that way. She dumped me."

"That seems awfully tacky. You liked someone who could dump you in an e-mail? What happened? Did she meet the guy who invented pantyhose?"

"I deserved that, Al. I know. I could have not mentioned it. She said I was much too married."

"What other way can you be married? She sounds like a moron," I said.

"I am so very, very sorry. Can we put this behind us? What can I do? Anything. Tell me anything."

"Everything."

I dreamed that Waldo brought Edith and Sheila/Shirley home to live with us. They had two dogs, and one of the dogs called Edith Mother. "Where is Mother?" the dog said. It sat on a stool in a cluttered kitchen. I was waiting for the dog to get off so I could sit down with Waldo and tell him that Edith, Shirley, and the dogs would all have to move out and take all their half-eaten cereal boxes with them. Waldo could talk to the dogs, but I could not.

• • •

At breakfast, Henry told Ezra, "I dreamed of the lady who went overboard last night. Ask Mom."

Ezra avoided my face. "I thought you never had dreams."

" 'It's the exception that proves the rule,' " Henry quoted.

"Everyone dreams," I said, not for the first time. "It's just that not everyone remembers their dreams."

"We know, Mom."

"Then you know that if you didn't dream you wouldn't be sleeping properly; plus, you'd have huge piles of unprocessed images and memories accumulating in your brain, taking up too much space and collecting dust."

Waldo walked in. "And that, boys, is science for you."

"Your father doesn't know everything," I pointed out.

"Just about, though," Ezra said.

Was it possible that for almost four years I'd listened to dreams and said things that dreamers wished to hear? How many times had I said that a body of water symbolized the unconscious? The unconscious we would drown in as the undulating waves of repression closed in over us; the unconscious we would swim bravely through, slicing the waves with the strokes of our imagination; the unconscious that was filling up the basement. But not to Henry would I say that.

I don't know how much later it was that Gunnar Sigerson called. "Waldo sounded rather strange on the phone last night."

"Funny," I said. "He said the same thing about you."

"Why would there be anything strange about me?" Gunnar said.

"I don't know. How would I know?" Dandy came over and nuzzled my leg and so I took the opportunity to check his gums. I pushed with my fingertip, because Donald had shown me that what really mattered was how quickly the gum refilled with blood after being depressed.

"So I was wondering how things are with you two."

"They're fine," I said. "We just got back from his brother's wedding. Did he tell you that? I thought his brother would never get married. I didn't think he even liked women."

Gunnar said, "Did you like the horse mushrooms?"

"We only got home last night. I haven't eaten them yet," I said. "What would I do with them?"

"Sauté them with shallots, or pine nuts, or just olive oil. And Alice? Don't worry about me saying anything. Anything at all." Gunnar was kind and reassuring, more than I could bear.

"I don't worry about you," I said. "I worry about me. Screwing up, that is. I told Waldo you were sweet on me."

"No wonder he was a little strange on the phone."

"I didn't tell him until after."

"But still."

"Do you think it will create a local scandal? Do you think we'll be written up in the *Sentinel*?"

"Don't get your hopes up!" He laughed. Gunnar thought I was funny?

Posey called. "There was another piece in the paper," she said. "They think it was an accident. Her mother said that she was a sleepwalker, and sometimes she lost her balance. Sleepwalkers do, she said."

"When they're awake? I've never heard that."

"That's what Margo Dilly told the police."

"Waldo's not home yet," I said. "Can he call you later?"

"I wanted to know about Ezra's cut. Mr. Cicero says you should be using arnica."

"We know that," I said. "And Bogumila agrees with you."

The boys went to bed, and still Waldo wasn't home. On his dresser I found some crumpled-up pieces of paper I didn't recognize. They were not in the trash basket. They were right on top of Waldo's dresser, in full view of me, or the boys, or anyone who happened to be in our bedroom. I knew I shouldn't look at them, but I did anyway. I had looked at his papers before, letters from the odious Edith Dilly, letters full of sex and longing, letters that I could never forget. I had read them and would always regret I had. Yet I would read them again if they were sitting there on the dresser top, calling out, *Read me! Read me!* I expected these crumpled-up papers to be something from Sheila/Shirley, something on her monogrammed stationery, or perhaps on a DSG memo pad. I hoped it would be something referring to the absolute end of their relationship. No, not a relationship, but a fling, a dalliance, a mistake.

I uncrumpled and smoothed out the papers. The Bug Harbor Yacht Club burgee was at the top of the page, and I read, written in pencil, in Waldo's handwriting:

There was a fair girl from old Maine
Whose tastes were a tad profane
Of Dick she was fond,
More than fond, but beyond.
That lovely young girl from Maine.

There was a young man called Dick
Who fell in love very quick-
Ly, Sydney was the girl
Who made his hair curl
And stroked the dick of young Dick.

Young Dick he loved his plants
Till Sydney came and put ants in his pants.
She fluttered her eyes
And breathed deep-felt sighs
Till Dick left his plants for her pants.

Richard and Sydney will soon be wed,
And after that they'll go to bed
Where we hope they will frolic
In settings bucolic
So it will be once the fair pair are wed.

Young Dick fair Sydney woo'd
Leave now if you don't like it crude.
For they screwed and they screwed
It was wonderfully lewd
They hoped for a Fairweather brood.

Said Dick to his Sydney, Let's fuck.
Life's too short to trust to luck.
For your body I lust
It's an absolute must
Therefore I repeat, Let us fuck.

There were lots of erasures and cross-outs, the creative process made manifest. Apparently he had tested out *woodchuck, horror-struck,* and *cluck* as rhymes for the irreplaceable *fuck.*

Were these all? I had expected—hoped for?—something racier, dirtier, something to warrant Posey's parental consternation.

I left the papers on top of Waldo's dresser, all smoothed out. They would say to him, *We've been read! Go to bed!*

Downstairs I sniffed and stroked the horse mushrooms Gunnar had left with Bogumila. They were more than usually rank and fungal. I stuffed them into the garbage.

I needed to get back to the Hagiographers Club. No, I needed a job.

Finally, finally, it was the morning of the last day of school, the longed-for day of no more school.

The telephone rang.

"Good morning, Posey," I said.

"Alice! Just the person I wanted to speak to! They found her body. Can you tell Waldo? He'll want to know."

I said, in a voice loud enough to be heard by both Waldo behind his newspaper and Posey in Maine, "Waldo, your mother wants you to know that they found Wendy's body."

Waldo said, "Who found it?"

I said to Posey, "Did you hear that?"

"Hear what?" Posey said.

"Waldo," I said. "Your mother is dying to talk to you." I handed him the phone.

Henry said, "Where did they find her?"

"Ask your father," I said.

Waldo spoke into the phone. "I'd love to talk, Ma. But I have to get to work. Today I'll be inventing cold fusion and a wind-proof umbrella. Can you give Al the details?"

The back door slammed behind him, and Posey was still there.

"She washed up on Slow Island," she said. "She was naked. There was an eel in her mouth."

I told the boys. Better to know than to spend the day with images of the floating body, the drowned body, the sunken body residing upon a shipwreck, the abandoned body eaten by fish and lobsters, ensnared by eels, inhabited by hermit crabs and barnacles, and cushioned by jellyfish.

24 ❧ The Persistence of Sharks

THE MEETINGS WITH the agricultural ministry had to be over. Maybe he was planting more coffee trees? Did that involve a shovel or a backhoe? What did I know? Or was he eviscerating chickens? No, I could imagine the boys and I eviscerating chickens (then throwing the offal to the dogs) a thousand times before I could imagine Lalo's hands slimed by chicken guts. That was not the point. The point was Tristána and whether her saintliness had performed any more miracles. The point was to be useful.

So I called Nicaragua. Nicaragua shared an area code with New Mexico (505) and in fact shared the code with the caves in New Mexico. This was not a coincidence, but it had to be something.

"Abelardo Llobet, *por favor,*" I said.

"*Momentito. ¿Quien habla?*"

"Alice Fairweather," I said. "In *Nueva York.*"

"*Claro.*"

I waited and listened to sounds of footsteps and voices in a tropical soup—the sounds of otherness. Then came Lalo. "Alice, finally."

"Hello, Lalo. I'm just wondering how you are. If you've recovered? And your aunt too."

"Your voice is marvelous, absolutely marvelous," he said. This was marvelous to hear. But I was having trouble hearing; the blood was thumping inside my ears. "I am fine now. I will stay out of snowstorms in the future. Snow blizzards and Abelardo Llobet are not meant to be together. But now you must tell me that you don't think I am mad, not altogether mad?"

"Oh, no, not that at all," I said. "Everyone has bad days."

"We can talk about it later," Lalo said. "Or perhaps you will prefer never to speak of it again. How are your friends in the ambulance?"

"Same as ever, I guess."

"Good. When are you coming to visit?"

"Oh, that's not why I called. I was just checking. And to tell you about the virgin saints. There are more than you ever imagined. Than you thought possible."

"How many had their portraits painted?"

"While they were still alive? None. That I know of. Or maybe Theresa of Ávila. I'll have to check. Does that matter?"

"Everything matters. It is up to us to make it matter, to make it a positive factor."

"I need to apologize, Lalo. Because I don't think I've been useful at all. I mean, I've loved reading at the club, and I really like Hubert even though he is rather unusual, and it's been great having a place to go and pretending that I was doing something useful. But deep down, I can tell you now, I haven't accomplished anything."

"Deep down, dear Alice, I can tell you that is not so. It will all be profoundly useful. So when are you coming?"

"Lalo, I can't come to Nicaragua. Just like that. The boys have stuff to do, and I have to take care of the dogs, and Waldo . . . even Waldo needs me."

"Of course you will all come. All the Fairweathers," Lalo said. Then he paused and disappeared into the space of a continent that separated us. "But now I must go, dear Alice. There is a problem at the *beneficio* and I must go. But soon we will speak again."

I was alone once more and shouted for Dandy and Flirt. We headed out and toward the woods. They ran fast, then faster, but always they circled back and returned to me. And I found that reassuring.

Waldo was reading *One Hundred Years of Solitude,* and I was close to sleep, next to him, when Abelardo Llobet Carvajal of Las Brisas and León, Nicaragua, called his old college friend Waldo Fairweather IV of VerGroot and Catamunk.

The kindest thing of all was that Waldo actually answered the phone.

"How are you doing, amigo?" he whispered.

I rolled onto my side so that I could hear.

"No," said Waldo.

But I couldn't hear. Waldo kept the phone to his right ear, and I was on his left side. He ignored my semaphored pleas to switch ears.

"So how's the coffee business?" Waldo said.

"Pésimo," Lalo said. Had he shouted that? Or had my hearing become suddenly acute?

I curled against Waldo's crème caramel back. His skin was too soft and warm for a man, too much like silk. Really, it was almost unmasculine. Except that it was so purely masculine. Except that it gave me such pleasure. I curled and warmed myself against Waldo's unfairly smooth skin, thinking of what a good dresser Abelardo was. How heavenly he'd looked in his blue suit. And how dreadful in a johnny. The one and only time I'd touched Lalo's skin was in the snow, trying to get him dressed.

What was Lalo wearing just then, as he spoke to Waldo on the phone, as he said things to Waldo that I couldn't hear?

I wrapped my left leg around Waldo's left leg, and gripped his Achilles tendon between my big and second toe, holding on for dear life to that brilliant tendon that could bear ten times his weight.

"He wants to talk to you." Waldo handed me the phone and promptly rolled over, detaching my leg and my toes from his leg.

"Dear Alice," Lalo said. "I apologize for leaving so precipitously earlier."

"Don't worry. Did you solve the problem, whatever it was?"

"Aha. The *secadoras* were overheating, and they have stopped overheating—for the moment—but I fear that problem will come again. I fear we have this to look forward to."

"Oh," I said. Though I doubted he was dealing with the clothes dryer, in which case I had no idea what he was talking about.

"Have I told you how lovely the climate here can be?" he said.

"I think it's pretty hot."

"Only in Managua. Here at the farm we have cool breezes. You can sleep in a hammock if you like. Do you like hammocks?"

"I'm not sure," I said. "Sometimes they make me motion sick. I have a tendency that way, but not like Ezra."

"Nicaraguan hammocks are the best in the world. That is not according to me. That is a fact. Our coffee is good but not yet accorded that status."

"I don't know anything about growing coffee," I said. This time I flung my right leg over Waldo's legs. He had abdicated this conversation far too soon. I could already feel the swaying hammock and my head was spinning.

"So when are you arriving?"

"Arriving where? Oh, Lalo!"

"Aeropuerto Sandino, Managua. Whatever the time, I will be there to meet you."

"I have no plans to come to Nicaragua," I said. "It's rather far away. I've never been that far south."

"I thought as much, and so we will make a special effort to show you volcanoes that are not erupting."

"You have volcanoes that are not erupting?" I was confused. Which was more desirable—the eruption or its cessation?

"Oh, Alice, this is important." Abelardo sighed.

I sighed back. What else could I have done?

"Once you meet my sisters, and the people here at Las Brisas, you will have a greater understanding of what we must do."

"But I haven't said I'm coming."

"All of you. Waldo and the boys. I am particularly anxious to meet Ezra, whose bed I slept in. We have lots to do in León. Do your sons like poetry? Rubén Darío was born here."

"They don't know very much poetry," I apologized.

"Ah yes, for gringos, it is not the breath of life it is for us Nicas," Abelardo said.

"They're still young. Give them a chance, and who knows? Maybe it will be their breath of life too."

"Forgive me, dear Alice! I forgot to ask if your dog is still alive."

"Dandy? Yes, he's quite alive. Knock on wood, he seems pretty healthy now," I said. "Thanks for asking."

"The best connections are through Miami."

"I've never been to Miami," I said.

"My sisters do all their shopping there," Abelardo said. "It's much cheaper."

"Cheaper than what?"

"Managua. Or Paris."

Afterward I said to Waldo, "Lalo wants us to come to Nicaragua. What do you think? It could be fun."

"I've been," Waldo said. "And it was loads of fun. But I can't go now. You should go."

"What was it like when you were there?" Was it possible I had never asked this before?

Waldo spread his arms wide, as if indicating an enormous fish. "It's a tropical paradise," he said. "At the farm. It's like stepping back in time. Managua is a dump though. I don't recommend Managua."

"I'm seriously considering it, Walds. I need to broaden my horizons!"

"I agree, Al. Go for it," he said. "How come you didn't ask him about the letter Carmen sent us? Or did you?"

"I don't know. I just didn't."

Then Waldo slept. No matter how I tried, I couldn't get close enough to his body, because I couldn't crawl inside his warm skin. "Hold me tight, Waldo," I said. "No, tighter."

Henry looked up from his bowl of Cheerios, the spoon poised before his open mouth. His morning hair ascended and aimed in several directions. All summer long the boys' relationships with combs became so strained that they often ruptured entirely.

"Mom, are you aware of the risks of going to Nicaragua? How am I supposed to sleep at night if I have to worry about you and Ez?"

"Who said I was going to Nicaragua? Who said Ez was going to go?"

Henry answered, "Dad and I can't go. He has to work, and I have stuff to do here. I have to take care of the dogs."

"And what exactly are the risks?" I asked.

"The sharks. They have freshwater sharks. You would have to stay really far away from the sharks."

"I have no intention of going near any sharks," I said. "Anyone for French toast?"

"Me," Ezra said. "Please don't use that crunchy bread."

"Lake Nicaragua is full of sharks. Bull sharks—the only kind that can live in fresh water. They get up these bursts of speed and then—*bam!* They get really aggressive in shallow water. Plus—get this—the females are biggest. Up to eleven feet. You'd have to stay really, really far away from them."

Ezra said, "I thought sharks only lived in oceans, in the deep."

"Everywhere in the world except Nicaragua," Henry said.

Waldo looked up from the newspaper. "Okay, Chief, tell us about the sharks in Nicaragua."

I said, "Who else wants French toast?"

"I told you! They only live in Lake Nicaragua, the big one. Lake Managua, I am very sorry to tell you, is biologically dead. Kaput. As a doornail."

"Where did you learn this?" I gave them French toast.

"The geology of the isthmus is fascinating," Henry said.

Ezra always cut all his French toast into small, evenly sized pieces before he poured on the maple syrup or took a single bite. He asked his brother, "Have there really been shark attacks there?"

"I told you, the bulls are angry types. You guys will have to be very, very careful."

Waldo said, "Abelardo doesn't even live near that lake. I think they should be more concerned about the volcanoes, or the hurricanes. What do you think, Henry? Don't volcanoes erupt all the time in Nicaragua? Henry's right, Al. You and Ezra need to stay away from smoking volcanoes."

Henry said, "But we don't have a family history with volcanoes. We do with sharks."

"Careful. You're talking about my mother," I said.

"Our grandmother," Ezra said.

"It was a great white that got Nana. Great whites are almost twice as big as bull sharks," Henry said.

"That's reassuring," Ezra said. "Not."

"When did we decide Ez and I are the ones going? Was I out of the room? Oh, I get it. Just because I don't have a proper job, I can just take off for Nicaragua."

"You're the only one who thinks that," Waldo said. "And what about earthquakes? Nicaragua has lots of earthquakes, and so does California. Do you have any family history with earthquakes?"

"I hope you don't think this is amusing," I said.

"Where does your friend live, Dad?" Henry said.

"León. It's near Chinandega, if that helps."

"There's a volcano near León that erupts every five years. Volcano Telica. I'll have to check and find out when it last blew its top."

Ezra said, "I wouldn't mind seeing a volcano go off. I think it could be beautiful."

"In 1992 León was buried under six inches of ash when Cerro Negro blew up. It wasn't the kind of eruption you usually think of, with molten lava, it was just gases and ash," Henry said. "I would hate to be covered in ash."

"Is there any more French toast?" Ezra asked. "At least you can wash off ashes. With lava you'd end up like a Pompeian."

"Sorry, Ez," I said. "Are you still hungry? Want some yogurt?"

"Which do you think is more dangerous?" Henry said. "An old volcano or a young one?"

"I give up," I said.

"Definitely the youngest," Ezra said. "So when are we going, Mom?"

I saw Hubert one more time. He and Camilla Hyde, the beautiful Camilla, Posey's erstwhile Ping-Pong partner, were deep in conversation. She didn't look remotely satanic. On this one issue I had to assume Posey was all wrong, all wet. There were even fewer lights than usual in the library.

Hubert popped up from their scrum of two and ejaculated, "You. I thought you'd be in Nicaragua by now."

"Why would you think that?"

"Abelardo, of course."

"And I thought I would be telling you. Ezra and I are going."

"Not a minute too soon," Hubert said.

"Christina has sold her novel for a vast sum," Camilla Hyde

said. She pursed her lips in delicate disapproval. It pained her to mention money.

"It's the monsignor we're worried about. He's been called back to Rome."

"Is that bad?"

"We don't think he is properly understood there. He's a terribly sensitive soul."

"Oh."

"Nicaragua is another story altogether," Hubert said.

"Did you by any chance tell Abelardo I knew something about the virgin saints?"

"I told him you'd been diligent in your research."

"You've misled him. You've led him sorely astray."

"I beg to differ. You have been diligent and Señor Abelardo needs an ally. Far more than he needs your expertise in virgin saints."

"Good, because I don't have any," I insisted.

"As I said, that is not what he needs. He needs your friendship. He needs to unburden his soul."

"That's even scarier."

"Think of it as a tropical vacation," Hubert said.

"Waldo said something like that," I said. But did he? Did I imagine it?

"Think of it as the antidote to Maine," Camilla said.

They were no help at all. "Have you read Christina's book?" I asked.

"Only parts," Camilla said. "She's captured Hubert perfectly."

Hubert actually blushed. "There are some who will be rather distraught. Who will, dare I say it, feel betrayed."

"Anyone I know?"

Neither answered. Hubert flicked the tip of his beard back and forth.

"What shall I bring with me to Nicaragua?"

"As little as possible," Hubert said.

"Antibiotic ointment, broad-spectrum antibiotics, water-purifying pellets, Lomotil, and morphine if you can get your hands on it," Camilla replied. "And do remember me to Posey," she added. "Such a dynamo."

I fell asleep on the train north. But I didn't dream. It was not a dream in which sharks stood on their tail fins and skated down the slopes of a perfect volcano.

Part III ❧ Life in the Tropics

25 ❧ Airborne, Then Tropical

> The contents of the narrative prove it to have been for
> the most part an audacious fiction . . . Its extravagant
> details are, of course, quite fabulous, but there is no
> reason to doubt St Amator's historical existence.
> — Alban Butler, "St Amator," *Butler's Lives
> of the Saints*

W E ARE ALL PACKED. Waldo and I are alone
in the kitchen, alone with Dandy and Flirt
and all the ghosts, memories, and leftovers. I
say, "Waldo, there is one more thing I need to be sure of."

"Shoot." An olive pit catapults across the kitchen and lands in
the soup pot on the stove. Waldo's aim is getting better and better. Soon this business of flinging small objects across the room
will be something he can list on his résumé. Unless it was not the
soup pot he was aiming for but the sink or the rosemary plant.

"This is serious," I say.

He rearranges his features: his cheeks flatten back and his lips
straighten out. The eyes he cannot dampen.

"Tell me you're absolutely, irrevocably, forever and ever done
with Sheila/Shirley."

"Al, I am done. I am completely and forever done. Believe it,
Al. It's true."

"Tell me it's never going to happen again. Because I couldn't
handle it, not ever again. I've exhausted my inner strength in that

department. But not my outer strength. Next time I will resort to violence."

"It might almost be worth it, Al. To see you violent," Waldo says. "But no, it won't happen again. Because I don't want it to. I can't completely explain it but that itch is gone. I promise you a thousand and one times. No, just once."

"Good. Now we can go. It seems that I really want to go down there, see a few volcanoes, broaden our horizons, glimpse Ezra before he's grown and gone. Then we'll come home and we'll all go to Maine."

"Maine's not going anywhere," Waldo says.

It is a truth universally acknowledged that the sight of a hugely overweight person lumbering down the aisle of the economy section of an airplane fills with guilty dread the heart of a passenger next to an unoccupied seat. Such is our dread as the young man soon to be known to us as Rodolfo Godoy makes his way past the first ten rows, then the second ten rows, then stops just before our row, row twenty-four. With fond trepidation I glance over at the empty window seat. Ezra is sitting on the aisle, the better able to observe the flight attendants as they attend to their rolling carts.

Rodolfo Godoy, who weighs three hundred and ninety-nine pounds if he weighs an ounce, says to the air above our heads, "I think that's my seat in there."

What else could we do? I unlatch my seat belt and stand, and elbow Ezra to follow suit.

The young man asks, "Do you have to be on the aisle? Do you think you could switch with me?"

I consider the question.

"I'm claustrophobic," he says.

This changes everything. He has a diagnosis. We move over so that Rodolfo can occupy the aisle seat. We all buckle ourselves in. I say, helpfully, "You know that you can tell your travel agent to book you an aisle seat. Or you can do it online. Given your condition."

"My parents made the reservation. I'm going home for the vacation."

"Don't your parents know that you're claustrophobic?" I ask. I am ready to write the derelict parents a note.

Ezra is reading the *Sky Mall* catalog; he is considering the merits of various wheeled suitcases, including the Animal Planet Pet-Wheel-Away for $99.95.

"Maybe all the aisle seats were taken," he says, dubiously.

"Exactly how claustrophobic are you?" I ask.

"I get very nervous when I'm hemmed in," he says.

"How do you feel about elevators?" I ask. I'm not crazy about elevators, but I dislike tunnels more.

"They don't bother me. Not much."

"What about tall buildings? Do you get nervous in tall buildings?"

"There aren't a lot of tall buildings in Florida. Or in Nicaragua for that matter."

"So is it only coach class in airplanes that bothers you? What about the back seat of an armored car?"

"Pardon?"

"You know," I say. "The kind with tinted bulletproof windows. Even I feel a little claustrophobic in those vehicles."

Ezra closes the *Sky Mall* catalog just as the plane takes off. He says, "We know someone who has just the opposite of what you have."

"The opposite?"

"She's agoraphobic. She's married to our vet."

Rodolfo's chubby intertwined fingers rest upon his vast stomach. His pale pink polo shirt is so large that it is actually loose on him. I watch his knuckles get whiter and whiter as the plane lifts.

"That means she doesn't like open spaces, or being outdoors in general."

"I know what it means," Rodolfo says.

"But she got a lot better during a snowstorm when everyone was snowed in. We weren't there for the snowstorm because we were spelunking, but we know all about it. Everyone knows about it. Everyone was stuck inside because the snowdrifts reached the chimney, and she wanted to go out. Things like that happen, you know."

"I don't think anything like that will happen to me."

"You never know," Ezra says. "I sleepwalk sometimes. Anything can happen."

My head snaps toward him so fast I pinch a nerve. That's twice this year. Ezra wrinkles up his eyelids and fixes a menacing stare upon me. The first and, before this, last person with whom he shared his sleepwalking was Wendy Dilly, and we know her fate. Now here he is slipping it into conversation with a morbidly obese claustrophobe on a flight to Nicaragua.

If Waldo were here, If Waldo were here. I love sitting next to Waldo in airplanes. If Waldo were here, I would drape a blanket over us and stroke his thighs. Touching Waldo in the presence of strangers—and inside a speeding vessel!—is an inexplicable aphrodisiac. If Waldo were here, I would refuse to consider all the other bodies this nubby fleece blanket has covered. Wherever my hands go, Waldo's face remains the same. He has a genius for arranging his features. *If Waldo were here.*

Now Ezra and Rodolfo are exchanging names.

Now they are talking about their animals. It seems that Rodolfo is devoted to his basset hound, Tommy.

Ezra says, "I will tell you the pros and cons of having two dogs. The pro is that they can play together, if they don't fight. The con is that you end up liking one better than the other. You might pretend that you like them both the same, but that's impossible."

In ten-plus years of cohabitation with him, I have never heard

Ezra refer to the pros and cons of anything. Ezra removed from his native habitat could turn out to be very different from Ezra in VerGroot. Ezra in the tropics could prove to be different from the temperate Ezra. Ezra under the meteorological pressures of El Niño could be totally unlike the Ezra basking by the Gulf Stream.

In the guidebook, I read about a certain eccentric millionaire who, in 1972, lived in the top two floors of the only decent hotel in the capital, the one shaped like a pyramid. He spent his days naked and watching James Bond movies. He was friendly with the dictator Somoza. Then came the earthquake, and he fled.

Elsewhere in this guidebook—I love my guidebooks—I read that Nicaragua is just about the most geologically active country in the world. We are flying at an impossible speed over land and water in order to arrive at a most geologically active place. An unstable place. I have no idea how fast the plane is flying. That is the sort of thing Waldo always knows.

Ezra is talking to Rodolfo Godoy. No, they are playing cards. Gin rummy. Ezra will win, because he always beats me. I read this: "Subduction of the Cocos plate underneath the Caribbean plate is at a rate of 8–9 cm per year, *the fastest rate of plate collision in the hemisphere.*" Did Henry read this book?

More than forty volcanoes are in a row. Volcanoes with names like Momotombo and Momotombito and Mombacho and Masaya. Names that will soon roll from my tongue like saliva bubbles.

Ezra says, "Mom, aces go around the corner *always. If I am not mistaken.*"

"They do when we play," I say. In our family, aces go around the corner, but this is not a universally accepted rule. Fairweathers are adamant on this point.

"They *always* do," he says with emphasis. For Ezra, emphasis involves drawing his pale blond, really almost nonexistent, eyebrows together. But no amount of facial contortions can connect his eyebrows.

"You're right, Ez, they always do."

Rodolfo leans over Ezra to say, "I never knew this rule."

"Ezra plays a lot of gin rummy," I explain. "His grandmother taught him, and she is quite strict about rules."

It hits us like a flying sauna: the tropical air and its potent humidity. This very instant when the door slides open and the Nicaraguan air meets the transported gringo air. We step down to the tarmac of the airport named by the revolutionaries for the same person who was their namesake, a young man tricked into leaving his hiding place by a promise of peace and then murdered. It is an old story. Atahualpa might have whispered a thing or two in his ear.

We do not follow the others, including the large and sweating Rodolfo Godoy, along the passage that leads to immigration and passport control. Before we even turn the corner Abelardo steps out of a doorway and greets us. He beckons us inside the room, identified by a small and mostly unseen sign as SALA VIP.

We negotiate a gaggle of bemused Americans clustered just outside the door. They will not enter the *sala* VIP. They are all wearing identical orange T-shirts that say *Tryon Calvary Evangelical Mission to Nicaragua* on the back. The fronts show a naïf-style sketch of a tall white man flipping hamburgers on a barbecue, surrounded by small dark children.

Lalo asks for our passports and luggage stubs, and I unquestioningly hand everything over to his sidekick, Rolando, a young man in a guayabera. Abelardo speaks *muy rápidamente* to Rolando. I am pleased to see Abelardo not in pajamas and not in the snow. I startle myself by being so pleased to see Abelardo in his own climate.

Last time I saw him he was recumbent in a hospital bed asking for fruit and confusing me with someone who'd lost a beauty pageant in Nicaragua. Last time he was getting to know a lacerated landscape worker in the next bed. Last time he was gone, disappeared without saying goodbye.

I want to grab the nearest telephone and call Waldo and say, *What am I doing here? Tell me what I am doing here. This is not a job. This is folly.* I will not cry, I will not weep. I am, after all, the mother here. Is this homesickness? How can I be homesick when Ezra is by my side, dear beloved Ezra, winner at gin rummy, master of surprises? Was I homesick when I was sleeping my way across Europe in seven languages? I was not. Was I homesick in Providence, foreign land of Roger Williams and Buddy Cianci? I was not. It is not homesickness that has my eyes and cheeks in its clutches. It is heartsickness. I want Waldo to appear and tell me that all is well, that I am his one and only. He can tell me in rhyme. Where is a telephone?

Abelardo says, "So this is the famous Ezra."

"Mucho gusto," Ezra says.

"I slept in your bed, I think it was," Abelardo says.

"That's what Mom told me. She should know. You left something in my room. Under my bed."

I say, "We can talk about this later."

Abelardo says, "Did I? I don't recall."

"According to my mom—"

"I've forgotten quite a lot. Perhaps you will help me to remember," Abelardo says.

"Maybe we could get him something to drink?"

Abelardo nods to a full-figured young woman, and lemonade materializes.

The *sala* VIP of the Managua airport came into being during the Sandinista time. Once inside the *sala* VIP you are spared the annoying details of immigration, baggage retrieval, and customs. Inside, lovely young women bring you a cold drink of your choice, shots of Flor de Caña, chilly Victoria, sweating Coca-Cola. Carmen tells me later that they are all former contestants in the Miss Nicaragua pageant. This is the consolation prize.

The difference is more than I can ignore. "The last time I saw you, you were so different," I say.

"That wasn't me."

"You mean, because you absconded? Flew from your mechanical bed?"

"No, because I was a penumbra of my former self, an inversion. What you see now is the real thing, and I hope it pleases you."

Ezra says, "Do you believe in ghosts?"

"I believe in the truth of what we cannot see, which is not quite believing in ghosts, young Ezra."

"I know the difference."

26 ❧ Heliconia, Agapanthus, Datura, and the Rain

> That this extravagant forgery, bristling with anachro-
> nisms and improbabilities, should have imposed upon
> an uncritical age is perhaps not to be wondered at: but
> it is surprising to find its genuineness still up held in
> certain quarters at this present day.
> — Alban Butler, "St Martial," *Butler's Lives
> of the Saints*

EZRA RIDES SHOTGUN in the Mitsubishi, next to Rolando, who is driving. I'm in the back seat with Abelardo. This is all so new, sitting next to him in a car I am not driving, feeling conscious of the different parts of my body as they accumulate sweat: forehead, backs of the knees, inner elbows. I should have installed one of those international chips in the cell phone so I could call Waldo; whatever made me think I could survive without speaking to Waldo several times a day? I am at sea. No, I am in a geologically active place. I say, "I don't want you to have the wrong impression."

"Of course not. Your son will enjoy the volcanoes very much. All the North Americans say it makes all the difference to see smoke coming from the crater. To look into a crater and see smoke."

"I mean about the virgin saints. I'm afraid Hubert has given you a very wrong idea."

"Hubert may be one of the few North Americans to fully understand what we are up against. One of the few persons anywhere."

That is not what I meant. What I mean is about Waldo, Waldo and me. I don't want Abelardo to think it at all strange that I came here to his country, this Nicaragua, without Waldo.

We are stopped at a light. This is the one and only road from the airport to the capital, and the one and only way to get from the capital to León, the city, and Las Brisas, the ancestral Llobet *finca,* and also to Granada, ancestral home of La Matilda and of Carolina Felicita de la Rosa Oberon and all the de la Rosas of lateral descent. Small children knock at the windows of the SUV and hold up plastic bags filled with peeled fruit. For Ezra, it is not necessarily obvious that the contents are fruit, or even edible. Other children hawk gaudy beach towels. Women wearing aprons over spaghetti-strap dresses sell mobile-phone accessories, leatherette cases and headsets. A scrawny man has a parrot perched on one shoulder and another outrageous bird in a cage that's dangling from his fingertips.

Ezra doesn't know where to look.

I say, "I like Hubert very much. Really I do. I think he is brilliant. But he lives in his own private world. You must realize that."

Abelardo smiles. "Do you realize to whom you are speaking? About living in a private world?"

We are driving north on the Carretera Norte (also known as the Pan-American Highway). Abelardo points out the baseball stadium where presidential inaugurations are held every six years, more or less.

The traffic was slow before, but now it is almost stopped. Rolando turns on the radio and we hear that Daniel Ortega is traveling to North Korea to discuss nuclear disarmament, and also that because of a confluence of El Niño and turbulence in the Gulf Stream, the hurricane season is beginning early this year. The first three names are Alice, Bernardo, and Chloe.

But Abelardo points to a pale blue vehicle with a woman driving. "This is marvelous," he says. "Do you know who that is?"

"How would I?"

"It is Carolina Felicita de la Rosa Oberon."

"Do I know her?" I know exactly one Nicaraguan in the world.

"La Carolina, she is second cousin twice removed of La Matilda Vargas de la Rosa, said by some—misguidedly—to be a likely candidate for Nicaraguan sainthood, because of her conversion from wickedness to sanctity."

"Oh, her," I say.

"So you do know her?"

"You told me about her, when you were in the Ginny O. You thought I was she. Which is flattering."

"I told you about her?"

"You did. You were lying on your bed underneath about ten blankets, and I was sitting in a very uncomfortable chair."

"You are thinking of someone else," he says, very softly.

"Seriously, Lalo. I remember. It must occur to you that you've forgotten things. Things to do with the snow and what happened in the snow."

"Memory is a very tricky thing," he says.

Ezra is talking with Rolando but I cannot tell in which language. Ezra's Spanish is rudimentary, and he eschews most verb forms.

Lalo's eyes remain fixed on La Carolina's sky blue SUV idling along with all the others. It idles primly amid the antediluvian American school buses from Mashpee County UFSD and Triple Forks Christian Middle School, the illegally imported luxury SUVs, the Japanese and Korean cars, the Yugoslavian and Russian cars on their last tires, the horse-drawn wagons, the donkey-pulled carts, and a pair of yoked oxen. We are just south of the red light next to the decaying hulk of the old National Cathedral, the one shaken loose of its theological underpinnings in that great earthquake of '72, the now desanctified, slippery pile of tessellated bits and iconic shards, the never repaired old cathedral.

"This really is remarkable, that we are seeing her, here today. I consider it a good sign," Lalo says.

"Beware of signs," Ezra says from the front seat. "Mr. Cicero says when we think we are seeing a sign, then we can be sure we are fooling ourselves."

"I never heard him say that," I say.

"Don't you think she is lovely?"

"I can't tell," I say. Why don't I simply concur? I can hardly be jealous that he finds another woman, someone he has known forever, beautiful. Lots of people are beautiful.

"Of course, she was always rebellious." Lalo stops in order to look over at this rival about whom he is rhapsodizing. Her lane of traffic moves forward about ten yards. Now we can see only the rear window of the sky blue SUV.

"Mom!" Ezra whispers urgently. "Do you see what I see?"

I follow the invisible line extending from his fingertip to a group of young men not much older than Ezra, walking in a cluster and carrying aloft a statue of the Virgin Mary. She looks like most statues of the Virgin, the pleasant but closed expression, the blond hair and blue eyes, except for two things: she is wearing a baseball cap, and over her white and cerulean robes is a team jersey. The Virgin has a large number 37 on her back.

Lalo looks too. I ask him, "Is that normal?"

"Is what normal?" he says.

"Baseball Virgin," I say.

"They must have just won a game."

We are making infinitesimal headway. This is unnerving in new ways. There is all the time in the world to watch the children selling Chiclets and random hardware items. There is ample time to see the mattresses piled up, for sale, on the sidewalk. There is time to scrutinize a man carrying a machete and a machine gun, to observe a tall gray stone statue in the neo-Hispano-Soviet style.

"Originally I was going to bring you to León, because—well, because it is a fine house and it is in the ancient capital, and you could visit the home of Rubén Darío and see his grave. But I have changed my mind. Quite possibly a hurricane is coming, so we'll go directly to the farm, which is on higher ground. Ezra will enjoy the iguanas and the howler monkeys. Are you fond of monkeys, young Ezra?"

"I am descended from monkeys," Ezra says.

We head for the countryside.

The colors are intense and the flowers unfamiliar. Not the flowers themselves but their Brobdingnagian scale. The ferns here are to the ferns of the Hudson Valley as a capybara is to a hamster. On the other side of us is the chaos and tangle of the rainforest with its one thousand shades of green. A bright blue butterfly hovers, swoops, and flits away. We drive uphill. We are among volcanoes. We are climbing a volcano.

Up ahead, a wooden sign hangs from a pole extended between two posts. It reads LAS BRISAS. We have entered the *finca*.

For a long while we ascend on this hairy dirt road, past thousands of shiny green coffee trees, through the *cafetal*, then level off at the village of many-colored cement workers' houses and a bright turquoise wooden church. The church, Santa Irena de Las Brisas (though there are many who hope it will one day be renamed for its local saint, not yet a saint), has vertical siding and stained-glass windows brought back from Prague in 1879 by a Llobet ancestor.

Lalo points to a smallish brown dog standing in the middle of the road. "Young Ezra, do you see that dog? He is a grandson of my Panchito. One of many. Panchito was prolific."

"What kind of dog was he?" Ezra asks.

"A mutt. A bit of everything. Panchito could go anywhere and never be a stranger. *Un extranjero.*"

"Lucky him," Ezra says.

Then we climb again and in a moment we are behind living fences and flowering hedges, we are climbing out of the SUV and standing breathless beneath the porte-cochère of a vast wooden *finca* house whose ends—like Patagonia—we cannot even see. Two seconds ago heat lightning splintered the sky. The heavy doors are carved with scenes of coffee pickers balancing *canastas* on their heads. I will never see a picker carrying a basket, or anything else, atop his head.

"So here we are," Lalo says. "I hope you will not find it boring."

"Even to say you are bored means you have no Inner Resources," Ezra says. He thinks he is quoting Mr. Cicero.

"I simply mean that we lead a very simple life here, growing coffee, among only family, talking coffee . . . you understand."

"Except your aunt," I say. "You talk about her."

"Yes, that is our great exception."

She emerges from the shadowy interior, a shape and then a slender vision in white, a tall woman with cascades of black hair, shocking green eyes, and cheekbones that announce themselves. Her cigarette pants and linen blouse are white, very white; her jewelry is gold, very gold. She walks effortlessly, on pointed and very skinny high heels, also white. How shabby do I feel in a skirt and Birkenstocks? Very shabby. Why did I give up high heels? Let me count the whys. Ezra gazes at the vision with what appears to be love.

Abelardo introduces us to his sister, the wonder in white, who is Carmen.

"I always liked Waldo so much," she tells us. "That northern sense of humor is charming. And so handsome."

I sneeze. Something is making me sneeze, twice.

"*Salud*," interjects Abelardo.

"You have your father's eyes," Carmen says to Ezra. "Don't you think so, Lalo?"

Normally Ezra would reply to this phrase with something along the lines of *No, I have my own eyes.* But this time, in Las Brisas, León, Nicaragua, he says nothing of the sort.

Carmen slides her arm through mine and leads me down the corridor that extends along this vast horseshoe that is almost a courtyard. We climb up broad, dark wooden steps that require an odd gait; the risers are uncomfortably short and it seems awkwardly ceremonial to be ascending arm in arm. She leads us to side-by-side bedrooms, cool dim rooms with dark wooden ceiling beams. In each one a woven and tasseled hammock hangs across the farthest corner. "My brother has told you everything about our Tía Tata?"

"Not everything. I'm sure *everything* would be impossible."

"He is obsessed. Now more than ever. You are kindness itself to come down here, but in reality I doubt anything will be accomplished." Carmen pushes a rogue strand of hair away from her face, then tilts her head slightly forward and with all of her hand sweeps her black mane up and back. "Reality? That is a lot to ask of my family. And Lalo is so brilliant. But so stuck on this."

"Where is your family?" Ezra asks.

"They are all here. Somewhere."

"Are they all like you?"

"No. I am unique."

"Technically, we are all unique," he says.

"Technically," Carmen says, "miracles are an impossibility."

"I meant like DNA," Ezra says.

"Aha." We must be visibly exhausted. I speak for myself. Carmen glides off, past the dark and mottled door. She says, "It's too bad about León. But the winds are bad now and the rain will get worse. In which case . . . Have you noticed how we always get too much or too little rain these days? It wasn't always this way." Carmen silently shuts the door behind her.

And now, before dropping off, I read in my guidebook that in León one can visit the home of Rubén Darío, the great poet who wrote an ode to a young Margarita Debayle, who would one day be aunt to the yet unborn dictator Anastasio Somoza, who, in retaliation for the city's rebellious behavior, would firebomb León's central market. While I'm asleep, a spider walks across my face.

Ezra pushes open my door. "We have to call Dad right away," he says.

"They're hunting fossils," I say to Ezra. I open my eyes. The guidebook is still open on the damp sheet.

"I have an idea for an invention." Ezra is wearing his bush poplin convertible pants, the ones with a zipper just above the knee to allow instant transformation to travel shorts. Ezra's pair has no fewer than seven pockets, in assorted sizes and shapes. The pants are held up at his waist with a canvas belt, because he read somewhere that bees and other insects find leather objectionable. His pale blue button-down shirt has two breast pockets and ventilation panels under the arms. Several of his pockets are already bulging with treasures and supplies.

"Now?" If I squint, I can read again about Rubén Darío's humble home on Calle Once, about wide wooden floors, and the *santos* in the corner. My ear is itching from a spider bite.

Ezra whips a mechanical pencil and an index card from his left breast pocket. He pats his right rear pocket reassuringly. "It's an instant anti-claustrophobia device."

"Can it wait?"

"He'll want to know," Ezra says. "Don't you want to know? I haven't worked it all out, but it gives you the illusion of space . . . you know, lots of room. Because if claustrophobia exists in the mind, then it must be combated in the mind. So this is virtual roominess."

"It sounds brilliant, but it'll have to wait," I say. "They won't be home. And I think I may have been drugged, this sleep is so . . . so perfectly sleepy." I want to roll over. I want to shut my eyes. I am very heavy and also I am surrounded by a heaviness that wants to sink into the mattress. Ezra needs me, I think. "We'll have to ask your father, but if something is virtual, can it also be a device? Are they contradictory concepts?"

"I'm starving."

"Go find Carmen, and I'll be out soon. I don't know what's come over me."

27 ❧ The Saltcellar

> There is little in the recorded history of Christina
> of Brusthem to make us think she was other than a
> pathological case.
>
> — Alban Butler, "St Christina the
> Astonishing," *Butler's Lives of the Saints*

LATER, OR THE NEXT DAY, it is dinner. Beneath the seductive rotations of this fan, we listen. Mostly, we listen. The mahogany, so highly polished, reflects the gleaming silver. Stray beads of water or wine wick off its surface.

It is a story that has been told countless times before. It is a story being honed and polished and shaped with each telling. It is a weighted story. It carries the weight of all the Llobet longings for immortality and justification and sanctity. It is a story well known to all its other tellers at the table. They too listen carefully for some nuance unheard in previous tellings that in a new light will make everything clear. They listen for the clinching detail that, forwarded immediately to the Vatican, will seal their case.

They are practicing for the real thing, for that moment when they face the grand papal inquisitor, that lean and beaky éminence grise in ecclesiastic robes of purple and gold, and with a kissable ring.

Meanwhile the eerily silent servants with broad Mayan features place gold-rimmed china bowls in front of the tiny and heavily sedated Doña Luisa, then me, then the sisters, Carmen, Emilia, and Olga. They serve Don Abelardo; and our host of hypothermic history, Lalo; and the son-in-law, Raimundo Vasquez de Soltera; and Ezra. Lalo's father is a large man, tall and barrel-chested. The painful incongruity of seeing him next to his diminutive wife with her bird bones and powdered cheeks is mitigated by his hands. Don Abelardo has the hands of a concert pianist or a courtesan, long, slender, and silken.

Tristána Catalina was born in 1896, the daughter and last child of Abelardo Llobet Uterbia and Doña Lili Otanguez de Llobet, younger sister to Rafael, Fabio, Martin, Esteban, and Juan. She would become aunt to Esteban, Abelardo, Alicia, Gertrudis, and about twelve more, and from then on be called Tía Tata by all. Later, she would be great-aunt to Abelardo; to Carmen, so beautiful in white and gold; to Emilia, Olga, and thirty-nine others. Tristána rejected five offers of marriage, not one of them from a mental defective, all of them from the cream of Nicaraguan society. Two in particular her father implored her to accept. First there was Carlos Chamaco, an amateur poet and brilliant coffee farmer. By the age of twenty-five he knew more about coffee varieties and advanced theories of cross-pollination than anyone in the country. He was particularly interested in taking the classic arabica Bourbon variety and injecting it with some of the hardier characteristics of the Brazilian. (This would prove impossible, and frustrating to the point of madness, but that is not our story.) He announced himself ready to commission a chapel on his *finca* to be dedicated to any saint Tristána cared to name. She cared to name not one. She told him he would do better to dedicate himself to saving his soul.

Olga, the youngest, asks me to pass her the salt. Her beauty is unlike Carmen's, perhaps because of the asymmetry of her face and her darting eyes. Her skin too is white, snow white, and her lips are red, ruby red.

Just like the fairy tale, if you believe in fairy tales. Which I do. What if Waldo is not my Prince Charming? I don't go to that place.

In Olga, the eyes seem an afterthought above her elegant broad cheekbones. The black neckline of her black dress incises a shocking V upon her chest. It is a low neckline but her breasts must be even lower because there is no visible cleavage.

The salt grains are fairly large. Were they gathered in the Salar de Uyuni, or from the Dead Sea? They cluster like miniature white boulders in a crystal dish fitted into a silver dish with four feline feet. I pass the dish down the table.

Carmen's look could bore a hole in Olga's wide forehead. Olga takes a heaping spoonful of salt with a tiny spoon just like the spoons that cocaine users dangle from golden chains around their necks. Olga creates a perfect white hillock on the rim of her plate, just inside the gold border. She takes a pinch between her thumb and index finger, sprinkles the salt on her left forearm, and rubs it into her skin in concentric circles. She rubs and she rubs, harder and harder.

It must be something they do in the tropics.

Months after Carlos Chamaco was refused, Tristána's father, Don Abelardo, lobbied for another suitor, Lorenzo Beckworth. When he wasn't tending his cattle or his vast holdings of sugar cane, Lorenzo traveled to distant bodies of water in search of the best deep-sea fishing. Tristána's father compared him to another fisherman, a fisher of men. Tristána said she would never again eat fish, flesh, or fowl. Nor would she marry. There were others, all summarily refused. Tristána told one and all that her body, along with her soul, belonged to Christ.

Carmen says, "I have always struggled with the bride-of-Christ concept." She looks directly at Ezra.

Olga smiles. "She always says that."

"My dear Olga." Carmen theatrically raises the three middle fingers of her right hand to her lips.

"If your struggle were doctrinal, I might understand."

"It's a contradiction. If the whole point is to be chaste and unmarried, to forgo the pleasures of the flesh and domestic life, then why even use the terminology of marriage? I would hope for irony, but I know how devoid of irony is the Mother Church."

"The church may be without irony, but that does not mean that its members in the Mystical Body of Christ are not ironical, even paradoxical." Lalo flutters his long lashes in all directions, but especially mine.

Carmen says, "As with Theresa of Ávila, who had sexual fantasies about Jesus. He pierces her with His burning lance." Carmen holds her knife aloft in her right hand.

"Why do you always insist upon misreading the nature of mystical experiences?"

Their mother, tiny Doña Luisa, interjects, "My family, on my mother's side, descends from poor dear Saint Theresa. The Cepeda-Ahumadas. We get our eyebrows from them. Strong, dark eyebrows. Fierce but elegant eyebrows."

"No one is descended from Saint Theresa," Lalo points out. "She was a bride of Christ. Even Carmen will tell you that."

"Pruning techniques for blueberries and coffee are not unalike," says Don Abelardo, the father. "Are you a proponent of *poda total* or *poda por mata?*"

The son-in-law says, "He's not coming tomorrow. Did I tell you? There was some mishap in Guatemala."

"Who's not coming?" Carmen says.

"The pruning consultant."

Doña Luisa says, "From one of her brothers. Her brothers came to Nicaragua, as you know. With the Virgin of El Viejo."

"That is very disputed, Mama," Carmen says.

"It is not disputed in my family."

Olga sits suddenly very straight. "No one ever told me we share DNA with Santa Theresa. That changes everything."

Emilia, who is beautiful in a wide-eyed, frightened sort of way, and almost never speaks, not even to her husband, Raimundo, makes a strange choking sound. She is much darker than the others and she has the square flattish features of *las indígenas,* except for her nose, which is petite and, as it happens, reconstructed. She and Raimundo also live at Las Brisas. Raimundo's face is sunburned.

"It changes nothing," Abelardo says.

"How can you say that?"

"Because it's probably not true."

"No one ever listens to me," his mother, tiny Doña Luisa, says sorrowfully.

Carmen says to Ezra, "It's true. No one listens to her."

Ezra says, "My mother would be very upset if we never listened to her."

There is a subtle vibration at this table. Naturally the first thing I consider is an earthquake. But that is not what is happening. For one thing, the vibration appears to be located only at this table. It is limited to Abelardo. Abelardo must be tapping his foot quickly and ferociously.

Abelardo is eager to get on with the story of Tía Tristána.

Until the incident with the portrait by Sorolla, Don Abelardo, Tristána's father, was universally regarded as a strong-willed man just barely on the acceptable side of tyrant. Until Tristána's adamant insistence on virginity. "What portrait?" Ezra asks.

"You must be joking," Carmen says.

Ezra said cheerily, "I would love to tell you a joke, but I have to check my notebook."

"You didn't tell her about the Sorolla? Lalo?"

"Perhaps not."

"That's a pretty serious omission," says Carmen. "Even for you."

"But he did," I say. I feel compelled to defend Lalo, though I have no idea what they are talking about. What makes me think he needs a defender? And if he does, couldn't he do better than me? Maybe he did tell me about Sorolla—whoever—and I wasn't paying proper attention. Maybe I was distracted by Dandy while he was distracted by the snow while we were both distracted by each other. This quickly gets complicated.

No one hears me. That seems a good thing.

The ferocious foot tapping ceases. Abelardo relates how Don Abelardo, his great-grandfather, lost his appetite, sat in a rocking chair on the veranda at Las Brisas overlooking the coffee trees, and murmured over and over to himself the tongue twisters he had learned from the Jesuits thirty-five years earlier. In Don Abelardo's youth all the best *colegios* for boys were Jesuit schools, and the Jesuits loved tongue twisters and riddles. They used them as mnemonics. Then in 1881 President Zavala banished the Society of Jesus from Nicaragua. The Jesuits returned early in the next century, but their stranglehold on the collective psyche of the country's elite young men had been shaken. Other orders (the Dominicans, the Salesians, the Ransomites) were ready and willing to fill the gap left by the evicted Jesuits. Like nature, religious education abhors a vacuum.

Emilia coughs and whispers that Tía Tata was trained by the Sisters of the Blessed Virgin of Saragossa, who, both individually and as an order, opposed meter and rhyme.

"What portrait?" Ezra asks.

Olga says, "*Señorita T.* Sorolla considered it his masterpiece. But that's because he fell in love with her."

"And Sorolla is?"

"The Spanish Sargent," says Don Abelardo. He exhales a perfectly cylindrical plume of smoke.

Carmen clarifies: "A Spanish impressionist: Joaquín Sorolla y Bastida. They called him the master of the impasto pigment."

"Who did?" Smoke still streams from Don Abelardo's mouth.

She does not deign to answer. "In 1912 Sorolla went to the States to paint commissions. He even went to Buffalo because there were many great ladies there; there were many fortunes made on the Great Lakes. But it was brutally cold, and Sorolla was not a native. He also knew Don Urbano Casares from Guatemala, a great coffee planter but, I am sad to say, a man of wicked impulses."

"He has nothing to do with this, Carmen."

"Don Urbano invited Sorolla to Antigua to paint his very, *very* young wife, and that led to more commissions. Sorolla was not reluctant to leave the city of snow."

"I love snow," Ezra says.

Abelardo shivers and pulls on his earlobe while the tip of his index finger strokes the outer edge of his left eye.

"Sledding is one of my five favorite things."

"Enough, Ezra. Not here," Carmen says. "So it happened that our great-grandfather heard—"

"Great-great," Doña Luisa corrects.

"He heard of Sorolla and invited him to Nicaragua to paint his daughter Tristána, known for her remarkable beauty. Then the trouble started."

"You mustn't say that," Emilia whispers.

"You mustn't say what I mustn't say," says Carmen. "Tristána had no interest in being painted. But her father was determined. Finally she agreed, but only if she could be painted in the habit of a Cistercian monk. Her father was enraged. There were no Cistercians in the family, none in all of Nicaragua, and it was a male order. At least a Carmelite would have made a tiny bit of sense, since there was a family tradition of unmarried ladies spending their dotage at the Convent of the Five Wounds in León."

Olga looks up from her salt pile. "Is that your plan, Carmencita?"

"*I* have not taken leave of my faculties. *I* have other plans entirely," she replies.

Their mother says huskily, "It's the loveliest convent in Nicaragua. They have a weeping virgin and several first-rate reliquaries."

"So how was she painted?" Ezra asks. His hands have been below the table for quite a while now, and there is no dog here, not that I have seen, not in this dining room.

"As a matador."

"A matador?" He gives his napkin a *verónica* flourish.

Lalo says, "She agreed to pose if she could dress as a matador. In those distant times, there were of course no female matadors."

"So there you are. It was Sorolla's masterpiece: *Portrait of Señorita T. upon the Plaza de Toros.* He fell in love painting it. He returned to Spain a richer but sadder man."

"I think it's cruel to kill bulls like that," says Ezra.

"You are young, and centuries of ritualized death are not flowing in your veins."

I am not going to mention Mami's side of the family, the Llovets of Barcelona. Not just now.

Ezra says, "There are cockfights in East VerGroot, but we've never been. They won't let strangers in because they're illegal."

How does Ezra know of such things? With each tiny hint of his hidden cache of secret knowledge, I am newly awash in anxiety. And then pride.

"But Tristána. The very next season her parents took her to visit Spain and there she saw a bullfight for the first, and only, time. Like you, Ezra, she was disturbed by the deaths. When she returned to Las Brisas, before she even took off her traveling clothes, she climbed a ladder, took the painting down, and turned it to face the wall. It stayed that way as long as she was alive, but now we have turned it back around, because it *is* a masterpiece."

Between profound inhalations, Don Abelardo says, "We kept it in Miami during the war, but the insurance was ridiculous."

I am listening carefully.

But how can I hear all that is said?

I am listening carefully.

I hear the shuffling of air molecules in the vicinity of my right thigh, a particularly sensitive area. Not unlike my left thigh in that regard. But tonight it is my right thigh that is closest to Lalo's left side, and that seems to be what matters.

I am discovering that Lalo is left-handed.

"Must we always speak of Tía Tata?" Olga addresses her plate and the geography of salt.

Her neck is sleek and narrow, like a heron's. How can something so delicate hold up her head, which, according to Henry, is the heaviest part of the body, weighing in at eight pounds?

"What would you have us speak of?" Her mother, their mother, is just so tiny; it is all I can do not to think of a stunted creature from a fairy tale.

"How was your flight?" whispers Emilia. She is the middle sister, like me.

Ezra replies, "We sat next to a claustrophobic man. I don't think he was so terribly claustrophobic. I told him about our vet's wife—she's agoraphobic."

Doña Luisa says, "What a smart boy this is to know all the phobias."

"His name wasn't Rodolfo Godoy by any chance?" says Carmen.

"It was. How did you know?"

"This is a small country. Is he still so large and round?"

"We thought so."

Carmen's eyes descend to half-mast and fix on Ezra. If she looked at me like that I would swoon. "Before this Saint Tía Tata stuff, we were a normal family, with normal hopes and dreams."

Emilia coughs and coughs. At first it seems a commentary cough, but she continues hacking and her face reddens. Something is wrong. No one pays the slightest attention. I pat her back, and she shoos me away.

Carmen just goes on. "Lalo was making great progress with the new pruning system for the coffee but now we have an infestation of nematodes in the Santa Rosa sections, we have dieback in the upper Teresita sections, and last season we couldn't get enough pickers."

"Everyone is having trouble getting pickers," Lalo says.

"My dad says that normal is in the eye of the abnormal."

Again those drooping eyes as Carmen says, simply, "Waldo."

Something crashes in another room.

With the soupspoon halfway to his lips Don Abelardo says ominously, "The weather report is not good." The soup's warm meniscus barely quivers.

Carmen says, "Are you watching CNN again, Papa? Natural disasters are their bread and butter."

"He is thinking only about the coffee."

"Did you know that coffee is a delicate plant?" Olga asks me. She's still rubbing the salt in circles. "Like me."

"Alice is gathering strength in the *mar* Caribe and heading westward," says Don Abelardo. "Of course I do not refer to you, my dear, but to the tropical storm that shares your name. A lovely name. What are your thoughts on blueberry pruning?"

"Papa, she's not a blueberry farmer," Lalo says.

"Of course she is."

"It's too early in the season," Carmen says. She whispers to Olga, "Stop that. Desist!" As she turns away her sleeve brushes against her sister's plate and knocks off the tidy pyramid of salt.

Ezra speaks directly to Carmen. "Does Abelardo mind hurricanes as much as snowstorms?"

But Lalo answers (and while he speaks Olga spoons more salt onto the rim of her plate), "Absolutely not. It is a matter of color and temperature. I am very sensitive to color."

"Abelardo used to be quite normal," Carmen says. "Even when he went to seminary he was normal."

Olga whispers, "You already said that."

"White is the absence of all color," Ezra says. He does not say that he rarely sees anything truly white, and that he sees colors that others do not see. He does not mention that a room of happy people will look pink to him, but if someone miserable enters, or if an argument starts, a blue tinge will seep into the room and turn the atmosphere purple. Like Abelardo, my Ezra is very sensitive to color.

"Exactly."

"But if you look at a snowfield, or just a photograph of one, you'll see that it's full of color."

"My eyesight isn't what it used to be."

"Ezra and his brother love the snow. They especially love snow days."

Complete darkness has overtaken the courtyard and all of Las Brisas. Lights twinkle down the hill in the village, but they will soon be extinguished. And finally, late at night, only the *beneficio,* the mill where the coffee is brought in and dumped into enormous squared-off concrete wells, and separated into floaters and sinkers, and then sent along watery courses, separated again and again and shaken to remove its thick red skin and then its finer parchment, and sent at last to the huge batch dryers or out to the patio to be dried by the sun, only this living, breathing *beneficio* will still be illuminated.

Olga stops impressing the circles of salt on her forearm and leans across the table. She whispers to me, "In the Yucatán the women don't get hot flashes. Never. They don't even know what hot flashes are."

"I didn't know that."

"It's true. I think hot flashes account for all sorts of things. Music, for one. And the way flowers smell."

Carmen says, "Alice is too young to be getting hot flashes."

Olga says, "I've always wondered about Tía Tata and hot flashes."

(Olga is only thirty-one but because of her medication she is already experiencing those inflammatory invasions of her body.)

Doña Luisa rasps, "Not in front of Ezra!"

Emilia rings a small bell next to her wineglass. She says, "Did Rodolfo Godoy tell you about his sister?"

Involuntarily, Olga laughs. It is meant to be a laugh but because her mouth is shut it sounds like she is choking. The specter of choking, or hiccups, is never far from the Llobet family.

"Surely not," Carmen says.

Ezra says, "He was pretty nice. We talked about our dogs. But he needs to get exercise."

Doña Luisa says huskily, "Exercise is a very modern idea."

Lalo says, "His parents are thin as rails. They were originally a Swiss family."

"What about his sister?" I ask.

"Some people believe she was miraculously cured through the intervention of Tristána. You may find it interesting, whether it was a miracle or not. But I don't know if I should tell the story in front of Ezra. He is so young and impressionable."

"I won't listen," says Ezra, who is devouring his passion fruit.

"I'm sure it will be educational," I say. Either Lalo is generating static electricity at an alarming rate or I am succumbing to the one and only tropical danger Posey failed to warn us about.

Lalo sips his demitasse. "Grace was a lovely young woman. Then sometime in the seventies—she was more than twenty years older than Rodolfo—"

Emilia whispers into her napkin, "People say it started with the earthquake."

"Whenever it started, Grace began to imagine things about men."

His mother interjects, "I will explain. Grace imagined things. She told her parents about men making improper advances, mostly married men. The parents prayed she would get married, and soon. One day after mass, Grace went straight up to Doña Margarita Hernandez—a timid, gentle person, who loved her lace more than anything—and Grace told her that Don Jaime—he was her husband—was in love with her, Grace, because Doña

Margarita was frigid. And Grace's voice could be quite loud. It got worse. Once in the parking lot of the country club she banged on the outside of Floridita Cabrera's car and said horrid things that I cannot repeat. The chauffeur was right there, but Doña Floridita told him to stay still and wait—she was a nice woman and by then it was pretty clear that Grace was deranged. But, oh dear, all the chauffeurs were there waiting in their cars. By afternoon everyone in the country knew that Grace Godoy was a hysterical madwoman in the grip of sexual frustration. There is a word for it, but I have forgotten. No, I never knew it."

Her offspring nod in disjointed unison. Not one utters the word in question.

Carmen says, "Young Ezra must be very tired, after his travels."

His eyes pop open. "I'm fresh as a daisy," he says. "My mother can tell you that sleep is not always my friend."

I will tell you no such thing.

"In the tropics you will sleep well," says Don Abelardo.

"Just finish what you started," Carmen says to her mother.

"Yes, please finish," I say.

"During Semana Santa, Grace came with her mother to wish me a good birthday. They brought Swiss chocolates. She remembered my birthday every year. I never remember anyone's. Perhaps it has something to do with being Swiss."

"They haven't been Swiss in a hundred years," Emilia says.

"As soon as they were inside Grace Godoy was taken ill. She excused herself and went off to the bathroom. Or so we thought."

She flutters her tiny delicate hand in the general direction of the front door. I notice the emerald ring surrounded by small diamonds. To the right are two doors close together. One leads to a lavatory of antique venerability. The other leads to the room where Joaquín Sorolla y Bastida's portrait of Tristána Catalina dressed as a matador hangs on the eastern wall. And that is the room entered mistakenly by Grace Godoy during that birthday visit.

Don Abelardo, who is able to smoke and drink his coffee simultaneously, a talent that will enthrall Ezra for days to come, says, "We will show you the portrait, but not tonight."

"Neither Señora Godoy nor I knew that Grace had gone into the wrong room, and then Olga thought someone should make sure she wasn't ill. The bathroom was empty. She found Grace on her knees before the portrait of Tía Tata. Grace stood up, as calm as could be. Then they made their farewells and never again did Grace accost another woman about her husband." Doña Luisa causes her crystal goblet to peal as she flicks her fingernail against the rim. "Thus was Grace cured of her intemperate lust and the imagined lust of others. It was miraculous."

All the Llobets suddenly look at me, which feels awkward, because I am thinking about food, about cuitlacoche and passion fruit and how they will affect our dreams. I need to focus. "As in a miracle?"

"By June she was married to Don Ignacio Gurdián, a widower with monastic leanings. They appear to be completely happy."

In a small silver bowl in the center of the table are almonds, each covered with chocolate and a thin pastel mint shell. Carmen places a lilac mint on the flattened end of her coffee spoon and very slowly she depresses the bowl of the spoon, testing her catapult.

This is very, very familiar. I have seen this a thousand times at our pockmarked table in VerGroot.

Carmen says, "Even if you believe in miracles—which I do not—according to your beloved Catholic Church, for a miracle to count it has to be prayed for. And verifiable."

Ezra appears to be asleep upright. It is time. This day started ages ago, certainly days or weeks ago.

Lalo readjusts his shoulders. "It is merely an anecdote. An

anecdote that may prove to be more than an anecdote when she is canonized."

"*If* she is canonized," says Carmen. "There is absolutely no evidence that Grace ever prayed to Tía Tata."

"She was on her knees, for Christ's sake," Olga says.

"She could have been searching for a contact lens," says Carmen.

"That's disingenuous."

"If you find me disingenuous, wait until you start talking with the Vatican. They chew up people like us every day, and spit them out after breakfast."

"Carmencita!" interjects Doña Luisa, but so throatily it is hard to believe she doesn't have bronchitis.

"I'm very serious. It is of course lovely to have Alice and Ezra here in time for the hurricane season, but I hope they were not enticed here by the false promise of a miracle." Carmen returns her concentration to the lilac mint at the end of her spoon.

When I go into the room next door to kiss Ezra good night, he is hunched over the bedside table, balancing a mint on the end of a spoon and levering the bowl back in order to catapult it across the room. There is nothing to say. I kiss the top of his head, his sweetly smelling head. Ez says, "I think I am going to like the tropics."

The rain is beating on the tile roof.

28 ✆ Ringing Carillon

The *passio* of St Quintinus is a worthless recital of tortures and marvels.
> — Alban Butler, "St Quentin," *Butler's Lives
> of the Saints*

I<small>N THE UPSTAIRS HALLWAY</small> Lalo startles me.
There is a faded photograph of pickers dumping their
baskets of coffee berries into the back of an ox cart.
Two women and a young man look oddly familiar. A dark dog
sits in the lower right corner of the photograph. I hope Lalo did
not see me testing the upper frame for dust—there was none.
This is unlike home in so many ways.

He says, "Do you remember Rubén Zamora?"

"Of course I do."

"His sister is very ill. She was. She had an inoperable brain
tumor. But she prayed to Tía Tata—her whole family prayed to
her and to no one else and now the sister is better. She's gone back
to the doctors and they've done tests, and the tumor is gone. Disappeared like the dinosaurs."

"You're sure she had it to begin with? This tumor? I've heard
of much stranger mistakes. Hairballs, hysterical pregnancies. That
sort of thing."

"As sure as I can be. The documentation is under way now.
It will naturally take a long time, because everything takes a long

time, and in the Vatican things take a thousand and one times a long time."

"Why are you telling me this? Before coffee?"

"Because it's good news. Because I want you to think about it as I think about it."

"You mean at the same time, or in the same way?"

"We're in this together, Alice dear."

"Oh, no, Lalo. No, no, no."

"How no?"

"I'm not like you. I don't believe, not in that. Not like you."

"I'll settle for your company," Lalo says.

Breakfast is almost over. I do not like having breakfast with people to whom I am not related. Breakfast is about caffeine, and listening to the rustling and crinkling of old papers inside my skull. Breakfast is about long silences that disappear into subterranean caves. Breakfast is not about the webs of emotions.

Ezra sees it differently. Ezra has been methodically eating *gallo pinto*. He is separating the red beans from the grains of rice, placing the beans on the left side of his plate and the rice on the right side. The only problem is that the whole point of *gallo pinto* is the rice and beans are mixed together. He finishes chewing, and then mouths something to me.

I shrug, and nod.

I say to Carmen and Emilia, "Ezra would like to tell you all his dream."

Emilia's eyes drill into Ezra and then me. She is wearing large round diamond earrings, and either the diamonds are very big or her earlobes are very small.

Ezra begins. It is known by all, and especially by me, that most people are uninterested in the dreams of others. Only Freud, Jung, and me. Well, Gordie, at WBLT, sometimes, and now these Llobet sisters. Something strange has happened and some seismic shift (perhaps the infamous Cocos plate) has rearranged the arrangements inside my head. In just two days in the tropics. No question that the weather has something to do with it. No question that I am susceptible to heat and humidity. Ezra finishes his dream and I didn't hear a word.

I had not seen Lalo standing at the far end of the dining room. He says, "That's all?"

Carmen says, "If I ever have a son, he will be just like you."

"He'll be a lot younger than me," Ezra points out.

Lalo says, "I told Mama that we will all stay here. That it will be safer here than in León. She wanted to go back for her ladies' book club because they are reading something by a handsome young Chilean writer. But it is out of the question. Alice is now a full-blown hurricane on its way in this direction."

"She hates all the ladies in that book club. She says they are ignorant and badly educated," Carmen says. "What was the name of the writer?"

"I have no idea."

"Roberto Bolaño," Emilia says. "He's already dead. At a young age. It is tragic."

Olga says, "I hate it when people die too young."

Carmen says, "We all do."

"No. Not like that. I hate it rather differently, because I will die young myself."

Emilia gets up from the table. "That's it. I can't listen to this anymore." She tugs on her earlobes, and the large diamonds send refracted light all over the room. "You'd think she was the only mentally ill person in this family."

"Clearly not," Carmen says.

I look at Ezra because I am thinking that he might prefer to be elsewhere. I might prefer he were elsewhere and not listening to this.

Who knows what Ezra is listening to? He is stroking the long white forearm of Carmen. If it were not such a cliché to compare pale skin with sculptural stone, I would say her forearms are like alabaster.

"How lovely that your mother belongs to a book club. Do you have many here in Nicaragua?"

"Many what?"

"Book clubs."

"It depends what you mean by *book clubs.*"

Thunder claps, and thunder barrels out of the sky with its mouth wide open. There is a thud, repeated irregularly, muted.

Olga jumps forward and says, "Did you hear that?"

Lalo takes her hand, so gently. "It's the *beneficio.*"

"No. It's the hurricane. *El huracán.*" She says it twice, first in English then in Spanish.

"No, *that* was the *beneficio.* We are having problems with the *secadoras.*"

Lalo is referring to the giant dryers for the coffee beans. They look like gargantuan inner drums of clothes dryers. Their heat is supplied from a furnace stoked day and night with *leña,* the branches from pruned coffee trees. This morning the *secadoras* sound like my clothes dryer sounds when I throw in wet sneakers: *slam slam, thump thump, clickety clack, slam* again, and again.

"What is the problem with the *secadoras?*" Carmen asks.

"They're out of alignment. And Misael is in León with his mother."

"Misael is the chief engineer," Carmen tells me.

"His mother has Parkinson's," Olga says.

"No, it's Alzheimer's. But that's not why he's in León. It's for the anniversary mass for his father's death. He told me last week. Do we remember to do such things, like anniversary masses?"

"Our parents aren't dead yet," Olga says.

Carmen taps her feet with rhythmic impatience. They are long, narrow, and naturally elegant. Her feet are not so much shod in her black Ferragamos as draped in them. Did Waldo ever suck on her toes? I wonder. I would rather not be wondering that, not just now, here, at breakfast. What I would really like are long, skinny feet of my own.

Lalo says, "First the *secadoras,* and then the hurricane. After the hurricane—what? The aftermath. We will advise Hubert how your research into Tía Tata's sanctity is coming along."

"It's not coming along at all," I say. "You know that. Wouldn't it be better if Hubert came down here?"

"I have asked him many times. I promised that volcanoes would erupt just to celebrate his arrival. But he refuses to fly."

"On principle?"

"He is terrified."

Ezra turns to Carmen and whispers, gleefully, "I knew it! You should have seen him when Flirt got skunked."

"Ah," says Carmen. "Since your Nine-Eleven, all sorts of people will no longer fly. But it is foolish. The odds are better for flying than . . . than so many things."

I say, "He should pray to Saint Joseph of Cupertino, the patron saint of flying. He was a big levitator and floater."

"In the matter of flying, I do not think Hubert wants any help."

Thump, crash, thud. The noises set in again.

"That's not the *secadoras,*" Olga says. "And I should know."

"Why should you know?" Carmen asks.

"My hearing is much better than any of yours. I have extraordinary hearing, and I can promise you, it is a curse."

"Then it must be Alice, the hurricane."

"Later," Lalo says, "I will show you the portrait. But first the *secadoras.*"

"I long to see it."

"She longs to see it," Olga repeats. Olga is a mystery to me.

"Can I go with you? To see the *secadoras?*"

"Of course," Lalo says. This surprises me. I expected to be turned down, and justifiably, because it seems impossible that

Lalo does not recognize that I am here on false pretenses. I will never help with the canonization of Tía Tata. At the most, I will clutter her narrative with vignettes of apocryphal virgin martyrs. Worse than my uselessness, though, is that I am succumbing to the luxuriant weight of the inevitable storm. I am no different from Lalo in the snow, and if I am, I am so wrapped up in the dripping foliage that I can no longer tell the difference. Worse still than the uselessness and the succumbing is that I am leaning toward Lalo. I am leaning toward his physical presence and his unswerving conviction that this is what he should do.

He does not turn me down. He says, "You should wear different shoes."

The *beneficio* is down the hill a short ways, in the center of the village, more or less across from the church. We could walk but we do not. Lalo goes off to talk to his second-in-command engineer and leaves me to wander around the cavernous, shaking room. In the middle of this room the beans are mechanically shaken over a grid that selects for size, and then they're shunted to long tables, where ladies pick out any last irregularities that have evaded the previous separations. Piled up along all the dark walls are sacked quintals of coffee beans. In front of each row is a hand-printed cardboard sign indicating the quality: CHORRO, CHORRO EUROPEO, and so on. The smell of old wood is admixed with the more pungent damp, ripe-vegetable odor that rises from the lower level of the *beneficio,* where the red beans are dumped into wells and then propelled along the watery canals by screw press to remove the skin, then the pulp, then the parchment. Up here in the shaking room, the rafters are home to Olympic-size cobwebs—whole other ecosystems existing comfortably beyond the reach of an indifferent broom. The randomly spaced fluorescent tubes flicker. In this way, the room reminds me of the Hagiographers Club; I don't know how the ladies can see well enough to distinguish one perfect coffee bean from its lesser cousin. They look at me but say nothing. I greet them guardedly. Even they can surely see that I am here under false pretenses. More so, since all the coffee beans look the same to me: like the dried brains of frogs or mice. Something very small with an even smaller brain.

"Coffee is in our blood." Lalo startles me by popping out from behind the *secadora,* in the company of a short man. He introduces me to Napoleon Something, who is missing the index and third finger of his right hand.

"Mine too," I say. "I can't stay awake without it."

He smiles. "Napo is an excellent engineer and *béneficero,* but he has never liked the *secadoras.*"

They rotate noisily. "What's not to like?"

"Their existence. He would rather we dried all the coffee on the patio. But the weather is too inconsistent these days. Nowadays." He pulls me to the edge of the *beneficio,* to the last place where we can stand under the roof, and indicates the vast cement patio where in years past the wet coffee beans were dumped and raked out to dry in the sun.

"It must have been so beautiful," I say.

"Let's go visit the church," Lalo says.

Inside it is dark, but not the same dark as it was over at the *beneficio.* The pre-storm sunlight filters in through the stained glass and flatters us both. The oddest collection of plastic flowers and real orchids crowds the altar. The crucifix above, while appropriately anguished and bloody, is also coyly modest—Christ is wearing a short sarong fashioned out of a denim-like material. Lalo slides into a pew on our left and kneels down. There is no good reason for this to be so surprising. But it is. I am adrift. It's been ages since I last knelt in church. Actually, I can remember exactly when: it was in Barcelona with Abuela. Abuela was a world-class kneeler—she put us Californians to shame. Should I kneel too? Or would it be too obvious that I am doing it only to impress Lalo, and because I am feeling dangerously devoid of any

Catholic credentials just now? But isn't it ridiculous—and solipsistic—to imagine he would think one way or another about my kneeling? To imagine that he would think about it at all?

"Would you like to go up?" he says, right beside me now. He points to the choir loft.

"Sure," I say. "You know what is wonderful? You. You believe in what you're doing. Have I said this before? I wish I had some of that. Some of your not-irony."

"Don't you understand?" Lalo says.

"Huh? No. Obviously not."

"I have to struggle all the time to believe in this. I know a saint would be good for Nicaragua. That I am sure of. I can't solve our poverty. I can't still the earth. I can't stop the avalanche of corruption. I can't control the rainfall upon the coffee. But I can further the cause of a Saint Tristána, who would be a huge boon to this country. After the Marines, the Somozas, El Pulpo, and the Ortegas, the country deserves some grace. So I keep at it, even though with each passing day it seems more far-fetched, and I am sure it has not escaped you that in my family the others who believe in Tía Tata are in various stages of crazy. Carmen is the only one of us who makes sense, and she's the one I have to contradict every day."

"You never said that before."

A young girl looks in from the open door at the back of the church, looks at both of us, crosses herself, and then heads back out to the church garden and the plaza.

"Do you know her?" I ask.

"I know everyone here. Her name is Flor Garzas. Her father was one of the best pruners we ever had."

"You should have told me," I say.

"About Flor? We only just saw her."

"No! About you."

"Let's climb up."

I follow him up the stairs into the choir loft, but we don't stay there. We climb the rickety, dusty ladder to the belfry. On the way up we pass the spire's single, singular window. I hang on tight and peer at the *beneficio* spread out below us and the *finca* spreading in every direction, an inexorable stretch of coffee trees climbing the sides of the volcano, plummeting into river valleys, and then climbing again.

Up in the belfry Lalo removes the square panel of wooden slats that—so it seems—is not fixed in place. And again we see the *finca* below us, farther below. I touch the rope dangling from the bell above us, and pull. It is heavier than I imagined—but not nearly as heavy as I should have thought had I recalled the contortions of Quasimodo.

Lalo pushes my hand away. "What are you thinking?"

I shrug. "I wasn't. But I've always wanted to ring carillon."

"Now is not the time." He points to the clock mechanism, a vision of notched wheels in countless sizes, all of them tiny, all communicating. As far as I can tell, *that* is a miracle.

On the lintel beam above our heads are names, carved and painted: Adolfo Ruiz, Kika Mas, Challo Pellas. Just names.

If I look straight down to the ground, I get very dizzy, so instead I look out toward the far horizon. Lalo says, "Have you ever committed a crime?"

An odd question for this vertiginous place. I have to think. "Sure. I smoked pot. I've sped. I've probably sped quite a lot. I used to shoplift red licorice. I need to think."

Lalo's face has taken on a masklike quality that frightens me. Either he is hiding himself from me or he is hiding something else from me. Default mode: I feel guilty.

He says, "I mean as in a mortal-sin crime. Something truly wicked."

"I need to think. If you mean murder, no, I haven't murdered anyone. Not yet. Have I coveted my neighbor's wife, husband, horse? I have. I've done wicked things but I'm not going to tell you about them. You probably wouldn't appreciate how wicked they were." I would love to ring the church bell just now. I keep my hands in my pockets and back away from the open square, the beckoning precipice. "Why are you asking?"

"Because I suspect you have never done anything truly wicked. That you just don't know how."

"You don't know me very well. Anyway, it probably depends on your definition of *wicked*. So, have you? Committed a crime?"

"I think I have. And I think I am about to."

"Now you've got me listening. Care to tell?"

"Lies, deceit, and falsehood," Lalo says. Then he touches my forehead and brushes back my flopping forelock. Just that: his cool fingertips making contact with my moist brow, and I'm ready to break as many commandments as I can remember. I could sink into the dusty planks right now. Tell me a crime, Lalo! Give me a chance! I will listen and then we'll fall to the floor and consummate forgiveness. I whisper, "I'm listening."

Three flights down a door creaks on its hinges. Lalo pulls on his earlobe, the left one.

"I don't believe you," I say. "I bet I would beat you hands down in the wickedness sweepstakes."

"Waldo is my friend," Lalo says. "Waldo and his family were very good to me."

From below a voice calls, "Don Lalo! Are you up there?"

"I have to go," he says. "That's Napo. I'll go first and you come later. Can you do that?"

"We haven't done anything wrong," I say.

"I would have," he says. "That's just the same." Then he climbs down the ladder.

29 ❧ Tropical Storm Alice Is
Not Named After You

It is the conclusion of the Bollandists that her story is an
empty fable, imitated from the last days of St Mary of
Egypt: "A pious tale fabricated by a man of leisure for
the gratification of simple religious people."
— Alban Butler, "St Theoctista," *Butler's Lives
of the Saints*

I AM SO PLEASED to meet you," Don Abelardo says.
I am standing in the middle of the living room, the
big room with its worn wooden statues of saints and
stuffed iguanas. There used to be stuffed monkeys arranged in
lifelike poses along the rafters: howlers, spiders, and cara blancas.
I imagine them casting shadows upon the ceiling, never being
entirely still and now aquiver with the storm approaching. "You
must be a friend of Carmen's. Olga would never allow her friends
to come here."

"I'm Alice Fairweather," I say. "I've been here for days. I'm
Abelardo's friend but originally he went to college with my husband, Waldo. Do you remember Waldo? All the ladies do."

"Then you must know Esteban."

"I have no idea who Esteban is. I'm sorry."

"I am delighted to meet you. I am Abelardo Llobet."

The cigarette in the corner of his mouth bounces slowly up
and down as he speaks. He may not know me but he never drops

the ash. I say, "We met yesterday, and also the day before and the day before. When I arrived here. With my son Ezra."

"I remember nothing of yesterday. But I do remember that Carmen and Lalo used to hide in Santa Irena's belfry and we never told them we knew where they hid. We let them believe in their secret. That was a hundred years ago. Please accept my apologies." He sits down in a vast leather armchair and turns on the reading lamp poised nearby. He shuts his eyes against the light and the tears.

"I miss you guys." I have finally reached Waldo. I am finally hearing his voice. I've been leaving messages, at home and on his cell. And no response. So this, this telecommunication linkup via satellites hovering somewhere either above or below the ozone layer, I haven't the foggiest which, this feels like an accomplishment. And that it should happen now, now that torrential rains are tattooing the roof and Niagara-ing down the chains in the courtyard, only heightens the sense of accomplishment.

"Ditto, Al," Waldo says.

"So tell me, how have you been? What are you doing? Anything new at work? How is Henry? Does he know everything there is to know about prehistoric creatures? How are Dandy and Flirt?"

"You've only been gone four days."

"It feels much longer," I say. I know as well as he does that in four days, continents can be crossed, lives can be created and lost, revelations can occur, and love can swoop down like a comet.

"How does Ez like life in the tropics?"

"He loves it," I say.

"How much does he love it?"

"You can ask him. If I can find him. Tell me about Henry, please."

Barking. The miracle of dogs barking on one continent being heard on another continent, or rather on the isthmus linking

340

continents, eliciting the reactions they would in the closest proximity. Are they hunting? Are they hungry? How is Dandy's blood?

"Henry has identified a new creature."

"What is it?"

"That's the beauty of it. We don't know. Henry believes he's found the fossilized footprints of a Paleolithic North American canine. But I think he should tell you himself. He's written to the NIS about naming it."

"Naming it? Does he get to do that?"

"If he really discovered something, you bet he does!"

"I miss you guys."

"You said that."

"I'll say it again."

"So what's with Lalo's aunt? Does she have a halo yet? Are they feeding you well?"

"No. Yes. I have serious doubts about this sainthood business. Even more serious doubts about me being here. It's not exactly a job."

"No one said it was a job."

"I think I need to get a job pronto," I say.

"You're in Nicaragua now. So enjoy the tropics."

"We're about to have a hurricane. This instant. It seems weird not to be able to go outside now."

"Wait till the calm after the storm," Waldo says.

"I thought the calm came before the storm."

Waldo says, "I don't think they're mutually exclusive."

"So. What does Henry want to name his creature?"

"Alicestodon. He wants to name it for you."

This makes me weep with an urgency compelled by distance and uncertainty. Though Waldo could very well be pulling my leg.

"He should tell you all about it, but he's disappeared. Missing in action."

"Really?" What is missing is Waldo's presence.

"Really it's no big deal. Seriously. How is Lalo?"

"Lalo is great. His family is great. The sisters are all beautiful, especially Carmen. But you know that. I hardly ever see Ezra, he's with her all the time."

"Give them all my best. You can tell them that Dick is growing coffee in Maine."

"How are the newlyweds?"

"As they should be. Blissful. I have no idea."

"You haven't spoken to them?"

"Al, it's been four days. Nothing has changed."

"I miss you terribly, Waldo. Didn't you know about the hurricane?"

"Unless Posey tracks me down, I won't hear a weather report until you return."

"Just this once, for me, check it out, *por favor*. If you want to know if we're still safe and dry."

"Okay. Just this once. Just for you."

"What are you working on?"

"This and that, the usual."

"I forgot to tell you that Ezra has an invention for you. Something about anti-claustrophobia."

"Adios, Alice. *Hasta luegito, amorcita.*"

And that is more or less it. One second we are talking and everything is normal, and the next second the connection is severed and I am on a coffee farm in a Third-World country best known for revolutions and assassinated dictators, and Waldo is in our home in VerGroot where I can visualize everything in its place and yet still have no idea what Waldo is doing and even less what he is thinking about. And missing him is a physical pain, a sharpness in my chest akin to the pain when you have swallowed ice water too fast and you have to breathe slowly and shallowly in order to bring in warmish oxygen, fast.

• • •

342

The house is trembling. My sheets rustle like waves. Earthquake. It must be an earthquake. Fuck, fuck, fuck. This is not the earthquake of my imagination. In my imagination I am the opposite of the naked American millionaire in the Managua pyramid, in druggy denial; I am alert and watching it all transpire. I am ready. In my imagination it is visual, it is the earth cleaving asunder in front of my eyes. I remain untouched. I need to find Ezra. I am not decent. Technically, I am not decent. But once I have located and pulled on my robe, Ezra is in front of me, awake and vivid.

"It's just the wind, Mom. It's the hurricane. Named after you," he says. "Just kidding."

Of course he is right. The trembling of gale-force winds is altogether different from the trembling of the earth's crust as it shifts and cracks open beneath you.

For the third morning in a row, there are pastel-colored mints all over Ezra's room. So much happens after I go to sleep. He must practice different techniques to improve both distance and aim. One day he will be an excellent golfer, but for now he does very well with a spoon of Taxco silver and imported French mints. He has not sleepwalked once since arriving in Nicaragua.

I miss Waldo like a finger, shocked to realize how essential even that small finger is, how much I rely on the ability to grasp an object and bend at my knuckles.

For the third morning in a row, Ignacia, the maid from Sutiaba, the indigenous town just outside of León that is even older than León, sweeps and tidies the room. She holds the broom with her fingertips, like a lover. She moves back and forth in a pattern both fluid and fixed. I suspect that she has swept up catapulted mints before, though not in this bedroom. Ezra has never had someone to clean up after him like this, and I would hate for him to grow accustomed to such a luxury. No, he will not. He is a Fairweather, and Fairweathers are independent, to the extent of preferring their messes untouched, their papers untidied, their noses unwiped, and their socks unpaired.

Why am I sleeping so far away from Waldo's warm flesh, from his smooth back, his furry chest, his energetic penis?

Why isn't Henry here being a know-it-all, a smarty-pants, a Mr. Knowledge, a Factoid Ferdinand? Whatever made me think it was possible to come down here without them? Without them, belief is not possible. Without Waldo to question everything and Henry to know the facts of everything, how can I believe in Tía Tata?

I have no idea where Ezra is. In an asymmetrical and pale room unconnected to anything else, I find about a dozen old leather suitcases with stickers from European hotels and spas. One has been energetically nibbled by an animal. A broom leans into an opposite corner. But the best part in here is this: a life-size statue of Saint Theresa of Ávila. She is dressed Carmelite style, in shades of black and white and gray. She is holding an arrow pointed at her chest from which the yellow paint is peeling off.

Dangling cuticles, canker sores, peeling paint: they all beckon me to fiddle, pull, worry. I do not resist. I flick off two larger pieces of loose yellow paint—*thwip, thwip.* This is probably art. I am defacing art.

Theresa Sanchez Cepeda Davila y Ahumada died late on October 4, 1582, but her feast is celebrated the next day, October 15. It happens that on October 5, 1582, Pope Gregory enacted the switch from the Julian to the Gregorian system and moved the entire calendar forward ten days. There was no October 5, 1582, nor was there an October 6, 7, 8, 9, 10, 11, 12, 13, or 14. Gone by papal fiat. The day after she died, Theresa's heart was removed from her body and found to have evidence of transverberation. It was pierced, just as Theresa had imagined herself pierced by the blinding arrow of Christ's love. Here in Nicaragua Rubén Darío's heart and brain were removed from his body, but no one seems to know exactly where they ended up.

And in the midst of the gully-washing rain, Lalo is quieter

than the *santos*. He is sitting in a rocking chair mere inches inside the protective roof of the courtyard, but he is not rocking. I want to slide into his presence without a ripple and be part of the stillness. What do I care about a dead aunt who refused to marry? I don't. I care about Abelardo. I think that if Abelardo could be the agent of Tristána's canonization, then . . . ? Then he would be satisfied. Then he might perceive me differently. Then we could go on to the next thing.

No resolve of mine to be silent has ever lasted more than moments. "So tell me more about Tata." (Distract me! Distract me!) "I'm having trouble when I think of her." (I'm having trouble not thinking about you.) "What did she do when it rained this much? Did she mind when her clothes were never entirely dry?"

"She was born here."

Lalo gets up from his motionless rocker and stands next to a wooden armchair lined with faded striped cushions, indicating that I should sit there. I have never looked at his face before. Have I? The squared-off chin, the feminine smoothness of his skin, the aquiline nose, the almost black eyes, and the vast anarchic eyebrows. It is something I would paint if I knew how to paint, or mix colors.

Just a few feet away the rain is hammering at the grass and pummeling the flowers of the courtyard. It is roaring down the chains and spewing from the drainpipes. Gargoyles would be very happy here, hunchbacked iguanas and harelipped cara blanca monkeys, spitting out streams of tropical rain. Lalo may lament the havoc it is wreaking on the countryside, but he does not mind his own proximity to the rain. I mind the proximity. I move my chair back toward the interior.

How long has it been since I last saw Ezra?

"What did she do all day? There has to be something I am missing. Because if the holiest thing she ever did was refuse to get married, well, if that's the case, then I think we have a problem, Captain."

Lalo smiles a smile of secret knowledge.

"It is true she refused to marry, but that was only in order to free herself for God's work."

So Lalo tells me how Tristána, after refusing all offers of marriage and refusing to behave like the wealthy young woman she was, agreed to stay here on the farm, Las Brisas—back then it was over ten thousand hectares of cattle and coffee and sugar—but only if she could live in a small worker's shack on the other side of the *beneficio,* the one he showed me. She dressed like a young man, in loose cotton trousers and a cotton shirt. There were stories that she wrapped long bandages around her breasts to flatten them, but Lalo says they are apocryphal. Every month she cut her own hair with her sewing shears. She was still beautiful. Perhaps in men's clothes and with inelegantly chopped-off hair, she was even more beautiful. She did not revisit the tight leggings of a matador that caused such longing in the heart of Joaquín Sorolla y Bastida.

I say, foolishly, "Hubert was a fount of information about the cross-dressers. Hildegund went on a crusade in 1106 dressed as a boy. Euphrosyne called herself Smaragdus, and lived in a solitary cell. He especially liked Saint Marina, who called herself Marinus. When she was accused of knocking up the innkeeper's daughter, even then she didn't reveal her true sex. She accepted her superior's punishment—like the saint that she was—and lived outside the monastery walls looking after the fatherless child. Only when she died was the truth revealed and her innocence declared."

"Hubert must be a wonderful man."

"He certainly has his qualities."

The constant drumming of the rain changes just this instant from a cacophony of individual raindrops to a vast sky-size bucket of water being emptied upon our heads, upon the roof, upon the village and the farm. The volume of water increases threefold or tenfold—who knows the exact multiplier? Perhaps one hundred times, which is the number of times I've thought about Lalo in the last hour. More or less. The sound is louder than anything else. To talk is folly.

And then the noise abates just enough for Lalo to continue.

She lived alone in that shack on the other side of the *beneficio*. It was not really a shack as in a ruin, just a shack as in a humble abode. Lalo wants me to understand the poverty and simplicity of Tristána's life, but also to know that the workers on the Llobet farm do not live in decrepit buildings. It is a fine line, but that is why we are here, because we want to draw a fine line all the way from this coffee farm to the Vatican's inner sanctum sanctorum sanctotum. Like the humble people, Tata ate fruits and vegetables, rice and beans.

The church of Santa Irena predates the current *beneficio*. It predates the advent of gourmet coffee. The parish priest was a young man from Nicaragua's Atlantic coast, named Oscar Felipe Franklin. Like most people on the Atlantic coast, Oscar Felipe was descended from Englishmen and English-speaking blacks, as well as Miskitos, and all his life he spoke Spanish with an English accent. Because of his popularity and because of the length of his tenure at Las Brisas, the *campesinos* to this day pronounce certain words with that same English accent: *almohada, ferrocarril, aguacate.*

When Tristána moved to the shack behind the *beneficio,* the one who was most uncomfortable was Padre Oscar Felipe. He had never heard of a young woman of good morals living alone on a farm. Especially a young woman of such a family. In all his life he had never been alone in a room with a beautiful woman, and here was Tristána, waltzing in and out of the tiny rectory he shared with a serving boy, Hugo. She alerted him to the material and spiritual needs of his flock, and questioned, again and again, the validity of coerced baptisms. That became a bee in her bonnet, and a thorn in his side. She'd read in a history book of all the Indians forcibly baptized by the Spanish friars and found it troubling. She dreamed of villages precariously clinging to the slopes of volcanoes, overrun with iguanas and inhabited by Indians who wore scapulas round their necks, prostrated themselves before the cross, and yet believed that milk and honey flowed from the veins of Jesus Christ. As soon as she woke from these dreams, Tristána rushed across the plaza to the rectory, awakened Padre Oscar Felipe, and asked him, again and again, what should be done about these poor Indians. The modest padre took to sleeping in his clothes. He was not much of a theologian, he told her. He preferred to leave such thorny questions to the Jesuits. As long as his flock didn't beat their wives too badly and kept all the saints' days and believed in the intercessory powers of the Virgin, Padre Oscar felt well satisfied with them.

Have I mentioned that Lalo has ridiculously long eyelashes?

"Alice," he says and leans toward me. How long have I been holding my breath? "Where is the irony in this? Tía Tata rejects all suitors, stays on the farm, tends the sick, and attends funerals. Then she dies and miracles occur. One miracle that we are sure of."

Is he referring to the hiccups or to Rubén Zamora's sister? Surely not the nympho Grace? I say nothing.

"It is the pattern of countless virgin saints—the ones you read about."

I chant, "Dympna, Werburga, Winifred, Begga, Paula the Bearded, Uncumber, and—"

Lalo stops me. "But something is missing. Some element of transcendence. You teach literature, do you not?"

"I used to. But only to high school girls." Hold on, Lalo. How does he know all those obscure saints that I thought Hubert was the only person in the world to know?

"You taught them about irony, did you not?"

"We grappled with irony every day. But we didn't always call it that."

"What did you call it?" What did we call it? Was it ironic that instead of performing exegeses on assigned texts we listened as the girls cataloged the horrors and indignities they had suffered at the hands of the men in their lives?

"Everything but," I say. "We called it afternoon study hall, or senior proms, or family dynamics. I don't think that's what you mean, or what you're after."

"I'm after what makes a saint."

Irony, shmirony, I want to say. *Let's go sit under a palm tree and eat a mango. Let's be tropical, we two.* But I do not.

The rain inhabits my skull. Record-setting rainfall is turning my cerebellum into unrecognizable dampness. The rain seeps out from the back of my eye sockets and coats my eyeballs, so I see everything through this film of an internalized tropical downpour. *Rain, rain, go away, come again another day, when we are far, far away, when donkeys bray, when lizards relay, their heartfelt thanks.* Lalo is the only thing I can see clearly in this courtyard. He alone is as exact as a Leonardo drawing. I say, "If you follow the Hubert hagiological curriculum, you will end up thinking that most saints are so called because of the times they lived in. There is this spectrum of behavior—and it's not linear—and depending on what the times are, the zeitgeist, if you will, if you exist in a certain place on that spectrum you get defined as a saint. All those hermits and ascetics and stylites who lived on water and pigeon droppings for thirty years while sitting on top of a pole: they would be diagnosed as asocial anorexics. And Christina the Astonishing, who levitated from her own coffin and ranted and raved about the revolting smell of humans? She's just like the bag lady who used to live in the doorway of St. Thomas's on Fifth Avenue. Or the bag lady was like her. What about Rose of Lima, who rubbed her face with pepper to disfigure herself? What was so holy about hating your body? And what is so intrinsically holy about refusing to get married? Or to get married and then essentially abandon your children, the way Saint Hedwig did, in order to start a bunch of convents? I think what I am saying is that sometimes a woman passionately spouting visions will be burned at the stake, and sometimes she will be sanctified, and other times, ours, as it happens, she'll be diagnosed and medicated."

He is leaning forward in his wooden chair, the rocking chair that stays still. "I had no idea you felt so strongly about this."

"Neither did I." It would feel wonderful right now to weep and wrap myself in towels. Dry towels.

"Tristána did not starve or whip herself. Not that we know of."

"No hair shirt? No cilice? Just a teeny-weeny barbed chain?"

"Alice, Alice. No, none of that."

"Right. She just refused to get married, and refused to dress according to her class." Too bad. A little kinkiness, some playful S & M, could be very appealing just now. At the very least, it might illuminate my foggy brain.

Lalo is elsewhere in his thinking. He says, "She went to funerals. She offered solace."

It is time for the rain to stop. There has been more than enough rain. Perhaps I will go to sleep and when I wake up the sun will be out again, and it will be possible to touch someone without being confronted with the essential liquidity of our bodies. I will wake up from a dream in which the hurricane takes place inside a house and then in a room and then inside smaller and smaller rooms until it is just a disturbance in a teacup on a chipped table.

"You don't think she can be a saint, do you?" Lalo says.

"I don't know what it means to be a saint, at this exact moment."

"To have a profound effect of goodness on other people. And then, of course, to have miracles occur when you are prayed to."

"She was an upper-class beauty. Men fell in love with her," I point out.

"That wasn't her fault."

The rain angles across the sky and into this courtyard where it smacks the tiles and the grass. Ezra walks by with Carmen. She glides more than she walks, and her left hand rests lightly on

Ezra's shoulder, as if she were blind. Ezra is carrying a terra-cotta pot incised with abstract shapes. "Pre-classic period, circa A.D. 900," he says. "Probably made by the Nicaraos. It was found on the upper farm about thirty years ago when they were planting new coffee."

"Don't drop it," I say.

"Carmen says the farmers are always digging up pots. It can be a problem if they're not careful. She has tons with three legs, and some with anthropomorphic designs." Ezra looks over his shoulder at Carmen, rapturously.

"Not tons," Carmen corrects. "The Llobets have always valued the *arte pre-Colombiano*."

"I like touching things this old," Ezra says.

Carmen's silk garments rustle audibly as she walks. Or they would were it not for the oceanic crashing of the rainfall. Today her jewelry is green. She is wearing a jade pendant in the shape of a jaguar, and jade globes hang from her earlobes. She never wears bracelets. I presume this is connected with Olga's habit of rubbing salt into her wrists and forearms.

"Where are you going?"

"Nowhere," Ezra says. Carmen extracts a long brown cigarillo and lights it. She does this in slow motion, shielding the flame from actual and imaginary winds. She inhales, and for a brief moment her face is entirely blank. Finally, she exhales and says, "It is so sad about the Cubans."

Carmen and Ezra walk away, connected, bearing ancient pottery, leaving us the quasi-fetid scent of her smoke.

Lalo leans back in his chair. His fingertips lightly touch each other, thumb to thumb, index to index, and so on. I make a physical effort to not imitate his gesture. The urge to do so is powerful. My fingers ache and twitch.

"The Cubans?"

He sighs. "There was a Cuban in her past."

"Where is he now, this Cuban?"

"Incinerated," Lalo says. "He was a volcanologist and one day he miscalculated and got too close to the crater."

"You're joking."

"He was with a group of Cuban scientists—we had a lot of Cubans here during the Sandinista period—you must know that?"

I nod, mendaciously.

Have I mentioned how long and thin Lalo's fingers are? They are still outlining the upper half of a ball, the dome of a cathedral. I wouldn't object if he chose to place them over my head, like a helmet.

A door slams. Graciela and Francia, the cook's helpers, run across the courtyard. They make no attempt to stay out of the rain, but they are running fast. Behind them is a chicken. Chasing them.

"What was that about?"

Lalo peers into the drenched courtyard. "It is always that way—"

"I've never heard of a chicken chasing a person." I wish Susie were here. She would know the name of the breed and what color eggs it might lay. "My neighbor in VerGroot is getting chickens. Maybe this very minute."

"Whenever it rains. It's either the chickens or the girls."

I am getting antsy. I don't have Lalo's capacity to sit still. "So? The Cuban lover?"

"He was passionate about volcanoes and we are a country of many volcanoes. Carmen met him at a party to oppose the visitations of the Fatima statue. He was also passionately anticlerical."

"The Fatima statue? I have no idea what you are talking about." Please, please, flap your hands like pennants atop a ship's mast, shiver with delight or horror. Is this what I want, for Lalo to lose control? Isn't that what happened before?

"There is a statue of the Virgin of Fatima, and it is a very holy and special statue, and once a year she comes to Nicaragua and all the best families vie for the honor of hosting her. They have a party in her honor."

"A statue?"

"As I said, a very holy statue. It was blessed by the three who had the vision at Fatima. You *have* heard of Fatima?"

"Yep. So Carmen met a fellow atheist? And fell in love?"

"She was planning to go to Volcán Monocromito that day, but something came up—something with Olga—and so she stayed behind. He went, lost his footing, slid down the scree, and was incinerated. I would think you read about it in the newspapers. It was a very big story, slightly different from the usual Nicaraguan news item but a disaster nonetheless."

"I definitely don't know how Posey missed it. It's a gruesome way to go."

"No worse than many of our early martyrs."

"Did you say that to Carmen? To put it in perspective?"

"Only to you."

"I'm honored." That sounds wrong. Will he think me facetious? I am anything but. I want him to tell me things he tells no one else. I want nothing more than to listen to Lalo's stories and secrets.

"Did the Cuban come before or after Waldo visited down here?"

"After," Lalo says. "How does it matter?"

"I don't know," I say. Because I don't. "I should probably go check on Ezra."

"I like Ezra," Lalo says. "His brain is compartmentalized, but that is not entirely a bad thing in a young boy."

"I don't think he's compartmentalized at all."

"Is his brother like that? Henry?"

"Henry is . . . well, Henry is more like Waldo. At least so it seems now. Maybe next year will be different. They switch on and off, you know. Good twin, evil twin, Jekyll and Hyde, apples and oranges . . ." Lalo stares. I think with kindness.

353

So I just go on. "Anyway. Henry is methodical. He has this laser focus. Ezra is more diffuse, he sees the bigger picture."

"He is like his father in one way."

"More than one, I'm sure. But Henry is more so. Or do you mean something specific?"

"I mean Carmen. He is taken with Carmen."

Waldo never clarified about Carmen. I am not supposed to mind, because it happened even before Providence. And I don't mind. I slept with seven men in seven countries who spoke seven different languages. But Carmen. Carmen is beautiful. Carmen is fearless, and I am anything but. And now this. Now Ezra!

"He certainly is. I should probably go see him."

"I will go back to the *beneficio*," Lalo says. And just like that he gets up. He levitates from the rocking chair and is on his way, through the downpour and beyond. I am still looking at my fingers.

30 ❧ *The Cross-Dresser,* Oil on Canvas, 65 x 50¼ In., 19–

The text, as we possess it, has certainly been rewritten
to suit the taste of later times. It contains extravagances
borrowed from other hagiographical fictions.
— Alban Butler, "St Mary," *Butler's Lives
of the Saints*

S OMEWHERE IN THIS HOUSE of coffee riches,
bad harvests, rain that won't stop, clothes that won't
dry, and delusions of sanctity, Ezra is alone with his
spoon and his dream journal.

From the veranda it is impossible to see the village. On our first
day here I stood barefoot on the cool tiles and inhaled unknown
flowers while Lalo pointed to the village below us. I didn't see
much past the *llama del bosque* tree, with its flaming red flowers
and its defiance.

Now I look toward the unseeable village and squint into the
stupendous rainfall and brace myself against the wind. I need to
stop shivering. Waldo would have something very funny to say
just now. He would make up a limerick.

> *There was a gringa from VerGroot*
> *A scorpion landed on her foot.*
> *The rain was eternal*
> *Its noise was infernal*
> *How she longed to be back in VerGroot.*

It is useless. Waldo has the gift. His meter generates spontane-
ously, like fruit flies in rotting tomatoes. I can keep at it forever
and I will still be counting syllables on my fingers.

"I bet he has not told you about her voices."

I jump at least a foot. It feels like a foot; it's probably an inch.
I knock my shin against a low table.

"Olga! You startled me!"

"Carmen just said the same thing. There are a lot of you with
uneasy consciences."

"I have a finely tuned startle reflex. What voices?"

"Tía Tata's. She heard voices telling her what to do. Saint Wal-
burga, Saint Hedwig, even Saint Winifred."

"He hasn't said anything. I'm sure he will. What else do we
talk about?"

"Winifred and Hedwig don't speak to each other, not even in
Heaven," Olga tells me.

"I don't understand," I say. But maybe I do. Thanks to Hubert,
I know Winifred was cruelly beheaded by the aspiring Caradog,
whose un-Christian lust she'd declined to gratify. Winifred did
not remain beheaded. Her Uncle Beuno came along and replaced
her severed head upon her shrugging shoulders. Meanwhile, poor
Caradog was swallowed up by the earth, and a stream sprang up
where Winifred's head had fallen. To this day, red-stained peb-
bles sparkle beneath the water. Hubert visited the shrine of Saint
Winifred in Holywell when he was an impressionable fourteen.
He dipped his fingers in the holy well, splashed water on his face,
and was cured of his adolescent acne. All I know of Hedwig is she
walked though Silesia with bare bloody feet, carrying her silken
shoes.

"Winifred speaks only Welsh. Hedwig speaks Polish and con-
siders Winifred to be a legend—pure fiction."

I understand even less. "Lalo hasn't said a word."

"That doesn't surprise me," Olga says. Her skirt is wrapped
around her many times. Today I can see how bony she is. "He

hasn't decided yet whether hearing voices is a good thing or a bad thing."

"Which is it?"

"Mostly, it's annoying. I hear voices all the time. Sometimes they make perfect sense. Other times they just tell terrible jokes and say nasty things about people. It can be hard to keep a straight face."

"I had no idea," I say.

"I'm a diagnosed schizophrenic, after all. Voices pretty much come with the territory. *¡Que barbaridad!*" Olga says. I think she is enjoying this. "More of you hear voices than will admit to it. I just admit to hearing them. I admit to everything."

"I had no idea."

"So you say."

"You seem pretty well to me," I say. When there are no animal-human mishaps to occupy her, Posey has been known to share tales of schizophrenics who stop taking their meds and slaughter their girlfriends, mothers. Beloved pets, whoever. In other words, anything is possible.

"I am the bane of my family. The black sheep. I am an embarrassment and a blot."

"That seems a little extreme."

She grips my forearm between her elegant bony fingers, stronger than hemostats, whiter than new-fallen snow. "What do you know about extreme?" she demands. Droplets of saliva extrude from the corners of her lips. "Here you are, frightened of the rain. Don't look at the ground! Your skin shrinks from the shadow of a puddle. If you think Lalo is in love with Tía Tata, you are wrong. She is the not the one for him. She is a distraction."

"A distraction? But he's devoted."

"You haven't even seen the painting yet, have you?"

"No."

"I never look at the painting," Olga says.

"We just haven't gotten around to it."

"Do you have any idea what happened when Waldo was here, when they were in college, when they were so very young and eager and dangerously handsome? Any idea at all?"

Where is everyone else? Where, oh, where is Ezra?

"I didn't know Waldo back then. That was before, before us."

Olga's face closes in on mine. "So you exist without history, without a past? I find that ridiculous. *¡Que barbaridad!*"

I step back. I am already against the wall. "Waldo told me Abelardo had beautiful sisters, and he wished he had a beautiful sister as well. To even things out." My neck feels very stiff. Gunnar Sigerson once explained to me that people with mental illness don't understand about personal space, about the impermeable bubbles we invisibly install around our bodies.

"I should probably go find Ezra." I am up against the wall like a dead fly.

She doesn't move. "Did you hear that the rescue teams can't even get into the airport? You were so lucky to arrive when you did. You and Ezra. Otherwise you might have had to return to Miami, or worse."

"And miss this hurricane?" I ask.

"Don't you ever listen to weather reports up there?" Is she genuinely perplexed? Do I have to defend my weather channel–surfing habits?

"Of course we do. But Nicaragua doesn't figure largely in our weather reports. If you can believe that."

"I know it for a fact," she says. "A fact, a fact, a fact."

"Please show me your aunt's portrait," I say to Lalo, I ask, plead, implore. Demand?

"We'll have to shut down the *beneficio* for the duration. It's not the worst thing. It's not as if anyone can pick coffee in this rain. But the wind is the worst thing. They say it is getting to a hundred and fifty miles per hour on the coast. *¡Que barbaridad!*"

"What coast?" Lalo has returned from the *beneficio* soaked to the skin, slick as an otter. In his entire body the only dry area appears to be his eyelashes. They constitute a separate ecosystem.

Hubert told me there are places on the coast of Wales that, because of the Gulf Stream, have a tropical microclimate. There are Welsh gardens that share a latitude with the frozen Hudson Bay and Siberian gulags, and yet palm trees, datura, heliconia, and agapanthus grow there, and thrive. Hubert is working on a thesis relating Wales's tropical flora with the golden age of Welsh miracles, the sixth century, when the place was chock-full of holy hermits, preachers, animal lovers, and dowsers (viz. Beuno, Winifred, Melangell, Dweywen, Illtyd, Cadoc, Cybi, David, and Seiriol, for starters).

When Lalo was running amok in the snow in his Brooks Brothers pajamas, did some part of him stay warm? Why doesn't he mind the rain-rain-go-away-come-again-some-other-day as much as I do?

I must be staring. Lalo says, "The Atlantic. All the hurricanes come from the east."

"I should have known that."

"Not necessarily. Here all weather is personal and immediate. Life or death," he says.

Does he remember the blizzard at all? What does he remember? Does he remember the dangerous umbles? COLD?

"You are thinking of earthquakes, volcanic eruptions, hurricanes. But the rain too is life or death. We are farmers here and too little rain can be terrible, but too much rain can be disastrous."

"Too much rain can certainly be disastrous. I'm terrible with rain. A failure. I can't tell you how many times a day I think about our tumble dryer."

Lalo says, "Perhaps you don't know your own Inner Resources."

"My Inner Resources are all outer," I tell him. "Because I am so very damp. And I'm not even outside."

"Tonight we will eat well and drink fine Argentine malbec, and you will be fine."

"I haven't seen your aunt's portrait yet," I say.

"The light is terrible."

"I don't care. I'd just feel better if I could see it, and then we can look again when the sun is out."

He takes hold of my elbow in a new gesture. New to me. "But first I must bring a message to my mother. Will you wait right here? Shall I tell Graciela to bring you a *cafécito?*"

I drink not one but three *cafécitos* while Lalo is off wherever he is with tiny, bird-boned Doña Luisa. I am sitting in the large living room. It is bigger than the entire ground floor of our house in VerGroot and I wish I could find a secret niche to curl up in. I am not agoraphobic or claustrophobic or any phobic at all, but here I am a shipwreck. Graciela comes in on marmoset feet bearing a *cafécito* on a tray. She departs, on tapir feet, and then returns with another *cafécito* at the exact instant I drain the coffee from the previous cup. I smile at her warmly. I want her to know I appreciate her attentions and that I am far from taking them for granted. I hear Ezra and Carmen in another room, playing cards, or an ancient game played with smooth totemic rocks. They will never tell me.

Lalo's been gone for a donkey's age. And then he appears.

"Do you have many vegetarians here?" Suddenly, I need to know this.

Lalo does this strange thing where his body takes on the shape we are speaking of, in this case, edible meat. His eyes enlarge and become bovine. The famous eyelashes flutter like those of a contented Belted Galloway. I don't believe I have perceived this before, seen the transformation of Lalo into a chicken or a melon; perhaps it is a phenomenon triggered by our crossing into the tropical latitudes. All I know is that Lalo as food triggers hunger. A Lalo transmogrified rearranges my cells into a gazillion arrows pointing straight in his direction. Suddenly I crave steak, and not just steak but rare steak, steak tartare, the unheated flesh of mad Nicaraguan cows.

"Not by choice. Our *churrasco* is second only to Argentina's."

"I didn't eat meat for almost ten years," I say. "When I was pregnant with Henry I craved sardines. Thank God for sardines."

"Waldo used to keep tins of sardines at Quincy House. They were his favorite. He ate them with popcorn and beer." He is doing it again. His arms press tightly to his sides and he is making himself as small as possible in order to fit inside a flat rectangular tin. A tin with a Norwegian sailor on its wrapping.

"He never told me," I say. For nine months I carried Henry and never once did Waldo mention his own fondness for sardines.

"We made him sit by an open window when he ate them. Even in the winter. Even in snowstorms."

(I have never drunk so much coffee in my life, strong coffee in little cups. I have never drunk coffee in sight of the trees that grew the coffee beans. If you told me Nicaraguan coffee had aphrodisiac properties, I might not argue with you.)

"I will tell Doña Odilia to make *churrasco,* and soon. Her marinade is so good, and so famous, that thieves once broke into the kitchen in a pathetic attempt to steal the recipe. As if she had a recipe! Fifty years ago half this farm was cattle. Now we just keep a few hundred head. Would you like to see them?"

"I think we should see the painting of your aunt."

"There are just one or two things you should know first. I do not exactly recall what I told you, during our pleasant conversations in VerGroot."

"Nothing. You told me nothing," I say. "It was Carmen who told me."

Have I made someone happy today? Oh, strange and wondrous phenomenon. Lalo is delighted. "That explains it! Now I understand! I'm not crazy after all!" And then he hugs me. Just like that. After all this, after madness and rain and longing for sainthood, his long arms go around me. They could go around me almost twice. It lasts for just seconds. If it lasted longer I might be able to feel dry.

"She probably told you Tía Tata was so beautiful that Sorolla went insane with love, and never painted properly again."

"No."

"She probably told you that Tía Tata had seen Julito Ernesto Julio San Felipe kill six bulls successively in Madrid and conceived a passion for him and that was why she chose to be painted as a matador."

"No!"

"She probably told you how Sorolla spent a winter painting portraits in Buffalo, New York, where they have the lake effect, which means they have more snow there than anywhere else in all of America, and that he spent no less than four hours a day weeping in a hot bath, looking at watercolors of the rainforest, and that was the only reason he did not go completely mad."

"No! Lalo! None of that. Please stop."

He sits down on one of the automotive sofas. He rests his elbows at the very tips of his thighs before they turn into knees. "I think I should have a *cafécito*," he says. "And you as well."

"I've had plenty of coffee. I have a gringo stomach."

Lalo says, "You are not as gringa as you think you are. Your mother was Spanish. My ancestors were Spanish. We are Iberians together."

Graciela slides in on capybara feet. Lalo drinks his *cafécito* in one delicate gulp.

With the palms of my hands I press my damp throbbing temples. Of course it is the rain and the humidity. I always get these humidity headaches in the summer in VerGroot.

"Are you ill?"

"No," I say. "Will you take me to see the picture?"

"Follow me."

I follow him along the veranda, past a wooden *santo* I don't recognize, past the open doors of the library. It must be the library. There are bookshelves from floor to ceiling and most of them are filled with books.

The next door is shut, and smaller. Lalo opens it. The painting is leaning against the far wall, and if it is life-size, then Tristána Llobet was about my height. But beautiful. You'd have to see it to understand. Even with that severe expression of someone about to kill or be killed, she is beautiful. The painting is beautiful. She is so long and graceful that you can't help but think of gazelles or greyhounds, although nowadays when I think of greyhounds it is as the donors for Dandy's blood transfusions.

She is standing sideways on the raked dirt of a bullring. Her gaze is directed out of the picture and out of the bullring.

Then there's the matador outfit: the body-hugging black jacket covered with embroideries or jewels. Beneath it is a white blouse so lustrous that it must be silk, so lustrous that you can't help but admire the silkworms who wove their cocoons of continuous silken thread six hundred meters long and then were plunged into boiling water to stop them from piercing the cocoon and emerging as moths because that would have cut short the precious long fibers. All to make Tristána's lustrous blouse.

Dangling from each tiny fruitlike earlobe is a single gray pearl drop. You have to wonder if oysters suffer with the irritation that creates those luminous orbs. You have to wonder how serious Tristána was about cross-dressing.

A cummerbund encircles her tiny waist. It is dark blue, neither navy nor royal, but the best of both. Like what we hope for for our unborn children. I've always found cummerbunds uncomfortable; they get loose and sag, or else they ride up, and either way, they end up looking sloppy. It seems an odd choice for a matador, who needs to be completely comfortable in his clothes because he is engaged in a life-and-death struggle with a bull. But

Tristána is not really a matador. A real matador might have his cummerbund sewn to his blouse so that it never rode up or down while he parried and thrust.

Without a doubt it is the pants—pantalets? capris? pedal pushers?—that introduce the element of sexuality. It seems ludicrous to say they look like they could have been painted on. They are painted on. They cleave so reverentially to the shape of Tristána Llobet that the viewer (me) feels the distinction between the painted art and the three-dimensional body getting fuzzy. So much is in the pants. They are short and black and tight. They cling to her bottom, which is like the bottom of a Greek athlete. Lalo never mentioned the shapeliness of his great-aunt.

"You haven't said anything." Lalo's face is barely three inches from mine.

"I haven't thought of anything smart to say yet," I say. "Scratch that. She's amazing to look at."

"Yes, we know that."

"And she never took a real turn in the bullring?"

"Of course not," he says. Lalo leans toward me and for a moment I imagine he wants to kiss me because the uncanny sexuality of his holy aunt has, like a Jesuit mnemonic, pricked his desire, and I am near at hand. I would not stop him. But that is not his intention.

Lalo just keeps leaning, as if into the onrushing bull. Both thumbs lightly touch both index fingers, and then pull back in a delicate *verónica*. He says, "I have this theory—no, *I believe* this bullfight business mattered enormously. She loved it and hated it. She could not stop herself from watching. But she was horrified. She connected that single bull's death with every bloody sacrifice of every innocent creature since, well, since the Crucifixion."

"She saw man's inhumanity, came back to Nicaragua, stopped dressing up, and set out to do good works."

"You're simplifying," Lalo says.

"No, I'm trying to give it a story line."

"Except it wasn't like that. When she returned, the first thing she did was turn her portrait to face the wall."

I say, "But she's so beautiful in the painting."

"She hated that. She never let them turn it around while she lived."

"I've never believed a beautiful woman who complained about how rough it is to be beautiful. *All that unwanted attention.*"

"She wasn't like that."

"You were never there when she walked into a room."

"Yes, I was. But she was very old, and I was very young."

"Isn't it enough to have such a beautiful aunt? Why does she need to be a saint?"

"Because she was one."

"I think her beauty could be a problem with the Vaticanistas, Lalo. Honestly. I had no idea she was this gorgeous. Even more than Carmen."

Napoleon of the Missing Fingers, in sopping clothes, jolts into the room, then comes to a halt. He is sucking up oxygen. He drips on the tiles.

"Don Lalo!"

"*Sí,* Napo." Lalo speaks softly. His voice is the volume control for every other voice around us.

Napoleon tells Lalo about an accident at the *beneficio.* A rotten wall has given way. It's been breached, and water is pouring into the shaking room. All those hundreds of quintals of dried coffee beans in jute sacks waiting to be loaded onto the trucks that, once the roads are again passable, will drive them to the Pacific port of Corinto to be loaded onto container ships for passage through the canal and up to the port of New Orleans.

The coffee beans will be ruined.

But will they turn into coffee? Don't be an idiot.

Lalo squeezes my shoulder hard between his fingers. He has incredibly strong fingers. It must be a Llobet trait.

He lopes out of the room after Señor Bonaparte, toward rain and wind.

"Can I go with you? I won't be a bother."

"Next time."

He is gone. I think he says, "Close the door when you leave." But he could just as easily have said "There are more in my sleeve" or even "Something, something before you grieve."

So I am alone with Tía Tata. This is my chance. To stare her down? To touch the paint? If I were to touch the applied paint of any Spanish Sargent in any museum, an alarm would wail and within seconds I would be dragged off to ignominy and shame. Here I can touch all I want. I can drag my oily fingertips around the canvas seeking bumps and ridges. I can lick the painting; I can go eyeball to eyeball with Tristána. I can lie on the floor and see how she looks from that angle.

But what's the point without Lalo?

I need to ask myself when I first knew of his existence.

I must have heard about him before Waldo called from DSG to tell me he was coming to stay, oh, by the way. *Oh, by the way, oh, wife, while the boys and I are caving you and the dogs will be alone with my old and dear friend, so old and dear that you have never before met him.*

Is that what he said? Did he say, *You remember him, my old roommate, my comrade in arms, my friend in need, my teammate and fellow drinker?*

The first time I saw him was at the VerGroot train station. I can swear to that.

Someone else, Olga or Carmen, will swear up and down that I had absolutely met Lalo before, in Cambridge or New York, that I expressed interest in all his family history, and that this had transpired in flawless Spanish. After they say that, I will be carted away to a sanatorium for those of us who are sloppy with memory. It will be located at such a high altitude that simply getting enough oxygen becomes a daily task. There will be pamphlets all over asserting the medical benefits of breathing hard to make you remember what you should have remembered in the first place.

When the rain comes down like this, it is as if it has rained since the dawn of time and will rain forever after. When the rain comes down like this in VerGroot, one of us makes a fire in the living room and we curl up in the sumptuously sagging chairs and read Roald Dahl or Edgar Allan Poe, and Dandy and Flirt take up the space closest to the fire, and the whole room smells like wet wool with a soupçon of canine musk. Ez and Henry play speed gin rummy. Then the rain can rain all it wants. But how often does it happen that we are all in the same room doing those things, each of us contributing to the others' safety and sanity? Not very often. Here the rain is coming down far worse than that, and I don't even know where Ezra is.

31 &✖ A Little Knowledge

> The story of Pelagia of Tarsus is one of those Greek
> romances which appear to have been originally
> fabricated to supply edifying fiction for the Christian
> public . . . The stories . . . are almost entirely legendary,
> and are confused one with another. No data are pre-
> served . . . The attempt, however, to reduce all these
> hagiographic fables to a recrudescence of the worship
> of Aphrodite is quite unreasonable.
>
> — Alban Butler, "St Pelagia of Tarsus,"
> *Butler's Lives of the Saints*

I WOULDN'T MIND EATING. But everyone seems
to have something else to do. Tiny Doña Luisa, with
her arms like dragonfly wings, has spent the whole
day in the kitchen with Doña Odilia, listening to the voice on the
radio describing the fury of the hurricane, denouncing the rain as
if it were Beelzebub personified. *¿Y los damnificados? ¿Que hacemos
con los damnificados?*

Ezra is teaching Carmen every card game he knows. Mami
and Tía Sofia taught me, and I taught Ezra all those card games.
Maybe he learned crazy eights from Posey. Waldo is indifferent to
card games, except fifty-two pickup.

Since Ezra is with Carmen it seems unnecessary to worry
about him. After all, she lives here. She knows where the kitchen
is, as does Ezra by now. I do too. Ten times at least I walk past
and listen to the voice on the radio rising and falling, about the

damnificados this, and the *damnificados* that. What does the devil, or his minions, have to do with a perfectly normal hurricane?

Graciela finds me. She slides in on poison dart frog webbed feet. Webbed feet would be lovely today. She hands me the cord-less phone.

It is Waldo, and he sounds—as they say—as if he is right next door.

He is fine. Dandy and Flirt are fine. The house is fine. The weather is lovely. The hydrangeas are bright blue. Susie's niece from Indiana came to visit, and she broke her leg while stand-ing still. Posey is fine. She is in the semifinals of the Maine coast seniors' table tennis tournament. She is favored three to one to win. Dick has called Waldo twice to expatiate on his newlywed libido.

This is not information freely given. This information is extracted from Waldo, like glass splinters removed with tweezers. He does not mind giving it up; it is the process that he recoils from: all those questions, all that poking with a sterilized needle.

"What about Henry? What's he up to? Has he discovered any more extinct creatures?"

"Henry has moved on to human experimentation," Waldo says.

I have to think. "On you?"

"On himself."

"I don't get it."

"He read an article in the *Harvard Health Letter* about bed-sores, which are easy to get if you absolutely don't move. If you can be completely motionless for just a few hours, the pressure on your back can squeeze shut the capillaries, and without fresh blood, the tissues start to degrade and eventually die. Hence a bedsore. Now, absent a coma, most of us move all the time, even when we're sleeping."

"Fascinating. But what about Henry?"

"He wants to see if he can give himself a bedsore."

"Let me talk to him, please."

"I can't. That would involve moving, and he's pretty determined."

"Bring the phone to him!"

"You don't get it—he can't move at all. Just talking to you would generate all sorts of movement. You can understand."

"You overestimate my capacity for understanding. It's pouring rain here. Nothing is dry. Towels in the bathroom never dry. You could get a bedsore in five minutes because of all the moisture in the air." I am standing by the window, looking through a wavy pane of glass into the penumbra surrounding the courtyard, the courtyard that is a deluge, Angel Falls, Niagara Falls, Iguazú, and Victoria, all bunched together and reduced to domestic scale. The storm drains in the center and corners of the courtyard are seething and frothing.

"But Henry's not in Nicaragua. He's here," Waldo says.

I have to ask. "What if something terrible happens?"

"It won't. Plus, you have to respect his research on the subject," Waldo says. "I think I can safely say that he now knows more about bedsores than anyone else in VerGroot."

"This sounds insane," I say. "A little knowledge—"

And then silence on the other end. *Is a dangerous thing* hangs unspoken between us, dangerously.

I would swear there is no sound other than our breathing for over a minute, but I have never been able to gauge elapsed time.

"Don't worry, Al. He'll be fine. He can write it up for a science project."

What am I worried about? All will be well. I adore Waldo, and Waldo loves Henry. Once he told me that Henry was like Dick, only with social skills. I disagreed. I think Henry is more like Waldo in his approach to science: he wants to know things and he wants to create things, and he wants results. He is not especially patient. As for his social skills, it is too early to tell.

I say, "You're right. He will be fine. And you love this stuff, don't you? This—this—myself as a guinea pig, my house as a laboratory."

"I wouldn't have put it quite like that."

"Maybe you two should come down here. When the rain stops. Or we should just come home, when it stops." Can he hear my breathing? I say, "I miss you so much."

"Me too. Can I talk to Ez?"

"I don't know where he is," I say.

"How is that possible?" I will not respond to this insinuation. I will not say, *Not only is it possible, it is true.* I will not say, *How is* what *possible?*

"He's with your friend Carmen, the babe. I have to assume she's trustworthy as regards ten-year-old boys."

"Are you crazy?"

How quickly it flees, the resolve to say nothing, *nada.*

"What are you saying?" A small fist tightens around one of my inner organs.

"Nothing, nothing," Waldo says, or chants. "I'm just pushing your buttons. Unwise at this distance."

"*Unwise* is just the beginning."

"Just tell him we miss him. Is he enjoying the saint stuff as much as you are?"

"Who said I was enjoying it?"

"Just an educated guess," Waldo says. "Speaking of which. Guess who called."

"Posey?"

"Nope. Someone I don't normally talk to."

"Most of the world's population? I give up. Come on, Waldo! We're having a hurricane here. I'm feeling very itchy in my skin."

On the other side of the courtyard is a *santo,* a life-size wooden statue of a gaunt man in a torn friar's habit. Some kind of animal crouches at his feet and looks up with adoring eyes. This is the first time I've seen this *santo* over there. Was it dragged out from elsewhere because of the rain and the wind? In order to watch the rain and the wind?

Waldo says, "Your friend. The merry monk."

"Hubert," I pronounce. "He's not a monk anymore."

"He was worried about your well-being. Ezra's too. He knew all about the hurricane."

"What else does he know?"

"He asked if you had a Saint Christopher medal."

"*Jee*-sus. Of course I do. I never leave home without it. Neither do you."

"I have no idea what you're—"

"There's one in your glove compartment. What else did he say?"

"He said he has an inside track on the competition."

It is possible that Waldo is making all this up.

There is a crunch, rather a loud crunch. "Are you eating an apple?" I demand.

"It's a cucumber. Too many seeds."

"Just tell me what he said."

"He has a friend in high places who knows something about somebody else's aunt, not Lalo's, who also wants to be a Nicaraguan saint. She just got a big leg up on the competition at the Vatican because she cured someone of deadly bee stings. If you get my gist."

"This probably sucks for Lalo. What else did he say?"

"I suggested he call you guys rather than expect me to explain. He said this other aunt, La Macarena, had better funding than poor Lalo's."

"La Matilda."

"It sounds fishy to me," Waldo says.

Kerspishhhhhoooompah. A watery, crashing, bellowing, head-thumping din. The telephone line goes dead. Briefly, I suspect Waldo of engineering the cutoff. I've seen him do that with Posey: quietly depress the button midsentence and then hours later pretend they were cut off by the CIA/KGB/FBI/RCA. But even Waldo could not have created the diluvial cacophony that I just heard. *Rain, rain, go away, don't come back for another day, when I'm far, far away, in Rome or Marseilles.*

There is no receiver, so I pocket the dead phone and go in search of Ezra.

No Ezra, no Carmen.

That evening Ezra tells me a dream: he had to collect DNA samples from a bedsore, but when he approached the bedsores with his instruments and his plastic bag, there was no person. It was an aquatic lizard, like those fish that grow feet and walk onto land in illustrations of the march of evolution. A huge wind knocked all the trees over on the river's edge so the walking fish had to climb over them, which it found almost impossible, so Ezra and Henry climbed down from some branches and helped it. The boys couldn't carry the walking fish because it was so slippery and slimy, but they had nets with them, and Carmen was there with a red plastic pail.

"When did you have this dream?"

"During my siesta," Ezra says.

"I can't believe you dreamed about bedsores," I say.

"You always said that was the beauty of dreams."

"What *did* I say?"

"That you don't have to make them up, and you don't have to believe them."

"I said that?"

"I need to tell Carmen something."

I tell him that I will kiss him good night, and then I do.

I wasn't dreaming. I don't know what I was doing but I wasn't dreaming because it is a fact that you can fall into a dream state only once you are in the deep REM sleep and you can achieve REM sleep only after a minimum of forty-five slumbering minutes.

It is not possible that Lalo is sitting at the edge of my bed, mere inches from not-dreaming me. So I must be dreaming. He is posing as a bedtime-story reader, and I expect a fabulous tale involving rabbits, large hats, loving parents, and cruel adversaries with speech impediments.

"You must have been having an amazing dream," he says.

"I wasn't dreaming," I tell him.

"You had the aspect of a dreamer," Lalo says.

"What are you doing here? Besides watching me not dream?"

"I could tell you that I was looking for something. But that would not be true. This is true: I thought I heard Ezra sleepwalking and naturally I was concerned."

"In this room?"

I am wearing Waldo's very faded, very soft Harvard crew T-shirt. I also have faded T-shirts from MIT and Tufts and Penn, because after a race the losing team has to give its T-shirts to the winning team.

"In his room. But he is not sleepwalking. He is engaged in catapulting." Lalo is wearing starched and ironed pale blue pajamas with dark blue piping. Brooks Brothers, it seems safe to assume.

"Lalo? Why are you here? It is not Ezra's room."

"You must know."

"I don't. You want to tell me what terrible thing happened at the *beneficio*? You want to explain the finer points of bullfighting? I give up! And I feel rather odd, rather . . . groggy. Or soggy."

"It seems to be the only way to be with you. Alone with you. Everyone else has to be asleep."

"I was asleep too."

"You must realize how I feel about you," Lalo says.

"You can't assume I know anything. I know less and less." I sit cross-legged and clutch the white linen sheets up to my neck.

"I think about you, your body, the way your ankles are crooked, the scab on your elbow, your hair in a bundle, your volcanic breasts . . . Call it an adulterous passion."

"Stop right there. That's not what you said before."

374

"Are you indifferent to me?" he asks with the most profound interrogatory inflection I've ever heard.

"It's a long way from indifference to adulterous passion," I say. "Is it technically adulterous if you are not married?"

Now I am awake. I am so awake my eyelids ache.

But not Lalo's lids. His lids are transparent skin behind the lush foliage of his lashes, lashes women dream of, kill for.

"Could I just kiss you?"

"There's a hurricane out there," I say.

"Precisely."

"Yes."

I lean forward and he does kiss me. And it is miraculous. All that focusing on his eyelashes, and I never realized what nice lips he has. We kiss for a while. His lips feel like a sigh. Then there is his tongue, a tongue simultaneously languorous and busy. He has a snail darter of a tongue. As if he has to memorize every single one of my teeth, and this is his only chance.

Lalo says, "This is *doloroso* on my back, right here." He flutters his hand in the general direction of that graceful swale. "We had to move about three hundred quintals of coffee, back there. Wouldn't it be more comfortable if I got under the sheets, with you?"

I nod. I have nothing to say. I just want those lips back on mine. I hear the rain thumping on the roof and gurgling down every gutter and chain. I hear the rich volcanic soil absorbing the rain. I hear wind and water, and Lalo's breath next to my ear. The insides of my ears are ticklish and eroticized. He is actually speaking words into my ear, but I don't hear them because his mouth is too close. I feel them. I turn my body toward his, and just like that, all stretched out, the length of me is attached to the length of him from his blue button-down pajama top to midway down the calf of his blue pajama bottoms.

"I'm going to take off your shirt," Lalo says. "You won't get cold."

I'm burning up. Did I say that aloud? No, I am incapable of speech. He slides the T-shirt over my head and along my arms. His fingers play with my nipples. "Like perfect coffee beans," he says. Even that doesn't make me laugh. I wrap my searing left leg around his right calf. I bring it up higher and slip my big toe inside his pajamas, clutch the waistband between my toes, and yank the pants down, down, down. It is a descent into weightlessness. It is like falling slowly into a well, with my eyes open, and nothing but delight on every side. Down, down the well, rounding the iliac crest, down the thigh and the tibia, and in the slippery beyond.

Lalo says, "You know that there are many different types of love: courtly love, romantic love, platonic love, agape?"

I nod and nuzzle my nose into his shoulder cavity, which fits me well.

His lips, which so recently molded my lips into any shape they liked, are now moving south, toward my breasts, which are not remotely volcanic. And when they arrive, and surround the nipples, the same thing happens, the thing that happened when he kept talking into my ear. I cannot remember who this is and why I am here.

Where is Ezra? Aloud, "Where is Ezra? Oh my God, this is demented."

"As I said, he is in his room, quite happily practicing some skill."

I sit up. The rain has softened; it comes down without rancor or fury.

"Exactly. Demented. I should go check on him. I need to be a good mother."

"You are a magnificent mother," Lalo says.

"You have no idea. What do you know about being a mother? Or a parent? Why don't any of you have children?" This has been below the surface for a while now, my wondering about the dearth of procreation around here. What's with four adult offspring and not one of them reproducing? Is there some weird genetic trait I have overlooked? Was their childhood too weird to warrant replication? "Not even Emilia, and she's married."

"Lie down, Alice. I can explain all that later. Ezra is fine. We will be fine. I adore your body."

"My body? My body!" Has anyone ever referred to my body like that before? Has Waldo? Is he differentiating it from my mind? Do I care?

"Explain now."

"There's nothing to explain, I just said that to calm you down." I am not calmed down. What if they've all taken vows of chastity? Or almost-chastity?

Hubert told me about Saint Thérèse of Lisieux, who went to the convent when she was just fifteen. Her two older sisters were already there, and later, three more sisters entered the convent. Poor Monsieur and Madame of Lisieux started out with six daughters and arguably a good chance of at least one or two grandchildren and ended up with none. Not only that, but all six entered a cloistered order. It was a tale of enchantment and sorrow.

His lips and mouth have wandered farther south, into the southern regions of white belly, lint-filled umbilicus, and even farther, into the tropics. We are in the tropics. I can hear myself breathe. I hold my breath and there is another sound, not the rain, nor my panting. It is Abelardo Llobet, humming softly as he moves his tongue in geometric patterns into the rainforest where my clitoris awaits him like a bride at the altar, just recently given away by her indifferent father, the Lord of Misrule.

"This is madness. This is demented. I can't do this." And then I do. Lalo holds my hips tightly with both hands. I whisper, "Ezra is next door."

Later the humming stops.

By then I hear breath and stillness, stillness and breath. I am voracious. Lalo breathes all the air in the room. He climbs. I sink. I climb. He sinks. I breathe all the air in the room.

And finally, stillness and enough oxygen for us both.

I hop out of bed and stand unsteadily. "You really have to go. We'll feel better in the morning. You'll see."

"You're brilliant, dear Alice. There is no other place in the world than here."

But he does get out of the bed. He reaches down to the far end of the mattress where his pajama bottoms were unceremoniously discarded, retrieves them, and pulls them on. At this instant, when the pale blue pajamas are midway up his legs, I see him as he was in the snow in VerGroot, in his pajamas, going mad in the whiteness. The instant passes, as déjà vus do, leaving a lingering taste of panic.

He stands next to me. Was this always going to happen? Was there a germ of this in the snow? In the Ginny O johnnies?

I adore Waldo. Let's not forget that. Waldo walks on water, on swamps, on puddles and pools.

"You know that Hubert called me?" Lalo says. "But I didn't speak with him. He left a message with Graciela. I would be very surprised if she got it correctly. Does Hubert speak Spanish? He never spoke Spanish with me."

"That's because your English is perfect."

"Like your nipples," Lalo says.

"Don't do that. This. I love Waldo. You love Waldo."

"Carmen loves Waldo. But she hasn't seen him in years. Waldo is beloved. Yes, that is all true," Lalo says.

"What was the message?" This would be easier if I had some clothes on. My T-shirt is somewhere in the tectonic folds of the sheets. I don't dare get near the bed.

"He told Graciela to tell me to read about Saints Marina, Pelagia, and Apollinaris."

"Is that all?"

"And some other saints, but she forgot." He cups my breasts in his hands. Not like before. Now they are foreign objects, experimental objects. "Can you think why I must read about those saints?"

"None of them ever existed? They are all legendary, conflations, borrowed from other saints or folklore."

"How can we ever say for certain that someone never existed?" Lalo asks.

"I don't know. I don't think of it that way. I'm not a philosopher. Far from it. Hubert called Waldo too. And told him something else."

"He did?"

"Yup. His sources told him your rival cured some bee sting."

"I know nothing of that, and it sounds highly dubious."

"See! Even Abelardo Llobet has his doubts." I am gleeful, giddy.

Then he disappears out the door, so silently, so graciously. *So like a gentleman* are the words in my head.

Was he ever really here?

I find my blue-striped cotton bathrobe—also Waldo's, a gift from Posey—and slip out, creep along the wall to the next door, Ezra's open door. I stand and listen. I need to filter out the rain and isolate Ezra's distinctive breathing.

Lalo was right. And also wrong. Ezra is not practicing catapulting. He is dreaming.

I tighten the robe's sash so that it cuts into my waist. Ezra sleeps on his back; his arms are bent, and both hands rest loosely on the left side of his chest, as if holding a small animal between them. Do I believe that a single saint ever levitated? Or walked across the bay? Or cured the halt, the blind, or the possessed? If I could do anything of that ilk I would gather Ezra in my arms right now and whisk him far above the stormy clouds and back to VerGroot, back to Waldo and Henry and our own barking dogs. I only kiss him.

"I'm not sleeping," Ezra says.

"Holy cow!" I jump and almost lose my death grip on the sash.

"But I was sleeping before. I had a dream. Do you want to hear it?"

"Always."

As his dreams so often are, this one is populated with Mr. Cicero, Waldo, and a strange woman on a train. Also dogs.

I say, "That is a great dream, Ezra."

"You always say that."

"That's because it's always true."

"My head hurts. I'm going to sleep now," he says.

"It hurts? Where does it hurt? Front or back?"

"I don't know. It's okay, Mom." His eyelids fall, and his body settles deeper into the mattress. Gravity prevails.

The bed I crawl back into is muggy and sticky. I am trying to remember if it was raining when we arrived. Yes, I believe it was. Maybe the first day the rain stopped and the clouds parted for three and a half minutes. Then it rained again and it has not ceased since. Or maybe I am confusing this with another visit to some other tropics. It is so slippery out there, and inside my head. The humidity is 100 percent, in this country, on this farm, in Las Brisas, in this room, this bed.

32 &c Take According to Directions

EVERY MORNING THUS FAR in the tropics, the tray with coffee, hot milk, and an orchid in a narrow vase, a lurid magenta cattleya, appears in this room within minutes of my eyes cracking open. It is beautiful, and it is a shocking affront: this flower of the jungle, with its two serrated petals framing the darker tongue, the challenge. It beckons the pollinating bees with their long tongues and kinky desires. These flowers grow alone in the ordered chaos of the rainforest. Why do they have to be so beautiful? I could get very used to this, this magical appearance of strong, dark coffee that I did not make.

I am assuming that Ezra ate breakfast earlier and that he's gone somewhere with Carmen. It seems a logical assumption. But it is wrong.

I can't look at the *gallo pinto* that ordinarily endears breakfast to me. The papaya and banana are chalk in my mouth. Lalo is nowhere to be seen. I am sitting here alone with Olga.

"Are you planning to starve yourself?" she asks cheerfully.

"No, of course not," I say. "Do you know where everyone else is?" *Rain, rain, go away, don't come back till I'm far, far away, in Utica or Canaday.*

"Anorexia has a bad name these days," she tells me. "It's been appropriated by models who sniff drugs."

"I think anorexia is a twentieth-century diagnosis," I say. "Where is everyone?"

"There have been several saints who survived on nothing but the Blessed Sacrament. I would try it, but I am so fond of fruit."

"God forbid you should get scurvy," I say, and I am gone. I scooch down the hall and then up the stairs, back to the upper story with its long loggia and bedrooms without end. I knock on Ezra's door, and go in.

Ezra is still in bed. He looks different. Still and pale. He looks at me without saying a word.

"Holy cow, Ez. What's the matter?"

"I threw up three times last night," he informs me.

"Why didn't you tell me? I was right next door."

"Every time I thought it was the last time."

"How do you feel now?"

"My head is pounding. And everything else hurts too."

I press my hand to his forehead, first pushing aside the locks of brown hair that are plastered there. "You're hot. I'm going to get a thermometer and some Tylenol. But first have some water."

He sips the water, stops to lick his lips, then sips again. He smiles at me, my beloved boy, and almost immediately his chest gives a hop, shifts location, and he starts heaving. He vomits the water and random bits onto the counterpane.

"Sorry about that."

"Never mind that. Oh, Ezra, Ezra." The rain is louder up here beneath the roof. Outside his window I see the vast hillsides of slick green coffee trees, just foliage. Everything is about to be submerged or washed away; I see that now. On the dark wooden windowsill I see the carcasses of three mosquitoes and one fly. They stick out because in this house I have seen no dust bunnies, no cobwebs, no dead flies, this being only one of the many ways that Las Brisas differs from the Fairweather Family Home for Stray Inventors in VerGroot, New York.

I clean up after Ezra, somewhat, and run to my room for the medical kit I prepared before we departed. It contains Band-Aids, a thermometer, aspirin, Tylenol, an Ace bandage, Deep Woods insect repellent, Benadryl anti-itch spray, Neosporin, Cipro, Lomotil and Imodium for diarrhea, Milk of Magnesia for its opposite, throat lozenges, and vaginitis cream (not for Ezra). His temperature is 103 degrees. I give him two Tylenol. That is the prescribed adult dosage. Ezra is not exactly an adult, but he weighs as much as a (smallish) adult, and 103 is a very high temperature.

He takes the pills obediently. Then he vomits up the white pellets, the water that washed them down, and unidentifiable mucus.

"You can't keep them down, can you?"

"Everything hurts, Mom."

I stroke him and hold him as if he might break. I tell him I am going to find Lalo or Carmen and call a doctor. Everything will be fine soon. He has a stomach flu. I can do this, I know I can do this. I can comfort Ezra and find the proper medicine. What I cannot do is stop the melodrama that is playing, end to end, back to back, in my head. I cannot stop the Worst Possible Scenario: Ezra is sick and all the medevac helicopters are lined up like toys in the airport in Managua, not going anywhere because of the hurricane. And they could never fly in the first place. I am weak in the knees. Of all the possible Bad Mother Moments, this is the absolute top.

What will I tell Waldo? Will Henry ever speak to me again? How could I have let this happen to him, here in an uncertain drowning banana republic? What exactly was I doing when Ezra was falling ill? When he was throwing up exactly three times all alone in his room? I know what I was doing, and it was a moment of insanity. Pure sanity.

No, it must have been after Lalo and after my visit to Ezra. That doesn't mitigate the Bad Motherness of it.

Downstairs Olga is at the dining table, drawing patterns with her finger in a plate piled with salt.

"Did you lose something?" she asks.

"Ezra's not feeling well and I need to call a doctor. Do you know a doctor who can come? Where is Carmen, or Lalo?"

"A man came to the *beneficio* a while ago, looking for help and a place to stay. Lalo is with him."

"Can we call the doctor now?"

"Our doctor is in León, and he never leaves the house before noon."

"But this is an emergency! Ezra has vomited five times now, and he has a fever. I take fevers very seriously!"

"Who does not?"

"Who doesn't what?" Carmen is standing behind me. The constant rain enables stealth.

"Ezra has a high fever and the vomits," I say. "I should call a doctor."

"The telephone lines are down but maybe the cell will work. What did we do before cell phones?"

"I don't care. I just want Ezra better."

"My poor darling Ezra," Carmen says. "I'll go call right now." Her perfume lingers when she leaves. Curare #4, or Andean Aphrodisia.

Outside the room I stop. The kitchen dog, yet another branch on valiant Panchito's family tree, limps close to the ground, comes round the corner, and stands still. Now I realize what Ezra looks like: Dandy when he was so deathly ill. Dandy when his red blood cells were disappearing and his bone marrow wasn't doing its job. Dandy before the first blood transfusion.

So much to refuse to think about.

Carmen leans against the *santo* and speaks a mile a minute into the cell phone.

"Fernando is an old family friend," she says to me, and inclines her head forward while the V of her thumb and index finger sweeps back her hair. She does this perhaps one hundred times a day. "He was at seminary with Lalo for a year, before they both left. His father delivered all four of us. But never mind. It is impossible to get here from León, but he can prescribe a broad-spectrum antibiotic and we can get it from the pharmacy in the village."

"But he hurts all over."

"I said we would call him back."

"Did you tell him about the vomits?"

"Most people who come here get diarrhea. Not only gringos," Carmen says. She touches my shoulder with either kindness or pity. She flips her hair back.

"Ezra didn't say anything about the runs."

"Fernando said it is probably either a stomach flu or malaria or dengue."

"Dengue! As in dengue fever?" Horrors.

Ezra looks the same, only smaller and paler. I was gone for mere minutes. He is talking to me but I am hearing Posey's voice saying something about dengue fever, scourge of the tropics.

Carmen standing in the doorway appears angelic, all white and luminous, framed by the dark wood. Ezra's eyes are drawn to her like iron filings to a magnet.

"I didn't say it was definitely dengue," she says. "Fernando was just tossing out some possibilities."

"How do you feel now, Ez?" I touch his forehead and imagine it is cooler, but I know it is not.

"Everything hurts," Ezra says.

I hadn't seen her, but Olga is here too, in a corner of the room. She's all in black, which makes it easy for her to sit unnoticed in corners for who knows how long.

"Malaria's the one you should worry about," Olga says. She's perched atop the convex lid of a massive wooden trunk with tarnished brass fittings, flaking leather straps, and the name LLOBET

OTANGUEZ painted between two wooden staves. "Healthy boys survive dengue. Malaria stays with you forever."

"Stop it, Olga!" Carmen hisses. "Don't listen to her, Ezra darling."

"Everything hurts."

I take his temperature and it is 104 degrees this time. What happens at 104? Do eggs poach? Do brain cells sizzle and sweat? Waldo would know. Which is why I love him. Which is among the reasons to love him.

Waldo would know that Herr Doktor Carl Wunderlich's nineteenth-century assertion that normal body temperature was 98.6 degrees was debunked more than ten years ago, and that our actual average temperature is a few tenths of a degree lower. This means Ezra's temperature is even more of a fever than it would have been ten years ago. Waldo would tell Ezra that Herr Doktor Carl Wunderlich traveled the length and breadth of Germany sticking his mercury thermometer under armpits, until he had racked up twenty-five thousand subjects. Waldo might compose a limerick about a comical German medical man, rhyming *armpit* with *nitwit,* and *mercury* with *fury.* I would fall in love with him all over again, and again.

There has to be an explanation for last night with Lalo. I need to explain myself to myself. But first Ezra.

Graciela brings me a mortar and pestle I do not remember asking for. It is just the thing to crush a Tylenol pill, which I dissolve in water and feed to Ezra on a teaspoon. He smiles and slurps it down. Three women watch the faint movement of his Adam's apple swallowing.

"Mom, I need the bucket." But I am not quick enough and he upchucks everything.

Ezra's eyelids sink. I lie next to him and tell him a dream he has heard countless times before. I dreamed it repeatedly as a child. It involves a bear, a canoe, and Pop. Ezra seems to like it.

Ezra's breathing is short and shallow. His skin is transparent in ways I never noticed before. The essence of Ezra travels along those blue veins.

I have no idea what time it is when Carmen stands in the doorway and tells me that Waldo is on the phone.

"I thought the phones were kaput," I say.

"He called my cell."

I tiptoe out. How did Waldo get Carmen's cell number? My Waldo dialed a series of numbers and was connected to a Nicaraguan cell phone?

This can only mean bad news.

"Can you hear me? Can you hear me?"

"I hear you perfectly, Al. How are things?"

"You mean you don't know? Why did you call?"

"I just wanted to hear your lovely voice. Anything wrong with that?"

"Nothing. But you can't be funny right now. Ezra's sick, you know."

"I didn't know." Waldo sounds aggrieved. "I thought Henry was the one with a bedsore."

That idiotic bedsore experiment.

"Don't tell me he is still doing that?"

"It was a brilliant success, as it happens. He got himself an incipient bedsore in about twelve hours. Now that we know he can stay perfectly still for that long, maybe we should exhibit him in a circus."

"Not funny, Waldo. Ezra is really sick. I don't know what it is and the doctor can't come. He can't keep anything—anything—down." The cell phone so close to my mouth, I could swallow it. It is warm. How long were Waldo and Carmen talking before? What other exceptions to standard operating procedure will Waldo make where Carmen is concerned?

"Make sure he stays hydrated, that's the key."

"Please listen. He can't keep even the smallest spoonful of water down. And he has a fever."

"What is his temp?"

"Last I took it, a hundred and four. Do they use centigrade here? What would that be in centigrade?"

"It's forty degrees."

"I should know that."

"Most of the world uses Celsius," Waldo informs me.

"But we're in Nicaragua."

"Ask Lalo what they use."

"He's disappeared," I say.

"Disappeared. Was he kidnapped?"

"No! He's just out somewhere. Probably in the *beneficio*."

"Forty is high."

"I know. He can't even keep a Tylenol down."

"Does Carmen have any idea what it is?"

"Did she say something to you?"

"No."

"She said Fernando—he's the doctor—thinks it's either a stomach flu, malaria, or dengue fever."

"Shit," Waldo says.

"He's going to be fine," I say. "He's still cheerful. You know how he is."

"I don't like being so far away."

"Me neither." For a few seconds neither of us speaks, and I notice the quickening of the rainfall, as if all those millions upon millions of raindrops are in a rush to get someplace else. "So really, how come you called?"

"Really? I just wanted to make sure you were okay. I heard on the news that there are mudslides in Honduras and Nicaragua. Big mudslides."

"You did? I hadn't heard that."

"I can thank CNN and the Magic Satellite."

"Of course I know we're in a hurricane. There is a ton of wind and rain. But it's not like home. It's lasting too long."

Waldo says, "It will be over soon. I have that on Channel Twenty-five's authority."

"Can I talk to Henry?"

"He's next door with Susie. Her chickens finally came. They are more amusing than bedsores."

"She got chickens while we're away?" Just a day ago this would have mattered.

"If Ez isn't feeling better I'll send in the medevac helicopters."

"Are you crazy? Helicopters don't fly in hurricanes. If there weren't a hurricane, the doctor could get here. He'll be better."

"He better be," Waldo says. "Better."

"Kiss Henry for me," I say.

Ezra's temperature is down to 103.5. I don't know what that translates to in centigrade. Less than forty. Graciela brings me a dish with green Jell-O. This seems an odd choice for someone likely to upchuck, but maybe Graciela knows something about tropical nausea I don't. I give him a couple of wobbly spoonfuls.

"Mom!" Ezra barely has time to grab the plastic bowl on the floor. The two spoonfuls of green Jell-O are regurgitated, up and out. "Never mind," he says. "I'm not hungry."

If Hubert were here he would pray to Saint John Bosco, who has all those boys' high schools named after him, or Saint Nicholas of Myra, who raised three pickled little boys from the dead after they'd been murdered and stuffed in a barrel of brine. Or Hubert might take the fever-patron tack and suggest praying to Amalburga. Better to pray to Mary of Oignies, who was especially devoted to lepers, ate no meat, and dressed only in white, like someone else I know. You would think that among all the thousands of saints there would be one who was once a sweet little boy who recovered from a tropical fever and then went on to spend the rest of eternity looking after other little boys with tropical fevers.

"How long have you been standing there?"

Lalo says, "The *beneficio* is flooded and the village is under mud. I opened up the church because it's on higher ground, but I'm afraid it won't be big enough for everyone."

"I must have fallen asleep with Ezra." Ezra's eyelids flicker, then settle back down.

"How is he?"

"The same. Sleeping. I told Waldo about it," I say.

"Why did you tell Waldo? We should discuss that first," Lalo says.

"He said to tell you his temperature is forty degrees Celsius."

"Oh. Ezra's," Lalo says. Light dawns over Marblehead. I could kiss him, again and again.

While I sit on this old trunk with its spalling leather straps and mottled brass hinges (formerly Olga's perch), Lalo tells Ezra about Tía Tata. They know I am sitting here, but Lalo has not spoken to me.

He tells Ezra about Tata's confidant, Padre Oscar Felipe. Ezra is immobile beneath the white sheet folded at neat right angles. His head creates a concavity in the pillow and is surrounded by a damp halo. His lips are slightly parted. He has the nicest teeth of all the Fairweathers.

It took years, but over time Padre Oscar got used to her outbursts and grew comfortable in Tristána's presence. Whenever there was a problem with a female parishioner, he went knocking at Tristána's door. Her shack was close by the rectory, near the church that is now sheltering villagers displaced by mud and water. They ended up becoming such good friends that in old age they looked alike: tiny, wrinkled, sunburned, and crowned with tufts of gray hair that resembled precious metal in the yellow light.

"Have I told you what she was most famous for in her lifetime? Besides being beautiful?" Lalo asks Ezra.

"Your aunt?"

"Great-aunt."

"She was famous for being your aunt. And Carmen's." I like the shadows in this room, because I can hide in them.

"Not that, my young friend," Lalo says. "She had a nose for death. She always knew when someone on the farm or in one of the villages was going to die, and she went straight to his house and stayed until he died. She arrived in her shabby pants and an overshirt, but once inside she would remove those outer clothes and beneath she was always in pure white. So naturally people thought she was an angel. I don't mean they thought she was really an angel, because our people know better than that.

"Her great task was to care for the ill, the dying, and then the dead. She was passionate about the need to respect the bodies of the dead so that they might look their best at the Last Judgment."

"Mom says you're not required to have a body anymore for the Last Judgment, because so many people get cremated."

Did I tell him that? Apparently I have not entirely neglected his religious education.

Ezra continues in his low, submarine voice. "My grandfather was cremated. But he didn't believe in a Last Judgment anyway. He believed in dust and ashes."

"I met your grandfather three times. Three times Three. He was a gentleman and a scholar."

Ezra's eyes are drifting.

Lalo continues. "Tata sang a cappella at the funerals of the workers, and not only the workers of Las Brisas but all around.

"There was a certain problem about having a nose for death, and I don't need to tell you what it was. So sometimes she walked in disguise."

Beneath his sheets, Ezra twitches at the word *disguise*.

Lalo says Tata occasionally accepted rides on an ox cart. When she did, she pretended to be mute, because her Castilian inflections would have given her away.

"If she was alive now, would she be here?" Ezra says. I hold my breath. Is this where we have been going all along?

Lalo is holding his breath also. Finally, finally, he says, "No, not here."

"I bet she looked like Carmen," Ezra says.

Carmen is in the doorway. There is altogether too much padding around on silent feet in this house.

"You're scaring him," she says. "And now we have something to be genuinely frightened of. I heard on the radio that Rio Santa Barbara has flooded. Two bridges are washed away. There are mudslides on Monocromito, bigger than the mudslides we had with Hugo. Two villages outside Granada have disappeared. Two entire villages. I'm going to take some aspirin."

Lalo turns back to Ezra. "Who's scaring who?"

"The problem with having a sister that beautiful is that you can't marry her," Ezra says.

I should be anywhere but here. But I can only be here, in Ezra's room.

"It has never bothered me. I cannot imagine the man brave enough to marry Carmen."

"I won't be young forever," Ezra says.

Carmen reappears at the doorway. "I forgot to tell you the most important thing. For you. Not for me. One of the disappeared villages was Tecacilpa."

I know the expression about the hair on the back of one's neck standing on end, but I can't say I have ever seen the phenomenon. Now I know. The short, neatly shorn hairs make a straight path across the back of Lalo's neck. The hairs that I knew between my fingertips are upright. They are Eiffel Towers, Washington Monuments, CNN Towers, and Cleopatra's Needles, all in a row.

"Tecacilpa is gone? I am sure that is an exaggeration."

"Unless they are doctoring the footage. The mud took everything in its path. I saw the gashed hillside. I saw the nothing that is left."

"But Carmen, you only heard it on the radio," Ezra says.

"He is brilliant, this child," Carmen says proudly. "Graciela has a television in the kitchen that runs on batteries."

"You know what this means?"

"What exactly *does* it mean?" Carmen says.

Lalo walks to the other side of Ezra's bed. Ezra looks better than I've seen him all day. His cheeks are pinkish. Later I will check his gums.

"Mostly loss and suffering. *Los damnificados!* But for us, it must mean something. I can only imagine."

"Am I missing something here?" I say.

Ezra says hoarsely, "It's the other one, Mom. She's buried there. Saint La Matilda."

"Your rival? She was buried there."

Carmen says, "Now under mud."

"Can I come watch the television with you?" Ezra asks.

Carmen answers. "Later. Not now. All the *damnificados*. The *damnificados*." She walks away.

33 ❧ *Los Gringos*

The account preserved of [Blessed] Ida of Louvain is,
it must be confessed, open to some suspicion, partly
because we have no external corroboration of any of the
incidents recorded, and partly because it abounds in
marvels of a very astonishing character.
— Alban Butler, "Blessed Ida of Louvain,"
Butler's Lives of the Saints

H OW DIFFERENT WOULD IT be to wake up inside Lalo's head? This question has been worrying
at me. Imagination can only get you so far.

Inside Lalo's head are his parents and his sisters, memories of
all those chaste aunts and celibate uncles. Inside Lalo's head are
the coffee trees, chicken farms, and sugar plantations. There are
the Jesuits who taught him tongue twisters and coached basket-
ball. There is the one and only year in seminary, the years at Harvard shared with Waldo. Inside Lalo's head is his conviction that
this great-aunt is something that none of us can ever be, worthy of sainthood. There is his belief in miracles. And now, inside
Lalo's head, is the man who crawled into bed with me, Alice, and
touched my body and confused me. This is where I will always
be, vis-à-vis Abelardo Llobet: outside.

I am awake now in the night, and something is different. I
touch Ezra. He is hot. With every third or fourth breath he shivers, as if trying to wake himself up. Otherwise, all is silence.

It's the rain and the wind. It is not the wind and the rain. It has stopped. It is quiet. It is the reason I can hear Ezra breathing so clearly. Outside this room and the house is perfect silence. No rain falls on the roof tiles or roars down gutters or hammers the ground. No record-breaking wind locomotives up and down the slopes of volcanoes.

The giant Mother Superior in the Sky has come out from her cloudy fastness and, holding her long, articulated index finger to her desiccated lips, hisses, "Shhh."

In the morning Ezra's eyes open with the sun as it slides like an egg yolk up and off the top of the eastern volcano. I lie here perfectly still next to him. But not as still as Henry incubating his bedsore. Oh, my darling, mysterious Henry. Why couldn't I speak with him yesterday? Was it yesterday? It is eons.

"Hi, Mom, what's up?"

"What's up with you? How do you feel?"

"Everything hurts, but it's different now. Sideways. Vertically. Horizontally."

"Your joints?"

"The hurt is connected to how they move."

I don't want him getting tired explaining the unexplainable. The sun is shining. The greatest impossibility of all seems to be the impossibility of understanding another human being.

"Try eating something? Or drinking?"

"Water."

So we do it again. I hold the glass to his lips, I hold my breath. He sips and swallows. We both wait.

And wait. Nothing.

Minutes pass and he has not rejected the water. His forehead is still so hot, but his temperature is now 102 degrees. Whatever that is in Celsius.

It is not as simple as making the world metric. Measurements are specific to what is measured. You have a *fanega* of coffee beans and a *bulto* of unrefined sugar, and not the other way around.

We have a gallon of American milk from New York cows in the Genesee Valley, but Jacques drinks a liter of milk from cows that chewed French grass in the Dordogne. They are not the same.

I don't see Olga until she is right here, standing on my toes and breathing my air. "Lalo has a bunch of gringos who need a place to stay," she says, and keeps walking.

"Gringos?"

"The same."

"Gringos," I repeat. "Gringos? How did they get here?"

"By jeep. Until it got stuck somewhere below the village. I bet I know exactly where. So they walked. They're a muddy mess."

"Does Lalo know them?"

Still moving, she says, "He says they know you."

I follow her into her room. Books are piled from floor to almost-ceiling. Just that, neat piles of books. I would do almost anything to know the titles.

"They know me?"

Deep inside I am overwhelmed with shame and fear. But what have I done?

Oh, that.

Funny how I didn't think of it. Funny how it doesn't seem entirely real.

Olga says, "Lalo said we had some Fairweathers staying here already, and one of them said, Fairweathers of Maine?"

"Where's Lalo now?"

"You really should consider wearing a hat. It would suit you. It would keep you dry."

"It's stopped raining."

"That was a metaphor."

"I am so confused," I say.

What am I so scared of? That some people who probably have never been to Maine in their lives will convict me of allowing Ezra to contract a tropical disease? While I was next door. With Lalo.

Exactly that.

"There is nothing wrong with being confused. It is often the holiest condition of all," Olga says. Her lovely long index finger strokes my forearm.

Waldo told me about Hindu yogis who create a layer of protective sweat that allows them to rest comfortably upon a bed of hot coals. I can feel Olga's finger incising a line along the inside of my arm. I am not unscathed.

Hubert told me about Saint Cunegund. Though chaste as the driven snow, she was accused by evil gossips of being unfaithful to her husband. She demanded the trial by fire in order to prove her innocence. *She* walked unscathed over the hot coals, and her virtue was made manifest for all to see.

It could be that a perfectly clean conscience allows one to perform great feats of endurance. Like sleep.

Ezra has not upchucked the most recent glass of water. This is progress.

In my room I examine the tiny lines of perplexity around my eyes. I watch myself say *How do you do? Pleased to make your acquaintance for the first time,* in English and Spanish. I tuck my shirt into a fresh pair of khakis, ironed by Nicaraguan hands, as they never are in VerGroot.

Once more I touch Ezra's forehead.

At the bottom of the stairs, standing next to a wooden San Antonio, Don Abelardo and the tiny Doña Luisa are standing almost as still as the statue.

"I miss you, *amorcito,*" she says.

"I used to know you," he says.

"I can't bear this."

"Tell me again who you are," he says.

She whispers, weepily, "I'm Lulu, your beloved wife."

He grins. "I knew that!" His gaze is transfixed by a distant object. The grin recedes. "Keep telling me. Please. Who you are."

I asked Carmen why they removed the stuffed monkeys and

kept the vicuña and guanaco. She said that vicuñas and guanacos were wild camelids.

Lalo and his gringos have not gotten very far beyond the front door. The gringos comprise two men in shorts. Their calves are spotted with dried mud.

The oldest man stands a bit apart from the others. He is craggy and sunburned, with washed-out blue eyes. His hands stay inside his pants' pockets except when his right hand emerges to pat down his pale blond hair. He has pronounced buttocks. This I can't help but notice. According to Three, New Englanders have no butts. He said that to me once, on the porch in Catamunk, while Waldo and Dick played Jenga with enormous concentration. "It has never been properly explained," Three had said. "The buttlessness of New England men. But it is worth study, don't you agree?" I'd nodded. I was going to marry this man's son. An uneasy silence descended over us. Since that time—*naturalmente*—I involuntarily examine the butts of men, and assess them. I can't stop myself.

So when this man, this gringo with pronounced buttocks, tells me he is from New England, I will be very suspicious.

But first I whisper, "Lalo, I think your father has forgotten your mother."

His face changes color and his eyes shutter. Did this need to be said? Now? How obvious is my desire to lay claim to Lalo?

"May I present our guest Alice Fairweather? Alice, these people have come on a mission to find the bodies. But now this man's wife is ill, and I have said we can put her up."

"I'm sorry to hear that," I say.

"Please tell me again your names," Abelardo says. They introduce themselves: Edward Flanz and George Glass. The absent, ill wife of George is Edith Dilly-Glass.

"We know the Fairweathers in Camden; are you one of them?" George says. "Edith's family have known them for ages."

I cannot look at him. There are embers inside my skull. I say, "Edith Dilly?"

"Yes! So you *do* know her!"

"I am married to Waldo Fairweather," I say. It would be perfectly fine if the rain started again. Now. This instant.

"Waldo. I've heard so much about him, but I've never had the pleasure," George says. "We had a small wedding, and then we've been doing mission work ever since. Edith is a saint."

Abelardo bristles and scratches his head. I want to gag. Not figuratively. No, nothing figurative about it. I am literally overwhelmed with nausea.

George still grins expectantly. Finally, with acute slowness, Lalo says, "They have a dog named Sam who goes with them around the world, sniffing out corpses. Have you ever heard of this?"

"Of Sam?"

The older man, Edward Flanz, says, "There was a piece about him in the *Times* last year."

"I must have missed it," I say.

George Glass says, "What a fabulous coincidence this is. Wait until I tell Edith. To meet people from home in godforsaken Nicaragua. Oh, sorry! I know she'll want to tell her mother. She's in Maine, you know."

"Oh." I have found the one completely blank spot on the wall, a spot with no cracks, no shadows of long-dead insects, no cartographic remnants of leaks and drips, and there I focus.

Abelardo, my friend, Waldo's friend, my mystery lover, appears ridiculously cheerful. He has recovered from the unfortunate saint remark. He invites the gringos to sit down. He directs Sam, the corpse-sniffing dog, to the kitchen, where Doña Odilia will feed him. Sam walks off in the correct direction. Abelardo asks where they are from, when they landed in Nicaragua, and how they made it to Las Brisas. They are from Delaware, Connecticut, and formerly Maine. Edward Flanz is the one with a shapely butt and he is the one from Delaware, state of no income tax, so I guess Three's dictum is holding fast. Edward Flanz and Sam arrived in Nicaragua only yesterday. He would have come sooner, he says, but he had to raise the money for his airfare. He raises all the money he needs from speaking engagements at churches and animal shelters, and he never takes a penny in payment for the work that he and Sam do. People are so very generous. The Glasses have been in the country for almost three weeks, on an outreach mission from their church. What kind of church? Pentecostal Congregationalists. Abelardo says softly, "This is a Catholic country." But even that does not dampen his cheerful demeanor.

They drove from Managua to León in their four-wheel-drive vehicle. In León the mayor directed them to the village of Santa Eulalia, on the slopes of the volcano, because that's where the worst flooding was, where the worst mudslides were, where a corpse-sniffing dog and two Pentecostal Confrontationalists would be greeted with gratitude. That is where poor Edith came down with dengue fever.

"What about—? That village Carmen was talking about? The village that disappeared?"

"That's near Granada," Lalo says. "In the other direction."

"Isn't that where they should be sniffing for corpses?"

"The *damnificados* are everywhere," Lalo says.

The stricken look on George's face is too perfect for my taste. "Poor Edith."

"She'll recover," Lalo says. "Since there is no cure for dengue, we have to pray."

"Carmen thinks Ezra has dengue," I say, and immediately regret it.

Suddenly Olga is there. "You probably want to know about Ezra."

"Always. I always want to know about him."

"Carmen is with him," she says. She rocks back and forth on the balls of her feet.

"What I don't understand is how *they* could get here but the doctor cannot."

"Our vehicle has very big wheels," says George Glass. "We were lucky to get it. We didn't make it all the way. We walked the last two or three miles. Even with dengue. There was no choice. Poor Edith."

Oh, yes, you had a choice. There is always a choice. Don't we always have a choice, especially when we don't recognize it? Isn't that what I said to Waldo? Back when he was choosing Edith Dilly over me? Back when he was screwing her front and back? Back before she joined the Pentagonal Confirmationalists and came south to behave in such a saintly way?

Olga addresses Lalo. "Do we know who these people are? Because the *beneficio* is a disaster."

"They came to find corpses. They have a dog that sniffs for corpses. Quite a famous dog."

"That's revolting," Olga says.

Abelardo shrugs. "Someone has to do it." Never before have I seen him shrug.

"We're on an errand of mercy," says George Glass. "Which makes it all the sadder about Edith getting bitten. By an infected mosquito."

Olga rolls her eyes clockwise *and* rocks on her feet counter-clockwise.

Olga says, "Who are you?"

I answer, "They're Penitential Conformists."

Lalo says, "His wife is ill and I said they could stay here. I told Graciela to put her in the old box room." To me, "That's on the other side of the upstairs."

I was spared Edith Dilly at Sydney Sweet's wedding because she was in some Third-World country doing mission work for a cult. Posey calls it a cult and she says the other Dillys are mortified. They should have been mortified years ago, when she seduced my Waldo. I was spared her at the wedding so that she could come here.

Is this the Edith Dilly who kept me awake nights, weeping? Death by earth, fire, wind, or water was too good for the Edith Dilly who alienated my Waldo's affections. What I wanted for Edith Dilly was a husband of her own who would betray her, break her heart, crush her tender emotions, and trample her affections beneath his indifferent hobnailed boots.

George Glass starts to speak, then changes his mind.

I still don't know what she looks like.

Abelardo was right, is right. There are no coincidences.

Dear Saint Tristána Llobet, hear my prayers. Grant me this miracle. Make Waldo love me and only me, forever and ever. Amen. And make Ezra better. Take away whatever fever it is that inhabits him. Is that too much to ask? Waldo and Ezra? And keep an eye on Henry. Henry is capable of doing anything, and he will do anything, and he doesn't know what he is capable of. Please keep a close eye on Henry. That's all. Just those three. Amen. And P.S., dear Tristána, put Ezra first. First of all I pray to make Ezra healthy again. Forgive me.

Nothing about Lalo. I don't know how to pray for Lalo.

I take the long way back upstairs. I take the route that goes past the kitchen. Don Abelardo and Carmen are watching the battery-powered television along with Doña Odilia and the others.

Carmen says, "It's worse than we imagined."

Graciela is weeping silently. "I knew it. I knew it."

"The death toll. The *damnificados*."

The image on the screen was shot from the air. It is awash in brown. At first. Then the image focuses and we see mud, streams and rivers of mud. There are tree trunks lying every which way, every way but upright, and there is debris. Lots of debris. They are filming the side of a volcano where mudslides washed away everything, every structure, every natural barrier, everything but the raw, gritty, slimy earth that remains. The engine's whir muffles the voiceover. Again and again, the *damnificados*. The damned. The damned ones. What did they do to be damned? To have attained damnation? Or damnification? *Millones des damnificados. Un montón de damnificados.*

Don Abelardo pulls out one of the wobbly wooden stools around the big central table, and alights.

Graciela chants names. "Pedro, Analuisa, Fabio, Rafa, Pedro, Analuisa, Fabio, Rafa, Pedro . . ."

Carmen says, "Erosion is a terrible thing."

I can't take it anymore. "Why do they keep calling them damned? Isn't it bad enough to be homeless, or dead, or washed away?"

"That is exactly what they are," Carmen says, and pushes her beautiful black hair back from her beautiful white forehead. "Graciela, you don't know anything yet. You always assume the worst. *Calmate!* The *damnificados* are not here. That is Tipitapa."

"We had chickens in Tipitapa," says Don Abelardo. "The chickens are drowning in mud now. My mother has special chickens. She keeps them near the house and feeds them *plátanos* and *pejibaye* and *palmito*. She will never recover."

"Papa! The chickens are fine and your mother is dead. Remember? She died twenty years ago, on Christmas Day. You must try and remember."

Ezra told me that Don Abelardo had a stroke two weeks before we landed in Managua. He told me that Carmen found her father sitting on the ground in the courtyard, touching his nose with the tip of his index finger and whispering to himself. His blood is too thick, Ezra told me.

"You keep telling me she's dead. I believe you, but I don't remember it," Don Abelardo says.

On the small television screen a woman in a short white skirt and décolleté red blouse is standing next to a large wooden box. Because of the angle, it isn't immediately clear that this is a coffin. Then it is. The lid is half off. The woman with cleavage and high heels speaks into her microphone with one hand on her left hip.

Carmen turns to me. "You know who this is, don't you?"

"Who?"

"It's La Matilda."

"I thought she was dead."

"She is dead. That is her coffin."

"I thought you meant the newscaster."

Don Abelardo smiles. "That's Maria de Torre. She has the most beautiful breasts in Nicaragua."

"Maria de Torre was her mother," Carmen tells me.

"Her breasts even smell beautiful." Don Abelardo holds his fingertips to his nose and sniffs.

"Stop it, Papa!"

This is my first time inside this kitchen. I can count exactly five fruits or vegetables I don't recognize. Which—in this small world/global economy of ours—seems rather a lot. They have lumps, protrusions, bristles, and hairs. They tend to tertiary colors. I have probably eaten them.

From the television comes the uniform newscaster's voice: "Local authorities are seeking help from the national government as people are flocking here from all over the country. There are no facilities to house or feed visitors, but still, the people want to see for themselves what is already being declared a miracle, the incorrupt body of Matilda Vargas de la Rosa, better known to all Nicaragüenses as La Matilda. As the whole country, and now the whole world, knows, Hurricane Alice's tragic mudslides of the past three days destroyed several villages along the slopes of the Mombacho and Santa Eulalia volcanoes, including Tecacilpa, the small village where Matilda Vargas has lain buried for these past twenty-four years. But now this mudslide that has wiped out the houses and the historic church of Santa Eulalia has created a different kind of havoc. The force of nature that destroyed structures also unearthed coffins, and one coffin in particular."

Maria de Torre of the magnificent bosom gestures operatically toward the mud-stained coffin with its lid knocked off.

"Here lies La Matilda. In deference to the sensibilities of our viewers, and also because the bishop has asked us not to, not yet, we are not showing footage of the actual body. But we are telling the Nicaraguan people and the world that something remarkable has happened here, because the body of La Matilda is as fresh as the day she was buried. Perhaps more so. According to several sources—and we cannot deny it—there is the unmistakable scent of gardenia emanating from inside the coffin. This is especially remarkable because of the blight of fungi isthmii that has lately attacked gardenias all over the country and seriously affected the cut-flower industry. Later today we will have an interview with Monsignor Roberto Ovadia, pastor of the Church of Our Lady of the Assumption in Managua and an expert in the miracle of the incorrupt body."

Carmen flips her hair back vehemently. "I know Roberto. Keep Ezra away from him. He likes little boys."

Don Abelardo ejaculates, "Pshaw! Everything he knows about incorrupt bodies he learned from Sister Maria Christina."

Graciela crosses herself.

Doña Odilia lights the gas stove underneath a large pot of black beans.

I have to go see Ezra. I am going to see Ezra. Abelardo is entertaining the gringos somewhere. How many *damnificados* has this hurricane created? Couldn't Edith be one of them? No, that's not what I wish for her. I want nothing for her. And Waldo all for me.

Ezra is awake. I open the casement window and breathe. I don't smell gardenias. I smell moisture.

"Ez, you're not going to believe what happened. I have a feeling it will change everything."

"I already know."

"You do?"

"Yup. Matilda's body smells like flowers."

"How could you possibly know that?"

"I just know. Maybe I dreamed it?"

"Carmen must have told you. Doesn't she tell you everything?" Oh, my sweet Ezra. He has such soft skin, and after three days in bed it's even softer. Softer than is safe in this world.

"I have a dream for you," Ezra says.

"First let me take your temperature."

"Are you okay, Mom?"

"I'm fine. Why?"

"You always want to hear my dreams. Before anything."

"I'm just trying to stay focused. To be vigilant." But he's right.

His temp is down to 100.5. Where are all the old mercury thermometers? No one shakes them down anymore. Here is what Waldo should create: a Museum of Lost Gestures. Shaking a thermometer. Dialing a rotary phone. Delicately placing the needle into the groove of a vinyl record at exactly the song you want to hear, again and again, "Sad-eyed Lady of the Lowlands." Cranking open a car window.

"You're not so hot," I say. "Are you hungry?"

"I had soup and Jell-O with Carmen."

"With Carmen? Oh." This is news. "Have you thrown up yet?"

"Nope! Isn't that great?"

"That is truly great, Ez. Tell me your dream."

"We can wait and I can tell Carmen too when she comes back," he says.

"If you want."

"Do you think I'll be better tomorrow?"

"I hope so, Ez. I really hope so."

"Carmen said there are some new people here. Gringos, she said. Have you seen them?"

"Some of them," I say. "They'll be gone soon."

I lie down next to Ezra. Whatever happens, I don't want him to see Edith Dilly. I cannot even wish for her prolonged ill health and misery, because what I really want is for her to be gone. Gone from this house, this farm, this country.

34 ❧ Translating the Relics

translate, verb: 1. *trans.* To bear, convey, or remove from one person, place, or condition to another; to transfer, transport; *spec.* to remove a bishop from one see to another, or a bishop's seat from one place to another [. . .] also, to remove the dead body or remains [relics] of a saint, or by extension, a hero or great man, from one place to another.

— *Oxford English Dictionary,* volume XI,
1933 edition

LALO IS STANDING IN the hallway outside Ezra's room. He is fresh as a daisy. There are no cobwebs gathered round him.

"He's better," I tell him.

"I've been praying to Tía Tata."

"You told me dengue goes away on its own."

"I am very fond of Ezra, so I am seeking insurance." He smiles and touches my cheek. Don't melt, I tell myself.

"You didn't know those gringos before, did you?" I ask.

Lalo says, "No. Isn't it extraordinary about them knowing Waldo's family? What a coincidence!"

"I thought you didn't believe in coincidences."

His eyes puzzle up.

"Why are they here? Really."

"Lovely Alice, is something wrong?" The tips of his ears are reddening. He strokes my forearm with his fingertip. This should not be allowed. This undoes every rational thought in my head.

"Why should something be wrong? Other than the hurricane, the *damnificados,* and Ezra, what could be wrong?"

"You seem agitated. Your cheeks are blotched."

"Blotched? Please don't tell me my cheeks are blotched. It sounds like the plague."

"I only mean—"

"I know what you mean." I am resisting with all my might. I whisper, "Could you give me a hug? Not here, obviously. Just in my room. Just a hug."

Across the threshold and behind the closed door of my room, and my temple rests against his chest. There is a world of difference between Lalo naked and horizontal, and Lalo clothed and vertical.

"Alice, Alice, Alice." It sounds new and wonderful on his lips.

"Now I can tell you." My mouth is pressed directly into the moist fabric of his shirt, and the warmth of his chest.

"Tell me what?"

"You don't know who this Edith Dilly is?"

"Are you referring to her unfortunate religious affiliation?"

"No."

"Please tell, dear Alice. I am not a mind reader."

"Waldo knew her. I mean, he *knew* her. They had an affair. While we were married. Around when Henry was born. I don't know her, but I hate her guts."

"This is terrible," Lalo says. His arms loosen their grip on me, and I tighten mine on him.

"I know."

"Hate is a poisonous emotion."

"Please, Lalo!"

"You need to keep your thoughts pure, your mind clear as spring water. I know you are like spring water."

"More like a mud puddle. Lalo! I shouldn't have told you. People don't like to know these things because they are so—so muddy."

"And she has dengue fever," Lalo says.

"I don't want Ezra to see her."

He is about to say something (the thing I want, I need, to hear) when Olga appears from behind the thrust-open door.

"I knew it," she says. I jump away from Lalo and his warm chest. My fingers cramp into claws. I am guilty, guilty, guilty.

"No, Olga," I start.

Lalo says, "Olga knows everything before it happens. What's the hurry, Olguitita?"

"Everything. The telephones are working and *La Prensa* called to ask what we think about La Matilda's ridiculous corpse. That's one thing. The other is that the back storeroom flooded—"

"Why should it flood now? The rain has stopped."

"A drain clogged. A dragon spit. A lizard fell asleep."

Lalo says to me, "She *can* make sense when she wants to."

"The suitcase. Paris 1912. You should consider translating the relics. Moving them. Pronto."

"I am going down now," Lalo says. "To rescue them."

"*¿Y los gringos?*" Olga says.

"You can have the gringos for now."

"Alice wants nothing to do with them," Olga says.

I want to shout, *Stop!* Olga knows everything before it can happen.

I forcibly straighten my gnarled fingers with the stiffened fingers of the other hand.

"You heard about La Matilda?"

"Yes."

"Do you know how many saints' bodies are incorrupt? How many smell like flowers?"

"No."

"They are legion. All the sweet-smelling dead scaring the living into devotion. They could populate a small country. A banana republic." She laughs.

"I know about incorrupt bodies," I say.

"Have you ever read the *Thousand and One Nights?*"

"As in Scheherezade? No, actually not."

"But you know how the story goes?"

"Of course."

"Then you know what I mean," she says.

"No. I don't."

"The story that won't die. Think about it."

"I thought it was that the storyteller would not die so long as the story went on," I say.

"Rubén Darío understood."

"I know who Rubén Darío is," I say.

Olga says, "If you followed the Incorrupt News, you would think that perfumed corpses were the standard."

"I should probably get back to Ezra."

"If I thought for one minute that my body would not disintegrate and that it would stay around past its usefulness to smell like a French whore, well, I would die," she says.

"Olga, can I ask you something?"

"You are asking me something."

"What do you think about Ezra? He's going to be fine, isn't he?"

"Ezra is fine. Ezra has never been the problem. He has never been other than fine. Are you by any chance worried about Carmen?"

This is what happened in 1912: In order to please Doña Lili, his beloved inscrutable wife, Don Abelardo Llobet Uterbia ordered from the renowned house of Louis Vuitton the most expensive and complete set of luggage possible. The set included, but was not limited to, steamer trunks of various sizes, suitcases of various sizes, cosmetic cases, hatboxes, and a custom-made travel writing desk. The leather was pale and soft. Every hinge, rivet, and nail head was of polished brass. The handles were carved from a single mahogany tree felled in the forests of Las Brisas. Inscribed on a golden plate were her initials: L. O. DE LL.

(Ah, the sad irony of luggage that no longer lugs in this brave new world of wheels and backpacks! And ah, what should have been obvious all along: in the rainforest, leather grows hallucinogenic mold, and brass discolors.)

Soon afterward, while the Liberals were still in power, Don Abelardo delivered two suitcases full of American dollars to the president, and when the railroad was built from the Pacific to the Atlantic, there was a spur right past the *beneficio* of Las Brisas, which meant that the Llobet coffee could be delivered with the greatest of ease to ships heading for the Port of New Orleans. The suitcases were part of Doña Lili's set.

This is what happened in 1982: Immediately after Tía Tristána died, quietly, in her humble bed, beneath her humble but colorful blankets, before rigor mortis set in, and before the doctor got there, her nieces Alicia and Isabella (Llobet cousins of Lalo's father; Alicia is now dead, and the senile Isabella passes her days as a guest of the Sisters of the Sad Redemption) entered her room and removed her bed sheets, her hairbrush, and almost all the clothes she was wearing. They knew exactly in which drawer to find her letters, neatly stacked and labeled by year, and also her diaries, kept in school composition books. Everything they gathered up easily fit inside two of the Louis Vuitton suitcases with their Grandmother Lili's initials. Unaware that the set had already been irrevocably broken up, that two pieces were mildewing in the old presidential palace, they called Hector, the gardener, to take the suitcases back to the main house and replace them in the back room in exactly the same position in which they had been stored for decades now. Isabella, who had been waiting a long time for this moment, said something about translating the relics. But Alicia smacked her forehead with the palm of her hand and muttered, "We are such idiots. We should have taken photographs. Who will believe us?"

Isabella did not answer. She was happily imagining the moment when she would kiss the pope's ring and he would congratulate her in perfect Spanish for having so wisely saved the holy relics of her newly beatified aunt.

And this is what happened in 1993: Waldo Fairweather III went into the hospital one day for a gallbladder operation, and while he was there his doctor and friend discovered that his body was riddled—as they bizarrely say—with cancer. Cancer was general throughout Three. The doctors sewed him up, and Three came home to die in his own bed with its view of the enormous white pine that had been struck by lightning the week his oldest son was born. I was pregnant with Henry, very pregnant. My ankles were very fat and swollen. Ezra was discovering his dreams. Waldo went alone to visit his ailing father. He sat by his bedside and played chess with him. When Three was well enough to walk, they strolled down to the harbor. One day, on the sidewalk in front of the hardware store, Waldo encountered an old family friend, a sailing companion and sometime tennis partner named Edith Dilly. He had not seen her in years. Her mother had died the year before, and the sympathy she offered him—for his father's imminent death—was perfect in every way. He fell in love. Just like that? Perhaps it took more than the week he was up there, but he made it sound pretty instantaneous.

Henry was born, big and beautiful. My ankles recovered their former shape. Waldo kept returning to Catamunk to visit Three. Three was doing just fine.

One night while Henry slept between feedings, Waldo told me about Edith, how he had re-met her and fallen in love. He couldn't help it. He still loved me too. The sex was great, he said. He didn't need to tell me that, but, he said, he couldn't help but tell me everything because I was his best friend. And I needn't worry that he'd be making any new babies anytime soon, he told me, because Edith was as fond of back-door sex as he was.

Afterward, I would ask myself what I hated most about his affair with Edith. Was it that she was born to sailing and tennis and Maine, and I was not? Was it the sex? Was it that it had happened when I was fat and pregnant? Was it all the lies he'd told? I began to have terrible jealous fantasies about how miserable Edith would one day be, as miserable as I was then with Waldo's heart elsewhere.

Years later, in one of our pillow-revelation marathons, Waldo told me he was attracted to motherless women. There was something about a woman with no mother, or a dead mother, that he found sexy.

He'd said, "I just thought you'd like to know. It's probably meaningless."

Nothing about Waldo was meaningless, as far as I was concerned.

Three lived another four years. Henry got a chance to know his Fairweather grandfather.

This armoire is big enough for three people. But no one is inside. My clothes are folded on shelves, hanging on hangers. My sneakers and flats are lined up below my suspended linen dress and jacket.

"I didn't hear you come in."

"I wasn't trying to be quiet," Lalo says.

Then I notice his feet. He has that toe fungus they advertise cures for late at night. So you know they don't work.

"I've been looking in on Edith Dilly-Glass."

"I thought you were translating the relics. Into Esperanto? I should be with Ezra this very minute," I say.

"She is practically hiding under the bed sheets."

"Where is her devoted husband?"

"I think he went off with the other man and Sam, the dog. I have a feeling she will be very nice when she is no longer sick."

"Are you saying that to upset me? Do you think I care if she is nice? I'm not nice! Why should she get to be nice?"

"I don't need you to be nice," Lalo says. "I don't even want you to be nice."

He wraps those long simian arms around me and I am lost, acquiescent to everything. Then the siren at the *beneficio* goes off and I jump and hit my head on his jaw and he slams his teeth shut on his tongue. Blood dribbles from the corner of his mouth.

"I'm so sorry, so sorry," I say. Do I kiss him? Do I attempt to lick away the blood?

"Don't worry, beloved," he says around his instantly swollen tongue. "That's the first time in three days we've heard that. It is a good thing."

"Your poor tongue."

He says, "I came to tell you about Tía Tata's letters. They are all wet and bleeding."

"Like your tongue."

"We have to dry them out. I thought we might read them together. This business with La Matilda's body is a terrible dilemma for us. Incorruptibility is not a miracle I place much faith in, but for many it's still a miracle."

"A miracle is a miracle is a miracle?"

"Please, Alice."

"I'm so sorry, Lalo. About your tongue, about everything."

He sticks his tongue out in order to view the damage. The bleeding has already stopped.

"I wish I could get Hubert to come down here and weigh in on the matter of miracles."

"I thought you wanted Waldo and Henry to come," Lalo says.

"I did," I say. When did I change my mind? "I do." But there is at least one and possibly two excellent reasons for me to no longer crave Waldo's presence in Nicaragua. "But Waldo doesn't know anything about miracles."

Lalo's hands are underneath my shirt, an ordinary polo shirt, formerly red, now faded to pink, a comfortable shirt with only one small tear at the left edge. His fingertips are cool. I tighten my stomach muscles and hope that he doesn't notice the excess avoirdupois. His hands move back and forth, but always north, until they are cupped beneath my armpits and he lifts me slightly off the floor. "Levitation can be a miracle," he says. "Except when it's a hallucination."

"Fevers can make you hallucinate."

"Will you come with me to see the letters?"

"First Ezra."

Carmen is with Ezra. She's sitting on a slipper chair upholstered in plain muslin that was not here before. Her elegant feet inside elegant white sandals are crossed at the ankles and resting upon the edge of the mattress. Ezra dozes while Carmen reads Sherlock Holmes.

"He's ever so much better," she tells me in a voice above a whisper.

"Thanks to you."

"Thanks to his constitution. Did he inherit that from you or Waldo?"

"From his grandfathers. On both sides."

"I should have guessed," Carmen says. "Did you know that Conan Doyle believed in levitation and bilocation?"

I whisper, "I had no idea. None."

"He was a rabid spiritualist. But not a Catholic. That would be too much to hope for. And he was friendly with Joaquín de Sorolla y Bastida."

"The Spanish Sargent?"

"Exactly."

"Does this have something to do with Tata?"

"It's not even true. I don't know what has gotten into me."

"Stranger things have happened," I say, softly. My arms long to stroke Ezra. My nose longs to nuzzle him, but mere minutes ago I was getting horny in the interstices of Lalo's arms. That old red tide guilt washes over me.

What is it about Lalo? Not the eyelashes, not even his body, certainly not the Brooks Brothers pajamas. It's his capacity for belief. He believes, believes, believes. There is not a cynical bone in his body. Unlike my body.

Carmen says, "I am so tired of Tata. I think when the roads are dry I will leave this place forever. I am thinking of moving to Budapest. Have you ever been there? I could be happy in a place of faded glory. Anything but this aching stretch for the unattainable future."

"Don't go to Budapest," Ezra says.

"You weren't asleep," Carmen says with mock alarm.

"Budapest is full of Huns," Ezra says. "Goulash-eating Huns. You wouldn't like it."

"You mustn't pay such attention to me, Ezra."

Finally, I reach out and touch his forehead. It feels warm.

"Do you want to try drinking something?"

"Ginger ale."

Before I can even turn on my heels to do his bidding, Carmen has summoned Graciela, through some mysterious silent communication they have, and told her to return with ginger ale.

Ezra sips, and does not vomit.

Carmen says, "I hear that someone else is sick here. The gringa."

"Who told you? What did they tell you?"

"Papa dropped by a few minutes ago."

"About your father," I say.

"I know. His memory is a wreck. He forgot the name of Emilia's husband. I told him it was fine—everyone forgets his name."

"But," I say.

"I know. Mama told me he's forgotten the names he used to call her, when they were young and delirious with love. So she starts crying and then he starts crying, and once he has started he can't stop. It's related to his strokes. That's what they say. But he was always like that. It's easier than real emotions. For instance, you may have noticed that I never cry."

"Never?" I ask.

Carmen says, "Things aren't looking good for Tata."

"You mean because of the body of La Matilda floating up? Doesn't it seem odd that her body pops out of its casket smelling sweetly while this other fellow arrives with his dog to hunt for missing corpses?"

"Where's the dog?" Ezra asks.

"In the kitchen. I guess."

"What kind is it?"

"I don't know, Ez. A hunting dog. A sniffer."

"Flirt and Dandy are hunting dogs."

"Only theoretically."

"I miss them," he says. There is a funny thing about enrouged cheeks: they can be a sign of health or a sign of fever.

"My poor Ezra," Carmen says. "As soon as you are well we can take horses and go see the high-altitude coffee."

"I've never ridden a horse," Ezra says.

"No problem," says Carmen. "The horses have never carried an American boy before."

"Is the doctor ever coming? Will he be able to tell us exactly what Ezra has? We really should know. I need to know."

"It *is* dengue. Dengue is endemic this week, this month. It only kills you if you're weak, or very old, or very young."

"What about the American woman? Edith Dilly?" I say. I slowly pronounce the syllables, because I know that naming things can take away their power. So I am naming Edith. Distinctly.

Carmen turns her face away from Ezra and whispers, "Waldo's former paramour, I gather. I hope she is attractive. I would hate to think he showed bad taste."

"I can't hear you," Ezra says.

Carmen smiles. "Perhaps she will die a painful death. But—oh, dear—I don't believe there is anything like justice in the world. And God forbid she should die here. What a nightmare. All the paperwork. A Canadian aid worker once had a heart attack in the village and we filled out forms for months. If that ever happens again I'll drive the body down the mountain and arrange it on a park bench in León, reading a newspaper."

I am undone. Should I be gleeful? Carmen knows about Edith, and Carmen is my ally. Carmen actually said *that*? About a painful death? How can she say aloud what I cannot express? Though what I wished for Edith were heartbreak and misery.

I had been so terribly jealous. Everywhere I'd looked (everywhere except sleeping Henry) spoke of Waldo's betrayal and my loss. Of course I had been melodramatic. Waldo was fucking Edith and I was leaking all over my flannel pajamas. Over and over, as I'd nursed Henry, as I'd inadvertently squirted milk all over his tender head, I'd muttered: "Here I am and Waldo is fucking Edith the fucking tennis champion. Or Edith the fucking sailing champion." I'd imagined Edith's head smashed by the boom at a yacht club regatta. I'd imagined Edith impaled on a tennis racket, a difficult thing to accomplish in the best of circumstances. I'd imagined Edith swathed and mummified inside endless yards of pink and green Lilly Pulitzer fabric, showing only the tips of her Pappagallos. Then I'd hated myself for thinking such thoughts as I cradled Henry. What anguish and future traumas were seeping into his psyche along with my milk? Was he doomed to spend years dissecting his dreams of mayhem as he reclined in a shrink's office? One of my early Bad Mother Moments.

It was all because I could not wish ill upon Waldo. Oh, no. I could not picture Waldo in any place except with us, in any attitude except as husband and father. That would have jinxed it, jinxed us. I'd wanted and needed Waldo back at his rightful place at the dinner table, constructing limericks and instructing Ezra about the arachnid life cycle and the many possible uses for bungee cords. I could not wish justifiable revenge upon Waldo because I'd wanted him back, loving me. So instead I'd imagined horrors for Edith Dilly.

Ezra has finished it all.

"Want some more ginger ale, Ez? Are you hungry?"

"Carmen's going to bring me some fruit."

She smiles at him. If there was ever a time when Waldo had weighed the relative attractions of Carmen and Edith Dilly, I certainly hope he went for Carmen. I have not seen Edith yet, but of this I am sure.

"Melon soaked in ginger syrup. There is nothing better for fevers, providing you can keep it down. Our young Ezra is ready for it now."

"Do you know where Edith Dilly is staying?"

"The room at the far end." She points toward the end of the upper loggia I have never visited.

"I want to see what she looks like," I say. Knowing Carmen is with me, knowing Carmen is with us, this must be what gives me the new courage to face Edith.

"Be my guest," Carmen says. "But remember that dengue is not flattering. Not even in our beloved Ezra."

"What do I care about flattering?"

"I'm just warning you." She smiles beatifically, a mother superior smile.

"Knock, knock."

Something falls to the floor. *Thud.*

"Knock, knock."

"Come in. *Por favor.*"

She is nothing like what I expected. I couldn't tell you what I expected.

"You must be Alice," she says. "George told me he met you."

"He did. How are you feeling?"

"Terrible all over. George says I have a fever." She raises or rolls her eyes, as if she might be able to see the reddish tinge of her forehead. Edith Dilly has a round face. Her watery blue eyes are unanchored in the face. In better times her hair is probably straight and blond, as befits her kind, but today it is damp and splayed across the pillow.

"Has he spoken with the doctor?"

"I don't know," she says. "It's dengue fever. There's nothing to do for dengue fever."

"I know that. My son had it. Has it. But he's much better now."

I have always imagined her taller, closer in altitude to Waldo. But now it's impossible to tell. There is the length of her along the bed, but I can't gauge her height. If only I'd paid attention in trigonometry!

We are silent. I am silent and Edith Dilly breathes audibly.

"I can ask Graciela to bring you ginger ale, if you want." I back away from the bedside.

"Don't go, Alice," she says.

I stop walking but a new thought occurs to me: What if she has something contagious, something airborne rather than mosquito borne? Do I bolt? No, I succumb to my personal version of tropical lassitude.

"George and I have only been married for two years," she says.

"Congratulations," I say. "A local fellow?"

"Not at all." She props herself up in her bed and reaches over to a glass of water. There is no wedding band on her ring finger. She sips, and I wait to see if she too will vomit up everything. She doesn't. "He's from Indiana, but I met him in Texas. I had never been to Texas before and I went to see my high school roommate because she had a new baby. A baby at last. A boy named Simon. He was born with six fingers on both hands and I wanted to be there for her while they removed them. She'd been trying for years to get pregnant, so this was a very big deal. A miracle, in fact."

"Why did they remove them? I would have waited."

"That wasn't for me to say. I was there to provide comfort. Then I met George in the waiting room. One of his colleagues had lost a thumb to a beer bottle."

"You were in the finger ward?" I say incredulously. How did we get to damaged digits in the state of Texas? How could she possibly know about my former student Angela Sitwell, she of the missing sixth? Stop, Alice! But Ezra knows about Angela Sitwell. Now that I think about it, before Carmen, Ezra was very fond of Angela Sitwell at Precious Blood.

"Of course not." Her eyes are watering. "George was in Texas doing training for his work with the church."

"The Pentecostal Conceptionalists?" I say.

"I don't expect people like you to understand."

"People like me?" I say. I should remember that she is sick in bed. With a dreaded tropical disease.

"People from Maine. People who go to the club."

"I'm not from Maine," I say. "You are. Your people go to the club. My people get bitten by sharks."

"I'm sorry," she says. "I just wanted you to understand about George."

"About George?"

"George changed my life. He helped me to see everything in a new light. George only wants to do good in this world. He doesn't have a cynical bone in his body."

Did she really say that? "What kind of good?" I say, because, yes, I have several cynical bones in my body.

"He wants to bring the light. He wants others to know the peace he has found accepting Jesus as his personal savior. But don't worry—he's not here just for that. He's here to build houses. He's a wonderful carpenter, you know."

"I see."

"George has barely been to Catamunk or Slow Island. He

knows who the Fairweathers are, in case you are wondering. But he's never met any of you. He's never met Waldo."

"I see."

"He and Waldo would be worlds apart, I'm pretty sure."

"Waldo has his good qualities," I say.

"I didn't mean it like that."

"How did you mean it?"

"Just that, just that," Edith repeats, and rolls her head back and forth on her pillow. "Just that Waldo is funny and George wouldn't get his jokes."

"Because he doesn't have a cynical bone in his body? Or just no funny bone?"

"The truth is, George is a saint."

"We don't bandy that word about lightly around here," I say. "Or don't you know?"

"Know what?"

"The Llobets feel strongly about saints. They have one of their own."

"I didn't know," Edith Dilly says.

"No reason you should," I say. "Especially since your own husband is a saint. So you say."

"What I mean is, he is very, very good."

"And that he doesn't know Waldo," I say. "And doesn't know about Waldo."

What I want to say is: *Waldo is mine, mine, mine. Even if I go straight to Lalo from your bedside, Waldo is mine.*

But I don't know if that is true anymore. Either the intensity or the possession.

"It wasn't my idea to come here," she says.

"To this house or to Nicaragua?"

"Both. But I meant this house. I certainly had no idea you would be here. You must admit that it's pretty unlikely."

"That depends. It's more unlikely that you would be here.

Because Waldo knows Lalo. Has known him for years, and so for us to be here is not entirely a stretch. Although someone might say it's more likely that Waldo would be here. In which case . . ."

"That was a really long time ago," Edith Dilly says. Tears dribble from her already liquid blue eyes. It probably has to do with the dengue fever, but it looks a lot like she is crying.

"I know."

"I always felt terrible about it. Not at the time, I admit. But afterward."

"I really don't want to hear this," I say. "I didn't come here for that."

"Is she telling you sad stories?" George Glass, the new and unfunny husband, is standing in the doorway. Because the light is behind him, his face is in darkness and I cannot make out his expression. "Edith has such a tender heart."

"I have to go," I say. "I promised Lalo." Then I flee. Now I flee. Behind me is the lava flow, the mudslide, the quaking earth.

35 ❧ The Decline of the Epistolary Art

There is, in fact, practically nothing known certainly
about him.

> — Alban Butler, "St Disibod," *Butler's Lives
> of the Saints*

THE LOGICAL THING would have been to put
the letters anywhere else. Somewhere high above
ground, like the church belfry. Someplace secure,
like a bank vault in Managua or Miami. Someplace dry, like the
Atacama Desert. Even more logical would have been to throw
away the ones that upset the apple cart. You have to wonder.

"What a mess. What a disaster," Lalo says. "*¡Que barbaridad!*"

"Is it true you've never read them before?"

"True."

"That is the most illogical thing I've heard all day."

"I never claimed to be logical. What does logic have to do
with it?"

I say, "I just assumed."

Lalo and I are sitting side by side on the largest LV trunk in
the room, a steamer trunk with hinges of surpassing loveliness and
delicacy. Two small adults could easily fit inside. Lalo and I could
not fit easily, because of his wide shoulders, his long feet, and, of
course, his regally erect penis. I must stop thinking like this: the
occupants of locked trunks, Lalo and I in locked embrace. Like all
the other pieces of luggage in this low-lying room, the trunk was
soaked in the hurricane. But unlike the others, it stayed shut, and

for all we know whatever is inside is Saharan dry. We don't know because it is locked, and the keys are lost, mislaid, or hidden.

"What a pleasure it is to do this with you," Lalo says.

"Sorting out wet love letters?"

"Anything, so long as it's with you."

"You don't know me. I'm a disaster."

"The hurricane was a disaster. You're beloved."

The edge of his thigh is touching the edge of my thigh. Given how wet the floor is, does that put us at risk for electrocution?

"Read to me, Lalo, please. I love being read to," I say.

"'*Querida Sor* Tristána,'" he reads.

"But she wasn't a sister."

"Only to her dissolute brothers," Lalo says. "'Today is the Feast of Santa Julia of Corsica. Like you, she had beautiful hair. It is raining again and I can count five different places where my roof is leaking. No, six. I would do anything to keep you dry. You are the castle I want to live in.'" Lalo stops. "The next part is smudged. Would you like to try?"

"No, thank you."

"Something something, 'when Doña Rosita came to my door I had to turn quickly. She brought me a chicken. She is so fond of her chickens. I had a chicken named Blue when I was a boy. He was killed by a jaguar that came in from the jungle one night, and my father beat me because I deprived us all of a fine meal. I was supposed to keep Blue safe, and I did not.'"

"Try another one," I say. He reads another, written on the Feast of Santa Eulalia, and then another sympathizing with Tristána because she has a fever and is spitting up phlegm of assorted colors, which Padre Oscar felt compelled to enumerate.

"I thought they lived close by each other. Why all the letters?"

"He was very shy?" Lalo says. "He was a writer manqué?"

"Please don't say something about the lost art of letter-writing," I whine.

Lalo strokes my head. "Tender, tender Alice," he says. What did I do to deserve this? "I imagine Padre Oscar was more comfortable expressing his feelings in writing. And he may have been awed by Tristána. Or struck dumb in her presence. What do you think, Alice? Will you be shocked when I cannot speak in your presence?"

"Shocked? I think my shock quota has been fulfilled. I am now officially unflappable."

"That sounds like Waldo," Lalo says.

Okay. *That* was not what I expected. Not what I had in mind.

"Sometimes written words express the otherwise inexpressible," Lalo says.

"Should we be inferring they were in love?" I ask. "That they . . . ?"

"Consummated their love?" The very word — *consummated* — agitates me. Lalo is as calm as the après storm. "I have no reason to think they did. A consummation devoutly to be desired . . . who said that?"

"Hamlet. Referring to death."

"This one was not. Desired."

"Desired by whom? Perhaps Oscar desired consummation."

"By me. By one who sees the larger picture." Lalo smiles.

"Can she still be a saint if they had sex? *Extra*marital sex? I love the implication of *extra*." What I love is talking about hypothetical sex.

"It all depends on the context," Lalo says.

"Whoa! That's a mighty situational answer. For a Catholic. Where are the absolutes when we need them?"

He stops my mouth with his mouth. His lips perfectly encircle mine and I could melt into the warmth of his mucous membranes. But I don't melt. I ignite. His tongue slides in like an animal in the night and scopes out the nether regions of my molars. His tongue lays claim to it all. My own tongue would happily reciprocate but his tongue rules, rules over the kingdom of melded mouths.

This is insanity. Moisture is everywhere. (And Ezra is sick upstairs with Carmen, happily with Carmen.) We are supposed to be drying out. But I don't stop. Not myself, not Lalo. (Ezra is better, and Carmen dresses always in white. Edith is upstairs, feverish and powerless.) Lalo's kissing is a miracle of pressure and motion and heat. It is a natural law unto itself, like gravity or thermodynamics. Or something like that. Lalo's kisses are dangerous and confusing.

Kisses from a man who wants to create a saint? Aren't there some very creepy kiss motifs in the Bible?

Lalo wipes his brow and leaves behind ink stains. "The Vatican is sending someone to check out La Matilda's corpse," he says glumly. "They don't do that lightly. So I need to be prepared. I need to find something here to help our case."

"Were you thinking about that while you kissed me? Honestly?"

He says, "Not entirely."

"Just read to me, Lalo, and I will listen."

He takes another sheet of thin paper and smoothes it upon his thigh, then pats it to absorb any moisture. The old letter leaves ink smudges on his khaki pants, stains that resemble remnants of a meal eaten long ago. "It's from Padre Oscar, but you know that. 'Some celebrate the Feast of Saint Peter today, but I am praying to Margaret of Cortona. Of course you know her. Tristána, can we not live as Elizabeth and Louis of Hungary, wedded and ministering to our flock? Or Clotilda and Clovis. Loving each other and loving God as well? Or Adelaide and Otto? Besides, inevitably, I will die first and you can continue in sanctified widowhood. Notice that I do not mention Blessed Delphina and Saint Elzéar—they made a choice I could never make. Do I have a choice? I know these saints do not interest you—I know you think their stories are fanciful—I know you think they are a distraction from any real work. And also young Diego Sanchez is extremely ill with marks upon his body. His mother is hopeless, I am afraid. She tears her clothes in grief, and he's not dead yet.' Then something I can't read. 'The altar linens are in terrible shape. Perhaps you could speak to some of your family. Your devoted servant, etc.' And here's another one: 'Beloved, esteemed sister in Christ, Today my whole body leans toward you like a sunflower toward the sun. Some things cannot be controlled and I cannot control this feeling I have for you.'"

"I hate to say this," I say.

"Say it, say it."

"I didn't think someone else's love letters could be so boring."

"Boring? I thought you were going to say something quite different."

"Please tell me you think they are too. Please tell me we live by the same boredom-o-meter."

"You have no idea, do you?" Lalo says.

"I don't mean to be insulting. It has nothing to do with her. She didn't write the letters. It's a generic response to other people's love letters. Mine would be riveting. Humorous and tender, with a soupçon of porn for titillation. Short and sweet."

"Yours will never leave my breast pocket," he says and pats his chest. "But these letters? These letters could be either very good or very bad for our case. Padre Oscar presents a problem."

"Because he was a horny fellow?"

"Because he was a priest, you blasphemous creature," Lalo says sweetly.

The whitewashed walls of the room are mottled with patterns in mold, with damp spots that resemble continents and inner organs. I can make out an enlarged appendix, and nearby a uterus. High up in the corner a calendar is tacked to the wall. It is too high to be useful to anyone but a giant. The year is 1944, the month November. Nothing of significance happened that year, that I know of, in Nicaragua. In the rest of the world everything significant was happening, and it was almost all bad.

"You really should get these transcribed, typed up, and put them on a CD. We shouldn't be touching them. Our fingers have oils that are treacherous to old paper."

Lalo wraps his fingers around my left wrist and brings my fingertips to his lips. When he starts sucking the tip of my index finger I almost jump from my seat.

"You have no idea where those fingers have been," I say.

"I can imagine," Lalo says.

"Every minute I learn something new," I tell him. This minute I am learning how his earlobes attach to his cheeks, and when he sucks my finger the movement of his jaw engages the cheeks, and the cheeks pull the earlobes ever so slightly. His ears wiggle when he sucks my finger. The question is: Is this normal? Or is this a Lalo Llobet specialty, like Waldo's limericks, and the late Three's ability to balance a spoon on his nose and recite the Lord's Prayer at the same time?

"Your finger has a hint of chili, and the sweetness of *miel de abeja*. Do you care to explain?"

"I care," I say. "I just care."

"One of the few things the Jesuits did not teach us was the miracle of sexual love. And its manifestations."

"Like finger sucking?"

"Exactly."

"What *did* they teach you?"

"Everything else," Lalo says.

This is nerve-racking. "Did you know that about your Tía Tata?"

"Know what?"

"That *she* wasn't a hagiographer? That she considered the saints a distraction?" Lalo releases my finger and holds both my hands on his lap, in bondage. I am beside myself with delight.

"That's only what Padre Oscar said. He is not wholly reliable."

"Shouldn't we keep reading?"

"I thought you found them boring," Lalo says.

"The sooner you get them read, the sooner we can—"

"Further our cause?"

I want to let my head drift onto his lap and nestle in there. I want to wake and sleep and wake and sleep, and never leave his lap.

He smoothes another letter and reads, "'It wasn't only the high and mighty who were married and holy. I almost forgot about Isidore's wife, Maria Torribia. She was very humble, and you are not very humble. You are in the sky above me. They had a child before they took that strange step that so many others took. How do I know it is strange? Because I wake every morning with your name on my lips where your lips should be.'"

"Strange step? What strange step? Are we finally getting racy here?"

"They swore a vow of chastity."

"Oh, that," I say.

Lalo keeps reading, but suddenly, in the midst of a letter, it occurs to me how easily I could tell George Glass about Waldo and Edith. I could let it slip. There are a thousand ways I could drop the bomb. With reminiscences of Bug Harbor, a day on the bay, or an oblique reference to Three's health and death, I could ruin everything for Edith. For Edith, with her new proselytizing husband. Her saintly Saint Joseph of a husband. She had just handed that to me. Handed me that power on a chased-silver platter. On a silver trophy for the yacht club's midsummer series championships. On a silver bowl for the biennial commodore's cup.

Was Edith looking to be a martyr?

"So. What do you think about the gringos?" I say.

"Not very much."

"I wish they had never come."

"But this way you can see Edith Dilly at last, and you can lay it to rest."

"Lay it to rest? I don't lay things to rest. I am a wretch that way."

"Waldo once told me that you were a bundle of contradictions," Lalo says.

"Waldo said that? When did he tell you that? I think if anything I am highly consistent."

"It was ages ago. Because of your Spanish mother and Welsh father."

"I fail to see what that has to do with anything." I jump up from the trunk and stand before him with my hands on my hips. It's a histrionic pose remembered from some melodrama, stored up all this time.

Lalo says, "Shall we read some more? Before I have to go and face the . . . the inevitable."

"Read away."

"I wish he had dated things. We had to date everything. The Jesuits were sticklers for record-keeping. I wonder where Padre Oscar went to seminary. I hate to think."

"Are you by any chance being a snob?"

"Most certainly. In this matter I am a snob. My standards are of the highest, beloved Alice." And then he reads from the multiply folded yellow sheet: "'I never met a matador like you. Yes, I know what you will say. I have never met any matador at all. I want to tell you that your secret is safe with me. I saw four hummingbirds this morning at the house of Doña Mirela. She wanted me to bless her pregnant dog. My mother said that keeping secrets was naughty and nasty, and she would beat them out of me. But your secret is lovely. Like you.'"

"Now that's exciting," I say. "A secret."

"It's probably nothing. I suspect this Padre Oscar liked a little drama in his life. Even to the point of creating the drama. And you, Alice, do you like drama?"

"I like you," I say. "Drama scares me."

Lalo reads more letters and I listen intermittently. I watch his lips. Are lips unique to their bearer, like fingerprints and retinas?

Ta-da! Olga appears, with flashing eyes and bits of hair sticking out from her head. "I consider them your problem," she says.

Lalo looks at her tenderly. "The letters or the gringos?"

"The gringos."

"Have they done anything wrong? Broken any pottery?"

"Pottery I can fix," Olga says.

Lalo says to me, "Olga is a genius with glue and epoxy."

"That's nice."

"How is the patient?" he asks.

"She is still sick. I looked into her room. She couldn't see me."

"Is that what you came about?"

"Of course not. Your friend Hubert is on the telephone. He acted as if he knew me. I don't know him."

"I'll go," Lalo says.

"Don't bother! We were cut off!" When she gets excited, Olga holds up her hands and shakes them. Her loose black sleeve slides down to her elbow, and the raw, salt-bruised skin of her forearm is exposed. "Do you know what I would do, if it were up to me?"

"No."

"I would burn them. But I would save the ashes."

"Why would you save the ashes?"

"Ash Wednesday," she says.

"I don't understand," I say. "I have to go see Ezra."

"Carmen and Ezra are playing that game. Though I doubt that he can ever win."

"What game?"

"Not Ping-Pong," Olga says. "Not ing-Pay ong-Pay."

Have we just discovered that Tía Tristána was not a virgin? After everything, is that what we have learned here? And was her non-virginity thanks to a consecrated priest, a priest of humble origins to be sure, but still a priest? Does that put my fornicating with Lalo into some kind of perspective?

I need to start answering questions.

It is only Scrabble. Carmen has set up the board on a small table by Ezra's bed and they are only playing Scrabble. Lovely, benign Scrabble.

"Carmen's ahead," Ezra says. "She got *dazzle* on the triple-word score."

"But there is only one *z*."

"She used a blank," Ezra tells me.

"Ezra has a marvelous vocabulary," Carmen says. "Look at this board. He made *scrofula* and *playwright*."

They're a mutual admiration society. They're a team of two.

"Who made *rivett*?" I ask.

"I did," replies Ezra.

"It only has one *t*."

"I was afraid of that."

"Well, it's too late to change anything now," Carmen says sweetly.

"Let me just take your temp, Ez."

"Don't worry. Carmen did. I'm fine. Getting better by the minute. She says that tomorrow I can have *gallo pinto* for breakfast and ride up the volcano."

"That seems awfully adventurous."

"He is better, and now that Edith is worse. Odilia said she was vomiting."

"Shouldn't someone call the doctor?" I ask.

"I did. Fernando says that of course it is dengue, because dengue is everywhere. He was not very worried. He has other things to be worried about. As do we all."

"But she's probably miserable."

"You can be sure of that," Carmen says.

(I suddenly picture Waldo and Carmen, standing side by side in an airport, an old airport, before security checkpoints and casual attire. A wizened redcap is hunched over with the weight of their three enormous Louis Vuitton suitcases.)

I am not eavesdropping. I can't help it if I can hear the cooing of George Glass, the saintly husband.

"Hello there!" he greets me loudly at the door. I exhale.

"I thought I'd check in on the patient."

"Come in! Come in! Nothing would please her more than to see you, a familiar face!" George shouts. I suspect he is one of those people who have difficulty modulating their volume.

"I'm not familiar."

Edith's face is small and ashen on the pillow. Gone are the red cheeks of fever.

"Poor Edith. She never complains. But I know that deep down she would always rather be in Maine."

"Can she eat anything? Or drink anything?" I ask George.

"I can't keep it down," she answers.

"My son was like that. Everything came back up."

"Ezra. You must be so pleased he is better," George says.

"We heard that Ezra is delightful," Edith says.

"Yes," I say. I don't want his name pronounced in this room, by these people. There is a limit.

They both smile, George transparently, Edith wanly.

"Where is your friend with the dog?"

"They went into the village to do something about the jeep. We got terribly stuck in the mud, you know. And then they were going to head over to the hills where the worst mudslide was. Sometimes it takes Sam a few days to get comfortable in his new surroundings. He's a terrifically sensitive dog. But you probably guessed that." George keeps his hands jammed into the pockets of his khakis, as if they need to be restrained from ecstatic gesticulation.

"I've never met a corpse-sniffing dog before," I say. "Are there many?"

"Dogs' olfactory senses are forty to fifty times greater than ours," George says.

"I know." Henry told me that, among many other facts concerning the wondrous abilities of dogs.

"George and I are here for the living," Edith whispers. "The survivors and the grief-stricken."

"They call them *damnificados*."

"We know," George says. "They are our mission."

"You could spend your whole life in Catamunk and never hear the word *damnificados*," I say. "I don't even know if Waldo has ever heard it. *Damnificados*."

Lalo would be so right to ask what I was doing, here, visiting with Edith. Lalo would be completely meet and right to demand an explanation, and I would be at a loss. Except that it feels right.

36 ❧ A Dime a Dozen

> It must be frankly admitted that the virgin martyr
> St Febronia is in all probability a purely fictitious
> personage, but she is venerated by all the churches of
> the East.
>
> — Alban Butler, "St Febronia," *Butler's Lives*
> *of the Saints*

DOÑA ODILIA MADE something special to-night," Olga announces.

"We have been blessed with her fine cooking for these many decades." Don Abelardo weeps into his soup. While smoking a cigarette. Not a simple conjunction of tasks.

"You mustn't mind his crying," Doña Luisa tells me.

"I had a stroke."

"She knows, Papa," Emilia says. I haven't seen her in days. I had forgotten about her.

"Hello, Emilia," I say.

"Where have you been?" Lalo demands of her. "Not . . . ?"

"I resent that," Emilia says.

"Where is Carmen?" Don Abelardo asks of the table at large. "Carmen has such a way with soup."

Across from me sits Edward Flanz and next to him is Olga. Don Abelardo regards his food with suspicion after praising it so highly. Lalo looks much like his father. They share the shape of their faces, their eyelashes, and their cheekbones. Don Abelardo's lips are thinner than Lalo's. I heard somewhere that lips thin and even disappear with age. Our parentage is inescapable, and just now the right side of Don Abelardo's face is drooping like an El Greco saint's. I look sideways at Lalo to reassure myself that his right side is intact.

Edward Flanz was probably a very unpopular boy. He grips his spoon with his entire fist and then ladles in the soup frantically, like one whose train is leaving in two minutes but who's determined to finish what he's paid for.

Olga stares. She spoons her soup and then dribbles it back into the bowl in a circular pattern. She says, "I met your dog in the kitchen. Did he find any corpses today?"

Reluctantly Edward Flanz stops inhaling his soup. "Today he, we, explored the area, we went to the village, yes, the village, we went there. We went to the village to see. We always do that first."

"Have you always done this?"

"This? Oh, I don't know. I don't know what you mean."

"Looked for corpses with your dog," Olga says. "I've never met anyone before who does that. Maybe there are thousands of you out there, but here, there is only you."

"I've always liked dogs, if that's what you mean. And dogs, well, they seem to like me. Sam, he was a police dog, but he ate too much, so they gave him to me."

"What does he do if a corpse smells like a flower?" Olga asks.

"Olga, Olga, Olga!" Doña Luisa cries out in consternation.

"It's a problem we are having in Nicaragua," Olga explains to Edward. "But the pope would tell you it's a worldwide phenomenon. The pope doesn't give much thought to the need for biodegradability. So I must worry about such things. The incorruptibles. All these saints who smell like flowers when they should be turning to ashes and dust."

Lalo returns from the telephone in the hall. "That was Fred Chavez at *La Barricada*. He wants to know if we plan to dig up Tía Tata."

"*¡Que barbaridad!*" Doña Luisa murmurs.

"Since you ask, that is, the question about the corpses." Edward's words come out in spurts, like a faucet coming to life after a long winter. "Sam, my dog, Sam, he doesn't care much about flowers, or so it seems. So it seems. He might not even find, wouldn't find it interesting, a body that smelled, that is, smelled like a flower. You could say, now, that depends on what flower, but I would say, any flower. Any flower at all."

Olga says to Lalo, "What did you tell him?"

Don Abelardo is weeping again. "Poor Tía Tata. She was so beautiful. And now they want to mummify her. How very sad."

"I told him I'd heard his sister Zoila was having an affair with Daniel Ortega. I asked him whether he was to be congratulated or offered condolences."

"Lalo! What is wrong with my children today?" hoarsely cries tiny Doña Luisa. "That is cruel. Everyone knows Zoila doesn't like men."

"He said nothing of the kind." It is Carmen waltzing in. On her, even the narrowest pants flow and waft in the breezes of her making.

Lalo says, "Carmencita, where have you been? We have been fractured without you."

"Fissured, crackered," Olga says.

"Ezra wanted to tell me his dream. Otherwise I would have come earlier. I wrote it down for him."

"Ezra told you his dream?" I say before I can stop myself, before I can imagine my way to masking the dismay in my voice.

"I will read it to all of you. He said he'd like me to, that it would be his contribution to our conversation."

"Ezra is an absolutely charming boy," Lalo says. He mouths, *And his mother.*

Carmen removes a lined sheet of paper from her sleeve, and reads aloud. "'My English teacher told us we were going to have to do a project on a saint, so I started to get irritated. I started a rebellion against my English teacher. We locked the basement door and formed a plan to get more people inside, and it involved a Lego robot, a ski helmet, and a lot of danger on my part. Then the door banged open and my English teacher and the kids who supported her came in. They ran up the stairs and started jabbing us with spears. I jumped from the balcony and grabbed my teacher's spear in midair. Around that time all the kids who were on my side changed to her side. She sent us to the principal's office and I admitted that the rebellion was my fault.'"

"That poor boy, all that violence," says Don Abelardo.

"That poor boy, with saints on the brain," Carmen says.

Emilia pipes up. "Don't get him started. Papa! It was a dream! Only a dream!"

"The worst kind," he says.

"I can't abide other people's dreams," says Doña Luisa, huskily.

Carmen snaps, "Not even Ezra's?"

"I never dream. Why should I listen to someone else's?"

I say nothing. A thousand and one times I've had this conversation with people who say they never dream. Of course they dream. If they didn't dream they would die. I am not inclined to contradict Doña Luisa tonight. This is not *Dream Radio*. This is a tiny country far from home, and I want Ezra to tell his dreams to only me.

Odilia taps Lalo on the shoulder and he gets up again.

I miss *The Dream Radio Show*, WBLT, 98.6 on your dial. I miss the early-morning commute, in darkness or dawning light. I miss the quiet energy of Grand Central Station at that hour, before volubility and panic set in. I miss the regular callers, the ones who believe in their dreams, the ones who believe that just putting a dream into words will get them over the hump of terror when it seems that morning will never be real. I miss the one-time callers who are so astounded by what their own minds have conjured up that the only thing they can do is call me, host of

The Dream Radio Show, and tell our listeners in the tri-state area. I miss the lack of commentary, the pure narrative.

"I heard that there is a dengue epidemic in Boaca," Olga says. I don't know how she managed it, but all the knives, from all our places, are lined up horizontally in front of her plate.

"Where is Boaca?" I ask.

"North of Granada, north of the lake. Cowboy country. Not far from La Matilda's village, in case you need to know."

He's crying again! And the soup has been removed. "It shouldn't be that hard to understand," Don Abelardo says. "But it's so very hard."

"What is so hard?" asks Emilia. I haven't seen her husband in days. Nobody has mentioned anything. Would it be polite to show some interest in his whereabouts and his well-being?

"The problem of Saint Tristána," says Don Abelardo.

Back comes Lalo. He rubs the top of his head and musses his silken hair. No, he is pressing down on the top of his head, keeping it from taking off like a champagne cork. I want him to make eye contact with me, and when he finally does, he mouths, *Hubert.* Does he want to speak with me? I push my chair back to indicate my willingness. Lalo shakes his head and walks in, sits down.

"That was Alice's friend Hubert the hagiographer," he announces.

"He was your friend first."

Carmen has a piece of speared meat on her upraised fork, and stops midair. "I doubted his existence until Ezra told me that, yes, he really does exist and he is deathly afraid of skunks."

Don Abelardo says, "There are no skunks in Europe or Africa. They are native to the Americas. Like potatoes."

Carmen says, "That's right, Papa. And Hubert is American."

Lalo says, "Of course he exists. *Someone* at this table is completely sane. He read about La Matilda's corpse on the Internet."

This seems a rather brave statement by someone who has

wandered lonely as a cloud in a snowstorm in his Brooks Brothers pajamas, even if that is the someone I can't stop thinking about with lust and longing.

His mother whispers, "Just because it's on the Internet doesn't make it true."

"It said her grave opened in the mudslide and the body is incorrupt. He gets e-mails and links from all over about saints, or would-be saints. It's his job."

"What else did it say?"

"Gardenias. That it smells like gardenias. And that the people are trying to get there but the roads are impassable."

"The gringo press always makes things sound worse than they really are," Carmen says dismissively.

I say, "I thought the roads *are* impassable."

"Some of the roads, some of the time," Olga says. Now the knives in front of her plate are arranged in crosses. Four crosses of knives; the juncture point is at the very base of the steel shaft, just above the silver handle.

Into the quiet, Edward Flanz speaks. "I know, that is, I don't know who these people are, who they are. I know a Hubert, he has a garage, well, it's more of a filling station, and it's probably closed now, but I knew him, and I think that is another one, another Hubert, not yours. Also Matilda I don't know. But I know a song about Matilda, a song everyone knows, those are the only songs I know, everyone's."

"Wrong Hubert," Lalo says to Edward Flanz. "He was concerned, which I thought very friendly of him. Thoughtful. 'Don't give up on Tata, incorruptibles are a dime a dozen,' that sort of thing."

A dime a dozen. A dome a dizzy. A Rome a raisin. A mime a mazes. Where, oh, where is Waldo when my brain is conjuring up nonsense? But if Waldo walked in right now, I might choke on my *palmito*.

442

"He must consider the situation to be dire," Carmen points out. "That he called at all."

"Not that you care," Lalo says.

George slips in and whispers something in Carmen's ear.

She turns to me. "Did Ezra have pain behind his eyes?"

"No. Not that he ever said. Behind the eyes?" She's asking me?

"It's a delicacy," Don Abelardo says. "When I was in Patagonia I was given the fat behind the eye of the rhea, because that is the choicest part of the bird, and my friend there was most considerate of my taste buds."

"Not the rhea, darling," whispers minuscule Doña Luisa.

"We're talking about pain, Papa. Our guest Edith has pain behind her eyes."

Emilia says, "She must have dengue fever."

"Of course she has dengue fever!" says Carmen.

"Would you mind coming up to see her?" George says. But he is not speaking to Carmen. It is to me.

"To see Edith?"

"If you wouldn't mind. She's terribly cold."

"I don't think I can help."

"If you wouldn't mind," he repeats. I grudgingly abandon the *flan de coco,* and follow George out of the room.

Piled atop Edith's narrow body are more blankets that I can count. She and George both tell me how horrid is the pain behind her eyes. Exactly where? Behind the eyeballs. If we had a plastic model of the skull she could take a long pin—like a hatpin—and show us exactly where the pain is. Ezra never said a word about anything behind his eyes. George asks me if I am sure he had dengue, and the answer is no, I'm not sure. It's just a name for a set of symptoms, for pain and fever and chills. George reminds me that a mosquito is involved, that there is a vector. I can't help him with the pain behind the eyes.

Edith says, "I think it's related to the chickens."

"What chickens?"

"I keep seeing chickens," she says.

"It must be because of the rooster. They cock-a-doodle-doo at all hours. Is there something wrong with Nicaraguan roosters that they don't know when to crow?" George says.

"Can she eat anything?" I ask.

Edith groans. "God, no."

"Is the pain better or worse?" George wants to know.

"Worse. Worse. I'm not sure I can do this."

"On a scale of ten to one, what is your pain?"

"Which is worse, high or low?"

"Ten is the worst pain ever," George says. The last time I heard that question asked I was in the Ginny O hospital with Lalo, but Lalo was not the one being asked to rate his pain. It was his roommate, Rubén. The nurse had asked Rubén several times, with Lalo translating, One to ten? First Rubén had asked the nurse what *she* thought was the correct number. And when she insisted on an answer, he'd said, One, maybe two. I'd averted my eyes from his bloody bandages.

"Eleven and a half," Edith says.

Why am I here? There is nothing I can do for them, for her. I don't want to see her, not even in pain. All those months when I craved to know what she looked like (Was she prettier than me? Skinnier? Chestier? Was her stomach flatter? Were her legs longer? How many times can those questions be asked? There is no limit, I learned), all those months when she was the toxic black cloud that threatened my marriage, my children, everything that mattered, and especially all the times I rubbed my wound raw by imagining exactly what sexual acts she might be perform-ing at any given moment with Waldo—and now this. Is this the anticlimax?

What does Lalo have to do with this?

Everything.

And nothing.

Edith moans again. "I told George about Waldo and me," she says.

My stomach grumbles ominously.

"She told me everything," George asserts.

"Are you sure there are no more blankets? An electric blanket? My toes are ice cubes."

"That was your decision," I finally say. "But Ezra doesn't know."

"Oh, don't worry!" George says. "It stays in this room. Between Edith and me there are no secrets. Otherwise we are silent as the grave. No one will know."

"Frankly, I don't care who knows what," I say. "It's only Ezra that matters."

"Don't mention graves." Edith moans.

Like my room and Ezra's room, presumably like all the rooms along the loggia here at Las Brisas, this one is airy and sparsely furnished. A hammock swings limply from two ceiling beams. Over the door frame is a smallish crucifix, nothing garish or bloody. It is positively tasteful, even Protestant, compared to the ones we stared at open-mouthed in Abuela's Barcelona apartment. The Virgin is over the bed, in Mestizo Baroque style. Nothing is awry. To the naked eye.

"We haven't even met Ezra yet," George says.

"You probably won't," I say. I don't know if this is true. I want it to be true.

George says, "The doctor says he doesn't need to come. That we should just go on as we are. Keep her hydrated, of course." He uplifts his hands theatrically. "I am beside myself! I don't know where to turn."

"You can always pray," I suggest. "To the saint in the family—Tristána Llobet. It's her territory."

"I've never heard of her. Or did you say something before?"

"She's Nicaraguan." I don't add that she's not exactly a canonized saint and unlikely to ever be one, given her letters, given the unfortunate fact of her sexuality that—I must admit it—I am delighted she experienced. It would be true to say I am misleading George Glass. "She's the object of a local cultus."

"Wow," he says. "I've never heard of a local cultus. Do you really think it would help? Praying to her?"

Edith shivers beneath her mound of blankets, opens and closes her eyes with obvious pain.

"It can't hurt."

"I don't normally pray to saints," George tells me.

"You're not normally in Nicaragua, and Edith doesn't normally have dengue."

"You have a point. So what about this saint?"

"She was a great beauty who forswore all her suitors and the world's pleasures. She lived in a small shack next to the church, and looked after the sick and dying. They say she knew when someone was going to die, and she would start walking to the house days before. Sometimes."

"Wasn't it pretty creepy to have her show up?"

Edith mutters something that sounds like *water*, and George holds the glass to her lips. Water dribbles down her chin. I stare at the Virgin: she has a tiny head and a huge tent of a gown.

"Not necessarily. Everyone has to die sometime. She sang hymns at their funerals. Everyone loved her."

"Kind of like Mother Teresa?"

"Kind of. Except that she stayed in one place, and she was beautiful, and she wasn't a nun and didn't start a new order of nuns, and no one has ever heard of her outside of Nicaragua. Her scale of operations was small, you could say, but her impact on individuals was great."

George says, "Why would she help Edith?"

"Why not? If you pray to her. Ask for a favor, a miracle."

Recovery from dengue would not qualify as a miracle, though. Even I know that. Ditto hiccups. The Vatican's standards are very high. They put would-be saints through rigorous background checks, and their miracles are subject to batteries of tests, panels of experts, and trials by fire. It is worse than applying for a job with the CIA. No, Tata Llobet still needs a major-league miracle. And Edith is not likely to be it. Back when, I had prayed for Waldo. For Waldo's undiluted love forever. Would that constitute a miracle? Be careful what you pray for.

Tata needs a miracle of her own. Or not, by my lights. No, I like her much better when I consider her now, nestled in bed with Padre Oscar.

George holds his hand over his mouth. "A miracle?" he spits out. "Is that what it will take? Oh, no, no, no." His sweaty face is awash in panic.

"Whoa. Calm down. I didn't mean it like that. People get over dengue. It only kills the old, the young, and the weak. Look at Ezra. Edith is a healthy adult. She is, isn't she?"

"I should never have brought her down here. It was my idea. You know—ahem—she feels so guilty about the thing with Waldo. I don't think that's helping her, feeling so terrible about what happened in the past, before she understood."

"I don't want to talk about Waldo," I say. I *don't* want to talk about Waldo because I need to think about Lalo and that is a lot to think about.

George goes on, "She told me it was like she was hypnotized."

I say, "I don't want to hear about it. It has nothing to do with dengue."

"I've never seen her sick before," he whines. "It's breaking my heart."

"Just keep her hydrated."

Edith moans from her pillow. "But the pain behind my eyes? Will that never go away?"

"Tell her it will go away, George. She needs to hear it from you."

"It will go away, Edith, darling. The Motrin will help."

The volume has diminished. "I can't take this pain. Oh, George, I'm such a weakling, but I can't take it."

George holds her hand but looks at me. "There must be something you can do," he says. "You speak the language. You know the people."

"I'm not a doctor, and even the doctor can't do much. Just get through it," I say. "Think of it as a boulder field you have to get across, full of rocks and crevasses. When you get to the end, well, then you're past it." Where did that come from? I have never crossed a boulder field. Does a rocky beach on the coast of Maine count?

George whispers to me, "That's easy for you to say. But I was a Christian Scientist before we saw the light and joined the Pentecostals. So I didn't do illness ever, back then. I'm at a loss."

"You'll be fine." The rest of the house is quiet and still. It is the time after eating and drinking and before the racket of early-morning birds and insects, and of course the Nicaraguan rooster. I don't want to spend this time in this room.

"I couldn't bear it if anything happened to Edith!" George ejaculates and lurches into my arms, weeping. He is larger than me. This is an awkward pose under the best of circumstances.

"Nothing will happen to Edith," I say sternly.

Through his sobs he utters, "Look at her. Hot—cold—cold—hot, and now this pain behind the eyes. What if it moves somewhere else? Somewhere worse?"

"George! Get a hold of yourself. She will be fine—don't let her see you like this. Remember, she's the sick one, not you. Give her water. Pray to Tristána. It will do you some good."

George bursts out weeping like a hysterical child, all runny nose and gasping intakes of air. He leans into my shoulder and sniffles onto my shirt. I can't step back because he might fall to the floor. "George! Cut it out! It's no good for Edith to see you like this. What will she think?"

448

"She'll think I am the unworthy wretch that I am." He sniffles.

"Take some deep breaths. Go splash cold water on your face."

He brightens, runs into the bathroom, and turns on the tap full force. Henry would say that George runs like a girl. When did I last speak with him? I am sure the bedsore experiment is over. I should be asking if the bedsore experiment ever took place. Could it be an elaborate construct of Waldo's? Was Henry off somewhere he shouldn't be, a parachuting academy or the shooting range? Or, worse, was he hospitalized with West Nile fever or equine encephalitis or a rare antibiotic-resistant strain of tuberculosis? Fever, fever, everywhere, but only if I blink.

"Why are those chickens bothering me?" Edith moans.

"There are no chickens," I tell her. "It's just the fever. Try to sleep."

"I won't eat meat anymore, if that's the problem," she says.

"No one cares if you eat meat."

George is still splashing his face. Such theatrics are not necessary.

"He's too sweet for this world," she says. "That's why all the bugs love him."

"You're the one with dengue fever."

"He had a terrible childhood," Edith says. She closes her eyes and tosses her pale perspiring face back and forth upon her pillow. George needs to cease his ablutions and come back to wipe her brow.

"He has you now," I point out cheerfully.

"Both his parents died," she whispers hoarsely. "His aunt adopted him. But she was a Scientist and didn't believe in death."

"Death exists whether you believe in it or not," I say. "George! Are you all right in there?"

"She didn't really like him, was the problem. She had always wanted a girl, someone she could share clothes and hair products with. Not that George has ever complained to me."

"Where is this aunt now?"

"On the dementia floor." Edith moans. "Poor, poor George."

"Edith needs you!" I shout. "And bring a facecloth."

At last. He is not running. He marches slowly, as if bearing the weight of the Virgin in a Holy Week procession.

"Just look at her," he says.

Edith says stagily, "The chickens are here."

"There are no chickens. Only we three."

"Can you ever forgive me about Waldo?" Edith says. Her eyes are locked on George. I assume she is talking to George. He wipes her forehead. "Can you?"

"Let's just not go there. Talk about it among yourselves, but not with me."

"Behind the eyes! Press behind the eyes!"

"I can't press any harder," George says. "I don't want to hurt you."

"I already hurt so much."

George is wild and panicked again.

"We need a helicopter!" he says. "To fly her to the capital."

I could tell him all the good reasons that is a bad idea—the mountainous terrain, the lack of a landing pad, the fact that all the helicopters in Nicaragua are Soviet army castoffs, the cost of fuel, the fact that she will be better soon—but I say nothing, because it is none of my business.

"Where have you been?"

George and Edith are serenely indifferent to his voice, but I whip around to see Lalo standing in the doorway. He is wearing a paisley silk bathrobe over his pajamas, and if I am not mistaken, they are a clone of the pale blue with dark blue piping Brooks Brothers pajamas he wore on the snow that morning in VerGroot. The men I know don't wear pajamas or silk bathrobes—such sartorial touches exist only in vintage movies. They are clothes for a fantasy. But now I know a man who does wear pajamas. And a bathrobe.

"I'm right here."

"How bad is she?" Lalo asks, from the doorway.

"Alice told me to pray to your aunt. And I plan to do it as soon as Edith falls asleep. It will be a first for me, but desperate times call for . . ."

"Desperate measures," Lalo completes.

"Exactly."

Lalo beckons me not with one finger but with his whole hand, with all the fingers together reaching toward me then arching back toward himself. I am drawn to that hand. Lalo's beckoning hand pulls me like the empty air past the edge of the cliff.

"I'm going to check on Ezra." I back out of the room.

Edith utters, "I hope to meet him one day."

I close the door behind me. No, no, no! Never.

Without a word Lalo kisses the top of my head, then pushes his hand down the back of my pants.

"Ezra is fine," he says.

"I thought so. I mean, I hoped so."

"Carmen says his temperature is normal."

"Carmen took his temperature?"

"You're coming with me," Lalo says.

"Where are we going?"

"Either to heaven or to hell. Probably both."

"You don't really believe?"

"In heaven? I was speaking in metaphors, dear Alice. Predicting," Lalo says, even as his hands are still burrowing under my pants and my waistband is digging into my belly and I am trying to suck in my petite pooch. "But yes, I do believe there is something after—if you really want to know."

37 ❧ Hubert's Nose

> The legendary or fictitious element is very conspicuous
> in the life of Hildegard . . . and the story cannot be
> trusted wherever it goes beyond the data furnished in
> the chronicles and other sources.
>
> — Alban Butler, "Blessed Hildegard, Matron,"
> *Butler's Lives of the Saints*

L ALO'S PREDICTIONS PROVED TRUE. The night
lasted forever, and it was too short.

One day I will apologize to Ezra, but not now.
Isn't he in love, loving someone, too? This state (of mind, of being)
we are in is tropical. And we temperate creatures are undone.
Does that constitute an excuse? Already I know that I will tell
Waldo. But I don't know what I will tell him.

In the morning, another newspaper reporter—also personally
known to the Llobets—calls for Lalo's comments on the fragrant
body of his late great-aunt's rival for canonization. He has none.

George appears briefly downstairs in search of coffee. When
asked about Edith's condition, he devolves into weeping and
handwringing.

Ezra gets dressed and presents himself to the remnants of the
assembled group in the dining room. He is paler and thinner
than the Ezra who sat here so many days ago and fell for Carmen,
but the luminosity has returned to his eyes. He delivers himself of
a dream that includes ice water, a beautiful woman in white, and
a steep cliff.

Olga asks, "Did the woman look like anyone we know?"

"No," says Ezra.

George says, "I saw Mary Baker Eddy in a dream once. She was wearing overalls and funny shoes with points and tassels in the front. Elf shoes."

Ezra tells him, "No one in my dreams ever has a name."

I should be loving this, a morning of dreams related. But I am edgy. There is no such thing as poison ivy in these tropics, so I am assured. But I feel the premonitory itch of urushiol gathering its strength just beneath the skin.

Lalo's eyes are darker and wider than ever, bright but focused elsewhere. He does not look like a man who didn't sleep last night, whereas I, I look like marmalade on a spoon.

Odilia beckons Lalo to another phone call. "No more news-papers, Odilita," he says.

"It's a man, a gringo," she tells him. We look at each other and mouth, almost simultaneously, *Waldo?* and *Waldo!*

While Lalo is talking out in the hall, the *gallo pinto* turns to unmixed concrete in my mouth. Ezra is explaining his theory about colors in dreams, and I cannot follow. George is a blur, Olga is a blur, even the exquisitely outlined Carmen has become impressionistic.

I picture Waldo at the kitchen table in VerGroot, holding the cordless phone discolored by beet juice. His bare feet are rest-ing on Flirt's soft back, and small fruits are scattered across the kitchen table. Henry is elsewhere. It's the words I can't quite imag-ine. Will Waldo tell Lalo I am a domestic tyrant who can't keep a job? Will he tell him that if I don't return to VerGroot pronto, he and Henry will disappear into a cave? Or has something hap-pened to Henry, something so dreadful that he felt compelled to tell Lalo first? Will Lalo tell Waldo that I have tumbled into his bed faster than lava flowing down the slopes on Monocromito? Will he politely and respectfully tell Waldo that my place is now on a coffee farm in Nicaragua? Will he even mention Tata?

The coffee is making me nauseated. Ditto the juice. What should go down is coming up. Ezra is explaining his theory of animal appearances in dreams. Ezra has much to say about chickens. George is massaging his temples. Ezra mentions Susie Crench. He describes Susie's pet chickens, their feathers and coloration. He has never seen her chickens.

Lalo stands in the doorway and fastens on my eyes. "Hubert would like to speak with you," he says.

"Hubert?"

"Your friend Hubert."

"On the phone?"

"He's just a little distressed," Lalo says.

I go.

"I steered you wrong. Re the virgin saints."

"Hubert! I'm so relieved it's you. What are you talking about?"

"It seems I steered you wrong. Had you barking up the wrong tree. Sent you off on a wild-goose chase."

"What are you talking about?" I am a broken record. But relieved, still terribly relieved.

"She wasn't a virgin after all."

"Lalo told you?"

Hubert goes on. "Which doesn't mean you should give up. Far from it. Sometimes the greater challenge—and thus the greater glory—comes from overcoming carnality to approach true godliness. To be saintly and human—there is perhaps the greatest challenge of all. Think Pelagia the Penitent. Think James of Lodi. Think Margaret of Cortona."

"Lalo told you about the letters?"

"He did. That's not why I called, though. I heard about La Matilda's incorruptitude. I saw it on my hagio-alert listserve."

"Waldo told me," I say. "It's probably hysteria. Don't you think?"

"Don't count on it. There are too many incorrupts out there to discount them all."

"More than there are UFOs?"

"As far as I know."

"Those are just the circles you run in," I say.

"Nevertheless, as I said, it's serious stuff. The Vatican's sending someone to verify the scent."

"The papal perfumer?"

"Very funny," he says, not laughing. "I told Abelardo he may want to change his strategy. Differentiate his aunt from La Matilda, and at the same time find some common ground. You just can't deny that this will give her a leg up."

"Not just a leg," I say. Silence at the other end.

"So. How is Christina the Astonishing?" I ask.

Hubert chirps, "You haven't seen the papers, have you? The reviews have been brilliant."

"I had no idea. It seems just the other day . . ."

"She was writing it. So I thought. So I thought."

"What's the title?"

"The Relics of Sadness."

"Catchy," I say.

"Do you think so? I think it's rather glum. Lacking specificity. And a tad melodramatic."

"Do *you* like it?"

"It has the earnest passion of youth," he says circumspectly. "And my character is rather heroic, which I don't mind one bit. But otherwise—it's a tad formulaic. Bats in the belfry. You know."

"I don't even know what it's about."

Hubert says, "I was expecting a plain old roman à clef. But this is full of arcane violence, along with the usual coming-of-age stuff."

"But that's not why you called."

"I told you why I called," he says. "And there's you and Abelardo . . ."

"Excuse me! What do you mean?"

"I have a nose for sexual peccadilloes," he says. "That's from the Latin for *sin, peccare.* The diminutive."

"I don't want to talk about it."

"That says it all," Hubert says, too gleefully for my taste. "Keep in mind the diminutive."

"There is nothing to talk about."

"Don't get so huffy, darling."

"Oh, Hubert, what if she doesn't get to be a saint? Will it break his heart?"

"I hope his heart is more resilient than that," Hubert says. "Besides, the process is interminable. The gears turn slowly in the Vatican. All those robes and miters, all that red tape in Latin. Any sane person will get bored before he is brokenhearted."

"But . . ."

"I know. There is nothing sane about this. Be of good faith, my dear. Your secret is safe with me."

I shout, too loud, "I don't have any secrets!"

"That's why she made me the father confessor character. Hugo von Coffin. Not very subtle."

The table is empty. Everyone is elsewhere. Lalo is on the far side of the courtyard, in conversation with Olga and Doña Odilia. I realize I cannot just walk up to him and touch him in the normal course of events. I realize I am an outsider here.

I don't know what else to do with myself. A radio show. A classroom of moody girls. But I have neither. Olga turns and says, "Papa forgot to put his pants on this morning. Doña Odilia wants to make him nettle tea."

Lalo says, "We are deciding about Tía Tata's letters. I think we should publish every one."

"But she didn't write them," I say.

"I think we should burn them. We haven't had a good bonfire in ages," Olga says. "I can think of lots of things I'd like to throw in."

Doña Odilia throws up her arms and then clasps her head with her hands. "What more can he forget?" she asks the flower border, the louche, pendulous datura and the stately agapanthus.

Lalo (those sinkable eyes! those earlobes!) informs us that the road is clear enough to get through and he is going to take Ezra and me to see some of the carnage and destruction from the mudslides. Olga says, "And the *damnificados?*"

Ezra is initially reluctant to go without Carmen, and Carmen says she cannot leave the house just now as she is in the middle of a project. Lalo does not ask. He is eager to set out; he taps his foot, then bounces on the balls of his feet. It is we three in his Mitsubishi, bouncing over the freshly rutted roads of Las Brisas, down the mountainside, and out the old wrought-iron gate. Then we hug the side of the volcano for an hour of gut-jolting and head up toward another crest of the volcano.

Everything is washed away. To describe the landscape as lunar evokes only its unearthliness. *Lunar* does not begin to address the mud. On both sides of the road, earth has been scraped away, rubbed raw by the mudslides. At first the earth is reddish, but as we climb it darkens to black. It is gouged. Occasional forlorn trees still stand, gathering round them sticks, plastic bags, and in one case a door. All the sad debris. It is the absence that silences us, for a time. Absence of trees, of houses, of vines and flowers, absence of the people who live here. This is an earth denuded and shorn of even its skin. When Lalo said the roads were passable, he was being optimistic. Even in four-wheel drive, in first gear, we groan and grunt along. Our wheels plunge into tire-eating potholes and spin. Lalo backs us up, repositions the jeep, and guns it. This works on the third try. The next time we get stuck, Ezra and I get out and dig at the mud with the shovel someone brilliantly keeps in the back of the vehicle, while Lalo carefully inches us forward onto harder ground. Ez and I climb back in.

Seeing this one mud-stripped slope of one volcano among

many volcanoes and mountains, it becomes easier to imagine the Tecacilpa cemetery ruptured with caskets tossed helter-skelter down the hill until they hit the immovable objects that jolt them open. Beyond that I can imagine only caskets filled with mud. Nothing smells sweet. There are no flowers.

"Where are all the people?" Ezra asks.

"We hope they're being properly buried," Lalo says. "But there are still many under the mud and the rubble."

"I guess Sam the corpse-sniffing dog will have to find them," Ezra says.

"That is what he's here for." Both hands grip the mottled steering wheel. The thumbnail of his left hand has been chewed to the quick, uncharacteristically. Lalo has such beautiful hands and lovely clean nails. Not like Waldo's.

"Poor Nicaragua is in the path of everything. If there ever was a country in need of a saint . . . we are it. But it won't be Tristána Llobet. I see that now."

Ezra pipes up. "Maybe someone else could be the family saint. You. Or Carmen!"

Lalo laughs thrillingly, softly. "I'd have to change my ways."

"You'd have to perform a few miracles," Ezra says.

"Carmen doesn't believe in miracles," Lalo reminds him. The road has flattened out, and with a grumbling of gears and spinning of wheels we are turning around. Farther up the mountain the road is much worse. The ruts appear as bottomless as volcanic craters. We descend in first gear. My right foot aches from pressing the imaginary brake.

"She just has her own ideas about what a miracle is," Ezra says.

Lalo grins at me. "We should have consulted this son of yours from the beginning."

Now Ezra's face is pressed against the glass of the back window. Quietly, I say to Lalo, "Did you mean that? About Tata not getting canonized? Hubert thinks you need another angle is all."

"I mean that without a verifiable miracle we are up a creek, as Waldo would say."

"Without a paddle."

"As you said long ago, hiccups don't count."

"Did I say that?"

"Mom! I saw a raccoon! I'm not supposed to see raccoons in the day."

Lalo says, "It's a pizote, and they are diurnal."

"I thought it was rabid," says Ezra. "Dad once ran away from a rabid raccoon in the middle of the day. Luckily, he's very fast."

"I never knew that," I say. "When was this?"

"Ages ago, Mom. In Catamunk. Posey watched the whole thing from her window upstairs."

"Where was I?"

Back at Las Brisas, Ezra says, "All that time I was in bed there was a hurricane named for you, Mom, and I never even saw it. Only today."

"You know perfectly well it wasn't named for me." He is already heading off to find Carmen.

How can we help? I mouth four of the paltriest words in the English language.

"Stay here with me," Lalo says, too quickly.

"I mean the country, the poor people hurt by the hurricane. The ones who were washed away."

"You mean the *damnificados*?"

"Do you have to use that word?"

"If that's what you're talking about, go home and persuade the U.S. Congress to send us more money and stop protecting the Florida sugar growers so that we can export to the American market. And, oh, yes, persuade American consumers to pay more for high-altitude Nicaraguan estate coffee. All of that would be helpful. But not helpful to me."

"Lalo, Lalo. I've been unemployed for too long. I need a task. And an audience," I add, shocking myself. Is this what it's been about all this time? Needing an audience? Has this been obvious to everyone else? To Waldo?

The office of the bishop of Managua calls to speak with Don Abelardo. Don Abelardo will not remember the bishop; he will remember only the slick-haired classmate from his Jesuit *colegio* who licks his pencil when he thinks. Lalo takes the call. It is an invitation to meet the special papal delegate at the bishop's palace in Managua, three days hence. It will be a private meeting, a meeting of substance.

"Normally, I would be more than delighted," Lalo answers. "But now I must give this some thought."

We are drinking *cafécitos* with tiny Doña Luisa when Graciela announces another phone call. Doña Luisa wears a dangling teardrop ring on her pinkie. It moves along with the frenetic movements of her tiny hands.

"It is the devil's instrument," Doña Luisa announces grimly.

"It is for Doña Alice," Graciela says.

For the second time I mouth *Waldo!* to Lalo.

Alone, I leave the room.

"Al, at last."

"Waldo! It is you. I was going to call later, when I had my wits about me. But you beat me to it. Oh, Waldo, Waldo."

"It's not the end of the world, Al," he says.

"How can you know that for sure? It's so hard to have these conversations on the telephone. I'm so scared."

Waldo says, "Al. There's nothing to be scared of, sweetie. I don't think she felt a thing. Flirt just—"

"Flirt!"

"Yes, it was Flirt. Teddy Gribbon was driving for the DPW, and he just didn't see her. It happened in seconds."

"You mean he hit her? Flirt?"

"I'm so sorry to be telling you this, Al. I was thinking not to tell you until you got back, so you wouldn't have to grieve alone. But somehow that didn't seem fair. To you or Ezra."

"Let me get this straight. Flirt is dead?"

"She is, Al."

"I'm going to have to tell Ezra."

"I know. Poor Al."

"Tell me again what happened." I have to sit and a chair is just not close enough to the ground. I drop all the way down to the hard wooden floor and pull my knees to my chest and grip them as tight as I can. Flirt! Darling, sweet, furry, ill-trained, lovable Flirt. Beloved, inarticulate, affectionate Flirt. Maybe I heard it wrong. "Tell me again."

"Susie saw it from her window. She ran out—"

"How could she run?"

"Maybe she walked fast. I wasn't there. She called me and Donald Eco. She said she couldn't get Teddy to speak a word. She's worried about him."

"This wouldn't have happened if I'd been there," I say. I am crying more than seems right. Today I've seen the landscape of destruction and loss, but the tears flow for my dead dog.

"That is the most ridiculous thing I've heard all week," Waldo says. "Take it back or I'll hang up."

I wail, "Don't hang up. For God's sake."

"Not everything is your fault, Alice. Think of poor Teddy. He's not exactly equipped to deal with this sort of thing. Emotions and so on."

"Yes, poor Teddy. But where is Henry? How is Henry? He didn't see her, did he?"

"Henry was on a geological expedition when it happened, so we had her wrapped up before he got home."

"I miss Henry so much."

"He misses you too. But you'll be home soon."

"I will?"

"Of course," Waldo says. "Herc called to offer condolences and personally apologize. Since it was a town truck."

"Tell me more about Henry."

"Henry is with Dandy. He said he would tell him. They're out back. They may even be asleep. After all that crying."

"I can't believe this."

"She had a good life, Al. As dog lives go, it was a good one."

"But short. Definitely short. Short is not good, in this case."

A damp chill seeps into my bones and I shiver. The earth is suddenly compressed and warped. What was far away is now closing in. What was immediate has receded toward a distant horizon.

"Al, are you still there?"

"I'm here. I think I'm right here."

"Tell me about Ezra now," Waldo says.

"He's much better. It's amazing how much better he is."

"I knew it! I've always had the highest appreciation for his recuperative powers."

"You have?"

"Both of them. It's a Fairweather thing. One of our few useful genes."

It is only when he says the name, our name, Fairweather, that I am reminded of Edith upstairs, feverish and suffering. And just now, mourning Flirt in communion with Waldo, I am not suffering. Not like that. I am a Fairweather too.

"Don't say that." Up to a point. Only up to a point can I ever be one of them. It's an illusion that comes and goes, a pushmi-pullyu. I say, "Ezra's going to want to know when you'll bury her."

"When you guys get back. Don will cremate her and then we'll bury the ashes next to Gertrude and Pilly."

"We'll have ourselves a regular canine necropolis back there." They already share a stone. And now Flirt. Three seems like a lot of dead dogs to share one gravestone. How is Waldo going to find and move a new gravestone all by himself?

He's not.

"So have you made your reservations?" Waldo says.

"No."

"I could do it from here, but I'm assuming you'd rather do it yourself. We can't bury her until you get home."

"Did Henry say that?"

"He doesn't have to," Waldo says.

"I'm going to have to get a job the second I get back," I say. This is the first I've thought of this. Thought of it in those terms.

"If you want to, Al, that's fine by me. Jobs aren't exactly growing on trees but I'm sure you'll come up with something."

On the opposite end of the courtyard is choreographed mayhem. Graciela runs from the kitchen wing to the shed. Olga passes her as she runs full tilt from the shed toward the kitchen. Even Carmen runs. The tall, white-clad, and unflappable Carmen runs—shockingly—like someone with two left feet.

"Make your reservations, Al. I'm going to find Henry."

I am sitting on the floor examining the smooth lines of the telephone I've replaced in its cradle. I have to find the number for the airlines. I have to tell Lalo we're going home. Does this mean I won't see him again? That we won't make love again? One more time?

The phone rings and unthinkingly I answer it.

"It's me again," says Waldo.

I panic. "What happened?"

"Nothing. I just forgot to tell you something. Something for you," he says, and then he recites, in the funny, somewhat thespian voice he saves for his lyrics, his doggerel, whatever you call them:

> *"Like the merry monks in their cloisters*
> *Our Alice is devoted to oysters.*
> *She likes them cooked and raw*
> *They slither down her craw*
> *And make her rather boisterous."*

"Oh, Waldo, I love it." Absent any handkerchief, I wipe my sniffling nose on my sleeve. This is turning into a three-star crying event. "I just love it. Can you say it again?"

"Nope. You'll have to come home for that. By which time I will have blissfully forgotten it."

"You mustn't."

"There are plenty more where that came from."

Now Lalo is running across the courtyard. Adios, Waldo. *Hasta luego,* Waldo.

Don Abelardo put his pressed blue shirt into the oven and turned it on to the broil setting, then swore undying love to Graciela. Only tiny Doña Luisa walks slowly and purposefully away from the kitchen and the uproar.

She says, "He will be fine. They make such a fuss, those children. They *like* drama, you know." She delicately pushes back a single stray strand of silver hair from her forehead. This must be the original template of Carmen's constant tossing-back of her jet mane. Doña Luisa's gesture is the ink sketch on paper; Carmen's is the fully fleshed-out oil on canvas. The pearl-drop ring flops silently.

Mami had a ring like that and I think Audrey has it now. I hope it's with Audrey. She has the nicest fingers. Will I have to call Pop and Audrey to tell them about Flirt? Will they assume I killed her too? I'll tell them I was in another country. I won't tell Annabel. What else will I tell them?

Shall I tell them about the earth denuded by the mudslides, and the *damnificados*? Or will I just stick to Ezra's recovery, and my return to bury the dog and find a new job?

38 ❧ Saint Radio

L ALO CHARGES IN. He's wearing yet another pair of pressed cotton pajamas. I am mentally packing my suitcase. "Are you really going back to New York?"

"How did you know?"

"Odilia told me."

"She speaks English?"

"She understands body language," he says. Body language? Did the Lalo I think I know just utter those words?

"There will be no Saint Tristána Llobet without you," he says.

"I thought you'd bagged that idea?"

"I would," Lalo says. "But it has a life of its own."

"Good. Let it. Then you can have a life of your own. But I need to go home and stop distracting you."

"Why didn't you distract me years ago?" Lalo says.

I say, "You're confusing me. You wouldn't have been interested in me. I was a shallow, flighty creature with perfect breasts. That's all. I promise. I can't remember the first thing I should."

"You remember the saints," he says.

"Only the ladies with beards or the men who roost on pillars. So you see, I am still a shallow creature. And Lalo, I have yet to see you with the hiccups."

"When I was cured, I was cured forever."

"That sounds like a miracle to me."

Lalo sinks to the edge of my bed. He pushes the hair back from my face while the other hand slides under my bottom. He kisses me. The warmth spreads down to his hand and then up to my tonsils. My priorities are completely reordered. Can I justify one more time? Oh, to be justified. (Back in the days of gainful employment, I lobbied Mother Superior to allow me to teach James Hogg's *Confessions of a Justified Sinner* to my honors English class. I was unsuccessful.)

"Does Ezra know you're leaving?"

"No. Don't stop."

We kiss again. I am thinking that the problem with celibacy is not going without intercourse, but without kissing. The whole mouth-to-mouth thing. This alone completes us, and to go through life—those poor, sad virgin saints—without it seems a rejection of the gift of life.

There is a slight pop of released suction as I pull back. "Were you seriously planning to be celibate? When you were in the seminary?"

"That was my plan. But it wasn't going to be possible."

"That wasn't why you left," I say.

"No. I was having trouble believing. I had doubts like anchors."

"But you believe so much. So well." I want to hold him and never let him go.

"I think you believe more than I believe," Lalo says.

"More than what?"

"More than has any basis in reality. Sweet Alice."

"I almost miss the rain. Or the noise of the rain on the roof."

"Be careful what you wish for."

"I've heard that before."

Lalo leans back again. "What are you going to do about Edith Dilly-Glass?"

"Nothing. I'm going to do nothing about her."

"Will you say goodbye?" he asks.

"I don't think so. Why would she want to say goodbye to her ex-lover's wife? Would you?"

"Oh, Alice, Alice, there is nothing shallow about you. You are so deep you can't see the bottom," he says.

"I love you for saying that! Even if it's only about sex in the immediate future, I love you for it."

His warm mouth refastens on mine, over and around mine. My hand follows its natural inclination to breach the elastic of his tidy pajamas and venture south. His low moan would cause anyone to give up religion. "It's a murky bottom," I whisper.

"How many times in life do you get the opportunity to do something for the last time and know it is the last time? Rarely. Let tonight be that for us."

Until this second I didn't know where this would go. Until this second I might have snuggled into his arms and curled up like a sleeping dog. But now I know.

"The last time was the last time."

"Oh. Are you certain?" Lalo asks, so very kindly. Kind because he must sense how uncertain I am.

"I am."

When we have disentangled, rearranged, and smoothed, I tell Lalo that Flirt died today. He couldn't tell the difference between Dandy and Flirt. Flirt was the healthy one, the risk-taker, the rambunctious one, the Puppy Kindergarten flunkout. Flirt stole food from Dandy's bowl. She caught baby rabbits and squirrels and proudly presented herself with a furry tail dangling from her jaws. The more I enumerate Flirt's infractions, the harder I cry.

We sit silently except for residual sniffles.

Lalo asks me if we will invite Hubert to the funeral.

No, I tell him, it will be a private, family affair.

Carmen asks George if Edward and Sam the corpse-sniffing dog have had any success yet.

Don Abelardo is spreading *guayaba* jam over his white cheese with painterly strokes. Without looking up, he says, "Did you say *sex-sex?*" He laughs to himself.

George looks straight at Carmen and says, "If you mean has he found any bodies yet, the answer is yes, and no.

"I should explain," George says. "Sam, who is a diligent dog, has identified remains beneath the mud and the rubble. All indications of there being remains are there. But not actually found. Dug up. So I think I can speak for Edward when I say yes, and no."

"You poor man," Carmen says. "Where are your theological underpinnings? Where is the absolute belief that leads to the crown of martyrdom?"

Doña Luisa, who chews very tiny bites to match her very tiny frame, chokes on her piece of toast. Her coughing would rack a much sturdier body, but she remains seated at the table, just this side of turning blue. Her family ignores her.

George says, "Did I say something wrong?"

His hostess continues coughing, and little projectiles of spittle fly from her mouth.

"Maybe I should leave now," George says. He bumps into Ezra, running at full speed, next to the scarred wooden San Raimundo Nonato.

"How can we leave when I've just gotten better?" Ezra demands. "I wasn't consulted!"

Carmen asks me, "Does he know?" At first I think she is referring to Edith Dilly and Waldo's past entanglement. But no, something about the hangdoggedness of her elegant eyes tells me she is referring to Flirt. Lalo must have told her.

What else does she know?

"Not yet. I was going to wait."

Carmen says to him, "Don't you miss your father?"

"He could come down here," Ezra says.

"He has a job," I say. A job, a job. He wakes up each morning with a problem to be solved, and he attacks it from all angles. Generally he solves it.

Doña Luisa's coughing dies down to intermittent gasps. Don

Abelardo says to me, "The next time you come you must bring the whole family, even the dogs." I nod dumbly.

Next to the pendent and rubbery heliconia, the one with pointy yellow tips, the one that always looks fake, George corners me. "I hope you'll come say goodbye to Edith. She has something to show you."

"To show me?"

"Nothing awful. Just come."

First I prevail on Ezra to let me pack his things.

Edith is sitting up in bed. Balanced on her knees is an atlas of Nicaragua on top of which she is playing solitaire with a pack of miniature cards.

"You see?" she says.

"You look better."

"I am."

George says, "Guess what."

"What?"

Edith continues peeling cards off the pile in her left hand.

"I prayed to your saint, the aunt."

"She's not my saint."

"It was my first time ever for that kind of praying, and guess what."

"What?"

"It worked."

"Huh?"

"You can see for yourself. I prayed for her recovery, and she's better," George says with a theatrical flourish of his long arms. His arms are exceptionally long and apelike. We knew a boy in high school whose arms hung down below his knees, and the other boys teased him by scratching their armpits and making monkey howls. He died of a drug overdose in college. Mami knew his mother from the garden club. After Ape-Boy died, all his mother's plants grew to enormous sizes.

"She would have gotten better anyway. I'm glad you prayed, but it's rather simplistic to think that's why Edith recovered from a perfectly recoverable fever. Look at Ezra."

"I don't think you understand," George says.

"What don't I understand? I need to go pack," I say.

"What I said. She recovered — *poof* — in a matter of minutes. One minute she was lying here with pain in every bone in her body — that's why they call it breakbone fever, you know — and the next minute she was sitting up and hungry and wondering where she had put her red skirt."

"You must be relieved," I say.

"There has never been a recovery like this before," George says. "So it must be because of the saint."

"She's not a saint yet. And probably never will be. Unless you want to write the Vatican a letter." I need to get out of here as fast as possible. I told Lalo I wouldn't see Edith again, and I should have stuck to that. It's important to stick to things: resolves, food preferences, vows.

Edith looks up from her cards but does not lay them down. "George, dear, she doesn't think it's quite as wonderful as you do. She is a skeptic. When she told you to pray she was mocking us."

"No, I wasn't. It's not skepticism," I insist. But isn't it? Has that been my problem all along? I am walking backward toward the door. "I'm going back to the States."

"How can you?" Edith says.

"You're not staying to help?" George says.

"There's nothing I can do. I can't make her a saint. My research was all misguided."

"I don't mean that! I mean with the hurricane victims, the corpses under the mudslide, the homeless and destitute," George says.

"Los damnificados."

"They are exactly who he means," Edith says.

"I need to be home with my family now," I say, picturing the four of us at dinner, playing Twenty Questions and eating spaghetti and meatballs while Dandy and Flirt slumber beneath the table. No. Flirt won't be there, won't ever be there again, and that deletion from our family circle is a fact I know and Lalo knows, but Ezra still remains innocent of. And Edith will never know.

"So you will see Waldo tomorrow?" Edith says.

"Yes."

"I'm not going to ask you to send him my best wishes," she says.

"Good."

"But you can tell him I am happily married to a good man. Because George is a good man, an excellent man."

"I'm not going to tell him anything at all about you," I tell her.

"That's okay too, if you'd rather not."

"It has to be okay," I say.

George says, "But you will tell our host Abelardo that Edith is recovered by virtue of saintly intervention."

"Nope," I say. "I think I won't be telling anyone anything."

"Of course it's your right, if that's the way you feel about it," George says. I am gone.

Waldo calls again. This is a record.

"Carmen told me," he says.

My heart stops beating.

"I can't hear you."

"She said Edith Dilly showed up. Of all the people in all the world."

It beats again. "She did. With her troupe. So?"

"So. I thought I had better call."

"There's not much to talk about."

"Did you at least curse her out? Poison her soup?"

"No."

"No?"

"Why are you asking me this?" I whisper.

Waldo says, "I wouldn't mind. I would completely understand. I'd rather you poison her than you sleep with Lalo."

"Well, I didn't."

"Didn't what?"

"Poison her," I answer.

Ezra climbs into the back seat of Lalo's Mitsubishi and opens up a book about Nicaraguan volcanoes that Carmen gave him. I ask if he would rather ride shotgun, and he says no. So for the drive from Las Brisas to León and then on to the airport in Managua, the one whose name has changed three times so far (from La Mercedes to Augusto C. Sandino to Managua International and back to Sandino) and is destined to be changed yet again, with a new regime and a new hero, Lalo sits up front with his driver and I sit in back with Ezra, who could never read in the back seat of a moving car without throwing up. Maybe this is the miracle.

I have to tell him about Flirt before we land in the States, and I have to figure out the best way to do it. Every way will, of course, suck.

Lalo points out volcanoes and names them. He tells us of the conquistadors who landed here half a millennium ago and took everything they could, and spawned little conquistadors and sometimes fell hard for beautiful Indian maidens and gave birth to the culture that would later give rise to Mestizo Baroque architecture.

Ezra keeps reading, if he really is reading. He is turning pages intermittently.

Lalo tells us that in 1522 or 1523 a Spanish adventurer called Pedrarias Dávila or Pedro Arias de Ávila or even Gil Gonzalez Dávila landed on the Atlantic coast with dreams of glory. Dávila had no qualifications for administration other than his marriage to one of Queen Isabella's ladies in waiting. He is the father of the national system of nepotism. Because of his advanced age when he came to the New World, Dávila brought an iron coffin with him. He died in León, where we are now, but the whereabouts of the iron coffin remain unknown.

"Like Rubén Darío's brain," I say.

Ezra looks up from a long description of volcanic activity in the nineteenth century to rub his eyes. He looks pale again. "Ez, maybe you shouldn't read in the car. Aren't you getting carsick?" He says nothing and returns to his reading.

Lalo says, "I presume you know how Admiral Lord Horatio Nelson lost his eye?"

"What?"

"Not you. Young Ezra," Lalo says to me.

Silence.

Finally, Ezra says, "We haven't done naval history in my school." Even to notice its absence seems to me pretty remarkable, but I hold my tongue.

"It happened right here in Nicaragua," Lalo says. "In 1779 Nelson was only twenty years old, barely twice your age, and already he was in charge of the British ships bombarding the Spanish settlements at San Juan del Norte; that's the Atlantic mouth of the Rio San Juan. Did you know that Spain joined with France in supporting the American revolutionaries against the British? No? He succeeded in his attack on San Juan and afterward continued upriver chasing pirates. And somewhere along the river an Indian shot an arrow that struck Nelson in the eye."

Lalo claps his hand over his left eye, and keeps it there as he talks. It is a painfully touching gesture. I realize I am in danger when such a simple gesture sets me tingling and aching for him. My whole system needs realignment. It needs to aim straight north.

"Nelson yanked the arrow, pulled out his entire eyeball, and threw it overboard. So now you know how Lord Nelson's eye came to rest at the bottom of the Rio San Juan."

Ezra says, "That doesn't seem possible. Your eyeballs are attached by lots of blood vessels."

"Well, I wasn't there," Lalo says.

• • •

We are back in the *sala* VIP with the would-be Miss Nicaraguas serving drinks. The flight from Miami lands, disgorges, and four priests enter the lounge, surrounded by assistants, factotums, translators, and bearers.

The man at the center of it all is tall and dressed in purple silks. A medallion hangs around his neck. I know this man. Holy cow, not only have I seen this man before, but I know about him and his sad story.

I tell Lalo. "That man. He's the monsignor from the club. The Hagiographers Club. What on earth is he doing here?" A young woman—her breasts defy gravity—hands me a glass of pale yellow fruit juice. It stings pleasantly going down.

Lalo says, "He's from the Vatican. I told you. They've come about La Matilda's incorrupt body."

"He used to cry all the time," I say.

"Who?"

"The monsignor. There was a terrible tragedy. A drowning at sea."

"I remember that," Ezra says.

"You do?" This should not surprise me.

"Dad said it had to do with his tear ducts, and something else I won't say." Ezra wears the biggest grin I've seen in days.

"I have no idea to what you refer," Lalo says in an attempt to sound testy. But I am unconvinced.

"He's a friend of Hubert's. At the club he read all day long, and wept because his entire family drowned off of Sardinia. They were sailing champions."

"They cannot have been such very great sailors," Lalo says. This too sounds out of character for Lalo. It is as if as we approach the plane he is inching toward another persona, a persona I can bear to leave behind.

"It was a terrible storm. Even champions get tossed in a storm," I say.

Ezra says, "He must be feeling better now."

"I'm going to say hello. Do you think he'll remember me?"

I hand my fruit juice to Lalo and walk over to the monsignor. He is the picture of calmness amid the clamor. He fingers the medallion. He looks like a Medici portrait.

"Monsignor Giacometti. Do you remember me? From the Hagiographers Club?"

He drops the medallion and gathers up my right hand and presses his lips to the air just above it. "My dear signora," he says. "Of course I remember you. Hubert was devoted to you and your cause."

I demur, "Hardly. But Hubert was a wonderful help. A great librarian."

"He has a gift," the monsignor says. "But tell me, to what do I owe this pleasure? To meet such a dear friend here, of all places. I can barely find this place on the map!"

I'm glad Henry is not here to hear him say that. Even if it's meant in jest. I explain about the Llobets and Tristána, briefly. I tell him that we are now returning to New York to bury a dead dog. I regret that. Ezra doesn't know yet. And it sounds so trifling compared to an entire family drowned at sea. He is nothing if not sympathetic. I take him to meet Lalo.

"Abelardo Llobet, *a sus órdenes.*"

"Paolo Giacometti, envoy of the bishop of Rome."

"You are here to examine the body of La Matilda, that they say is incorrupt."

"Among other things. Many other things," the monsignor says.

"I am afraid we have nothing to compare with the splendors of Rome, but you will still find much to interest you in our little country."

"I have no doubt. I have no doubt," the monsignor replies. "And now, before I return to my labors, please tell me about our dear Hubert."

"He's terrified of skunks," Ezra says. Where has he been? Consorting with the ex–Miss Nicaragua runners-up?

"I see the resemblance," the monsignor says. The ways in which I resemble my sons are not visible to the naked eye. "A handsome young man."

Lalo speaks solemnly. "While you are in my country, you must visit the Virgin of El Viejo. She resides outside of Chinandega, upon an altar of chased silver unrivaled anywhere except Potosí. The Virgin came here with Rodolfo, the brother of Santa Theresa of Ávila."

"I will certainly make every effort to see this Virgin," says the monsignor. "So that I can better understand the Nicaraguan church. I am always happy to learn the truth of local devotions."

"Perhaps you will," Lalo says. This all sounds way too subtextual for me.

And then formal pleasantries are repeated and Monsignor Giacometti is gone, reabsorbed by his posse.

"Why didn't you say something about Tía Tata?" I ask Lalo.

"What would you have had me say? That she loved a priest and he loved her?"

"I think you're overreacting to those letters," I say. "I thought some of them were very sweet. And not incriminating."

"So you say. I saw Carolina de la Rosa when we entered the terminal. She must be here to meet the papal delegate."

"You saw her? Did she see you? Why didn't you say something?"

"She was distracted. She looked radiant. I wasn't inclined to speak just then."

"Oh."

"And now your flight is boarding."

We say goodbye. Ezra is right here, but that is not the reason we say nothing at all about our love, if it was love, and lovemaking in the darkness. Lalo says nothing about my perfect breasts. I say nothing about his perfect skin and throb-inducing eyelashes.

Neither of us alludes to a future meeting. I do not reveal that the bottoms of his cotton pajamas are in my suitcase. Ezra says nothing about Carmen. The tropical air between us swallows it all like quicksand. Ezra and I step out into the torrid Nicaragua afternoon and cross the steaming tarmac.

When the pilot announces that the coast of Cuba can be seen from the left side of the plane, I know it is now or never.

"I need to tell you something before we get home."

"Shoot."

"There was an accident in front of the house. The garbage truck hit Flirt, and she was killed. Flirt is gone."

"Flirt? Are you sure?"

"Ez, honey, your dad told me."

"Dad wouldn't lie about that," Ezra says. He turns away to gaze down upon the island of Cuba and the shimmering blue Caribbean. "Why does everyone like Dandy best? Flirt was bigger and stronger."

"You're right, Ez. She was our alpha dog. People always prefer underdogs. But someone had to be the alpha. And that was our Flirt."

Ezra bites his lip and presses his forehead to the porthole. He can press hard enough to make a red rectangle on his forehead, press with all his might, but the window won't budge. Poor Ezra, he can't get off this plane until Miami, and he can't make Flirt come back. That seems like an overdose of reality for a little boy who just a few days ago had pain in every bone in his body and couldn't keep down a thimbleful of water.

"Will that make Dandy the alpha now? What if he doesn't want to be an alpha dog?"

"I don't know. I don't know if he has a choice."

"Carmen had a dog once, named Wally. He was a German shepherd and they had to shoot him after he took a bite out of someone's leg."

"She had a dog? When was this?" Nothing about this should be so very surprising. Lots of people have dogs, and some of them even have German shepherds. So it was with Carmen sitting by his sickbed that Ezra has already plumbed the sorrow of a dead dog, while I was elsewhere.

I need a job.

Over the Florida Keys I remember Edith. But the power of Edith is gone. Somewhere between the coast of Cuba and the U.S. mainland, it dissipated. I am lighter now. So light I may need to nail my feet to the ground.

In customs in Miami, I phone Waldo and read aloud to him the sign above the baggage carousel:

USE THE RED LANE IF YOU HAVE:
1. *Dogs*
2. *Cats*
3. *Nonhuman primates—monkeys*
4. *Turtles, turtle eggs, tortoises, terrapins*
5. *Etiological agents and vectors:*
   (a) *Any living insect (bedbugs, fleas, lice, mites, etc.);*
   (b) *Any animal known to be or suspected of being infected with any disease transmissible to man;*
   (c) *All living bats;*
   (d) *Unsterilized specimens of human or animal tissues (including blood, body discharges or excretions, or similar matter);*
   (e) *Any culture of living bacteria, virus, or similar material;*
   (f) *Snails and mollusks.*

"Well?" he says.

"Well what?" I demand. "Isn't that extraordinary? The possibilities."

"Do you have any? Etiological agents or vectors?"

"Poor, lonely, sad Dandy. Is he bereft?"

"Henry says he is grieving. To me he just seems quiet."

"Waldo, guess what. I have an idea for a new radio show. The name will be *Saint Radio,* and Hubert would be the hagiographer on call."

"Have you asked him?"

"No, but I'm sure he'd love it. What do you think?" The truth is, I have just conceived of this radio show this very minute, standing here sweatily holding our passports.

"It sounds . . . You can explain it when I see you. You might want to ask Hubert first."

"Fine, they're calling our flight."

"I have news for you too," Waldo says.

"Tell me!" I shout. Really, it's more of a bark that involuntarily erupts from the pit in my stomach.

"Sydney's pregnant. Dick is going to be a father. More little Fairweathers are on the way."

"Posey must be ecstatic."

"Don't miss the plane."

We fly up the eastern seaboard in mostly darkness. Somewhere over the nation's capital, Ezra asks me about etiological agents, and points out that no one would willingly, or knowingly, travel anywhere with bedbugs or fleas. Which makes the sign rather dopey, or illogical.

Ezra tells Waldo and Henry about how Admiral Lord Nelson lost his eye in the Rio San Juan, the southern border of Nicaragua.

Individually, silently, alone in corners of the house, we each hold Dandy and whisper words.

And then at last, sleeping next to Waldo is like finding a pocket of air that is my shape exactly.

• • •

The next morning, Waldo sits on the edge of Ezra's bed. "Fezzy Ezzy, do I have news for you. And Abelardo."

"I'm asleep, Dad."

"That Nelson story is hogwash. Baloney. Hooey. Pure fiction."

"Huh?"

"Nelson did lead an expedition to Nicaragua and he caught yellow fever there. They all did. But he recovered and returned to England with all his limbs, and both his eyes, attached. Later, in 1794, at the siege of Calvi—half a world away from poor muddy Nicaragua—he damaged his right eye and lost his sight. He was fighting the French, not the Spanish, not pirates. These are all facts. Sorry to have to break the news."

"I'm still sleeping, Dad. And you're not sorry."

I call to Waldo. He sits on the edge of the bed, rocking back and forth.

"Isn't it a little early for history lessons?" I ask.

"It's never too early for history," Waldo says. "Left to our own devices, Henry and I ended up reading the *Guinness Book of World Records* at dinner. Sad, huh?"

"Where's Calvi anyway?" I ask.

"Corsica, the northern coast of Corsica."

"Oh. Isn't that near Sardinia?"

"Next door," Waldo says. "Why? Do you have more travel plans?"

"No. Far from it."

At dusk we bury Flirt's ashes in the backyard. Susie and Bogumila come to pay their last respects to a dog they trusted with chickens. I am wearing black, but I am dry-eyed and distant, with *Damnificados! Damnificados!* playing in my head like a top-forty song that will not quit, until Henry takes my hand. Those five strong fingers, that palimpsest palm, those dirt-filled fingernails grab hold—and I am back on firm ground, I am linked to metamorphic and igneous rocks, to once-tilled Hudson Valley soil, to the parched grass, the poison ivy vines, the spartina and the anthills.

Susie suggests we sing a hymn, and Waldo, naturally, is rolling his eyes. Out of the blue, or rather, out of a DPW truck, Teddy Gribbon shows up. Poor Teddy. His eyes are red, and he is carrying a bouquet of carnations. His arms reach toward Waldo, then he withdraws and hands the carnations to me. "Flowers are a universal sign of respect at a funeral," he says.

"Thank you, Teddy. You didn't have to."

"You don't hate me?"

Before I can utter the appropriate platitudes, Henry pipes up. "Teddy, do you know about catharsis?"

Teddy smiles ruefully. "I know about transmissions and carburetors, but not that one."

Henry says, "I read about it in the grief manual. It's what we're doing here. By crying and expressing our emotions, we end up feeling better. So it's a good thing you are here."

Now Susie rolls her eyes.

Waldo is still reading *One Hundred Years of Solitude*. This pleases me because if he were reading a new and strange book I would not have known how to proceed. He rolls toward me and says, "I almost forgot. A rather interesting new book is out."

"You mean the one about the Hagiographers Club? Hubert told me."

"I have no idea about that. It's about the invention of the telephone." Waldo pauses. I think I can hear the barking of dogs in the backyard, but I am wrong. "You'll never believe this. But you of all people should believe it. After all the grief I've taken, it turns out the telephone really was invented by Henry Fairweather."

"Holy cow." I stare at the blackness of the individual windowpanes. "Oh, I get it. You made this up."

"Al! That's the whole point. I did not make this up. That's

what you've thought all along but now it turns out I was right and there is even proof. Some guy from Delaware has discovered that Bell stole all the ideas of Great-Great-Uncle Henry. And then manipulated the story." Waldo is grinning, grinning. "This will change everything."

"Like what?"

"Don't be so literal. And guess what else. I can't come up with a limerick. My brain just freezes when I try to rhyme *telephone* or *invent* or even *Graham Bell*. Odd, don'tcha think?"

"How about *fishbone? Chaperone?* How about *serpent? Incandescent? Rodent?* Leave it to me, Waldo!" I say. And he does.

It's the Feast of Saint Margaret of Antioch, who escaped from the dragon's belly by tickling his tonsils with the cross she carried. She's one of the Fourteen Holy Helpers, who were ever so popular during the black death. She was an apocryphal virgin, and I need to expand my repertoire beyond virgins. Waldo asks if I have called Hubert, to tell him about the likely noncanonization of Tía Tata and my idea for *Saint Radio*. Not yet, I reply. Waldo asks if I have called Lalo to let him know we arrived safely in New York, and to thank him for his tropical hospitality. Not yet. Before I call Lalo I will tell Waldo, and I don't know what will happen then but I am not racked with guilt, not about Flirt and not about Lalo.

Waldo asks what I have been doing. There was a message from Gordie at WBLT, I tell Waldo, and when I returned the call he told me that Trudy had been fired for sexual misconduct (details at a later date) and that he is now producing the morning shows. Do I have any ideas?

I have just the thing.